MEDITERRANEAN VOWS

PIPPA ROSCOE

JACKIE ASHENDEN

MILLS & BOON

First published in Great Britain 2024
by Mills & Boon, an imprint of HarperCollins*Publishers* Ltd,
1 London Bridge Street, London, SE1 9GF

www.harpercollins.co.uk

HarperCollins*Publishers*, Macken House, 39/40 Mayor Street Upper, Dublin 1, D01 C9W8, Ireland

Mediterranean Vows © 2024 Harlequin Enterprises ULC

Greek's Temporary 'I Do' © 2024 Pippa Roscoe

Spanish Marriage Solution © 2024 Jackie Ashenden

ISBN: 978-0-263-32011-4

06/24

This book contains FSC™ certified paper
and other controlled sources to ensure responsible forest management.

For more information visit www.harpercollins.co.uk/green.

Printed and Bound in the UK using 100% Renewable Electricity
at CPI Group (UK) Ltd, Croydon, CR0 4YY

GREEK'S
TEMPORARY 'I DO'

PIPPA ROSCOE

MILLS & BOON

For Amy Andrews.
Not only an amazing author and a wonderful woman,
but also an incredible friend.
Thank you so much for sharing your beautiful home
with me.
xx

PROLOGUE

Eleven years ago...

HELENA WIPED HER damp palm on the silky material of the black dress her best friend had picked out especially for this moment. She wanted it to be just right, which was why she and Kate had talked about it non-stop since Helena had got back to boarding school in September from the summer holidays.

Spending Christmas on the Liassidis private island, just off the coast of Greece, was the best present her parents could have given her. Getting to see Leo and Leander in between the summers she and her parents spent here in Greece? A Christmas miracle!

Helena checked herself in the reflection of the mirror in the hallway outside Leo's bedroom. She'd put her hair up in a fancy bun and even made an effort with her make-up. Her mother had raised a critical eyebrow and deemed it unsuitable with a single word that had cut like a knife. But her father had patted her on the shoulder and told her she looked beautiful—*'very grown-up'*—salving the dull ache her mother had caused.

But that was what she'd wanted, right? To look grown-up. She was fifteen now, not the little kid that Leander and Leo always joked about her being. She pressed her lips together. She knew why she didn't want them, want *Leo*, to see her as a 'little kid'. And she wasn't stupid either. She knew he had a girlfriend, that he would never be interested in her in that way. But there it was…that little candleflame flicker of hope that wouldn't quit, no matter what she told herself.

Her fingers clenched reflexively and accidentally crinkled the carefully wrapped present she'd spent ages choosing and personalising. She pressed a hand to her chest to soothe the funny, turning twist it did at the thought of giving it to Leo, reminding herself to breathe.

She looked up and saw the boughs of rich green foliage Cora had decorated the house with just for her. Helena knew that in Greece they didn't traditionally decorate their homes with holly and mistletoe in the same way that they did in the UK, but that Mrs Liassidis had done that—for her—touched her deeply. Helena *loved* the Liassidis house with its incredible view over the Aegean that she couldn't get enough of.

But really, the best thing about it was Leonidas and Leander. The twin brothers might have been six years older than her, but they made her feel like family. Leander made her laugh and laugh and laugh, but Leo…

'Helena, really. Isn't it time for you to stop being so foolish? Leo's six years older than you.'

Helena felt a painful blush rise to her cheeks. Despite her mother's words, she wasn't actually stupid enough to think that she'd marry him like her father and Uncle Giorgos joked about. Giorgos Liassidis wasn't really her uncle but her dad's business partner. Only he felt like an uncle and Helena loved the way he was with his wife, Cora, the easy affection between them. And she liked how her parents were when they were here. Because when they were back in England she didn't really see much of them.

Helena shook off the thought and focused instead on the Christmas present she'd bought Leo. It was completely different to the one that she'd bought Leander, which she knew he'd like, but…the one for Leo was different. It *meant* something.

He'd been so different since arguing with Leander a few years back and starting work at Liassidis Shipping. She'd wanted to make him *happy* and had thought that her present for him might at least make him smile again.

She got to the landing outside his room, her heart pounding in her chest and her palms a little damp again. *Nervous.* Why was she nervous? She smiled at herself for being silly and went to knock on the door, but…

'It's fine, I don't know what you're worrying about,' she heard Leo say in a tone Helena didn't recognise. It was joking…but patient?

'I just want to make a good impression.'

Helena scowled at the whining tone she recognised.

'Mina, you've met them loads of times before.'

'But this is different. It's *Christmas*.'

Helena leaned closer to the door and realised that it was open a sliver. Her heart shuddered as she saw Leo pull his girlfriend into his arms and she willed back the hurt. She was being stupid again. Of course, Leo would be with his girlfriend.

'I suppose that *she'll* be here. Helena.'

For the first time, Helena almost regretted learning Greek. A part of her wished she couldn't understand the conversation, but she couldn't make herself turn around and leave either. The bitterness that Mina had spoken with had cut Helena. But not as deeply as realising that Leo didn't come to her defence.

'Of course she'll be here. My father invited her parents.'

'She's such a brat.'

'Mina, she's harmless.'

Helena's throat was thick with hurt and her cheeks hot from a painful flush.

Harmless.

'I've seen the way she looks at you. That's not harmless. I know, I was that age once.'

The present crumpled in her hands as Helena clutched it tighter, shame burning into her skin.

'She follows Leander and me around like a puppy,' Leo dismissed.

'Then train her better,' Mina's voice snapped out.

'Mina, she's just a child.'

'Trust me, that's something you have to nip in the bud. And it's really unfair of you to lead her on.'

'Lead her on?' Leo asked, the confusion in his tone clear. 'Mina, I think you've misunderstood. She's nothing to me. Just the daughter of my father's business partner. That's all.'

Unable to see past the tears in her eyes, Helena spun away from the door and down the corridor. She pulled up short at the top of the stairs.

She's just a child. She's nothing to me.

She clenched her jaw so hard her teeth started to ache, and furiously wiped at the tears in her eyes. How could her heart hurt and pound so much at the same time? She took a shuddering breath but it did nothing to ease the pressure in her chest. Another tear fell down her cheek and she wondered why it felt as if a rope tying her to shore had been cut. As if she were a boat drifting out to a stormy sea without an anchor.

She looked down at the present in her hands, the box slightly crumpled, and knew she couldn't give it to Leo. Not now. Humiliation crept across Helena's skin and settled into her stomach.

She thought of the cubbyhole that Leander, she and Leo sometimes used to leave silly notes or treats for each other. It was hidden behind a small painting just down the hall. With a numbness creeping over her, she went to the painting and shoved the present into the hiding cubbyhole, hoping that no one would find it for a very long time.

Her throat thick with hurt, she forged that feeling into resolve. Mina had nothing to worry about. Helena wouldn't look, or think twice, about Leonidas Liassidis ever again.

But as she wiped her eyes and made her way downstairs she didn't see Leander step out from the shadows, concern and sadness flicking between Helena and the door to his brother's room. He shook his head, before slowly following Helena down to where the rest of their families were gathered.

CHAPTER ONE

'TELL ME AGAIN that I'm doing the right thing.'

'You are doing what you *need* to do.'

'Am I?'

'Helena, if you want me to talk you out of this, I can…
I don't care about the guests, the church, the press interest all of this hoo-ha has gained, or the damn money.'

'Hoo-ha?'

'Yes, Helena. Your wedding is a load of hoo-ha,' Kate
said with such seriousness, Helena didn't know whether
to laugh or cry.

Groaning, she turned away from her reflection in the
mirror. 'You're right. It is a load of hoo-ha. Just think
what would happen if they all knew the truth,' Helena
said as her heart lurched guiltily.

That this marriage was a farce, a sham, utterly fake.
But it was also the only way to fix the terrible situation
she was in—the only way to save her charity, Incendia.

'If only they hadn't been whipped into a frenzy by *Leander the Lothario*,' Kate joked.

Helena smiled at Kate's teasing. Leander Liassidis
might have been the eternal playboy cruising through
life like he didn't have a care in the world, but for Helena, when she needed it, he'd been her rock and her sav-
iour. She loved Leander like a brother and the only thing

that ever caused her any worry was the hope that one day he might find someone that he could love sincerely. Which was perhaps a tad ironic, considering that in less than twenty minutes Helena would be walking down the aisle to stand beside him in front of one hundred and fifty guests, where a priest would declare them husband and wife.

'If only my inheritance didn't have the most ridiculous strings attached to it,' Helena wished out loud.

'What on earth was your father thinking?' Kate demanded. 'As if access to your inheritance should ever have depended on a man.'

Helena's heart turned as it always did when she thought about her father. He had passed away just after her sixteenth birthday and not a single day had gone by that she hadn't thought of him, hadn't missed him.

'To be fair, if I could have waited just two years until I was twenty-eight, none of this would have even been necessary,' Helena countered.

'Of course. Also, perfectly reasonable,' Kate said sarcastically. 'A woman matures only when she marries a man or when she's nearly thirty!' she cried.

Helena couldn't help but smile. Their unwavering defence of each other was what made them strong, their bond closer than family because it had been chosen. And Helena would choose Kate every single day.

'I'm sure my mother would have helped me fight it, if there had been time,' she insisted, missing the sceptical look that passed across Kate's features. 'But challenging a will in the courts would take too long and draw too much attention. The financial review of Incendia is due in December. The police have advised that they won't have caught Gregory by then, and even if they do, they won't be able to return the money he stole until after a full investigation and a lengthy court case,' Helena said, shaking her head.

Helena had never believed that she'd one day get to work at the charity that had been a lifesaver to her when she'd needed it. After the loss of her father, her abrupt return to boarding school had been hard. Her fear of falling asleep and never waking up—just like her father had done one awful June night—was at risk of becoming full blown and permanent insomnia. So her tutor had recommended Incendia to her. There she'd received grief counselling and support while she underwent the genetic testing to see if she had inherited Brugada syndrome, the disease that had killed her father.

While the test had eventually come back negative, it was with Incendia that she'd got to see first-hand how much good that charities could do, how integral they were to providing support for people in need. It had inspired her so much that she'd changed her study direction immediately to focus on attaining a business degree at Cambridge, swiftly followed by her master's in Non-Profit Management.

Her mother thought that she was being foolish, throwing away financial security for misplaced altruism, but Helena had found her passion, and not only that, something she was good at.

Her first job had been with a small charity start-up and she'd relished the opportunity to throw everything she had at it. It paid off and she soon became known for having a head for business, and a fresh, exciting approach to gaining partnerships that were relevant and contemporary to younger generations. Connecting people who were sincere about helping, rather than seeking out borrowed kudos, was what made her unique. Her hard work made her peerless.

And then six months ago it had happened; Incendia had asked if she might be interested in a role as their CEO. It had been the most amazing moment of her life. She had celebrated with Kate and even Leander had made a special trip to London to take her out and treat her to a congratulatory meal that had ended up—as it usually did—with him seeing her safely home in a taxi, before he escorted whatever woman had taken his fancy back to his London apartment.

But within a month following her start at Incendia, the CFO had quit and disappeared with nearly one hundred million pounds in investment funds. Shocked and horrified, she'd gone immediately to both the police and the charity commission. She'd spent days locked in meetings with Incendia's trustees, where she discovered that the previous CEO had failed to renew the business insurance that would have made this painful rather than disastrous.

Because if there wasn't a way to cover the shortfall in money, Incendia wouldn't survive long enough to see what the police could recover. A financial review at the end of the year would declare them bankrupt and all of the people they could help, all of the families Incendia supported, the research into medical conditions that affected millions around the world...would be left with nothing.

Helena *couldn't* let that happen. Incendia had been there for her when no one else had been. She'd *needed* to find a way to fill the hole made by the missing money and there was only one way she could think of.

The shares her father had left her in Liassidis Shipping.

Staring at her reflection in the mirror, she felt that

sense of loss keenly. The shares were the last piece of her father that she had left, and she'd never wanted to part with them. She'd hoped to leave them in the business now run almost completely by Leonidas Liassidis, simply content for that to be her connection to the company her father had founded with Giorgos Liassidis. That was all she'd wanted. To know that her father's legacy lived on. To know that a part of it still belonged to her. But now she would have to let them go. Let *him* go.

A little piece of Helena's heart broke under the weight of the sob she kept locked in her chest.

She felt two slender arms come gently around her shoulders and looked to the mirror to meet Kate's eyes in the reflection.

'It's the right thing to do,' Helena said, unsure who she was trying to convince more, herself or Kate. It was what her *father* would have done, Helena was sure of it. 'I can sell the shares as soon as the marriage is registered in the UK and there will be enough there to cover the shortfall in Incendia's accounts.'

'Do you think you could buy back the shares, once you have what you need?' Kate asked gently.

Helena bit her lip and looked down at her feet. 'No.' She wouldn't lie to herself about this. She couldn't afford to. 'Only a fool would sell shares in Liassidis Shipping,' she explained. Only a fool or someone extremely desperate. And she was extremely desperate.

'Well, then,' Kate said in her no-nonsense way. 'We have a plan, we're going to stick to it and we're going to get it done!'

Helena smiled at her best friend. 'I really like that colour on you,' she said, glad that she had chosen gold for her only bridesmaid; Kate looked absolutely radiant.

Kate smiled, shrugging a delicate shoulder to the mirror and pouted. *'Merci!'*

There was a knock on the door and Helena turned, hoping that it might be her mother, but it was just the officiant letting them know they were ready.

Helena turned back, masking the hurt before Kate could see it. Yes, it was foolish to hope, and she probably should have known better after all these years, but she felt peculiarly alone standing in the small church library that had been given for her to get ready in on her wedding day, without either of her parents there with her.

Pushing that thought aside, she looked at herself in the floor-length mirror.

The deceptively simple wedding dress suited her slim figure. She'd been teased as a teenager for resembling a kitchen towel tube and had never really liked her lack of curves, but the dress by a new Spanish designer—Gabriella Casas—made her look and feel beautiful. A puff of laughter left her lips at the irony. It would be utterly wasted on Leander Liassidis, who had never looked at her as anything other than a little sister.

As Kate told the officiant that they would be right there, Helena touched the silver bracelet her father had given her on her sixteenth birthday. It was the last present he had given her, barely weeks before he'd passed. She was both sad and relieved that he was not here today. Sad because even though this wasn't ever going to be a real marriage, the small child in her still wanted her father here on her wedding day. But she was also relieved, because he didn't have to see what she was about to do. Shame stung her skin as she fought an internal battle of wills. She wanted to be a businesswoman that he could have grown to respect, that he could be proud of. And she could still do that. But only if Incendia survived.

'Are you ready?' Kate asked from behind her.

Helena nodded.

It was a short walk between the church library and the entrance to the rather grand chamber of the Catholic church in Athens. Helena might have wanted to have a small ceremony with very little grandeur, but Leander had his way in the end.

'It's going to be my only wedding—we might as well make it a party!' he'd exclaimed.

She just hadn't realised that Leander's 'party' would attract so much attention and so much 'hoo-ha', as Kate had said earlier.

If she was honest, she'd been utterly thrown by the press interest in them. Yes, the Hadden name had notoriety in the UK, but in Greece, the Liassidis name was on a whole different level. The press had been stalking them ever since the news became public, each subsequent headline more hysterical than the previous one, the whole of Greece and beyond taken by the friends to lovers fairy tale.

Anyone who was anybody was there, wanting desperately to be seen. In truth, Helena had only cared about a handful of people. Her, Kate, Leander, obviously, and his parents, Giorgos and Cora. She wasn't naïve enough to think that his twin brother would come. Leander and Leo hadn't shared a single word in the last five years. Her heart pulsed once. She hadn't spoken to Leo since the bitter confrontation he'd had with her mother nearly ten years ago, after Gwen had naïvely thought she could continue her father's work with Liassidis Shipping.

She would be there in the church, with her second husband John, who had reluctantly agreed to interrupt his golfing holiday, and Helena tried to tell herself that it was enough that they had come.

She and Kate paused outside the large doors that would open to the nave of the church, listening for a moment to the gentle hum of conversation and the soft sounds of string music. Helena wasn't religious, but she couldn't help but wonder if it was sacrilegious to marry in this way, in this place, for reasons that had nothing to do with love.

'We could run, you know. I've got the car keys,' Kate whispered as if sensing her hesitation.

Helena laughed and turned to see Kate's reassuring smile, the easy confidence she had radiating over Helena like a balm.

'No. I'm good. But thanks though,' Helena said.

'Loves ya,' Kate said, causing Helena to grin at the favourite phrase passed back and forth between them.

'Loves ya,' Helena replied. 'Now, let's do this.'

The wedding march started up and unseen hands opened the doors from the inside. Kate began her procession down the aisle and Helena's heart started to pound. Even though it was silly, it wasn't ever going to be a real marriage, nerves dotted her skin with pinpricks. Helena locked her gaze firmly on the bouquet in her hand, which was why she didn't see the way that Kate stiffened and almost missed a step.

Helena didn't, in fact, see much until she was nearly halfway up the aisle because it was only when Kate stepped to the side, glancing in panic between her and the man at the top of the aisle, that Helena realised that something was wrong.

Something was terribly, horribly wrong.

Because standing at the top of the aisle, the six-foot-four-inch dark-haired, bronzed Adonis wasn't the man who had promised that he'd do everything in his power to help her. No.

Standing at the top of the aisle was the last man she'd ever expected to see.

Leonidas Liassidis.

Leo stared at the closed doors of the church, silently cursing his arrogant, reckless brother to hell and back, utterly uncaring that he did so in a church.

He was furious. How *dared* Leander do something like this?

If Leo hadn't picked up the message his brother had left him little less than three hours ago, he wouldn't have even been here. As it was, he'd barely made it on time.

Leo cursed silently again.

He hadn't spoken to Leander in five years and *this* was the first thing his brother had asked of him?

'Be me.'

There had been more on the message, but now as he stood at the top of a church aisle in front of one hundred and fifty guests, it was all Leo heard.

'Be me, be me, be me.'

They hadn't pulled this stunt since they were boys. Back when he'd still considered Leander his brother, before his lies had betrayed the future that Leo had thought he would have with Leander by his side. The future Leo had wanted.

Time hadn't dulled the memory of the day they had turned eighteen, when their father had offered them a choice: inherit Liassidis Shipping, beginning a three-year handover period from him to them, or take a sizeable fortune and strike out on their own.

They'd spent *years* of their teenage lives talking about what they would do with Liassidis Shipping. Years, planning how to make it the industry number one, how they would rule together, side by side, sharing all decisions and doing it all together.

And right up until that moment, Leo would have sworn he knew his brother better than he knew himself. But when their father made the offer that had been made to him by *his* father, Leo had looked at Leander and seen a stranger staring back at him.

Even the thought of it rippled tension across the muscles of his back. Betrayal, fury, a potent phosphoric taste in his mouth. Leo clenched his teeth together, painfully aware that he was the sole focus of the entire congregation at that moment in time. And in that congregation were his parents, staring at him, looking horrified.

Because although he and Leander were truly identical—to the point where the number of people that could tell them apart could be counted on one hand—his parents had recognised him the moment he had entered the church.

But he had been ushered immediately up to the top of the aisle before he could tell them what was going on. And even if he *had* been able to speak to them, what would he have said? Would he have repeated what his brother had said when he'd left his message?

That Leander had 'needed time'?

Time for what, the *maláka* had not even bothered to explain.

Leander had insisted that he would be back by the

end of the honeymoon, but Leo didn't believe him for one second.

Helena needs this. Really needs it. So please. I'll ask... beg. But please, don't leave her alone on the wedding day.

Leo clenched his teeth again, a thin lightning strike of tension spreading up his neck and jaw. Of all the women in the world, his brother had chosen to marry Helena Hadden? Leo would have been happy to have lived the rest of his life never seeing or hearing of a Hadden woman ever again.

There had been a time when things had been different. When he'd enjoyed Helena's company, when he had almost thought them friends. But that was before Helena had taken Leander's side following his betrayal, and things had only become worse three years later, after what her mother, Gwen, had done to Liassidis Shipping following the death of her husband.

Whether it had been grief or sheer stupidity, Gwen's actions had nearly destroyed Liassidis Shipping for ever by engaging the competitor of an existing client at a knockdown price. It had taken everything, *everything*, Leo had had in him, to pull it back from the brink of ignominy.

Christós, what was he even doing here?

He looked back at the church doors. No matter how much he resented the Haddens, and hated his brother, he couldn't have left Helena alone to face down a near obscene number of wedding guests, let alone the press corps camped outside. No, only his selfish, uncaring brother would do such a thing. And he—Leo assured himself with an almost violent intensity—was *nothing* like his brother.

The sound of the doors opening screeched against the

floor, causing him to wince momentarily at the shocking intrusive sound. And then, just for a second, he saw her centred in the doorframe, smiling at her bridesmaid, her face filled with hope and excitement, and it cut through the red haze of his anger.

That wasn't Helena Hadden, his body roared.

The effect she had on him was instantaneous, his stomach tensing against a punch to the gut, as heat worked its way around his system. The woman standing in the ivory sheath was statuesque tall, beyond beautiful, and barely reminiscent of the gangly girl he'd last seen ten years before. The sheer marked difference between what he saw and what he'd been expecting destroyed any instinctive barrier against seeing the intense feminine beauty of the woman standing at the opposite end of the aisle and he was frankly relieved when the bridesmaid came to take her place in front of the bride.

Get yourself together. Right now.

Reminding himself who she was, what her mother had done—what his brother had got him into—tuned his feelings back to where they should be. Right around the time that the bridesmaid stepped aside and Helena caught sight of him.

He was staring at her so intently he saw the exact moment she realised it was him standing at the top of the aisle, not his brother. Shock and horror morphed quickly into anger, the fire in Helena's startling blue eyes burning him as badly as that first impression of her had.

And yet he could do nothing—say nothing—until she reached his side. And even then? They were facing the entire congregation and because *someone*—probably his egotistical brother—had the genius idea to have the priest stand with the congregation rather than with them, as tradition would dictate, they were in full view of absolutely everyone.

Helena needs this. Really needs it.

Leo bit back a scornful laugh. One look at the sheer panic in her eyes was enough to tell him what he needed to know.

This was no love marriage. Not that he'd have believed it even if they'd tried to deceive him. There had been absolutely no trace of such feeling between her and Leander in all the years that the Haddens had spent with his family. So Leo could be forgiven for thinking that it was a joke when the wedding invitation had first arrived. He'd left the thick embossed cream paper on the corner of his desk, almost needing to see it again and again just to believe it.

That was until the press and the gossip magazines had started to whisper rumours that 'Leander the Lothario' was finally settling down.

What had started as a few pieces in lifestyle magazines had taken Greece by storm. The Liassidis family name combined with, Leo would grudgingly admit, Leander's own achievements were lauded throughout the country. It should have come as little surprise that this mockery of a love story would have captured the nation's attention.

But Leo had seen members of the international press right by the steps of the church. Was that why his brother had decided to cut and run? Or was there another reason? Did it even matter, Leo asked himself, as his brother had once again proved that only his own needs and desires mattered, uncaring of who he hurt in the process?

He turned his attention back to Helena, who was mere steps away, and she was *still* glaring at him with a fury that promised nothing less than hellfire.

Finally, she stepped up beside him, her eyes locked onto his face as if *he* were the one who had put them in this situation, rather than his brother. As if he didn't have better things to do with his time than to play groom in whatever scheme Helena and his brother had cooked up.

She pasted a smile over exquisite features and hissed out from between her teeth, 'What are you doing here?'

'Your beloved fiancé has done a runner,' he returned with an equally false smile and gritted teeth, aware that the gaze of every person in the room was on them. If he hadn't been the employer of nearly twenty thousand staff around the globe, he might have found the experience a bit intimidating.

He looked back at Helena to see that the blood had drained from her creamy complexion.

Malákas.

This time, he wasn't sure whether he was cursing his brother or himself.

'He said he'll return before the end of the honeymoon,' his hitherto unknown conscience prompted him to add.

In her wide eyes he could see her thoughts churning like a sea swell in the Aegean, but they were just as unfathomable to him.

'Smile,' he warned as he registered a ripple of unease pass across the guests in the church.

She flashed another glare at him that didn't need translating. It was the eye-squint equivalent of *Don't tell me to smile, damn you*. But she did exactly as he'd said. She turned to face not only the priest but also the guests, the delicate rosebud of her lips widening. And Leo could have sworn he heard a collective sigh pass across them as if she'd bestowed them with a gift.

The priest welcomed the guests in English and began

the wedding service, but he could have sworn that he felt Helena's panic tugging at his senses, inflaming his own frustration that his brother had involved him in such a scheme.

And as the choir began the first of what he hoped was only a few carefully selected hymns, Leo only had one thing on his mind—getting out of this ridiculous situation as quickly as possible—which was why he went through the process of saying what was needed to be said, when it needed to be said.

Honeymoon be damned, the moment this ceremony was over he was done. Out. Back to his apartment in Athens, back to Liassidis Shipping, where several important meetings and events would consume his thoughts. Not the quagmire of chaos that surrounded both Helena and Leander.

The priest gestured for them to enter the vestry, where they would sign the marriage document, and if anyone thought it odd that Leander Liassidis had grasped the hand of his soon-to-be wife and rushed her away from the view of the congregation it was only put down to just how passionately he loved the beautiful Helena Hadden.

CHAPTER TWO

'DON'T TOUCH ME,' Helena commanded in a harsh whisper, painfully conscious of the guests not terribly far away, her head swimming and panic crawling across her skin.

'I'm not,' Leo growled, his hand hovering near the base of her spine having the same impact as a red-hot poker would have. He turned back to the priest and his parents, following just behind.

'*Parakaló*, Father, Mamá, Patéra...would you give us a few minutes? We would like to just take in this beautiful moment.'

This beautiful moment?

Leo's words tripped around her head and she thought it half a miracle that they couldn't hear the insincerity dripping off them like poison.

Cora glanced between them and Helena nodded to let her know that it was okay. Helena hadn't seen as much of Leander's parents as she would have liked since the showdown between Leo and her mother following the mistake Gwen had made with Liassidis Shipping, and Cora's concern touched her deeply. But if Helena had even a single hope of figuring out what was going on, and how she was going to fix it, she would have to talk to Leo. Right now.

She watched the priest and Leo's parents leave the small, ornately decorated room. Turning away from the powerful impact his mere presence had on her, she was confronted with the cloth-covered table—a large book open to display the marriage schedule detailed in beautiful calligraphy. And there, mocking her, were empty spaces waiting for their signatures. No, not theirs, *his*.

Leander's.

Without that, she would never be able to access the shares that she needed to save the charity.

Oh, God, what was she going to do?

She spun back to face Leo, taking a step closer than she had intended, her worry, her concern so strong.

'Where is he?' she demanded, unable to keep the panic from her voice.

'How should I know?' demanded Leo, as if affronted she would even ask that of him.

He peered down at her, apparently uncaring of how close they were standing. And she hated the way her body responded, as if he were the man of her dreams instead of her nightmares. They were almost chest to chest, pressed against the superfine of the dark impeccable wool of his three-piece suit, the pristine white shirt that smelt of cotton and sandalwood, and she fought the temptation to inhale deeply. Because if she did breathe in, her chest would push against his and—

Leo stepped back so suddenly she nearly stumbled forward. Humiliation coursed through her as she regained her equilibrium, turning away from him to take that much needed breath.

'There must be some mistake,' she insisted.

'The only mistake you made, *agápi mou*, is trusting Leander for even a single second.'

'Don't call me that,' she lashed out, resenting the affectionate moniker that had no place between them.

She leaned back against the table and looked resentfully at the man who was seemingly unaware that he was standing in a sunbeam that picked lovingly over such incredibly handsome features. Helena knew that most people had a hard time telling the Liassidis twins apart, but she had never fallen foul of mistaking one for the other.

It was as if she could sense their personalities as much as what they looked like. Leander was playful, fun, irrepressible to the point of distraction. The week that she, Kate and Leander had just spent together in the lead-up to the wedding had been full of parties and fun, drinking and dancing. They'd been staying at the private island owned by the Liassidis family while his parents were away and she'd sensed absolutely nothing wrong with Leander. No, as always, he'd been his larger than life, gregarious self.

But if Leander was the life of the party, then Leo was the hangover in character form. The painful reminder of the morning-after, of earthly responsibilities and recriminations—that mistakes must be punished and paid for.

And while their features were near perfect symmetry—the thick, raven-dark hair almost wilfully unruly, the patrician nose, the savage cut of cheekbones regularly wept over by models, the closely cut beard that looked insolently stylish and the broad determined forehead—there *was* a difference.

Leo had always held himself back. He was just that little bit more isolated, that little bit less gregarious than Leander, a trait that had only increased with time and their separation, as if their differences had become more marked.

Because Leander had *never* impacted her the way Leo did—like her breath had been stolen, like flames heated her skin, like her pulse, her body even, was attached to the snap of his fingers, ready to leap at his whim.

Helena cleared her throat, suddenly painfully aware that she had been staring at him.

'What did he say to you?' she asked.

'Here. You can listen for yourself.'

Leo pulled his phone out of the pocket of his trousers and pressed the screen. Within seconds, Leander's voice filled the small room.

'It's me. I know we've not spoken for...well. You know how long it's been. I need you to do something for me. I have to go away. I just need some time... I'll be back by the end of the honeymoon, but until then I need you to do something for me. I need you to be me. I know you're not going to want to. But Helena needs this...'

Leo pressed a button on the screen, stopping his brother's message.

Helena frowned. 'Is that all there is to the message?'

'All that's pertinent to this situation,' he replied, not entirely sure why he had cut off the message there. But he knew instinctively that she wouldn't have wanted to hear Leander beg him not to leave her alone on her wedding day. Not because she wouldn't appreciate Leander's concern, but because he, Leo, had heard it.

She was staring at his phone as if there was more. As if there was some kind of explanation still to come.

'He wouldn't do this to me,' she said, lost in her thoughts. 'He knows...'

'He knows what, Helena? Why you're performing this absolute scam of a marriage?' Leo asked, refusing to disguise the scorn and disdain he felt for her and his brother in that moment. He hated lies, detested dishonesty, and it didn't get much more dishonest than this. 'What is it? What could you possibly hope to get from this?' he demanded, finally at the end of his patience.

Helena bit her lip. He could see the struggle in her eyes. Azure blue, misting over with sea spray.

'The *why* isn't pertinent to the situation,' she had the audacity to throw back at him.

'Fine. It doesn't matter anyway. The moment that the priest comes back, I'll tell him I'm not signing it and I'm done. Out,' he said, cutting through the air with his hand.

The effect on Helena was instantaneous, as if she'd been burned by fire. She launched herself across the vestry, her hands in little fists, raised as if she was holding herself back from actually clutching onto the lapels of his suit jacket.

'Please, Leonidas, please. I... You can't,' she said hopelessly. 'I... I need you.'

The words seemed to shock them both.

'Then tell me what this is all about,' he demanded.

She nodded fast, and a thin tendril of wheat-blonde hair unwound from the chignon. Helena began to pace and he began to feel uneasy for the first time that day.

'Helena—'

'I'm thinking!' she exclaimed. 'I'm...trying to figure out where to start.'

She turned on him mid-stride.

'Do you remember the shares my father left me?' she asked, her eyes bright shards of blue piercing him straight in the chest.

Of course he remembered the shares her father had left her in Liassidis Shipping. They tormented him each shareholder meeting where decisions were made that determined the future success of his company.

After Leander had taken his father's money and disappeared, Gwen Hadden's ignorant and stubborn decision had nearly destroyed the company, and it was Leo—alone—who had poured blood, sweat and tears into returning Liassidis Shipping to its rightful place as the number one company in the global industry. He had worked furious hours, with no one and nothing to guide him but his grit, instinct and determination. And he alone was responsible for the outcome.

In the years since he had fully taken over from his father, Leo had built up a global client list, with even more desperate to work with him. But the knowledge that anyone, let alone a Hadden, would one day inherit the thirty percent of Liassidis Shipping shares that her father had left her in his will had *tortured* him. He hated that, like her mother, Helena could impact the company's decision-making process. He hated that he didn't have complete control over a company that should be entirely his.

'*Naí*, of course I do, Helena,' he bit out.

She pulled her top lip beneath her teeth. 'The terms of my father's will state that I will inherit those shares—'

'When you are twenty-eight years old. Yes, I know. Two years' time.' The date had been indelibly printed on his brain ever since he'd heard the terms of the will. It had been like a bomb, ticking down until the day he no longer had a decent grasp on his company.

'Do you remember the caveat?'

Leo frowned. 'No, I… What caveat?' he asked, his stomach beginning to shift uneasily.

Helena swallowed. 'I can inherit those shares earlier than my twenty-eighth birthday if I marry.'

Leo felt as if he'd been slapped. Shock poured into every cell of his being.

'Why do you need the shares, Helena? What are you going to do with them?' he asked, realising suddenly that, no matter what played out here today, no matter where his brother was, whether he came back at the end of the honeymoon or not, his own life was about to change irrevocably.

Helena squared lean shoulders and faced up to him.

'I'm going to sell them,' she declared mutinously. 'As is my right.'

Helena had heard the phrase *a face like thunder*, but never actually seen it until now.

'You're going to sell the shares,' Leo repeated, almost word for word, as if making absolutely sure that he'd heard her right. 'Do you have *any* idea how that could impact Liassidis Shipping?' he demanded hotly. 'Any at all? How could you be so—'

'Keep your voice down,' Helena hissed.

He inhaled an angry breath and turned around, but Helena didn't miss the way that his fists clenched as if he'd hoped they were wrapped around her neck, before he plunged them into his trouser pockets.

She watched the shift of the wool suit jacket over the shoulders he rolled and as he cricked his neck from one side to the other. He stood so tall within the vestry, he nearly took up all the space.

'Who?' he asked, without bothering to turn and look at her.

'Who what?' she responded, not quite sure what he meant.

His exasperated sigh echoed around the room. 'Who are you selling the shares to?'

Helena frowned. To be honest, she hadn't thought that far ahead. She didn't need her business degree, or her master's, to know that the moment she had access to the shares there would be a feeding frenzy. People would bite her hands off for Liassidis Shipping shares.

She should have been pleased, but she wasn't. The thought of selling the shares her father had left her in a company he and Giorgos had built from the ground up devastated her. It was her father's legacy—the only thing of his that she had left, after her mother had sold the house and everything in it while she'd been away in her last year at boarding school, 'desperate to move on with my life,' she'd explained in the phone call that had taken away the last of what had once been Helena's entire life.

'You haven't decided yet,' he accurately guessed, pulling her back into the present.

The hairs on the back of her neck rose in warning. She could see the wheels turning behind Leo's fierce eyes. The intensity in them was as hypnotic as it was unbearable and she had just realised what he was about to say when the words came out of his mouth.

'Sell them to me.'

'No.'

Leo laughed, cruelty masked by remarkable beauty. 'It's not as if you're in a position to refuse me.'

'What are you going to do?' she demanded. 'Marry me? It's Leander's name on the register, not yours,' Helena pointed out.

'And the only people that know I'm not my brother are you and my parents. And it's in none of our interests to reveal the kind of fraudulent activity we're about to embark on.'

'You're mad. Crazy. You would never put Liassidis Shipping in such a risky position. What if we were discovered?' she demanded.

'The reward is worth it.'

To have you removed from anywhere near my company, she all but heard him add in the silence.

An ache bloomed deep within her heart from one too many rejections but she told herself it didn't matter.

'And you're desperate,' he pressed. 'I don't need to know what you need the money for, whether you spent too much on pretty clothes, or whether Gwen has tried to destroy another company,' he dismissed, uncaring of the effect his words had on her. 'All that's important is that you need to sell the shares, and I am in the position to buy them the quickest. So, tell me what you need in exchange for them.'

And at that moment she truly hated Leonidas Liassidis. Of all the things he'd ever said about her, of all the things he'd done after her mother had made an easy mistake for someone utterly new to business, *this* was what Helena would resent him for the most.

Making her feel weak and vulnerable, *to him*.

'It's not just the wedding,' she finally admitted through gritted teeth. 'It needs to be unquestionably a marriage. Leander...before he left, arranged for us to attend events throughout the next week—'

'The honeymoon?'

'Yes. We're supposed to attend various events to be seen, to prove that this is a real marriage. So that when I register the marriage certificate in the UK there are no questions then about me accessing my inheritance.'

'You need me to pretend to be him.'

'I need you,' Helena grudgingly explained, 'to pretend

to be the affectionate, playboy, charming husband that Leander would have been.'

'I can do that.'

'You have as much charm as a venomous snake,' she hissed. And while everything feminine in her roiled at pretending that Leonidas Liassidis was her 'loving husband', she couldn't deny that he could give her what she needed quickly and without fanfare.

'How much?' she asked, cutting to the heart of the matter. She thought she saw a flash of surprise, but it was gone in the blink of an eye.

'Fifty million. For *all* your shares.'

Helena nearly choked. 'That's nearly a third of their market value, Leo. That's daylight robbery,' she accused, horrified. She'd expected to make nearly two hundred million from the sale.

He shrugged as if to say *take it or leave it.*

'Absolutely not!' she cried out angrily as pinpricks of sweat dotted the back of her neck.

It wasn't enough. Not nearly enough to replace the money stolen from Incendia.

'Okay,' Leo said amicably. 'It's your call. I'll just slip out the back and you can explain to all the guests that my brother has disappeared to leave you stranded and alone on your wedding day. I'm sure that the press will have more sympathy for you than him. But, to be honest, none of this will affect me in the slightest.'

He turned and before she could stop herself she'd reached out to grab his arm. He paused, looking down at where her hand had grasped onto his sleeve as if he couldn't believe she'd dared.

She removed her hand and he turned slowly to give her his full attention. How could she have ever thought there was anything remotely decent about this man? It had been years since they had properly spoken, more years before that since they had laughed together. Just the thought of it seemed nearly impossible. And now? She couldn't ever imagine laughing with this man again.

He was blackmailing her with an offer that was so offensive it made her feel nauseous. But what choice did she have? If she didn't agree to his offer, then there was no way that she could hope to plug the shortfall caused by the CFO's theft. And if she didn't, then the charity would be declared bankrupt by the financial review in December. Millions of people, families experiencing loss and devastated by cardiac events, would suffer. All because she hadn't been able to fix it.

'I don't need to know what you need the money for... All that's important is that you need to sell the shares, and I am in the position to buy them the quickest.'

Leo was right in one way. But he had also made a big mistake in revealing how much he wanted to have the shares for himself. It was a weapon. Small, and not enough to beat him, but enough to get what she needed.

'One,' she threw out between them.

'One what?'

'One hundred million.'

His head snapped back as if he'd hardly expected her to even think, let alone dare, to actually counter his offer.

'No.' The word was a full stop cutting through the air.

'Okay,' Helena said, putting her hands on her hips. 'You're right. I'll call this off. I'll figure out a different way to solve my issues. And I'll *still* have thirty percent shares in Liassidis Shipping,' she taunted.

Tension snapped across those broad shoulders, making him appear to loom more imposingly over her. He went very still, as if fearful that if he moved the wrong way he might lose the one thing he most wanted. Those shares.

'And then, when I'm twenty-eight, just think of what I could—'

'Seventy-five.'

'No.'

Leo slammed his teeth together before he could say another word. Helena Hadden had learned how to negotiate. There had been a time when her face had been so expressive that he could have sworn he'd all but seen her words before she said them, but now? Staring back at him was a fury who had chosen the hill she would die on. He couldn't afford to underestimate her like he had with her mother, or this time the damage could be fatal.

And really, if he was honest, offering fifty million for thirty percent shares in Liassidis Shipping was almost disgusting. One hundred was still nauseating. But it was a drop in the ocean of what Gwen had cost the company, so Leo told himself that the deeply unfair price was nothing but compensation years after the event.

He could have let her sweat a little more, but they didn't have time. He could feel the restlessness of the guests waiting in the nave, the concern building between the priest and his parents.

'One hundred.'

She held out her hand as if to seal the deal.

'I'll have my people email you the contract,' he said, ignoring her hand and turning back to call for the priest, missing the way that Helena masked the jagged edge of pain that crossed her features.

His parents, thankfully, remained studiously quiet while the priest went through the legal requirements.

Helena was first to sign the register, her gaze flicking to his one final time before the pen flew over the dots beside her printed name.

Unaccountably, his pulse picked up. Looking down at the piece of paper, the jarring sight of Helena's name beside that of his brother tightened a grip around his chest. Recognising it as a reasonable response to the chaos his brother and Helena were dragging him into, he placed his pen on the paper.

Signing this was the height of stupidity. If they were ever discovered, it would absolutely destroy his reputation and in all likelihood be the very end of the company—and after he'd worked so hard to bring it back after near bankruptcy.

But if they *weren't* discovered then he would finally have the whole of the company to himself. Without another thought, Leonidas Liassidis signed the register as his brother.

Five minutes later, he took his place beside Helena in front of the priest and the wedding guests and counted down the minutes until he could get away from the church and Helena and get a drink in his hand. The reception would at least afford him some space from her, he prayed, as the priest's words washed over him. Until…

'In the sight of God and these witnesses, I now pronounce you husband and wife! You may now kiss!'

His mind went utterly blank for a moment, the pulse of blood rushing in his ears became thunderous, even as he leashed himself back under control. He turned to face Helena, studying her carefully, her eyes wide with shock and something close to fear, but not quite. He half-expected her to run, but she didn't. She simply watched him, her gaze a physical touch against his senses.

He raised his hand to the side of her face as if to cup her jaw, but stopped short of touching, and he chose to ignore the ripple of response across Helena's features, chose to ignore his body's instinctive response to her as a woman. Because his brain had absolutely no trouble remembering just how far he needed to keep from Helena Hadden.

She watched, wide-eyed, as he dipped his head. He felt the entire congregation in the church hold their breath in anticipation, surprised to realise that Helena had done the same—the blue depths of her eyes beginning to disappear beneath the black of her pupils.

Leashing an instinctive response, he dipped his head deeper, cutting off the line of sight to their lips from the guests in the church, and lowered his thumb to Helena's mouth. He slid the pad of his finger across the slick surface, blurring the gloss coating of the flushed plump lips, trying to ignore the subtle flinch that pulled at Helena's body as he did so.

Oohs and *ahhs* filled the nave of the church and the only person who would ever know that they hadn't kissed was his fake bride.

CHAPTER THREE

'WHAT THE HELL is going on? Where is Leander?' Kate demanded as she drew a still reeling Helena away from the reception. The loud voices of guests could still be heard at a painful volume to Helena's sensitive ears. But the small cloakroom was thankfully quiet and empty of guests, who were being distracted with canapés and chilled glasses of champagne.

She felt... She shook her head, still trying to rid herself of the humiliation that had stung her cheeks irrevocably with shame. She had *wanted* Leo to kiss her. With an old familiar need that had filled her senses and overwhelmed all rational thought, she had wanted him to kiss her and, as if unable to bear even the smallest of touches, he'd only made it *look* like he'd kissed his bride.

'Helena? Are you okay?' Kate tried again, pulling Helena around to face her. 'You're beginning to worry me.'

Helena was worried too. She pressed her fingers to her lips, hoping to feel something other than Leo's thumbprint there. A shudder rippled through her. Disgust, she told herself. Anger.

'Helena!' Kate cried, finally pulling her back to her senses.

'I'm sorry,' she said. 'I'm... Leander's gone,' she admitted helplessly, without realising that Kate had somehow recognised that the man standing at the top of the aisle had been the wrong Liassidis.

'I know that. But where?' she demanded.

'That's what I'd like to know,' Leo said, standing across the threshold as if as reluctant to enter as she was to have him there. As it was, he filled the doorframe of the small cloakroom, stifling the air and making Helena feel claustrophobic.

Kate glared at him. 'Actually, that's not important right now. Are you okay?' Kate demanded of Helena.

Being cut off by a complete stranger, being told that what he said wasn't important, left an almost comical look of shock across Leo's features and Helena enjoyed every single moment of it. Bastard. It was the least he deserved.

'Yes, I'm okay,' she told Kate. 'I don't know where Leander is, but Leo is going to stand in for him while he's away.'

'Away? This isn't making any sense, Helena.' Kate's pretty features scrunched in confusion.

'He just said that something came up and that he'd be back by the end of the honeymoon,' Helena explained.

'That's it? He didn't say anything else to you?'

'It wasn't said to Helena, it was left on my—'

'Well, we have to find him,' Kate announced, cutting off Leo once again.

Leo's response was a glare that would have felled many a man, but Helena's best friend couldn't care less.

'Do you know where he'd go?' Kate asked Helena.

'Why would she know where—' Leo tried before Helena cut him off this time.

'He could be anywhere, but I'd imagine he's in one of his properties. He's probably thinking that there are too many for us to check them all. But I need him. He needs to be here,' Helena said desperately.

'I'll find him, Helena. I promise,' Kate swore, the look in her eyes telling Helena that Kate knew how much this meant to her. So much was on the line—and just because Leo had promised to cover for his twin didn't mean that he'd actually be able to pull this off. If people found out—the press even—it would be a nightmare of unholy proportions.

'My jet will be at your disposal,' Leo informed them.

Kate looked at him blankly. 'Is that supposed to impress me?'

Leo glared at her. 'I don't like you,' he said boldly.

'That's okay, I don't like you either,' Kate replied, turning back to Helena. 'If you can give me a list of his properties, I'll take the jet and find him. I'll go now.'

'No. Not yet. You're supposed to be giving a toast. If you disappear it would look like something's wrong,' Helena said, thinking through the rest of the reception. All she had to do was get through the next few hours and then, when she got to the villa on the Mani Peninsula that Leander had booked for their honeymoon, she could breathe, think and plan.

She had this. She would get through this and get what she needed, because she was a Hadden. She was her father's daughter and people counted on her. Incendia counted on her. She wouldn't let them down.

Kate nodded in understanding. 'What about after the toasts?' she offered and Helena agreed.

Helena desperately didn't want Kate to go. As the only person who knew the whole truth about why she needed the money, who knew how much it had hurt to discover that someone had abused the charity that had meant so much to her in such a way, who had taken advantage of her new appointment to do so, Kate being away at a time that she most needed her would be terrible.

'Just think of it as practice for Borneo,' Kate replied, alluding to the fact that her best friend was finally achieving her dreams, having secured a permanent position as a vet at an orangutan sanctuary in the Southeast Asia island. Just the thought of her friend being so far away caused a pang of hurt to unfurl within her. But she pushed it aside. Kate had wanted this for so long.

'Okay, but if you don't find him in three days, that's it. You've got too much to do before Borneo and I can't let you mess it up.'

Kate gave her the dazzling smile that soothed her more than Helena could say. 'It's all done! I'm ready. Packed and everything. And don't worry. I'll probably find him hiding out at the first place I look.'

Leo had taken out his phone and was typing away. Both of the women looked at him expectantly—and when he looked up, he simply stared back at them blankly.

'Do I have permission to speak now?' he asked drily.

'Don't sulk,' Kate replied. 'It will give you wrinkles.'

Leo's eyes flashed, but Helena cut off whatever he was about to say with a question.

'Is the jet nearby?'

'Yes,' he replied, frustration clearly still simmering in his gaze. He turned to Kate, handing her a card, both reluctantly and resentfully. 'Give this to the pilot and crew. They'll help you with whatever you need, they'll take you wherever you need to go. Just…be nice, okay?'

Kate flashed him a sugary smile. 'I *am* nice,' she replied sincerely. 'To those who deserve it,' she said, before slipping out of the cloakroom and back to the reception.

Helena didn't bother hiding the smirk on her lips. It was nice to see someone put Leonidas Liassidis in his place for once. Especially as she couldn't do it herself. No matter what she felt towards the man, she needed him. At least until Leander returned.

'What did you tell her about me?' Leo demanded.

'Nothing but the truth,' Helena replied tartly, before slipping past him to follow Kate back to the reception.

Leo was getting a headache. Sitting at the head of the top table next to Helena, the sunlight bouncing off starched white linen, glistening glass and pristine silverware combined with the noise from the guests made him grimace.

'Could you at least try to smile?' Helena whispered angrily.

'It's a little hard to find something to smile about at this present moment,' he whispered back.

'Just think of all those shares you're getting at a bargain price,' Helena hissed through gritted teeth and, much to his surprise, he did actually smile. Something that seemed only to anger Helena more. So much so he could have sworn he heard a growl coming from her, which in turn only made him smile more and her scowl.

Looking out across the room, he could have counted the number of people he recognised on one hand. He had become such a stranger in his twin brother's life that the only people he knew were the bride and his own parents. Not that he cared. If these people valued his brother in spite of his selfishness and his ability to betray in a heartbeat, then more fool them.

Because wasn't this the ultimate betrayal? Not even turning up to his own wedding.

A wedding Leander had agreed to only to help Helena access her inheritance.

He was stopped from following that chain of thought by the way that Helena was craning her head to search the room.

'Is something wrong?' he asked.

'No, I just…' Her voice trailed off when her eyes settled and a small hopeful smile crossed her features. Her hand rose in a half wave, as if unsure how it would be received, and when he turned to look he found Gwen, acknowledging her daughter with a barely cracked smile.

He watched, leashing an old familiar anger as Gwen leaned to say something to her companion—her second husband, he presumed, the one she'd married about a year after her debacle with Liassidis Shipping. The man—John, if he remembered rightly—was something in banking.

As she came to greet her daughter, Leo was struck by the impression of seeing Helena in thirty years' time. Blonde hair adeptly highlighted with elegant silver streaks. High cheekbones and a strong jawline that had resisted age's pull. Gwen Hadden was slightly smaller than Helena, who had inherited her height from her father, but the poise was inherent to both women.

'Darling,' Gwen said levelly. 'The dress looks beautiful,' she went on with no tone of warmth in her voice at all, 'despite being from such a relatively new designer.'

Helena gazed carefully back at her mother, as if waiting.

'But really, having Kate dressed in gold,' Gwen added. Leo was surprised to feel the scold in her words. And Helena, who had been so fiery, who had been so full of life demanding he increase his offer for her shares, biting back a hurt Gwen *must* have been able to see.

'I'm so pleased that you and John could make it,' Helena said with a sincerity that seemed wasted on the woman.

Leo looked back to where John remained at the table, still eating his starter and engaged in conversation with another guest.

'Well, it did interrupt his golfing holiday, but he'll make up the time later. Will we be seeing you at drinks in October?'

Helena blinked. 'I'm not quite sure yet—the end of the year is a busy time at work.'

'Well, it would be good to see you there,' Gwen said before turning her attention onto him.

'Leander,' Gwen finally acknowledged.

Helena placed her hand on his, and to the world it would look like the affectionate connection between a newly married couple. Obviously, they couldn't see the crescent moons digging into his palms from her nails. He managed to keep the smile on his face despite the scratch of pain.

He nodded in return, suddenly unwilling to risk opening his mouth.

Gwen turned back to Helena one last time and Leo thought he saw the shadow of emotion flicker in her gaze.

'Your father…' She stopped, pressing her mouth into a firm line before pushing on. 'He would have been happy today,' she said, nodding to herself as if she had done some great maternal duty.

And, for just a moment, the years dropped away, the arguments, the feuds, the recriminations, and Helena was a little girl again, looking for her parents' approval. He saw it in the sheen across her eyes.

* * *

It was enough, Helena told herself through the dull ache that edged her breathing. It was more than she'd expected, she reasoned, and then told herself off for being silly. She had to remind herself that this wasn't a real wedding. It shouldn't mean anything to her that her father *had* joked about joining the families together. And she shouldn't be wishing for more than her mother was capable of giving.

Helena watched Gwen return to her table before daring to cast a look at Leo, whose expression was unfathomable. It was, she realised, the first time he'd seen her mother since the argument between them that had resulted in Gwen quitting and selling her Liassidis Shipping shares back to the company.

He reached for his wine glass and took a healthy mouthful as she remembered the awful heated words from that night. The ones that had excommunicated her and her mother from the lives of all but one of the Liassidis family.

'What do you want me to do?'

'I want you to go back in time and not have done it in the first place!'

'Don't be so juvenile, Leo.'

*'I want—*the board *wants—you to sell back your shares and leave Liassidis Shipping completely. And then? I want never to see you again.'*

More words and more anger had filled the room that night, all of which had been shocking to the sixteen-year-old, already grieving Helena, so much so that she rarely thought about it. Leander had been the only member of the Liassidises to keep in touch with her afterwards. Helena had sometimes wondered if it had started to spite

Leo, but theirs was a true friendship, a bond that had strengthened into one of love. Just not *that* kind of love.

In her heart, she'd always believed that Leander and Kate would make the perfect couple but, despite all her best intentions to get the two together, they had only met last week when she and Kate had travelled to Greece for the wedding.

But they'd had such a great week together, Helena thought. So she couldn't understand what had caused Leander to disappear. It hurt that he'd not been able to tell her. Leander was her friend, one she loved like a brother. Yet, instead, he'd chosen to rely on the person he hadn't spoken to for five years.

'And now we welcome Mr and Mrs Liassidis to the dance floor for their first dance as husband and wife!' exclaimed the wedding planner, pulling her awkwardly back to the present.

Leo had stood and was gesturing her towards the dance floor and suddenly she wanted to be anywhere but here. She didn't care about the money, she didn't care if she failed as the charity's CEO. She just couldn't be this close to Leonidas Liassidis, who had made it painfully clear how much he disliked even the thought of touching her.

But she didn't have a choice.

They approached the dance floor as the opening bars of *At Last* by Etta James played out across the reception hall and she determined to get through it without incident. But when she placed her hand in his and he slipped his arm around her waist, his palm splaying delicately at her back, a shiver rippled through her. He couldn't have missed it, yet his focus was firmly, almost disdainfully, on the guests.

And, just like that, she was a fifteen-year-old girl again

and he was the older boy she had a crush on. The one whose girlfriend had spat venom and caused her friend to become a cold stranger. One who couldn't bear to even look at her.

'And you thought I was going to be the one having trouble keeping up this façade,' he whispered and it was all the warning she got before he pulled her against his chest, much to the tittering delight of the guests watching.

Her breasts pushed against his firm chest, the outline of his body indelibly inked on her skin, the heat of his palm on her back pressing her gently against him, keeping her there even if she could have pulled herself back.

How could her body betray her so? Her pulse leapt to his touch, arousal filling her core with an ache that was indecent. She leaned back to glare up at him but was struck by the unflinching intensity in his gaze. His eyes glowed, shards of gold pulsing deep within the rich mahogany of his gaze.

Could it be that he felt it too? The wicked energy in the air between them. The *want*.

In response to the shift in their positions, his hand curved around her ribcage, the tips of his fingers perilously close to the underside of her breast. She felt the flush of heat on her cheeks and hoped that no one could see as he bent his head to the shell of her ear.

'Just think of all the money I'm going to give you,' he whispered, returning her earlier taunt back to her. And, just like that, whatever sweet heat had built in her body flamed to ash. He had misread her body's reaction as anger? Had *she* been fool enough to misread his anger as something else entirely?

Perhaps it was better that way, because he was right. She *did* need to think of the money he was going to give her. Money that she would use to save the charity that had once saved her. She used that thought to give her strength. She needed to get access to those shares. And to do that she needed this marriage to seem real.

Leo clenched his jaw, bracing against the impact of soft, warm hands on his body. He might not remember the last time he'd held a woman like this, but he knew it hadn't felt so...incendiary.

He'd not quite been able to give his trust to another woman after the breakdown of his engagement to Mina, but that hadn't stopped him from engaging in mutually pleasurable affairs with women who valued discretion and honesty.

Helena was as far from those two things as he could imagine. But as she pressed one hand against his heart and raised the other to curl her fingers in his hair, his body didn't care that it was a calculated move for appearances' sake.

And his mind and heart wrestled between pulling her closer and pushing her away.

He risked a glance down at her, a flash of silver catching his attention. He nearly tripped when he caught sight of the silver necklace Helena wore.

'Leo...' Helena whispered, her grip tightening on his hand.

Pasting on a bright smile for the guests, he shrugged and twirled her away from him and back to buy his racing thoughts some time to calm.

'What is it?' Helena asked, settling back into the rhythm of the music, her face flushed from the dance.

'I'm surprised you're wearing that today.'

Helena's gaze snapped back to his, holding just a little

too long before she looked away, cutting him off before he could discern her thoughts.

'My necklace? Why wouldn't I? It was a gift. From Leander.'

From Leander?

And, just like that, he remembered. He remembered how his brother, at home during one of his rare visits since he'd left, had ended up claiming responsibility for the Christmas present he'd bought the fifteen-year-old Helena all those years ago.

The box, with the inscription 'From L', had contained a simple peony pendant that Leo had bought her, because they were her favourite flower. But on that last Christmas they'd all spent together—before her father had passed, before Gwen had nearly ruined their company—the argument he'd had with Mina had made it impossible for him to claim responsibility for it.

While everyone had oohed and ahhed over the pretty pendant Helena had received, Mina had already been fuming—smarting over the fact that the small blue box he'd given her contained earrings rather than the engagement ring she'd been expecting. She would have made a scene of epic proportions if she'd discovered that it was he who had bought the necklace for Helena. And in what had perhaps been their last moment of twin sense, Leander had stepped in to help him and taken credit for the present.

'It's a peony,' Helena explained, as if he didn't already know.

'Mmm,' was all Leo was capable of replying. It was something he'd completely forgotten about.

'Something old,' Helena continued. 'I guess blue is the feeling I got when Leander didn't appear and 'new' would be you? Or would you be borrowed?' Helena said, smiling sadly.

'Borrowed would be the shares,' he snapped, feeling utterly thrown by the memories beginning to resurface.

'Of course,' Helena replied, fake smile back in place, while her eyes glowed with accusations and recriminations. 'Because you insist on conveniently forgetting that my father helped Giorgos not only found Liassidis Shipping, but also broker many of the deals that made it an international success in the first place. Your revisionist history wouldn't account for that, would it?' she demanded hotly through her teeth.

'Revisionist history?' he demanded, intensely disliking how well her verbal blow had struck.

As the song drew to an end, Helena's fingers tightened at his neck. The smile trembled for just a second before firming.

'We're done here,' Helena promised and slipped from his embrace, waving to the guests as she exited the reception through a door where Kate waited anxiously.

He was left for a moment, standing in the middle of an empty dance floor, one hundred and fifty pairs of eyes on him and none meaning a single thing to him.

'Be me.'

Leo forced a broad smile to his lips, took a comically dramatic bow and returned to the table, needing as much space from Helena as she apparently needed from him.

The whirr of the helicopter blades filled Helena's ears and she welcomed it. Welcomed the way it blocked out her chaotic thoughts and filled the silence that had descended over Leo the moment they had left the reception.

Helena had bid a tearful goodbye to Kate, unsure

whether she'd get to see her best friend again before she travelled to Borneo and hating that the parting had been so focused on Leander.

God, she hoped that Kate would find him. Being around Leo was stressful enough. Every time she looked at him, all she could think of was how he was all but blackmailing her for her shares. If she hadn't been so desperate there was no way she'd have ever agreed to such a low price. Not as a grieving daughter and not as a grown businesswoman.

'We're coming in to land,' informed the pilot on the open channel in the headsets.

Helena nodded to show her understanding. She'd warned Leo already not to say anything revealing on the open channel—the pilot knew Leander well—and Leo had apparently taken that to heart by not saying a single thing. Instead, he'd spent the entire journey looking out of the window, his expression grimly guarded.

They came to land on the small helipad at the back of the beautiful Mani Peninsula villa. Their suitcases had been sent ahead earlier that morning so their belongings would be waiting for them, and all Helena could think about was getting out of her dress. It was beautiful, quite possibly the most exquisite thing she'd ever worn, but it was too much now.

The co-pilot slipped out from the front of the helicopter and slid the door open for her, holding out his hand. Helena gratefully took it, wanting to leave Leo in the damn machine to fly off God knew—or cared—where.

Kate was gone, Leander was gone, and she was alone with the bastard who had bartered her inheritance for a pittance.

Now that the guests were far behind her, now that the

stress of the day was nearly done, she could barely keep the tears back as she hurried towards the villa Leander had booked with her in mind.

'It will be our refuge for the week. Here you can finally let go and just be yourself.'

But it wasn't. It wasn't a refuge but a prison, and she couldn't let go at all—not even for one second. Because Leonidas Liassidis would be there, waiting around every corner.

'Where are you going?' Leo asked, his tone unusually blank.

She felt his gaze on her as she grabbed the bottle of champagne from where it had been placed in an ice bucket by the open front door.

'To bed. Alone. With this,' she said, holding up the green bottle, purposely keeping her back to him as the first tear rolled down her cheek.

CHAPTER FOUR

HELENA WOKE UP feeling awful. She peered at the clock on the side table next to the large bed she barely remembered collapsing into last night. She closed her eyes against the glowing display announcing that it was seven in the morning and cursed.

The last thing she remembered was promising herself that she'd just close her eyes for a short nap, but she'd slept for twelve hours. For most people that would probably be a good sign, but for Helena Hadden? Sleep was her stress response. Her body's default protection setting, a primal act of self-preservation that should have been warning enough.

She passed a hand over her face and hauled herself unsteadily to sit on the side of the bed, surprised by the cool touch of platinum from her wedding ring glancing over her skin.

Married. She was, for all intents and purposes, now married to Leander Liassidis.

Only it wasn't Leander who was here with her, but his twin brother.

Not that it mattered. Because as long as the press continued to believe that it was Leander with her, then she still had a chance to make this marriage believable. And as long as it was believable she could still save Incendia.

That thought kept her going while she showered and dressed in a long cream muslin dress, reminding herself that Leo wouldn't much care how she looked. She walked out onto the balcony of her room, the view of the Mediterranean Sea a dramatic display of sheer beauty, glittering like diamonds on silk rippled by the wind. Raising her face to the sun, she inhaled the sea salt and rosemary that always reminded her of Greece.

Her heart said *home*, but her head chided her for being fanciful.

What part did Greece play in her desire to be a successful CEO and businesswoman? To prove herself worthy of her father's name? What part did Greece play in her life when everything she knew now was in England?

But that wasn't true, was it? Not any more. Kate would soon be in Borneo, and Helena would be alone. But she told herself that it would only give her more time to focus on Incendia. On its future success *after* she had ensured they passed the financial review at the end of the year.

She sighed and prised open her eyes, the sound of something down below drawing her attention. There, powering through the gentle waters of an infinity pool that merged so well with the sea beyond she'd not even seen it, was Leo.

Dark head of hair, seal slick, and powerful muscles undulating across his back, his arms parted the water like a sea god. The glory of his easy movements, the breath he took with each alternate stroke, the backs of his thighs, the cut of his calf muscles, defined, solid, slid through the water with enough grace to barely mark the surface of the pool.

Her cheeks warming and her pulse flaring, she could no longer deny her body's response to him. It wasn't anger that made her heart pound painfully in her chest. It wasn't resentment that caused heat to burn through what little common sense she had when it came to him. The effect Leo had on her was overwhelming. The throb between her legs, the dampness even. No one had *ever* made her feel this way.

But the person she wanted to be with, to give herself to, would do more than make her body sing. They would make her feel loved, cherishcd, wanted because she was enough, just as she was.

And that could, she assured herself, never be the man currently in the pool below. Because the cold and aloof Leo Liassidis only wanted one thing from her: her shares. And once he got them he would leave her life, just like he had before—without a backward glance or a second thought.

Leo had devastated her teenage years and she wouldn't let that happen to her twenties. So she would stay out of his way until she couldn't avoid him any more.

Leo hauled himself from the side of the pool for the second day in a row, after eventually realising that, no matter how many times a day he swam, no matter how many laps he did, it wouldn't resolve the frustration that had plagued him for the last two days.

Helena's absence suggested that she was hiding from him. Which, if he were being honest, suited him just fine. He'd taken several meetings online both the day before and earlier that afternoon but, despite insisting that very little needed to be changed, his assistant had, for the duration of Leo's absence, taken it upon himself to 'lighten his load'.

And he didn't like it one bit. Over the years he'd developed a routine that he was happy with, that worked for both him and Liassidis Shipping. Full days and ferocious focus to the exclusion of all else was what had saved the company once, and what ensured that it was still at the top of its field today.

Leo rolled his shoulders, relishing the ache brought by his morning swim as he stood there staring out at a view that looked similar to the one from his parents' island. He hadn't been back there for quite some time now. Before, he would have blamed it on work. But was that true? Or had he just been trying to avoid his brother?

Whether it was Helena, seeing his parents at the wedding, or a strange mixture of both, his memory was tiptoeing around things he'd rather forget.

'Have you made your decision?'

'Yes, Patéra. I'm going to work at Liassidis Shipping.'

At eighteen, he'd been so excited to accept the mantle his father was willing to pass on. Wanting to make him proud. Wanting to work with his brother, to stand by his side as they became men.

'And you, Leander?'

'I...' He'd not even been able to look Leo in the eye. *'I want to take the money.'*

Leo clenched his jaw, braced against the memory of that day. But, in truth, it wasn't that moment that had been the fatal blow to his relationship with Leander. It had been the days, weeks, months of daydreams leading up to it. Of his brother pretending to support his plans for their future. The *years* of believing that he and his brother shared one thought, one desire, one goal.

And none of it had been real.

It had been him alone in that daydream. And him alone to bear the weight of the damage caused by Gwen three years later. By that point, he hadn't even expected or wanted Leander to come home to help. But it had also been him alone to pull Liassidis Shipping back from the brink of absolute disaster.

And it had taught him an invaluable lesson. If he couldn't rely on his twin, he couldn't rely on anyone. And he'd honed that independence into a skill. That way, he didn't have distractions, he didn't leave himself or his company open to other people's incompetence or betrayal. No. It was far better for him to go it alone.

Leo shook off the water from his hair and dried himself with a towel when his mobile beeped. He stopped to check the message.

We have the gallery event.

Frowning at the message from Helena that could just have easily been said in person, he typed back irritably.

Yes?

The car is coming in thirty minutes.

His hackles rippled at her clipped tone, but he restrained the urge to snipe back. Yes, Helena needed him. But he also needed her. If he alienated her, he might never get hold of those shares, and he'd never have what he'd always wanted: complete control of Liassidis Shipping.

He reached his room and peered at the wardrobe, filled with clothes that belonged to his brother. Clearly, when Leander had left, it had been with nothing but his phone and presumably a passport.

But the moment Leo caught himself wondering what had possibly made his brother do such a thing, he stopped himself. It made no difference to him. He no longer allowed himself to be tormented by the whys of his brother's behaviour.

He showered quickly, dressed and was buttoning up the crisp white shirt when he realised he was standing in the one place in his room where he could see through his own door, down the hallway and into Helena's room.

From this exact point, he could see the corner of her bed, and Helena looking at her reflection in a floor-length mirror.

Leo turned his attention to the cuffs of his sleeves. At home, Leo had rows and rows of cufflinks on display. They were the final touch on an appearance that mattered to him as the face of Liassidis Shipping. And while Leo knew Leander wouldn't wear them, he purposefully retrieved the pair he'd worn the day he'd arrived at the wedding and fastened them in place.

He glanced back up to catch Helena putting in an earring. Her head was tilted to one side, her hair styled in a pretty, messy knot high on her head, showing off the slender arch of her neck. It was such a simple moment, but one that felt oddly private, as if it were something he shouldn't be witnessing.

But his gaze still consumed the sight of her, dressed in the floor-length, high-necked green velvet dress, as if she were a feast. His hungry imagination, delighting in this moment of voyeurism, offered up suggestions for what his eyes couldn't see and what his subconscious desperately wanted.

Inches of pale skin glowing beneath jade-coloured lingerie filled his mind. He saw his hand slide across that skin, felt it shiver beneath his touch, tasted the heady scent of her as he pressed open-mouthed kisses to her breasts, relished the damp, wet heat of her as he delved between her legs.

His pulse tripped and sweat broke out across his neck. Locked in that moment of erotic images, his famously quick brain made a million and one connections, all hurtling towards fierce arousal as if it were a race.

So attuned to her body, he felt the moment she realised that he was watching her, the way that tension pulled like a thread across her shoulders. He forced his gaze away and stepped from view, taking ruthless control over his wayward body.

Helena was a means to an end. Nothing more. She could never be anything more. And he didn't *want* anything more, he told himself. This was nothing but an aberrant response to the female form. And it wouldn't happen again, he warned himself.

By the time he'd regained his composure, Helena had retrieved her clutch and was making her way towards him down the corridor.

'You shouldn't be wearing cufflinks.'

Biting back a response, because right now anything that came out of his mouth would either sound petulant or lecherous, he simply stated, 'We'll be late.'

'Leander is always late,' she dismissed easily. 'You shouldn't be wearing cufflinks.'

'I should be about two hundred and eighty kilometres away and not here, involved in this farce, but...' And he shrugged as if to say, *here we are*.

Helena glared at him. 'Fine. But please remember. If people don't believe that you are Leander and that we are happily married, you can kiss your shares goodbye.'

* * *

The car pulled up at the red-carpeted entrance to the gallery in Kalamata for the opening night of an exhibition by an up-and-coming artist garnering deserved amounts of attention for her unique subversion of the male gaze. Helena had been more than happy to support the event when Leander had chosen it, but with Leo beside her she wanted to be anywhere else but here.

She just couldn't imagine how he would respond to the detailed and graphic images that had prompted extreme responses in both the media and the public. But, Helena supposed, she would soon find out.

Leo slipped wordlessly from the car and came round to her door, holding it open and offering his hand. The smile on his face shocked her for a moment after the cold silence between them since leaving the villa, but then the first of many flashbulbs erupted and she remembered that he was supposed to be Leander.

She stood and he placed her hand in the crook of his arm and gestured towards the length of red carpet, where the three-deep crowd of paparazzi waited impatiently. As always, she felt assaulted by the bright flashes of light directed their way. In England, her family wealth and name had always drawn attention, but her marriage to a Liassidis had launched the attention into a whole new stratosphere.

'Leander, over here!'

'Helena, Helena!' another called.

From somewhere in the mass of dark shapes looming behind the bright flashes, questions were hurled their way.

'How's the honeymoon going, Helena?' one voice jeered, but she kept her smile.

'Is it true what they say about him, Helena?'

She swallowed at the crass comments, distaste and disgust crawling over her skin. She felt the flex of Leo's forearm beneath her palm. Unlike his brother, Leo had never courted the press. Especially not after the months and months of speculation and derision at his leadership fail in the early stages of taking over Liassidis Shipping. A hounding scrutiny that he had protected her mother from, even as he'd engineered her removal from the company.

'Helena, are you here for pleasure, or are you hoping to gain a brand ambassador for Incendia, perhaps?'

Seizing on the sanest question of the evening, and the opportunity to increase awareness for her charity, she paused and found the reporter amongst the masses, allowing a genuine smile to spread across her features.

'I would be incredibly lucky to do so, but for tonight we're just here to enjoy the exhibition. Efi Balaskou is a fascinating artist and I can't wait to see her exhibition.'

'*Efcharistó*, Helena. Leander? If you have a moment?'

Leo's focus had been on the crowd until the mention of Incendia. She couldn't have explained why, but she felt it. His attention had zeroed in on it, as if it were a vulnerability he could take advantage of.

And the horrible truth was that it was.

'Congratulations on your wedding. It was a beautiful event.'

Leo smiled broadly, setting off another round of flashes from photographers who knew bankable good looks when they saw them.

'Oh, that little thing?' he said, full of tease that felt just wrong coming from Leo's lips. 'It was perfect, wasn't it, *agápi mou*?' he went on, turning to Helena.

She smiled, despite a strong suspicion that he'd used that term precisely because she'd told him not to.

'But your brother wasn't there. We've all heard the rumours of the rift between you, but how did it feel for him to have missed your wedding day?'

Helena's mind went blank. She just hadn't expected the question. This time, the pause, though infinitesimal, seemed to stretch out before them like eternity.

Leo narrowed his gaze at the reporter and, in a panic, Helena tightened her grip on his arm.

'You know what Leo Liassidis is like,' Leo dismissed, after an eternal moment of near deafening silence.

The reporter laughed, clearly thinking he was in on an inside joke of some sort.

'*Naí.* The words *stick up* and *backside* come to mind,' the reporter said in Greek.

Helena flushed. It was one thing to think it, but another entirely to say it. And accidentally to the man's face? Breath rippled in her chest, making her light-headed enough to want to come to Leo's defence.

'I—'

'It would take an act of God to remove that stick,' Leo interrupted, leaning towards the reporter conspiratorially. 'He had *very important business,*' Leo mimicked and for a moment Helena was so lost in Leo being Leander, being Leo, that she simply stared at him. 'I hear that he's so wedded to his office chair, he takes it home with him.'

The reporter laughed again as she forced an awkward smile to her lips.

'Helena, were you offended by your brother-in-law's absence?'

Leo looked at her, the challenge in his eyes wicked. As if he were saying, *Now's your chance.* A wickedness that cut through the years, the bitter recriminations between them, to before her mother's mistake, before the loss of her father, before that horrible Christmas, to when she'd felt safe in their relationship, when she'd felt she'd known him. And that he'd known her.

'I'm usually more offended by his presence, so for me his absence made a pleasant change,' she announced loftily, holding Leo's gaze.

Leo threw his head back and laughed. A genuine, full-throated laugh that caught almost everyone's attention.

She couldn't help but let a smile curve her lips. It wasn't every day she managed to score a point against Leo Liassidis, but to make him laugh like that? Like he used to? A round of flashes went off and it was as if the stars had fallen from the sky to land at their feet. Leo recovered himself and gestured for her to continue down the carpet and she followed, dazzled not by the lights but by *him*.

Leo hadn't expected to laugh. He'd expected to be angry. He'd expected to use her as a foil to vent his frustrations. But she'd surprised him. And he hadn't been surprised for a very long time. He strangely welcomed the moment to move beyond all the anger from the past, even if just for a while.

They navigated the small bottleneck blocking the entrance to the gallery and each accepted a glass of champagne from the wait staff. Making sure that there were no reporters hidden behind corners waiting to catch him out, he finally took a sip of his drink as he turned back to the larger-than-life photograph they stood before and promptly choked.

Bubbles ran simultaneously down his throat and up his nose, blocking off his airways.

There was a distinctly unsympathetic smirk across Helena's features as, without taking her eyes from the gallery piece, she passed him a napkin. Leo's eyes watered as he vainly tried to contain all the liquid trying to leave his body at the same time, while he avoided the image that had caused this disastrous incident in the first place.

'Helena, what the hell have you brought me to?' he whispered the moment he regained the ability to speak.

'It is called art, Lee—Leander,' she managed, spinning his name into his brother's in case anyone was listening.

'That,' he spat, 'is pornography.' It didn't seem to matter that he'd glanced at the photograph for less than a second—the image was indelibly inked on his brain. But, what was worse, it was now irrevocably linked to Helena. *Gamóto.*

The last thing he wanted, or needed, was to be thinking of Helena in any correlation to the image of a pair of lips utterly encasing a rather turgid part of the male anatomy, in such close proximity that the photographer made the viewer feel less observer and more participant.

One quick glance around the other images adorning clean white gallery walls confirmed his fears. They were everywhere. Every possible sexual act imaginable seemed to be blown up in extreme detail and pasted all over every wall. He could turn a corner and fall headfirst into a *ménage à trois* if he wasn't careful.

'I didn't take you for such a prude.'

'I'm not,' he assured her. 'In the privacy of my own bedroom.'

And suddenly the air thickened between them, heavy with the implication of what *did* happen in his bedroom.

Helena's teasing lips wobbled a little. Lips that he had swiped with the pad of his thumb. Lips that he now associated with the large photograph directly behind her. And it was as if that thought lit the touchpaper that had been the last barrier of his restraint.

Helena broke the connection between them, taking slow steps from one large canvas to another. Amongst the black and white images on display and the monochromatic style of the other guests, she stood out like a shard of jade. He followed behind her, stalking her, past pictures of increasingly detailed sexual acts that merged with his earlier fantasies about the woman mere inches away from him. It was a very fine line and he was hovering dangerously close.

'You look like you're angry with me,' she said, her gaze in a reflection of glass covering a sculpture of twisting limbs in marble.

'How do you want me to look at you?' he asked before he could stop himself, the question unspooling a dangerous arousal between them.

She stilled, the pulse flickering at her throat daring him to push further, the tremble of her fingers on the stem of the champagne flute urging him beyond his usual self-control.

'Like I'm your newly married husband?' he pressed, leaning over her shoulder to whisper into the shell of her ear, unable to help himself. 'Like I want to do these things to you?'

The sharp inhalation of her shock was both a warning and a temptation, but when she stepped away from the heat of his body he let her go. He took a mouthful of the champagne but it did nothing to cool the ardent heat coursing across his skin.

What was wrong with him?

There was too much at stake to play silly games like that. He blamed it on his body's primal reaction to her as a woman, the shocking difference between the girl he'd once known and the incredibly beautiful adult before him. He then spent the next twenty minutes wandering the gallery as far from her as possible while he struggled for the control that he was so famous for.

By the time he'd reined himself in he found Helena standing by the window that looked over a stunning Greek nightscape.

'When can we leave?' he asked, clearing his throat.

'Soon,' she said without looking at him. And he was thankful that at least one of them had sense enough to maintain the barriers between them.

He took another careful sip of his champagne, searching for something safe for them to discuss, rather than the dangerously sensual play they should most definitely not be engaging in.

'What is Incendia?' he asked, expecting her to respond with some bland explanation of her day job.

He knew Helena well enough that the evasive shoulder shrug and moue she made with her lips was as red a flag as any.

He nodded to himself and pulled out his phone.

'What are you doing?' she asked, turning her attention finally away from the view from the gallery window.

'Looking up Incendia.'

She pushed down his phone with a sharp slap of her hand, catching him completely by surprise, red slashes on her cheekbones, and not through pleasure but anger.

'What do you want to know?' she demanded in a low voice.

'What you're trying to hide,' he returned, just as low, sliding his phone back into his suit pocket.

Helena had never been one for deceit and, on reflection, even the idea that she would actually marry Leander to access money was so uncharacteristic he couldn't believe he hadn't seen it before.

'I'm not trying to hide anything,' she said with a shrug. 'I'm CEO of Incendia, a—'

'Oh, Christ, Helena, don't tell me you're trying to prop it up with your own money,' he interrupted, his hand bracketing his temples.

The shock in her gaze, the fear as she looked around to make sure that no one had heard him, made him even more furious.

She grabbed him by the arm and pulled him into a corridor away from the main exhibition.

Anger crawled up and bit into whatever peace had been found between them as he yanked his arm back. What she was doing was immature and reckless. Dangerous even, and not just for her company but for herself.

'Didn't you learn anything from your mother?' he demanded.

'My mother made a mistake,' Helena hissed. 'She thought she had learned enough about business from listening to my father for years. And you punished her terribly for it.'

The accusation was both unjust and true at the same time, but Leo couldn't leave it at that.

'She didn't just make a mistake, Helena. She expressly went against the wishes of not just me but the entire board of Liassidis Shipping. She engaged one client—a fierce competitor of an existing one—to make herself feel like a businesswoman, and nearly bankrupted us in the process.'

Helena's defiance faltered. It was just a second, but it was enough.

'You didn't know that?' he asked, before he could take it back.

'I knew enough!' Helena cried. 'I was there when you yelled at her and called her stupid, and foolish, and a liability. She was a grieving woman, Leo,' she accused, 'and you cut her off from everything and everyone she knew.'

'And you're still making excuses for her,' he hit back, wondering if she would ever stop searching for something that Gwen would never give her.

'She's my mother,' Helena replied, unable to stop herself from feeling all the hurt, anger and confusion from that time building up all over again. When everything she had known had been slipping through her fingers—she'd lost her father, her mother had made a terrible mistake and then Leo was pushing them out of his and his family's lives as if they were nothing more than an inconvenience.

'Then how could you possibly even contemplate making the same mistake again? If the company is failing, it's failing,' he announced with a fatal finality.

'It's not failing,' she slammed back. 'It's employee theft. All we need to do is survive the financial review at the end of the year,' she insisted.

Leo shook his head, that same look of disappointment in his eyes now that she remembered from when her mother had messed up.

'You cannot put your own money at risk like this,' he warned.

'Why not? *You* did,' she accused.

'Because it was *my* company, Helena. This? It's just a job. A CEO's position.'

'Even if it *was* just that, why is it okay for you to do it but not okay for me?'

And that was when she saw it. The answer that she feared the most.

'Because you think I'll fail,' she correctly interpreted. A sob rose in her chest. To see him staring back at her, disappointed and disapproving, it was her worst imaginings come to life. 'Thank you for your vote of confidence, Leo.'

She pushed past him and out of the gallery, the cool of the night biting into her heated emotions. As she messaged the car service, she told herself that Leo was wrong. She wouldn't mess this up. She would save Incendia and prove him wrong. She knew what she was doing. All she had to do was stick to the plan and it would work. She knew it would.

Her phone buzzed in her clutch and she read the message from Kate with a strange mix of relief and resentment. And felt immediately bad. Her best friend had travelled halfway round the world to help her. Leander had to be in some sort of trouble to have done what he'd done. And all she could think of was that it wasn't enough.

Oh, why was this such a mess?

Leo came to stand beside her just as the car pulled up. 'Kate's found Leander.'

'Hopefully, she can bring him back before it's too late,' Leo said.

But Helena feared it already was.

CHAPTER FIVE

WHO OPENED A club on a Wednesday night? Leo wondered as he looked at the wardrobe with neatly pinned paper cards informing the wearer of the date and the event. Leander's assistant needed a pay rise. Leo would never have asked his to do such a thing.

He doesn't have to, because you never go out, a distinctly Helena-sounding voice said in his head.

Leo rubbed a hand over the closely cut beard on his jaw. It had been two days since the gallery opening. Two days before that had been the wedding. If it followed this pattern, he could avoid Helena for another two days, starting tomorrow.

Because you'll say some other appalling thing to her and cause her more upset.

That voice sounded like his brother.

The fact that Leo had been right about everything he'd said that night at the gallery hadn't quietened his conscience. If anything, it had only got louder and louder as time wore on. He'd catch glimpses of Helena around the villa, the trail of a scarf, or a pair of sunglasses lying around. A book she'd left on a lounger that he'd been curious about and looked up. Little pieces of a girl he'd once known.

At least their argument had drawn a line under whatever had invaded his senses that day. Not that he'd forgotten the words he'd whispered to her, how close he'd come to crossing the invisible line between them. He assured himself that he was cured of that momentary madness as he considered the deep ochre-coloured T-shirt and dark maroon linen suit Leander's assistant had chosen for tonight. A pair of sunglasses were tucked by an arm into the breast pocket and a leather belt hung over the suit shoulder. He frowned at the casual attire.

'Be me.'

Kill me, thought Leo as he reached for the clothes that would turn him into Leander.

As he buttoned his shirt and tucked it into the waistband of his trousers, he racked his brain for why he had suddenly become so responsive to Helena. Yes, it had been a while since he'd last spent time with someone.

But after Mina he'd had absolutely no intention of making himself that vulnerable again. Since then, women had been an *as and when* for him and certainly no more permanent than a night or two of mutual pleasure. Despite his reaction to the pictures in the gallery, he wasn't a prude. Far from it. He enjoyed pleasure, his partner's and his own, greatly. He just didn't have to splash it all over the papers like his brother.

With one last look in the mirror, he went to the living room, to find Helena looking at her watch.

'So "Leander the Lothario" wanted to take you to a club opening on your honeymoon,' he stated, trying to warm the chill in the air between them and ease his conscience at the same time.

'Travi, the owner of the club, is a business associate,'

she informed him in a clipped tone that he should be thankful for.

'Of yours?' Leo asked, confused.

'Of *Leander's*,' Helena replied disdainfully, as if she were reproving him for how little he knew about his brother's life.

As if it were *he* that had caused the separation between them.

'I thought Leander is into web-based app development.'

'He is. Travi is an investor.'

As they left the villa and made their way to the helipad where the helicopter would fly them back to Athens for the evening, the blush-pink sparkles covering Helena's dress glistened in the setting sun. Before him was a kaleidoscope of golds, yellows and pinks that struck him in full Technicolor. Where the dress from the previous event had been long, this one stopped barely at where her fingers reached her toned thighs.

He clenched his jaw and slipped the sunglasses over his eyes.

'So, you know Travi well?' he asked as he followed, trying to watch where he was going and not the backs of Helena's well-defined thighs.

'Reasonably. But not as much as Leander. You're going to have to concentrate this time.'

He nodded, though he already knew that hemline was going to be a major problem.

'I'm surprised you know so much about my brother,' he observed out loud.

'I'm surprised you know so little,' she snapped back in a rebuke he felt to his core.

The helicopter was waiting for them, the door slid

back and the blades at a standstill for the moment. He waited while they took their seats and the headsets were in place. The co-pilot talked them through what channels to use and what to do in an emergency and Leo only heard every other word over the pounding in his head as the vee of Helena's dress gaped just enough to reveal the gentle slope of her breast.

Skatá, he was turning into a pervert.

'We kept in touch.' Helena's words came through the headset, bringing him back to their conversation.

He didn't miss the unspoken accusation that *he* hadn't bothered to keep in touch with her.

You cut her off from everything and everyone she knew.

Had Helena just been talking about her mother? Or had she also been talking about herself?

'Do you see him regularly?' Leo asked, choosing his words carefully, wondering how much of an answer he really wanted.

Helena smiled and her face lit up. 'We find time to celebrate the milestones. I don't get to come to Greece that often any more, so he'll usually fly to London. He was...' she looked up at him and then away '...there when I needed him.'

The sting of jealousy surprised Leo and it covered everything. Not just the fact that Leander was there for Helena in a way that Leander had never been there for him. But because there had once been a time when Helena had come to *him* and not Leander. And the way she talked about what they had made him curious about the man he'd cut from his life.

'Is he happy?' Leo asked, unsure of the answer he wanted to hear.

Helena looked at him from across the helicopter. 'Yes,'

she said with a small smile. 'But sometimes I get a sense that there's something missing from his life.'

'What?' Leo couldn't help but ask.

'You.'

He couldn't say anything to that.

Helena felt unusually self-conscious entering the trendy nightclub owned by Travi Samaras. People turned to stare, but she was under no illusion as to who it was that drew their attention. She was standing next to a man who looked like a Greek god worshipped by mortals, rather than one himself.

She would have laughed had she been with Leander, but standing beside Leo, seeing the impact he had on other women, feeling the impact he had on her *without even trying*, was making her feel distinctly on edge.

'What's wrong? Are you nervous?' he asked, dipping his head to her ear, once again playing the doting new husband.

'No. Just curious as to how on earth you're going to succeed in pretending to be your party animal brother,' she replied, wondering how he'd noticed her discomfort.

'You don't think I know how to party?' came the amusingly indignant reply.

'I don't think you'd know a good time if it came up and slapped you across the face,' she said as she stalked towards the bar. He kept pace with her as she made her way through a sea of people that parted for Leo as if he were Moses.

'I do,' he insisted as he reached her side at the bar.

'You *did*,' she countered, his persistence softening some of her defiance.

'What's that supposed to mean?'

She deliberately caught the eye of the barman rather than look up at Leo, whose famous focus was now intently on her.

She shrugged. 'Once upon a time you knew how to have fun. Now? Not so much.' Turning a smile on the barman, she ordered a bottle of champagne.

'You can put it on Leander Liassidis' tab,' she told the barman sweetly.

Leo's eyes widened in realisation, his lips curving into a wicked smile just before asking the barman to make it two bottles.

'Just the two?' Helena asked as she found a standing table at the edge of a dance floor while the bar staff set up tall buckets with ice and two glasses.

'I'm ordering a bottle of vodka next,' he growled.

Helena found herself smiling despite herself. The merest hint of the boy she remembered from her childhood was enough to warm her. Back then, he'd been funny, irreverent. More grounded than Leander, yes, but so much less serious and sombre than the adult Leo.

She was about to reply when she saw Travi making his way towards them.

'The man in the white suit and dark shirt? That's Travi. You've known him for three years, ever since he approached you looking for an investor,' she whispered hurriedly. 'You decided against the first project, but liked an app designed by one of his young techs and invested in that instead. You tried to pinch the tech, but Travi made him an offer he couldn't refuse to stay. You said at the end, *At least the kid is finally being paid his worth.* You joke about it regularly.'

Leo stared at her, his gaze halfway between surprised and impressed.

'What?' she asked, wondering what she'd done, but before she could ask, Travi had arrived at their table.

'So, you incorrigible flirt, you finally bit the bullet and settled down with this unimpeachable goddess who is worth ten of your weight in gold,' Travi announced, grabbing Leo by the shoulders and nearly wrestling him into a headlock.

Helena pressed a hand against her mouth to try to stop her laugh escaping from the shock on Leo's face, until he managed to regain his composure, or at least recall that he was supposed to be Leander.

'Hey, *maláka*, I know exactly how much she's worth,' he said, turning in the man's hold to accept the hug in a way that seemed utterly alien to Leo, but absolutely one hundred percent Leander. '*Everything*. She's worth everything.'

Although Leo was looking at Travi, the words struck Helena hard, catching her breath in her chest. Because wasn't that what she'd always wanted? To be someone's everything.

'But if you call her goddess again, we're going to have words,' Leo added with a warning bite that sounded foreign to her ears as she hastily pushed down the sudden bloom in her heart.

'Helena, *angelí mou*, light of my life, why did you pick him? You know I would have married you in a heartbeat,' the other Greek male complained.

'Travi,' she said, taking his face in her hands, the smile on her face only a little forced. 'You know how much I love you, but he has a bigger bank account,' she teased.

'How very dare you?' Travi cried in a high falsetto and a cut glass English accent. 'I expect you both to be the last couple standing,' he commanded with a finger pointed right at them, before he left to meet and greet his other guests.

One after the other, many familiar faces from amongst Leander's crowd came and went, Leo seemingly relaxed and easy, mimicking his brother so well that even Helena nearly forgot. But it wasn't just the smiles and jokes. Talk quite often turned to business—and she suddenly realised how many of Leander's acquaintances he'd actually met through business. Someone needing investment advice, or wanting the 'in' on his latest app development.

Leo handled each and every one with an ease and confidence that surprised her, the marked difference from the man who could barely bring himself to touch her at the wedding, who was more relaxed and freer somehow.

When someone tapped her on the shoulder she turned and found herself immediately wrapped in the warm embrace of Serene, a friend of Leander and Travi that she'd spent some time with in London when she'd visited for work.

'Man, you tamed the devil,' Serene teased in English, nodding to Leo and mistaking him, just like everyone else, for Leander. 'I didn't think anything would make him settle down.'

'Neither did I,' Helena replied, feeling a little guilty for the deception now that she was with friends.

'So, what is it like?' Serene demanded as Helena passed her a champagne flute. 'Married life! Gah, I can't think of anything worse.'

Others around the table joined in the conversation, affectionately shouting her down, but Serene remained beautifully and happily adamant.

'Go on,' she taunted Helena. 'Hit me with it. What's the best thing about being newlyweds?'

'Oh, I don't know...' Helena hedged. 'Morning breath?'

she offered, determined to hold onto the humour in the conversation.

'Picking up someone else's dirty laundry,' another of Leander's friends contributed.

'Argh.' Serene grimaced, the look of horror on her face comical.

'Having to put the toilet seat back down,' another woman added.

'Okay, no. If you're not going to be serious about this, then I'll ask him. Hey!' she shouted, pulling at Leo's arm. 'What's so great about being married, Leander?'

Leo looked at the expectant faces around the table. He knew they'd all been laughing about it, but as he looked at Helena he didn't want to laugh it off. He had once believed in the sanctity of marriage. He'd wanted it, hoped for it. Thought he'd nearly had it. Helena's smile faltered just a little and he forced a smile to his lips.

'The best part about being newly married is that I get to dance with my wife whenever I want!' he said, reaching for her and pulling her away from the crowd to the celebratory yells and encouragement of Leander's friends.

As he led her to the dance floor Leo felt drained from having to pretend to be his brother for the last two hours. He hadn't realised how at the wedding no one had actually said anything more than congratulations. And at the gallery they hadn't spoken to anyone after the red carpet.

But this had been different. These were Leander's friends. And Leo liked them. He could see how easy they were around each other, how supportive, how interconnected. Business was business all over the globe, so he could field any specific work-related questions with ease. The loyalty these people had to Leander—who, in Leo's considered opinion, had the staying power of cheap Sellotape—surprised him. He was struck, seeing his brother through other people's eyes. But he was also struck by how *he* was seen.

As a man who didn't show up to his brother's wedding.

A man with a stick up his backside.

A man who couldn't relax.

In truth, he was a man who couldn't remember the last time he'd come to a club or been out with his own friends, and it was that realisation that had made him want a moment away from Leander's friends, so he'd clutched at the opportunity to draw Helena on to the dance floor.

But then the music that had been full of wild beats and chaotic chords had changed and morphed into something deeper, with a bass line that rolled over the skin and senses like a promise. The track poured sibilance into the air like a thousand whispers and the hyperawareness of earlier became almost painful.

Helena looked up at him uncertainly. She looked at him like he was Leo Liassidis, not his brother. And it was a smile he didn't want anyone else to see. He led her deeper into the dance floor to find just a little anonymity, a little breathing space, he told himself. He wanted to explain himself to Helena, why he'd brought them to the dance floor, but when he turned he realised his mistake.

Swaying to the beat of the music, she unfurled beneath the dim blue lights throbbing from above. She reached up to sweep her hair from her neck, eyes closed, her rapture was all her own and it was the most erotic thing he'd seen. Even after the gallery exhibition.

As she shifted from foot to foot, the hemline of her dress, that had been barely decent before, became nothing but temptation, sliding across thighs that he wanted to grip and pull against him. Hot pinpricks of desire broke out across his shoulders and the base of his spine. His breath was staccato in his chest.

This wasn't some artful moment of manipulation. There was no intent or thought for anyone else, he could tell. Not because she just wasn't that type of person but because her focus, one he could feel almost instinctively, was on herself. Her pure enjoyment of the moment.

Just at that moment she opened her eyes, unerringly finding him without having to search, and all the blood rushed from his head. The crowd on the dance floor grew bigger and someone jostled him, but he still couldn't look away. Just as the music built to a crescendo, the girl behind Helena careened into her from behind and Helena was thrust forward, Leo only having enough time to reach for her as she crashed against him.

Suddenly, his hands were full of soft, hot skin and sequins. Her breasts pressed against his chest, her hands, one palm to his heart, the other clinging to the lapel of his linen jacket. His breath left his lungs, and instinct took over. He pulled her more firmly against him, his fingers flexing against her body. Neither of them moved, a breath held, shared between them. Helena leaned back and this time when she looked at him there was something beneath the trepidation: *want*.

He was jostled again and the moment was cut short when she pulled out of his arms and laughed a little, perhaps at herself, perhaps at him. But whatever it was that had passed between them was over. And he couldn't work out whether that was a good thing or a bad thing.

Helena left the dance floor without looking to see if Leo was following her. She needed some time and space to sort through what had just happened. Or at least what she had just wanted to happen. She pressed the back of her hand against her flushed cheek and turned towards the table when a hand caught her wrist.

Leo looked at her with no trace of a reaction to what had just taken place on the dance floor.

'Travi wanted us in the VIP section?'

She nodded reluctantly. She wanted to go home. Not just to the villa, but *home* home. To England. But even that was no longer the refuge it had once been, everything tainted by Gregory's theft and Kate's soon-to-be absence.

She wanted to hide from everything that she was feeling, but instead she followed Leo past the suited bouncer who unhooked a red velvet twisted rope, up the stairs and over towards a red velvet sofa.

They had barely sat down when a waiter appeared with a silver bucket, a bottle of champagne and two flutes.

'With the host's congratulations on your recent nuptials.'

The flourish was so extravagant she bit back a laugh and allowed the distraction to smooth over the tension from the dance floor. Leo graciously accepted as Leander and the waiter disappeared, but he looked strangely disappointed.

'What's wrong?' she asked.

He scratched his chin and winced. 'I was hoping to buy the entire club a round of drinks. On Leander's tab, of course.'

Helena smiled. 'It would be the least he deserves. I mean the least *you* could do,' she hastily corrected.

Leo poured them each a glass and offered her one.

'A toast.'

'To?' she enquired.

He paused, looking at her a little too intently. 'To new beginnings.'

She grasped it like a lifeline but, clinking her glass to his, she couldn't hold his gaze for long. She looked down over the crowded club and wondered what that might look like.

New beginnings.

Unable to stifle her curiosity, she turned back to him, the question in her eyes finding its way to her mouth.

'What would that look like? To you?'

The hand holding his glass paused halfway to his lips, his gaze locked on hers, until it refocused on something—someone—over her shoulder.

Leo cursed.

'So, "Leander the Lothario" finally settles down?' the woman said when she arrived at their table.

Helena swallowed, genuinely incapable of speech in that moment. Panic swelled and her heartbeat thundered in her ears. She couldn't believe what she was seeing. Of all the people they could have run into.

'Mina,' Leo greeted through clenched teeth. 'What are you doing here?'

They were going to be found out. There was no way that Mina would let them leave without creating the biggest scene she possibly could.

'Don't be silly, Leander, you're not the only one who moves in these circles.'

It took a moment for Helena's brain to catch up because she genuinely couldn't believe the woman that Leo had been engaged to couldn't tell the difference between him and Leander.

'Just because your brother doesn't deign to come down off his lofty mountain to have some fun, doesn't mean that I don't. But Helena?' she said, still directing her conversation to Leo, as if even now she was beneath Mina's consideration. 'Of all people, you chose to marry *her*?'

'I'm sitting right here, Mina,' she said as calmly as she could, but her pulse was wildly erratic and her hands fisted.

'Yes, you are. But I don't understand why,' she dismissed with a shrug. 'Everyone knew you had a silly schoolgirl crush on Leo.'

Humiliation crawled up Helena's skin in angry inches, hating that Leo was sitting right there hearing everything she said. 'That was a long time ago. Things change.'

Leo cursed. There had been a time when Mina was the woman he'd wanted to spend his life with, to have a family with. Back then, he'd found her avarice amusing; it had been tempered by youth and her insecurity was much better hidden. But age had only made her worse. And that she couldn't even tell that it was him was shocking.

Mina's jealousy of Helena was as blatant as it was unpleasant. Looking back, he remembered the shame and embarrassment he'd felt at the conversation they'd had that last Christmas the two families had spent together before Helena's father had died. At the time he'd thought the feeling was because of his awareness of Helena's feelings for him. He now realised in a shocking moment of self-revelation that he'd been embarrassed by Mina. And himself, for letting her say the things that she'd said. His stomach turned and he looked at Mina, truly looked at her, trying to find some semblance of the young woman he'd spent nearly three years of his life with, but he found that there was nothing of her left.

'Things don't change that much, Lena,' Mina spat.

'Don't call her that.' His tone was as definitive and unquestionable as his swift and sudden dislike of her use of the nickname for Helena that only he had ever used. And from the look on Mina's face, she didn't like it one bit. He should have known that she'd turn on Helena in response.

'So, when you couldn't get your hands on Leo you settled for the "other" Liassidis instead?' she threw at Helena.

Leo barked a laugh and leaned back into the sofa. *'Other?* There's nothing *other* about me, darling,' he said, perfectly impersonating his brother.

'I. Don't. Believe. It,' Mina said, leaning forward, wafting alcohol over them with every word. She was drunk, Leo realised. Very drunk. 'Whatever this is,' she slurred, 'I hope you get found out.'

Warning her to keep her voice down wouldn't work in the slightest. But he couldn't let her run around thinking or, worse, saying this to others. He just had to make her believe it.

'There's nothing to find out, Mina. This is the woman I have pledged to love for the rest of my life. And I intend to do just that,' he said, reaching for Helena and hauling her into his lap, facing him.

The look of surprise on Helena's face lasted a breath's length before understanding dawned in her gaze. He raised an eyebrow in query. If she wasn't with him in this, he'd leave her alone, he'd stop the charade and leave the club that very moment.

Subtly, Helena nodded and with his eyes on Mina's over Helena's shoulder, he brought her closer and deeper into his lap with his hands on her backside.

Helena pressed her lips together as if trying to control her response to him, but there was no controlling his response to her.

Slowly, so very slowly, he leaned towards her, wanting to give Helena time to stop him if she needed to. But she didn't. He became aware of the scent of her perfume, something heady and full of citrus, teasing his senses just as much as the heat of her body against his.

His lips were mere inches from hers and Mina no longer existed. The busy, crowded bar receded, the blood rushed in his ears and his heart pounded in his chest so violently he feared the world would hear it.

Want.

He could lie to himself, justify a kiss with the need to keep up the pretence, but he wanted this. He wanted *her*.

His lips met Helena's in what was supposed to be just a kiss. But there was nothing 'just' about it. It exploded through his body, his lips not content with a simple press, as he gently teased and prised her mouth open to his. Her gasp—surprise or pleasure, he wasn't sure—poured into his mouth and he was done.

He pulled back, shocked, trying to understand what was happening, but the sight of Helena staring up at him, wide-eyed, flushed and kiss drunk, meant he couldn't have held back for the world. He claimed her mouth again just as Helena's hands came to his jacket, clinging to the lapels as if needing an anchor.

Bringing his hand to cup her jaw, he angled her to him and took full advantage of the position. Open-mouthed, his tongue claimed her, thrusting deep into a soft, wet heat that was instantly addictive. He plundered like a Neanderthal, while holding himself back with a ruthlessness that bordered on masochism. She became fire in his arms. Heat and passion rippled between them like a wildfire and it was only the desire to do so much more that brought him to his senses.

CHAPTER SIX

HELENA'S HEART POUNDED as if she'd run a marathon. Breath heaved in and out of her chest. Every part of her was vibrating at an almost invisible level, but altogether it made her whole being hum at a frequency that only Leo could ignite.

The first kiss had been a shock—an assault to her senses. She had fantasised so much and for so long that she couldn't believe it was happening.

But it was the second kiss—the one that hadn't been Leander kissing his wife, but Leo kissing her—that shifted the sands beneath her feet. It was a drugging kiss, lowering her defences and igniting her desires. His tongue stroked her into submission, filling her in a way that only partially satiated her desires, whilst igniting more. She *felt* how much he wanted her. Straddling his thighs, the hard ridge of his arousal pressed heavy and hot against her core and it wasn't nearly enough. From this position she was above him, Leo reaching for her, pulling her down onto him, and it made her feel invincible—wanted and needed in a way she'd never experienced before.

When he finally pulled back, desire blazing in his eyes like a forest fire, one that matched her own, flame for flame, it was *she* that wanted to go back for more.

Until she heard Mina saying, 'Get a room.'

Shock snapped her back into the present, back into the VIP room, where a few other guests had seen them and broken into gentle giggles and one wolf whistle.

'Careful, Mina,' Leo warned his ex-fiancée over Helena's shoulder, desire morphing into disdain. 'Your jealousy is showing.'

'Me?' Mina practically screeched. 'Jealous of her? You're kidding, right? She was never anything more than a puppy that followed you and your brother around, picking up whatever scraps of attention you dropped on the floor.'

And just like that, Helena was back outside Leo's bedroom, listening to the conversation that had broken her teenage heart. Hurt bloomed beneath the truth of Mina's words. She *had* followed them around, desperate for whatever attention the Liassidis twins would give her.

'Mina,' Leo warned, the tone of his voice enough to raise the hair on the back of Helena's neck.

But it was too late. Helena's memories crashed around her in a red haze, the desire filling her chest replaced with a thick, painful ache. That last Christmas she had spent on the Liassidis island with her parents before everything changed. Before Leo started to treat her like a stranger, before he and Leander began to argue in earnest. Before her father had passed away and her mother had ruined everything.

All of it followed on from that one overheard conversation that had fed painfully into insecurities already burgeoning within her teenage sense of self.

'She's just a child. She's nothing to me.'

Helena clenched her teeth to stop the tremor of tears from creeping onto her tongue, to keep her mouth from wobbling.

'Do you have to dress like that?'
'Do you have to wear that?'
'Do you have to want so much, Helena?'
'You should be able to do this on your own. I can't do everything for you.'

Her mother's voice mixed with the memory and it became louder than a drumbeat. She slipped from Leo's lap, cold and shivery from the stark difference in mood and tone, and looked up at the woman currently glaring at her with such undisguised jealousy it actually hurt to look.

It was clear that Leo's ex-fiancée had her own demons and it wasn't Helena's responsibility to carry them. But she wanted Mina to know. To know that she had heard what Mina had said that day. And perhaps a small, devastated part of her wanted Leo to know too.

'Well,' Helena said to Mina, finding her strength, 'I guess someone *trained me better* in the end. Because even though I'm *just the daughter* of Giorgos's business partner, *I'm* the one wearing a Liassidis ring.'

Mina's eyes flashed in the dark of the nightclub, clearly realising that Helena had overheard her conversation with Leo. It was a petty shot and she shouldn't have said it, but Helena was hitting back at all her childhood hurts any way she could.

Beside her, Leo flinched but Helena didn't pay it heed. 'It takes a really troubled woman to blame a girl of fifteen years old, Mina. And as for Leo. If I remember rightly, you left him. You chose to walk away from him because it looked like he could lose his company. You walked away because you couldn't see his worth. It had nothing to do with me.'

'Nothing to do with you? You and your mother—'

'Enough,' Leo said, standing up, cutting off Mina's

words before she could do any more damage. 'He knew, Mina,' he announced with cold disdain. 'Leo knew what kind of woman you were. He might not have realised it at the time, but the moment you left, it was a blessed relief for him.'

His words caused goosebumps to scatter over Helena's skin, beginning the healing of a part of her she had refused to acknowledge. Leo turned and held his hand out to her and she took it, leaving Mina, open-mouthed with shock, watching them as they left the club.

They stepped into the night, emotions so thick between them they were almost visible, like hot breath on a cold winter's night. She could all but feel the fury rolling off Leo in waves.

'Leo?' she asked uncertainly as he pulled her along practically at a jog out into the night.

'Not here,' he growled. 'I will not talk about this here,' he went on, his words harsh and final. A car pulled up to take them back to the helipad and Leo was silent all the way back to the villa.

Leo stalked into the villa, wanting to slam doors and punch walls. He hadn't been like this since those first few years after Leander had walked away from everything they'd planned—from the company that they were supposed to take over from their father together. From the *lives* they were supposed to lead together.

And somehow all of it had been made worse by the Haddens and it had just become a jumbled mess in his mind that he'd refused to think on. Only now it seemed that the fates were conspiring against him and finally forcing him to face it all.

He crossed the living area to the wet bar in quick

strides, wanting only to feel the burn of the alcohol in his throat rather than the aching hot twist of shame that had sprung the moment he'd realised where he'd heard Helena's words before. *When* he'd heard them.

'Why didn't you tell me?' he demanded, unable to look at her, staring at his white-knuckled grip around the glass.

'Tell you what?' Helena asked from behind him.

He clenched his jaw and turned, pinning her with a stare. He hadn't bothered to turn the lights on when they'd got back, but the gentle glow of the solar-powered garden lights lit the room through the floor-to-ceiling windows, picking out the glittering sequins on her dress and the sparks of defiance in her eyes.

'Why didn't you tell me that you overheard our conversation that day?'

He watched her expression change into something like incredulity. She let out a burst of air that sounded alarmingly like a scoff, but he could still see the pain she was valiantly trying to hide from him.

'What?' he demanded.

'You're angry because I didn't tell you?' she asked.

'Yes,' he slammed back. Knowing that it was a lie. That wasn't why he was angry at all. He was angry because he'd been in the wrong that Christmas Eve. He should never have said those things to Mina about Helena. And he should never have allowed his girlfriend to say such things. But being in the wrong didn't fit the story that he liked to tell himself about what happened back then—that every wrong thing was Leander's fault and that he had been the innocent victim.

'Why on earth would it have been my responsibility to let you know that I'd overheard you and your horrible girlfriend comparing me to a dog?'

Shame was a hard slap across the face that might as well have left red palm prints across his cheek, the fierce blush there was just the same. He braced himself against the sight of the tears welling in her eyes. He deserved every minute of her pain. And that wasn't even the worst thing he'd said.

'I wasn't… I didn't. Ever.' Not the way she'd made it sound.

'A puppy following you around? That was what you said. Those were your words, Leo,' she returned, and he couldn't deny it.

'I was twenty-one years old,' he defended.

'And I was fifteen! I looked up to you!' she cried.

'But I didn't know what to do with that! You looked at me like I hung the damn moon and I didn't know why.'

The confession burst out of his chest from a place he'd never looked at, never wanted to see. Because Leander had turned his back on him only three years before, and he'd still been searching for a reason why. Helena had openly adored him and it had been confusing and painful and joyous all at the same time. He'd relished those moments, he finally allowed himself to remember now. But then, Mina had noticed.

'Our families always joked about us getting married. And I didn't even care that they teased me about your crush. But Mina did. And when she did, I just…needed to keep you at arm's length.'

'Oh, so you treated me like a stranger for my own good?' Helena demanded. 'Do you think that I didn't re- alise you weren't interested in me in that way?'

'Lena, you were a child,' he said, his stomach twist- ing. 'I never once—'

'I know that!' she yelled. 'I know that you and Leander saw me like a sister. And yes, I may have had some silly crush—'

'You barely saw us two months out of the year, Helena,' he dismissed.

'Don't do that. Please don't do that,' she all but begged. 'Don't undermine what having you and Leander in my life at that time was like,' she said, and her words struck him hard. Her words conjured the past he had kept hidden behind a locked door because he hadn't wanted to acknowledge what he'd lost—Leander *and* Helena.

Those summers had been endless and idyllic in a way that seemed remarkable now. Lazy days spent out on the Aegean, the sea breeze and sounds of laughter, the seagulls flying overhead and the simplicity of eating fish caught from the back of the boat.

But then he remembered why it was that he and Leander would take Helena with them.

Because her mother had been too busy focusing on her own interests, and her father had been more interested in business. Yes, they'd entertained her in a kind of absentminded way, but while her father had softened Gwen's coldness, both brothers had felt their rejection of her and tried to protect her from that.

'It devastated me, losing your friendship,' Helena said, unaware of the blows that she was landing on his heart. 'Losing what I looked forward to the whole way through the crappy school year at that god-awful boarding school. No, Leo, I didn't have schoolgirl fantasies of kissing in the rain or something stupid like that. I had dreams of coming to the island and playing on the beach. Lighting fires and swimming in the sea with you and Leander. But when you two fought, all that stopped. There was nowhere to hide from the tension between you, and no way to avoid the heated conflict that would come any time you were in a room together. Which meant that there was nowhere to hide from the fact that…the fact that… my parents didn't treat me the way that Cora and Giorgos treated you. Didn't treat me as if…they wanted me there.'

His heart twisted and turned to see her eyes glistening at her confession. He'd always wondered how much she'd been aware of her parents' casual neglect. He'd hoped that he and his brother had countered it in some way, but now he was realising that the consequences of his fight with Leander had stretched beyond his family. Her emotional confession was raw in her eyes, as if admitting their fighting had cost her too. And he hated seeing that in her, the price she'd paid for their mistakes.

'Lena—'

She shook her head, as if trying to navigate around the emotional boulder that must have been far too heavy to bear. And watching her pull herself together was both remarkable and painful at the same time.

'That was why I hoped you and Mina would work out, even though I didn't like her,' Helena pressed on, breath coming harder and quicker. 'No, she didn't make you laugh like Leander did, but she made you smile again after the separation between you, and that was enough for me. You seemed almost happy again.'

Christós. He'd thought he'd hidden his feelings better. He'd had no idea how obvious he'd been. His parents hadn't wanted to speak about the separation widening between their sons, hoping that it would blow over. Leo had told himself he'd hidden the wrenching pain that was threatening to tear him apart at having been severed from the person he'd thought he knew better than himself. The person who had been almost half of himself.

'I really didn't mean to overhear your conversation,' she said apologetically.

He huffed out a painful laugh. He should have been the one apologising.

'What were you doing there anyway?'

Helena bit her lip. 'I wanted to give you your Christmas present.'

He frowned, remembering more of that day than he had before. 'You didn't get me a present that year.' He'd remembered it because...because of the present he'd bought her.

She inhaled a shivery breath and gave him a sad smile. 'I didn't really feel like giving it to you after...'

Leo nodded. 'I can see that,' he admitted roughly. 'What happened to it?' he asked, curious.

She shrugged, sending a ripple of glitter across the sequins. 'I put it in the hiding place.'

The cubbyhole. It was a place where he and Leander used to leave messages or stupid little things in the house on his parents' island. They'd shown it to Helena when she was little, but he hadn't thought about it for ages. He certainly hadn't looked in it since well before that Christmas.

'It's probably still there,' Helena said as she walked past him to gaze out at the nightscape beyond the window.

He shook his head. Presents, painful misunderstandings. He thought of the peony necklace, the one that Helena thought was from Leander. The delight that she'd expressed in that moment, looking up between him and his brother; he remembered it now like a punch to the chest. It was the last time he'd seen her look like that in his presence.

'I'm sorry,' he said, the words shuddering out of him. 'There is no excuse for my behaviour that day or for what I said.'

* * *

Helena stared at the small circles of light punching holes into the darkness, illuminating unfamiliar shapes of shrubs and flowers that were beautiful and bright in the day and bleached and alien in the night. Her arms wrapped tightly around her waist, holding herself together, holding the tears back.

She'd never said that out loud. About her parents. Certainly not about the father that she'd hero-worshipped. Not even to Kate, who seemed to understand without her having to explain. But Leo had been there, he knew. And she wasn't sure that she could hide it any more.

But acknowledging it didn't change anything. It didn't stop her still hoping that one day her mother might soften just that little bit more. Like she had at the wedding. Each time she saw a glimpse of it, of the love there, she wanted more, like an addict only given enough to get by. So, was it naïve to keep hoping for something that might never happen?

Was it naïve to let Leo's apology soften the blow of his words that day? Because if she let that happen, if she allowed him to soothe that hurt…then what would be left to keep her feelings in check? What would stop her from—

She shook her head at the thought. The seesaw of emotions from that evening alone were almost enough to knock her out for a week. Seeing Leo at the club, relaxing and talking to Leander's friends—even if it was just for show—it had seemed for a moment that he was almost having fun. Then dancing with him on the dance floor, running into Mina, the kiss…

She hadn't even had time to think about the kiss.

A kiss that was just for show.

It hadn't felt like it was just for show.

She had felt wanted. Desired. Needed.

But hot on the heels of such an argument? She shivered, tiredness and cold creeping up her skin, wrapping around Leo's apology. There was too much past between them, too much hurt.

'You were having a private conversation with your girlfriend, Leo,' she said in response to his apology. 'There's nothing to apologise for. It's not your fault I overestimated my value to you in my imagination,' she said quietly, making it easier for him. For them. Because now, when Leo was more dangerous to her than ever, she had to have done that. *Had* to have overestimated her value.

Leo pulled her back round to face him, a frown marring those startlingly gorgeous features. 'You didn't. You should never think that. You were hugely important to us.'

Then why was it so easy for you to push me away?

Helena couldn't bring herself to ask the painful question. In part, because she didn't want to hear the answer. It was a question that was all too familiar to her, one that had littered her childhood, not about the twin Liassidis brothers but her parents. When her father was too busy to come to piano recitals and ballet performances. When her mother was present, but so much more absent than her father. Each time they'd failed to show up for her making it both worse and easier to bear at the same time. And then Leo had pushed her away and even now, with Kate—

No. She wouldn't let herself think that. Kate was following her dreams and nothing, *nothing*, would make Helena begrudge her that.

'Helena...' Leo tried.

She shrugged him off. 'It's fine. It was a long time ago,' she said, looking down so that he couldn't see how much she lied.

He placed a finger under her chin and lifted it so that her gaze met his. 'It doesn't matter how long ago it was. I hurt you and I'm sorry.'

His words were a balm she didn't know she'd needed and certainly not one she'd expected, shifting old hurts and unfurling old feelings. She bit her lip to stop the emotion from escaping, but when his eyes dropped to her mouth, she remembered.

She remembered *everything* about the kiss in the club. Her heart pounded in her chest, a flush crept up her body inch by startling inch, and all the while he watched her with an intensity that she couldn't hide from.

He was barely touching her. Just one point of contact, the tip of his forefinger, but she felt *him*. The way that he'd taken possession of her, the way that she'd not cared if she took another breath, the way he'd made her feel alive. Her nipples pressed against the inner lining of her dress, and damp heat spread from her core. The way he'd made her feel, the things she wanted him to do, they all crashed together in a want, a desire so strong that it stole her breath.

His gaze flickered between her eyes and her lips as if he were unable to help himself. Her hands gripped her waist to stop herself from reaching out to him. But it didn't make a bit of difference. Because in her mind erotic images flickered against the backs of her eyes like a multicoloured kaleidoscope... Her hands thrust into his hair as he teased her nipples with his tongue. His open mouth against her skin, his hands around her chest, holding her to him as she rose above him, the shift of his legs as he settled in between her thighs...

Her eyes drifted closed against her will, desperate to cling onto the images for just a little longer. A sigh escaped her lips at the same time she imagined her name falling between them. But that's all it must have been her imagination. Because when she opened her eyes Leo released the tentative hold he had on her and took a step back, and the draught of cold air left in his wake was enough to return her sanity to her.

What was she thinking?

She had married Leander. Even if it was a fake marriage, even if it was just so that she could access her inheritance, and even if, for one second, Leo felt just half of what she did, she had just married his brother in front of one hundred and fifty guests and it had been covered by several international news outlets. The press had been filled with stories about their childhood sweetheart marriage. And if there was even a chance they were discovered it would ruin them both.

And even had she not married Leander, this was *Leo*.

Leo, for whom nothing was more important than Liassidis Shipping, including his brother and his ex-fiancée. Leo, who would ensure that nothing, *nothing*, jeopardised the company he had given so much to, certainly not her. Wasn't that precisely why he was doing all of this? To get her shares away from her?

'We should talk about the kiss,' Leo said as if it were the last thing he actually wanted to do.

'There's nothing to talk about,' Helena replied, drawing a line that couldn't be crossed, no matter how much she wanted to. Because, as she looked into his eyes, she saw that he knew it too. It couldn't happen. Nothing could happen between them. 'I'm going to bed. I have an online meeting in the morning.'

Leo saw the resolution in Helena's eyes and didn't like the frustration he felt because of it.

'Helena. It can't happen again,' he ground out, the words burning his mouth as they came out.

'I know. It was just for show. Don't worry. I didn't mistake it for anything else,' she said, her words scratching against his conscience. 'You did what you had to do because we both thought that Mina was going to out us in public. So, no. It won't happen again.'

But that was the problem, wasn't it? He *wanted* it to happen. Needed it like a feral thing in his blood. It was a ferocity that shocked him to his core. He'd never felt like that about a woman before, not even his ex-fiancée. It felt stronger than a craving. An addiction even. Which was what made it so dangerous. A thing that needed to be leashed. Because he knew what was at risk. His company. *Hers.*

It had taken years to crawl out of the damage done to Liassidis Shipping's reputation after the betrayal of a client was made public knowledge. Years of not putting a foot wrong, or stepping once out of line. He'd been the perfect businessman, determined, focused only on his company and his clients. Focused on doing it his way and by himself.

Even if Helena and Leander publicly split and waited *years*, Helena would be seen as his brother's wife for ever. And really, there were only a few sins greater. So, no. It didn't matter what he wanted, or what Helena wanted.

It was simply an impossibility.

The realisation felled him. And he wondered whether, if he was able to go back in time, would he do things the same way that evening? Would he kiss her the way he had?

Yes. A million times yes.

The answer was swift, determined, ruthless, and demanded more. But Leo had more control over himself than most and he wouldn't give in to a selfish desire that would burn through the fragile hold both he and Helena had on the situation that Leander had thrust them into.

'It's okay,' she said to him with a brave smile. 'Tonight we drank to new beginnings, remember? So that's what tomorrow will be. A new beginning.'

She was offering them a lifeline. A fresh start without the weight of the past or the intoxication of the kiss between them in the present. And he both wanted it and loathed it, but it was what they both needed if they had any hope of getting what they wanted from the future.

She held his gaze for one more second before turning to leave the room.

Clenching his jaw and unable to watch her go, he turned back to the window, reaching for a glass of whisky that was now an unappealing room temperature. He heard her steps on the marble floor, taking her further and further away from him.

But, before he could let her go, he needed to know one thing.

'They were good times, though. Weren't they?' he asked her before she could completely disappear.

'Yes,' she said after a moment. 'Yes, they were.'

'You had fun?' he pressed. He held his breath.

'No one made me laugh like Leander did,' she admitted, and he waited, knowing there was more, and knowing that he wouldn't like it.

'And no one made me cry like you did.'

With that final, devastating blow to his heart, she left the room.

CHAPTER SEVEN

FOCUS, HELENA ORDERED herself as she dabbed BB cream under her eyes, trying to cover the dark circles that had formed from too little sleep. A little blusher and a swipe of lip balm had put a little colour back into features paled from tossing and turning all night.

'I was twenty-one...'

'I'm sorry...'

'It can't happen again...'

Leo's words were background music to images of a kiss that was so carnal, so intense she'd woken up damp, exhausted and miserably unsatisfied. And she would stay that way, she reminded herself, because acting on whatever this was between them would ruin them both.

But at least she wouldn't have to worry about it for much longer. The message she'd received from Kate at some ungodly hour of the morning had put an end to that.

Leander has promised to return to Greece on Sunday.

It had taken Helena a moment to realise that what she was feeling wasn't relief but a sense of loss that shocked her to the core. But Leander was who she needed, so she sent Kate back a series of praying hands emojis.

The alarm on her smart watch beeped with a ten-minute warning and she used that time wisely. She'd set up her laptop under the shade of the thatched pool house awning, aware that Leo would be done with his morning swim. She chose to forgo the peaty Greek coffee she loved to have semi-sweet and opted for an espresso, taking it out to the table, where she made sure that the sun wasn't shining on the screen or the camera.

She flicked through the dossier she'd brought with her on Jong Da-Eun, the German-born Korean actress who had recently gained an international following with a part in a major Hollywood blockbuster. But beyond her celebrity, Jong Da-Eun had a history of charitable partnerships proving her more than capable of being a brand ambassador for Incendia.

She had met Jong Da-Eun about a year ago and, discovering that they had both lost family members in a way that had changed their lives irrevocably, they had formed a fast and firm friendship. Now she wanted to make that relationship professional too.

Helena closed her eyes and inhaled the sea-salt air, taking the time to appreciate the moment. She loved this part of her job—finding the right people for the right role, knowing that it would positively impact not only the charity but the people that it could reach, knowing what good it could do. And she *had* to believe that Incendia would continue. She *had* to believe that she would fix it. That all this was not only worth it, but would work.

The sound of the video call interrupted her thoughts and she settled into the chair and hit the accept button.

'Helena! It is so lovely to see you.'

'Likewise, Jong Da-Eun,' Helena replied sincerely.

'Please, Da-Eun is fine,' the actress assured her. *'Kamsahamnida.'*

Da-Eun laughed easily. 'Your accent is getting better.'

'I've been practising,' Helena confided.

'It's paying off. But Helena, we shouldn't be speaking on your honeymoon,' Da-Eun chided. 'Though,' she added, peering at the background behind Helena, 'it looks incredible.'

'It *is* incredible,' Helena replied, allowing the natural excitement of the location to fill her voice, happy to avoid discussion of the actual honeymoon.

They caught up a little on the details of each other's lives. Helena asking about her latest drama series and the male lead she was paired with, and Da-Eun asking about Incendia and the wedding. Helena hated being evasive, hated having to pick and choose her truths, but if she didn't then neither Incendia nor a possible partnership with Jong Da-Eun would even be possible next year.

Helena's chest ached. She desperately wanted Incendia to be a success. She had worked twice as hard as many of her fellow students, volunteering in the charity sector throughout her studies and beyond, for no extra credit. She had developed her skills until they were honed to a fine point, studying business leaders in the sector and beyond, understanding how their minds worked. She *wanted* to be seen as an excellent businesswoman, just like her father. He had been a titan in his industry and paired with Giorgos Liassidis they had been unstoppable. It was a legacy that she'd wanted not just to be a part of, but to be worthy of.

And she *was* good at what she did. But ever since Gregory's theft she had begun to wonder if she did actually manage to make it through the financial review would that finally be enough to appease the yearning in her heart? For more. For belonging. For *love*.

Yanking her thoughts back to the present, Helena wasted no more time. 'You know how much I've wanted you to work with Incendia, but I really believe that this campaign is the right one for you,' she said truthfully.

'So do I,' Da-Eun replied with a smile.

'Wait...what?' Excitement unfurled like a whip within her. 'You're going to do it? You're in?'

Da-Eun laughed. 'That is why I like working with you, Helena. You can be all work one minute and then a ball of excitement the next.'

Helena blushed and tried to apologise.

'No, don't be sorry. It's refreshing,' Da-Eun insisted. 'This is a cause you not only believe in but have personal experience with. It's so much better than these po-faced men who would do absolutely anything just to make money.'

Helena hoped Da-Eun didn't see the way her words had caused her to pale. Didn't realise how close she had come to the truth. Because wasn't that what she was doing? Absolutely anything to get her hands on her inheritance.

No, she assured herself. It wasn't like that. She wasn't doing it to put the money in her back pocket, like Gregory had, or like countless others who took advantage of any loophole they could find. This was different. Yes, she was doing a wrong thing, but it would achieve the right thing in the end for Incendia, and that was all that mattered. She closed down the call with promises to send contracts and set up meetings for when she returned from her honeymoon.

The shares are yours. The money is yours. Your father made silly, outdated stipulations on your inheritance and you're doing what you have to, in order to save a charity you believe in.

A very Kate-sounding no-nonsense response sounded in Helena's head and she let it soothe her doubts. After all, she had just managed to secure Incendia's first international brand ambassador!

Leo hung back from the threshold, watching Helena's video call, struck by how natural she looked. In control. Powerful in an innate way that he hadn't seen before now. It reminded him of watching his father and hers doing a business deal over lunch.

It wasn't arrogance that had given them a near lazy sense of 'ease', but belief. Belief in their skills, belief in their company, and knowledge. Knowledge that they were the best in the business. And, watching Helena now, he was surprised to find himself enjoying that about her too.

And, just like that, he was regretting not having done his research on Incendia. The way she had talked so passionately about it couldn't be faked. Whoever she'd been speaking to knew it, and so did he. But the person on the call had called it a 'cause'. And although he loved his company, he had never met anyone in business who called their company a *cause*.

What was it about what this company did that made Helena so desperate that she would marry his brother to access money to cover the financial hole? The questions that he'd managed to keep at bay until now began to burrow through his mind like woodworm, burrowing little holes into every conversation they'd had before now.

He watched as she wrapped up the conversation, the sun catching the golden glints in her hair, the oversized shirt hanging from her shoulders, indolently revealing the smooth skin he'd spent an alarming number of hours thinking about. A gentle tan had sun-kissed her skin with freckles that looked wholesome, even as his body responded to the near primal passion he had glimpsed the night before.

It seemed that, despite the warning his brain had been given, his body still hadn't got the message. All night he'd been tormented by impressions of a kiss that was just as real as his erotic dreams had provided. He'd woken up, his body on fire and full of a tension that wouldn't quit until Helena and this entire situation was firmly in his rear-view mirror.

He was about to turn away when Helena got to her feet and he realised that the shirt, which stopped midway down her long thighs, was all she was wearing. Whether it was a shirt or a dress, he didn't give a damn. He would go out of his mind if he spent the next few days in close proximity to a woman who was his every fantasy come to life.

He tried to leave again, when his attention was snagged by her cry, 'Yes!' He turned back to find her dancing up and down as if she'd won some great victory.

'Yes, yes, *yes*!' she cried again.

As she punched a button on her mobile, he wondered when he'd last felt like that about a deal or a contract.

Never, he realised with a start.

Gwen's damage had happened too soon after he'd stepped up to take over the helm from his father for him to ever fully trust or feel such pure easy joy or trust in a new deal again.

'Megan, we did it!' he heard Helena cry into the phone. 'Jong Da-Eun is coming on board.'

Even from here he could hear the high-pitched scream of the person Helena had called, especially when Helena had pulled the phone away from her ear to laugh, and he couldn't help but smile at their exuberance.

'Yes, yes, I know. So can you move forward with the contract? Absolutely… No, that won't be necessary, just send it out to the list in the dossier.'

There was a pause and some of the joy dimmed from her features. 'No update? Nothing from the CPS?'

Leo frowned, recognising the acronym for the British Crown Prosecution Service.

It's not failing. It's employee theft.

'Okay… No, that's okay. If you can just chase Dr Matheson for his research proposal, then we can begin to create the fundraising plans.'

And once again his interest was piqued.

What did Incendia do?

Helena raised her gaze and it clashed with his in shock as she discovered him standing on the threshold.

'No, that's it, thanks, Megan,' she replied, without taking her gaze from his. 'Have a great rest of the day.'

She hung up the phone and now he didn't know what to do. Come out onto the deck? He could hardly turn and leave.

And just when had he become so indecisive and weak-willed?

Throwing off the awkwardness, he brazened it out onto the deck.

'Am I right in thinking that congratulations are in order?' he asked, hating the hesitation between them, the wariness heavy in the air awkward and uncomfortable. He'd almost preferred the intense sexual tension to this.

Slowly, she nodded, the smile on her lips pulling to one side. 'Yes,' she said with quiet confidence, unable to quite hide her excitement. 'I've just secured my first brand ambassador and she's going to be great.'

'Then that *does* deserve congratulations. We should celebrate,' he announced before frowning. 'Or do we have another social event to attend?' he asked with distinct displeasure.

'Celebrate?' Helena asked, as if confused.

'You know, celebrate. Do something special to mark the success,' he offered at about the same time as he re-alised that it was something she usually did with his brother. 'Unless you want to wait for Leander?' he asked, wondering why that thought filled him with a strange kind of resentment.

'Well, I suppose I could. Kate messaged. Leander's coming back on Sunday.'

Her words had the same impact as a stone thrown into a lake.

'*This* Sunday?' Leo asked, unable to hide his surprise.

'Why? Is something wrong with that?' Helena asked, picking up on his shock.

'No, I just…hope that Kate got him to sign in blood. I'm about done with this whole affair,' he dismissed, de-spite the bitter taste in his mouth.

Only to see Helena's expression morph into hurt.

'You're not the only one,' Helena grumbled as she made her way past him.

'Wait,' he said, reaching out to clasp her by the arm.

Everything stopped. His heart, her steps.

Slowly, she looked down at his hand, where his fingers had wrapped around her bicep, and he released her im-mediately. He'd done it without thinking, but the tremors rippling through the air and across his skin warned him it had been a mistake.

'I'm sorry,' he said. For the snarky comment, for grasping her arm. 'I'm…' he took a shaky inhale '… I'm trying. I'm not used to…' he pressed his lips together '… modifying my behaviour. Having to, or even wanting to. Usually, people just do what I say and don't really ask questions,' he admitted hesitantly.

Or talked back, Helena guessed. Because Leo seemed to be talking only about professional interactions. The confession pulled at her heartstrings as she began to see, really see, how the separation between the two brothers had impacted *him*. But even what he had just said seemed much more like the old Leo than the still aloof Leo she had met on her wedding day.

'So,' he tried again. 'Leander's coming back on Sunday. But it's Thursday today and I feel like we should celebrate sooner than that.'

Helena could see that he was trying. That it was an effort for him, but he was doing it for her. And even just the glimpse of what he could be like when he wasn't so angry and rooted in the past made her want to pull him out fully into the light.

'You know…' she said hesitantly. 'I saw that Leander left his prized convertible here in the garage,' she went on, remembering how much Leo had loved to drive. To be in control, but also to be *free* in that control. 'It would almost be a crime not to take it out for a spin on such a beautiful day.'

'Now that, Helena, is an excellent plan,' Leo replied, with a spark in his eyes that she hadn't seen for years.

As Leo manoeuvred the car along the coastal road leading away from the Mani Peninsula and upwards, Hel-

ena couldn't help but smile. The powerful car practically
purred under his command.

The wind roaring in her ears and whipping at her hair
meant that conversation was almost blissfully impossible
and she was surprised by how content she was to simply
be there in the moment, the sun falling on her shoulders
and the stunning coastline a picture of intense blues, startling yellows and rich greens.

This was the most relaxed she had seen Leo since he
had burst back into her life and she was glad of it. As he
changed gear, the convertible leapt forward, restrained
by his control but eager to show its power.

In tan trousers and a white linen shirt, rolled up to his
forearms, he looked every inch the powerful Greek bil-
lionaire with the world at his feet and Helena revelled in
being beside him. His eyes firmly on the road, his eyes
hidden behind a pair of sunglasses, she watched his lips
curve into a smile hooked at one side.

'What?' she couldn't help but ask.

'That,' he replied, nodding towards the downward tra-
jectory of the road, at the end of which was a small fishing village. 'Are you hungry yet?' he asked.

Oh, yes. She was very hungry. Just not for what he
was able to offer her.

Half an hour later, they were sitting under a blue and
white fluttering awning, protecting them from the fierce
heat of the sun. The table was one of only about six on
the small terrace of the main, and quite possibly only,
restaurant in the small village stuck like a barnacle to
the side of the coast.

'Are you sure this is how you want to celebrate?' Leo
asked, as if he wasn't sure it was enough.

'Yes!' she insisted with genuine sincerity. 'Because honestly, if I have to smile at another reporter, or give another red-carpet interview, I think I might actually murder someone.'

'Well, if it's my brother, then I'll happily help,' Leo replied with a humour that was usually absent when talking about Leander. She ignored the slip, all the while hoping for more. Because she would love nothing more than to help the two brothers find their way back to some semblance of a relationship. Somehow.

The waiter arrived to pour their wine, promising that the food would be with them shortly. They had ordered a fish platter and side of fresh salads, pitta and the hummus she had been lusting after the moment she'd seen another couple dining in the late afternoon sun indulging in the chickpea dip.

'To your new brand ambassador,' Leo toasted.

Helena clinked her glass to his and took a sip of the cool white wine that instantly burst with tart, delicious freshness on her tongue.

'And can I ask what she will be branding for you?' Leo enquired.

Helena swallowed, the wine going down the wrong way and causing her to cough.

Apologising and spluttering, she didn't know why she was reluctant for him to know, even though she was aware that she'd been keeping it from him.

'It's a medical charity,' she started.

Leo's head cocked to one side in curiosity.

'For heart conditions, mainly. But it's one of the only charities supporting the families of people with—'

'Brugada,' Leo correctly concluded.

She clenched her jaw, surprised that Leo had realised,

had even *known* the name of the disease that had killed her father. She was touched—moved. They hadn't really been talking that much back then.

Shock rippled through Leo's body with a shiver that raised the hairs on his arms and neck. Brugada syndrome was what had caused Michael Hadden's heart to stop one night in his sleep and never start again. There were rarely any symptoms of the genetic disorder that caused irregular heart rhythms that were often catastrophic if left undiagnosed.

Malákas.

'I didn't know,' he confessed.

'Why should you?' she asked defiantly.

'Because if I had I would never have offered such a low price for the shares. *Christós*, Helena.' Leo's conscience sucker-punched him in the gut so hard he was winded.

'Don't do that,' she commanded. 'I made my choice that day. I knew what I was doing,' she whispered angrily.

'But *I* didn't,' he fired back.

Helena let out a cynical laugh. 'Whether you like it or not, I *made it* as a businesswoman. If you change your mind because you feel sorry for me, you're undermining me and patronising me. On the day we're supposedly celebrating me.'

Realisation dawned in his gaze and he started to shake his head in denial, but stopped as he fully understood what she was saying.

'That wasn't my intention.'

'But it was what you were doing,' she pointed out gently.

'It's not a good deal for you,' he said again.

'Then maybe, in the future, you'll think twice about

the deals you offer,' she said, leaning back into the chair, clearly aware that she'd made her point.

He'd been so hell-bent on getting all the shares in Liassidis Shipping that he hadn't even bothered to do his own research. Research he was usually absolutely meticulous about. He didn't like it, the effect she seemed to be having on him. The way he was behaving out of character. But he also didn't like the discord between them. Not after how much he'd enjoyed the peace.

'How did it come about? You and Incendia,' he asked both carefully and curiously.

She could have sniped back at him, he certainly deserved it, but he sensed that she wanted it too, the fragile truce between them.

'After my father passed away, Mum was…pretty difficult to be around.'

Helena had always found it difficult to talk about Gwen. It was as if it were a betrayal to reveal some weakness in her mother's character. Especially to a man who had been so devastatingly impacted by her already. But was grief really a weakness? It affected everyone in such different ways and none that could be predicted until it was felt, experienced.

'At first, Mum was determined to continue on as if nothing had happened. Yes, her husband was gone, but she could cope with that as long as everything else remained the same. And she did that first by trying to carry on with his work.'

Which had been disastrous.

'I…knew that she had made a mistake that had cost Liassidis Shipping greatly, but…' she trailed off, shaking her head '… I didn't know that she'd gone expressly against your wishes, or those of the board. I didn't know that at all. I just thought she'd made a mistake and that you'd...'

'Exiled her?' Leo asked, his eyes lit with a strange mixture of understanding and lingering resentment.

Helena pressed her lips together and nodded guiltily. She understood a lot more now than she had then, as to how damaging that would have been for his company. How it would have felt to have his decisions questioned like that, and to have been so publicly defied. In a way, wasn't that what Gregory had done by stealing such an obscene amount of money from Incendia on her watch?

'We shouldn't have let it happen,' Leo said of himself and his father.

'No one expected her to throw herself into it to that extent,' she admitted. 'But I think it was because... Well, I think because if she could keep everything the same, then nothing had happened. She hadn't lost the man she loved. She wasn't drowning in her own grief. If she was busy, if she was doing something, then she didn't have to think about it. The only problem was...'

'That if she wasn't managing her own grief, she wasn't managing yours either,' Leo concluded correctly again.

Helena nodded. It was strange how much he seemed to understand her without her having to explain. It was familiar, and it both soothed and hurt at the same time.

'My grief was a reminder of things she didn't want to acknowledge. And it made an already difficult relationship painfully strained. One of the teachers at my boarding school referred me to Incendia and it was there that I got some support for myself, rather than having to neglect my feelings in order to try to protect my mother's. Their help was a godsend.'

But when grief had entwined with the loss of the Liassidises from her life—the anchor that had seemed to hold her little family together—it had felt as if everything had slipped through her fingers. After her mother had failed to navigate her own grief with her husband's work, she had returned to England and thrown out everything that had ever belonged to him. She had put the house in Mayfair on the market without even telling Helena and although it had never really felt like a home it had still been a devastating blow.

Helena had clung to Kate in those early months, and even Leander. But the people she'd missed so terribly, her father and…and Leo, she forced herself to admit, were gone.

'I worked with one of their counsellors, and then began volunteering when I had started to find my feet again. Knowing first-hand how important their work and the funding they raised for such specific research was—the kind that big pharma doesn't have any interest in because the conditions are so specialised there is little financial incentive—just made my work there more important.'

Leo was listening intently, impressed beyond belief at the kind of strength it must have taken to work at a charity where every day she must be reminded of the loss of her father.

'So, after my A-levels, I went to study business management at Cambridge Judge Business School.'

'That's incredible,' he said.

'You sound surprised,' she accused.

'Not in the least.' And he wasn't. Because he had always known, really, that whatever she put her mind to, she could achieve.

'I did my master's there too. Did a few years in the sector, worked as a consultant across a few startups. I won a few awards,' she admitted, as if it were something to be shy about rather than proud, and Leo was back to cursing the mother who had taught her daughter to expect so little.

'And when Incendia approached me about the CEO's position it was… It was a dream come true.'

Leo wondered whether she realised it—how passionate she sounded when talking about Incendia. Helena shone the moment she talked of it, her eyes bright and powerful, the flush on her cheeks nothing to do with anger, or sexual tension. Just joy and inner pride that made her more beautiful than he'd ever seen her.

His conscience twisted painfully in his chest as he realised not only how much he'd missed, but the active part he'd played in her isolation during such a painful and grief-stricken time. He knew then that no apology could cover his behaviour. But he found himself wanting to explain, to justify.

'I had no idea. About Gwen. About…'

Helena bit her lip, but he pressed on.

'About how difficult that time must have been for you.'

'I don't know how you could have. You were too busy trying to save a company my mother nearly destroyed.'

He nodded. 'It's no excuse, but that was a really hard time. Dad had just stepped down from the day-to-day running of the company, and I was working flat-out.'

Mina had broken off their engagement and he hadn't even had time to work through that. He'd been pulling nineteen-hour working days to retain the few clients that had stayed, to keep the workforce on so that when they did get new clients they could fulfil the work orders. He'd refused help from his father, because to accept it would admit that he was failing, and he wouldn't even let himself think about asking for help from the brother who had all but disappeared from his life.

'I wanted to prove myself. I shouldn't have taken it out on Gwen, I know that. Even though I'd told her not to do it, to engage that client, I think that Gwen saw me as a child, an upstart and that she knew better.'

'A little like how you see me?' Helena asked, her tone light, but something serious in her gaze.

And he realised then how truthful that statement was. He felt the sting acutely.

'A little. Yes,' he admitted. 'I still think that you're playing a very dangerous game in trying to plug the charity's financial hole yourself, I won't lie to you. But I understand why you're doing it. And, ultimately, it's your choice as CEO.'

She nodded, but didn't look convinced.

'What is it?' he asked.

'I… What if…?'

He waited. Whatever her fear was here, it was important to her and he couldn't rush it.

She looked down at the table. 'What if it's not enough?'

The desperation in her tone cut him to the quick.

'For who?' he asked.

'The board. My mother.'

The latter was a near whisper that broke what little was left of a very cold, hard heart.

'It needs to be enough for *you*, Helena. No one else.'

Leo knew that better than anyone, because he'd learned it the hard way.

CHAPTER EIGHT

WRAPPED IN A TOWEL, wet hair piled into a messy bun on top of her head, Helena looked tiredly at the dress she was supposed to wear to the lunch Leander had arranged for them at a trendy restaurant that also just happened to be owned by a potential client for his company.

Helena hadn't for a second begrudged Leander using these opportunities to drum up prospective business, at least...not until he had disappeared and left Leo and her in this mess.

She let the printed silk of the dress slip through her fingers as she wondered what would have happened if Leander had stayed. What if she had arrived at the church to find him rather than Leo waiting for her at the top of the aisle?

Yes, everything would have been easier. She and Leander would have smiled and pretended to be the perfect couple. Kissing Leander would have felt silly and stupid, and not far off what it would have felt like to kiss Kate!

But kissing Leo...

Goosebumps pebbled the skin on her forearms.

It can't happen again.

She forced away the throb of desire that undulated through her body like a wave against the shore. Three days. She just had to get through three more days. As long as they kept to the schedule, she'd be able to make it.

She'd won a huge victory with Jong Da-Eun and Leo had wanted to celebrate that. Yesterday had been wonderful, she admitted to herself. Seeing Leo like that again, talking to him like she once had. He'd been impressed by her, she'd seen it. And that meant more to her than he'd ever know. So much so that she'd confessed her secret doubts—that saving Incendia wouldn't be enough. To make up for the board's doubts in her, her mother's rejection.

He'd told her that it needed to be enough for her, but she couldn't help but feel that nothing she did would fill the hole created by her mother's mental absence and the loss of her father.

Helena shook off the sad thought. What point was it yearning after things that could never be?

Throwing on a pair of loose trousers and a short shirt-top, she went to have breakfast, to find Leo wheeling a cabin bag into the living space.

He was leaving? Now?

'What—' She stopped herself midsentence because she didn't even know what to say. She'd thought that yesterday had brought them closer. At least to a point of understanding. And now he was leaving?

Leo looked up and must have seen the shock pass over her face.

'What's wrong?' he asked, concern stark on his features.

'Why do you have that?'

He looked down, said, 'Oh…' and grimaced.

'Look, if you have to leave—' Helena said, trying to sound nonchalant rather than panic stricken.

'Leave? Why would I leave?' he replied, confused.

'You have a packed case!'

'Yes,' he answered as if she were missing something.

'Why?' she nearly cried.

He smiled then and the sight was so at odds with the entire exchange she wanted to throw something at him.

Oh, this man!

'We're going on a trip,' he announced.

'What trip? We're having lunch at Thentroliváno.'

'*Leander* wanted to have lunch at Thentroliváno, but us? Not so much.'

'We don't?' Helena asked, feeling, against all odds, the tug of Leo's good humour working on her.

'Nope,' he said, shaking his head. 'We do not.'

'So, what is it that *we* want to do today?' she asked, playing along.

'We are going on a boat trip,' Leo announced with an uncharacteristic flourish. 'So go pack a bag,' he commanded.

Helena's mind completely blanked. 'What am I packing for?'

'Swimming, sun, sea and an overnight stay.'

'O-overnight?' Helena stuttered, never once having suffered from the affliction before in her life.

Leo looked away, hoping that Helena didn't see his body's reaction to her simple question.

'Yes, just a change of clothes,' he confirmed as he fiddled unnecessarily with the handle of the case.

Gamóto, he was behaving like a schoolboy.

He glanced up at Helena, who was staring at him, an unfathomable look on her features. He paused, fearing that he'd done the wrong thing, that he'd made a terrible mistake. All he'd wanted to do was to throw Leander's damn agenda out of the window. They'd been playing by the rules of a games master who wasn't even here. And if they only had three days left, then Leo didn't want to waste them doing things that would only benefit his brother.

Yesterday had been a breath of fresh air for him and he was surprised to find he wanted more. It had nothing to do with the fierce arousal which was banked, as much as was humanly possible, by what couldn't be. He had enjoyed spending time with her. Talking to her. Hearing about her life. And, masochist that he was, he wanted more. If this was all they could have, he would take it *all*.

'Why a boat trip?' Helena asked.

'Because whenever you visited the island it was the first thing you'd ask to do. You'd run straight up to us and demand to know when we were going to take you out onto the water. We used to call you—'

'*Delfíni*. You used to call me dolphin.'

Leo nodded, his lips curving into a smile against his will. *'Naí.'*

Helena smiled. It started off small and slow, but grew until he felt it in his heart. There were many things that he could never give to Helena or be to her. But this? This he could do.

'Go pack. We leave in ten minutes.'

The look of excitement that lit her features stopped his breath. Eagerness, joy, a flush that was so damn innocent he nearly choked.

She spun on her heel and ran off to her room, giving him a brief respite from the impact of her presence, and time to calm his body's innate response to her.

And then, with startling clarity, he realised just what kind of hell he'd let himself in for over the next twenty-four hours.

* * *

The driver let them out at the large marina where the
yacht Leo had organised last night waited for them. It
wasn't presently on the market, but the owner was a
friend and Leo had paid an exorbitant price to have the
yacht's staff sail through the night to have it here on time.
And while he'd seen pictures of it, knew its reputation,
even Leo couldn't help but be impressed by the thirty-
three-metre-long yacht.

Helena drew up beside him and stared, eyes wide and
mouth open.

'Boat trip.' The words fell from her lips.

'Mmm?'

'You said boat trip. *That's* not a boat,' Helena said, the
awe in her voice making him smile, giving him exactly
what he'd wanted when he'd first had the idea.

As if in a daze, Helena drifted towards the yacht,
where a uniformed staff member waited at the plank
with a smile on their face.

'Mr and Mrs Liassidis? Congratulations on your recent wedding.'

Of course, Leo had told his friend that it was a wedding gift for Leander and his new bride. But he'd forgotten what a nuisance it would be having to keep up the
pretence in such close quarters. And he'd wanted this to
be a true escape for Helena. A chance for her to just be
herself. As he hastily looked for a way round it, Helena
let herself be guided onto the yacht.

As directed, he left their bags by the gangplank and
followed Helena for a basic tour of the beautiful yacht.
Split over three levels, the lower, main and upper deck,
the yacht could comfortably house eleven guests along
with the five crew members serving on their trip. There

was a Jacuzzi on the back end of the main deck and a dining area on the upper deck.

'Your bags have been taken to the master suite on the main deck, but we'd first like to welcome you with a glass of champagne,' the staff member offered.

Helena's eagerness was immediate and infectious, and Leo smiled, enjoying the excitement rolling off her in waves. He gestured for them to lead the way towards the glorious view from the back of the upper deck. The Captain joined them for a toast, congratulating them on their nuptials, and then returned to the cabin, where she piloted them out of the marina and into the Mediterranean.

One by one, the staff members retreated unobtrusively, leaving them alone on the deck. Helena leant against the rail, the wind playing with the strands of hair that had come loose from where it was held back. He wanted to see it down, he wanted to run his fingers through it, grip it in his fist as he…

Maláka.

He needed to have better control over himself than this. Much better.

'How long do we have?' she asked, without turning to look at him.

He wanted to say as long as she wanted, he wanted to give that to her. But he couldn't.

'We'll return to the marina tomorrow afternoon. But if you want to return earlier—'

'No,' she said, interrupting him. 'No,' she repeated, as if wanting to hold on to this moment as much as he did.

He nodded, and even though she didn't see it, he sensed she knew in that strange shared understanding that existed between people who had spent so long together it didn't matter how many years had passed since they'd seen each other.

Needing to break the moment, he excused himself, heading off to speak to the Captain about the arrangements for that evening.

Helena gazed longingly at the horizon for just one more minute. It was perfect. There was nothing marring the clean sliver of sea beneath the weight of a sky so blue it almost hurt to look at it. She had only ever felt this kind of serenity looking out at the sea. Maybe Leo and Leander had been right, maybe in a past life she had been a dolphin, content to swim the oceans.

She laughed, knowing that if she'd said as much to Kate, the veterinarian would have reeled off facts and figures about their lifestyle and personality, and the pods they swam in. Kate would have been in her pod, Helena decided. And Leander, of course. But might there be space for Leo?

And there, looking out at the clash of deep oceanic blue and light denim sky, she inhaled deeply, easily, for the first time in what felt like months. Despite her ever-constant awareness of Leo, here, out on the Mediterranean Sea, at least there were no reporters. There were no staff members, utterly ignorant of the perilous state of the charity, no terrified board members looking to her to save them. Nothing to fix, and nothing to prove to anyone. She hadn't realised how exhausting that had been for her. But here, just like it had been when she was younger, was refuge given to her by Leo Liassidis.

The sun had shifted and was no longer so harsh on her skin. It felt warmer, softer, almost as if it had known that she'd needed comfort rather than ferocity. She heard Leo's steps on the wooden deck behind her.

'What has you sighing like that?' he asked, and she sent her smile out to the sea.

'The realisation that I needed this,' she lied. Because the truth was, it was the realisation that *he'd* known she'd needed this that had caused her heart to turn.

'It's so peaceful out here,' she observed.

'It wasn't like that when Leander and I used to take you out in the boat when you were younger.'

'No,' Helena replied with a laugh. 'No, it was not.'

She would shriek with delight as they guided their speedboat into a crashing wave, scream as the boat jerked and dipped beneath her, loving the salt on her tongue and the gleam of pure delight in the brothers' eyes, and cry out for more.

'You were the only ones to do that. Take me out on the sea,' she confessed, remembering that her parents would have rather spent time with Giorgos and Cora than the child they barely saw through the school year. 'I don't think I ever thanked you for it,' she said, frowning, trying to remember.

'You never have to thank me for that,' he replied.

Helena turned to look at him as he came to stand beside her at the rail. Her heart stopped for a beat. He was utterly devastating. The close-cut beard against his jaw, dark and inviting. A pair of sunglasses, hiding his gaze, his emotions from her. His cream linen shirt was open at the neck, just enough to tantalise with the dusting of chest hair she'd not seen on him as a younger man. This Leo was even more *male* to her. Age had honed his features to perfection and it was hard to ignore the impact he was having on her.

'But this is wonderful,' she said, forcing a bright smile to her lips as she looked back to the sea. She closed her eyes and inhaled slowly. 'I think it's the first time since discovering the theft of the money that I've actually just taken a breath.'

Leo's heart went out to her. He could see what a struggle it was for her, not just because of how much the company meant to her, but because she was a young businesswoman who wanted to prove herself so much that she'd gone to such extreme lengths. Lengths that were dangerous, both financially and emotionally.

Surely it would have been much simpler just to borrow the money? Or was he just looking for something, anything, that would have removed the barrier of her wedding to his brother?

'Why did you ask Leander to do this for you?' he asked, struggling anew with the resentment he felt about this entire situation. 'Did he not offer to lend you the money?'

'Of course he offered to lend me the money,' she explained. 'But I *have* the money. It's *my* money. I just… don't have it *yet*.'

Before him was a woman who had to fix things herself. Who didn't want to rely on someone else, who had learned from her father's absence and her mother's neglect that she could only rely on herself. Didn't he know that for himself? But why, when he thought of Helena being like that—like him—did it feel like a punch to the chest? To the *heart*?

'But as to why Leander,' she went on, interrupting his thoughts. 'Because I trust him.'

Leo couldn't help but scoff. 'Trust? Leander?' he demanded, his tone harsh, his instinctive reaction to his brother's betrayal near primal.

'Yes. Trust. I knew that he would be discreet and I knew that he would be there for me when I needed him.'

'That's just wishful thinking. As evidenced by the fact that he's *not* here when you need him,' Leo replied hotly.

But Helena shook her head. 'I know him. I know that whatever it is that came up, whatever it was that he needed space for...it was something incredibly important.'

Leo shook his head, a bitter sneer across his face. 'Leander is selfish. He will always put himself first, make choices that benefit him most, without any compunction or thought for anyone other than himself.'

'That's not true,' Helena replied gently. 'It's just what you want to see in him.'

Helena's open expression and flat denial floored him.

Hot anger, old, dark and thick, something *nasty*, built in him. He'd been softening towards his brother. He'd felt it. Not because of anything he'd done, but because he'd seen how others saw Leander. Right up until just then, when Helena had said that she trusted him. Because Leander had lied to him. Made Leo believe that his brother wanted what he wanted.

Right up until the moment when his father had asked the question, Leo had thought he'd known how his life would be. What it would look like, how it would go. Throughout their teenage years they'd developed a way of thinking that completed each other, balanced each other. Applying that to a business context for their family company would have made them unstoppable. But, beyond that, Leo had believed that they wanted the same things.

He'd believed that he'd had companionship, trust, *safety* with his brother. It had been them against the world.

'I want to take the money.'

That was what had been more important to Leander than *he* had been.

The shock, the pain, at discovering that everything he'd thought about his brother had been wrong was devastating to him. It had shaken the foundations of what he believed in, and the only way he had been able to survive it had been to cut Leander from his life. To cauterise the wound with abject denial.

He had taken the tattered ruins of his plans for Liassidis Shipping—the only thing he'd had left after Mina had abandoned him—and forged a path ahead alone. Until he'd eventually forgotten that there was a time when he had shared everything with his brother, and instead now shared nothing with anyone.

'Leander,' he told her hotly, as if he could convince her as much as himself, 'would, and *did*, sell out his own brother for his own selfish whims.'

'In the last ten years, Leander has made time for me to celebrate the wins and commiserate the losses. He's been there to take me out for dinner, or dancing or whatever, because he knows that's something that I need. He has given me so much and, in return, all he got is a forced fake marriage.'

Leo clenched his jaw against the picture she was painting of his brother. Trying to cling to his anger instead of the memories of the times that Leander had tried to reach out to him.

'He was there even when I tried to avoid him because of how embarrassed I was over what happened with Liassidis Shipping and my mother,' Helena said, looking at her hands.

'That's because he didn't have to clean up the mess,' he bit out without thinking. But the moment he saw Helena pale, he regretted it instantly.

'That's because he valued my friendship. So please don't undermine my relationship with your brother just because you don't have one.'

Her words sliced clean and deep.

'It's not like that,' he dismissed instead.

'You could probably say that to anyone else, but I know what you two were like before your father offered you the choice of inheritance between the family business or a financial lump sum.' Her gaze on him was steady and knowing. 'I know how close you were, how sometimes you were so similar only your parents could tell you apart. That kind of connection doesn't just disappear.'

But she was wrong. He admired that Helena was someone who could grow up with parents like hers and still hope for more. Still reach for, *want*, that familial connection. But he couldn't.

No. From that first moment, from the *second* that Leander had chosen to walk away, Leo had drawn a line. A *hard* line between them. He hadn't wanted to speak to, see or hear from the person who had once been half of him. Leander had come home occasionally so he'd been unable to avoid him completely, but five years ago even those sporadic visits had stopped and Leo had refused all contact since then.

That was how he worked, that was what worked for him. That stubborn determination was how he survived.

Yet still Helena pressed on, unaware of his thoughts. 'But I also know that Leander would have been miserable if he'd worked with you at Liassidis Shipping. And I'm pretty sure that you know it too.'

Everything in him wanted to deny her words. Refute them with all his might.

'What I know is that my brother gave me absolutely no warning. The coward let me think that he was going to come with me and then took the money and ran.'

'What do you think would have happened if he'd joined the family company with you?' Helena asked. And his mind went utterly blank. 'Would you have had help? Would you have had someone to talk to? To share your burdens and your fears?' she asked.

Yes, he answered mentally. *Yes*, to each and every one of those questions.

As if she'd read his response in his face, she nodded. 'But all those things are about Leander helping you, not Leander making his own life a success, doing the things that make *him* happy. Believe it or not, but your brother's purpose is not to make *your* life easier.'

He wanted to be outraged. He wanted to be furious. But he couldn't deny what Helena was saying. He couldn't deny the hurt and the shock and the pain that her questions had uncovered. And he couldn't stop his next words from falling from his lips.

'He left me.'

'I know,' Helena replied sadly. And in her, he saw the pain of a daughter who'd lost her father too young and whose mother had barely been present for her.

'But he chose to do that,' Leo insisted, clinging desperately to his resentment, terrified of what it meant if he didn't.

'Yes,' Helena agreed. 'He had a choice to go it alone, do it the hard way and make something from nothing…

rather than slowly lose pieces of himself working in an industry he had no interest in, for a company that would have ignored him in favour of you. What choice would you have made?'

He was prevented from answering by the appearance of one of the yacht's staff.

'Mr and Mrs Liassidis? A sunset dinner has been prepared for you on the lower deck.'

Helena wasn't sure that she could eat at that moment, but didn't want to offend the staff, who had created a feast of absolute deliciousness. Laid out on the table that looked out over nothing but sea and sky were what looked like twenty or so plates of different Mediterranean delicacies.

Absently, she ran the little silver peony pendant across the chain at her neck as she took in the prettily set table and the romantic candles illuminating the deck. The sun was beginning to set, casting streaks of pink and ochre across a sky turning a shade darker with almost each breath she took.

She felt Leo's presence behind her, the warmth of his body like a physical touch against her skin. Despite the difficult conversation they'd shared there was no animosity between them, but she could tell that Leo's thoughts were heavy.

That wasn't what she'd wanted or intended. But she could see the pain the separation between the two brothers was causing each of them. If she could do anything for either of the men who had been such important figures in her life, it would be this.

To bring them back together.

Once again, petals had been scattered across the table and the deck itself, but this time, when she looked closer, she realised that they weren't rose petals. The shades of white, violet and red struck her immediately. Peonies. The colours of native Greek peonies.

Helena turned to look behind her as the Captain appeared on the deck with the other staff members.

'We'll be heading to the mainland now. Just call when you want us to return.'

Leo nodded as if he knew that this was going to happen.

Something like alarm rushed through her, not from fear of him, but from the thought of being alone with him out here. She could barely trust herself with people around. As if sensing her concern, he placed a hand on her shoulder, as if to anchor her, to reassure her, but that didn't make it any better.

The Captain looked between them, and Helena forced a smile to her lips. 'Thank you so much for all of this, it looks beautiful. I hope you have a lovely evening.'

Reassured, the Captain nodded and took her crew down to the main deck, where a small speedboat idled, waiting to take them back to the mainland.

'I thought it would be easier not to have to pretend that I was Leander and we were married, so...'

Helena nodded, but was instantly regretful having lost the security that the staff members had provided. The *barrier* they had provided to her wants.

She looked back at the peonies on the floor and her heart hurt.

He remembered. He'd always remembered that they were her favourite flower.

Why did he have to do that? she thought, even as the lump formed in her throat.

'What's wrong?' Leo asked.

Tears pressed against her eyes. She couldn't let them fall, but it was all too much. Every time she wanted to put Leo in a box where she couldn't touch him, he did something like this. He showed her that he was more than the unfeeling, cold, aloof man he pretended to be. Instead, he was a man who wanted her to have some fun, who had celebrated her success, who'd been devastated by his brother's choice, and who still remembered her favourite flower. All of those complexities made it impossible to ignore her feelings for him. Feelings that she should deny, but she didn't want to. Not any more.

As she ran the silver pendant across the chain again Leo's gaze centred on it.

'Thank you,' she whispered.

'For what?' he asked, his voice as low as the last of the sun's rays on the horizon.

'For this,' she replied.

He looked away to the table and took in the petals on the floor.

'No,' she clarified. 'For *this*,' she said, holding the necklace with her fingers and his gaze with her eyes.

The muscle at his jaw flexed as his eyes blazed with golden shards.

'You knew?' he asked. 'All along, you knew it was from me?'

Helena smiled, a little rueful, a little sad. 'Leander said he'd picked it because it was a pretty rose.'

'It's not a rose,' Leo replied almost indignantly.

'I know,' she said, his response almost making her smile. 'It was only you that ever remembered I loved peonies so much.'

'Why didn't you say something?'

'Because at first it was easier for me to pretend and not cause any trouble for you.'

'And then?' he asked, his tone hesitant, as if he almost didn't want to hear the answer but couldn't help himself.

'And then it was easier for me to pretend that it was Leander and not you who had given me such a significant present, when it was so easy for you to cut me from your life.'

The truth sobbed in her chest. She no longer wanted to hide anything from him, to protect him, or herself. If this was all she was going to have with him, if this was all they would ever get, she wanted him to see and know even the most dark and vulnerable parts of her. She wanted to be known by him, completely and utterly.

Only by him. Only ever by him.

'Why did you wear it to the wedding?' he asked. 'Before you knew I was going to be there.'

She looked to the ground. 'Because I wanted something of you that day.'

He lifted her chin with his forefinger, pulling her gaze back to his, the question in his eyes not needing to be spoken.

'Because,' she said, drawing on her courage, 'because it's always been you.'

CHAPTER NINE

NOTHING COULD HAVE undone him more in that moment. Nothing had *ever* undone him more. The naked want he saw in her eyes, the yearning. No one had ever looked at him like that. Not Mina, or any of the other women he'd spent time with.

She had kept his secret—the Christmas gift—at first to protect him and then later to protect herself, and he didn't know what was worse. No one had tried to protect him before. Not his brother, or his ex-fiancée. An ex-fiancée who had not even recognised him when they'd collided in the club. But Helena had. The moment she'd seen him at the top of the aisle, she'd known who he was. She *always* had.

It's always been you.

Deep down, he'd known that. He'd felt it but never wanted to look too hard or too closely at it because he hadn't wanted to lose her too. But her desires were written in her eyes and he wanted, so damn much, to give in to all of them.

'The world just watched you marry my brother,' he said, still desperately clinging to the last remaining barrier between them.

Helena nodded, agreement and understanding shining in the depths of the tears that hadn't yet fallen.

'We can't...' he tried again. Tried to convince himself. Tried to lie. When all he wanted to do was take her into his arms. 'It would ruin us both if it were found out.'

Helena bit her lip, her gaze dropping to the floor as she nodded in a way that twisted his gut. She turned to leave and the sudden wrench in his heart nearly killed him. It sliced clean through every and any objection that he could make, any fear for the future or of the past. He couldn't let her go. He just couldn't.

Leo caught her wrist and pulled her back to him and when she crashed against his chest he held her there, caged within his embrace, half terrified that she'd escape.

His entire body tensed against the shock of her against him, so close that he could feel the beat of her heart against his chest. Neither of them moved, barely breathed even, until she sighed and relaxed against him and he felt a victory like he'd never known.

Her head came to just beneath his chin, and he felt the puff of her breath against his neck. Goosebumps unfurled across his skin at the proximity of her lips to his skin, arousal coming for him hard and fast. His pulse raged in his chest and for a moment all he could hear was the sound of blood rushing through his veins.

His entire being wanted to hold, cling, delve, grip, any part of her he could claim. Possession, not sexual, but primal. He wanted her to be his in every way and it shocked him. Shocked him that he could feel something so animalistic when what he held in his arms was so fragile and precious.

She shifted in his hold and for a horrifying moment he thought she wanted to pull away, but when she settled herself against him more securely, when she seemed to relish the press of her body against his as much as he did, his breath eased.

Tentatively, she leaned into him and pressed her lips against his neck and, *Christós*, he'd never felt anything so pure and so wrenching at the same time. The constant tug, back and forth, suddenly stopped the moment he felt her lips pressed against the column of his neck. Arousal shot through him like an arrow, but he held himself back, fiercely curious to see what Helena wanted to do, content and excited to let her lead.

Her hand came up between them and splayed the shirt open at his neck, releasing a button to give her more skin to caress. His fingers gripped her hip reflexively and she pressed herself against him in response.

When she kissed the top of his chest, her tongue swept out and he nearly jumped out of his skin in desperation to join with her, to meet her, to give her even just a taste of what she was doing to him. But he couldn't move. He was under her spell and helpless to stop her sensual explorations.

'Helena...' he tried, his voice coming out on a croak and momentarily unsure as to whether her name was a plea or a prayer on his tongue. Until he realised. It was a plea. It would always be a plea—because he would never need permission to worship her.

She leaned back, still holding on to him by his shirt, her lips not even remotely as swollen as he wanted to make them, the flush on her cheeks nowhere near what it would be when they were done. Her large sapphire gaze, open, vulnerable and showing all of her wants, was utterly irresistible.

'Please, Helena,' he all but begged. 'Stop me now.'

Helena dropped her gaze to his chest, her brow just slightly furrowed.

'Is that what you want?' she asked, refusing to meet his gaze.

'Not for the entire world,' he answered with raw honesty.

He watched her response, the slow close of her eyes, the breath caught in a chest pressed against his so that he could feel the slightest movement, the heady fragrance of crushed peonies beneath their feet and the soft scent of *her* reaching up to bewitch him.

'Then no,' she said, opening her eyes and locking her gaze with his. 'I won't stop you. Do what you will.'

Need clashed with the last vestiges of his control, thrashing against the leash of his restraint.

'And what is your will?' he demanded, his voice harsh, but broken by the strength of his want. Needing to hear her desires, needing her to be in this as much as he was.

'My will is that you take me, own me and make me yours so that I will be ruined for any other man to come.'

He searched her eyes, her face for any sign of fear or insincerity, but there was none. She meant what she said. And it was a command that he would follow to his last breath.

'As you wish,' he replied, before claiming her mouth with his. As his tongue thrust between lips opened on a gasp, meeting the push of hers, his fingers flexed and fisted, the silk of her printed dress sliding over skin he needed to touch as much as he needed oxygen.

She moaned into his mouth and his chest nearly burst with need. His hands came up to cup her face and he angled her beneath him, taking full advantage of his height, bearing down on her with all the need and passion he was so desperate to share. Her hands came to his wrists, not to stop him but to keep him there, as she opened herself to him in utter and complete surrender.

'Don't hold back,' she whispered against his lips. 'Please don't hold back,' she begged.

Helena's body was on fire, everything burning for him, from him. She didn't think her heart would ever recover, her pulse, her breath would be ruined for ever by the sheer power of her need for him.

He pulled back from a kiss that was so overwhelming she had to steady herself against his chest. The incessant pulse between her legs, the ache low in her core, the dampness on the silk of her panties, Helena swore he knew it all.

He held her gaze as his hands dropped to her thighs, fisting the silk of her dress in his hands, inch by inch, the sensual glide against her ankles, her calf muscles, her knees and upward to her thighs. She pressed her legs together as he pulled the silk higher and higher, towards her hips, and shivered not from the cool sea air that hit her damp sensitive flesh but from the promise in the dark swirling depths of his eyes.

His fingers gripped the flesh of her backside and slipped beneath the bunched dress, the silk falling over his hands as if hiding the deliciously wicked things he was about to do from the world behind a veil of civility. His palm rounded the curve of her bottom, his thumb playing with the string of her silk thong, pulling it taut against her clitoris, and fire exploded across her skin and ignited a deep need in her soul.

Her head fell back and her mouth opened on a cry as his other hand slipped beneath the front of her panties, one long finger gliding down the centre of her slick folds, slowly back and forth, the palm of his other hand still pressed against her, while his gaze still held hers captive, as if demanding that he see every single expression that he wrought from her.

A sob fell from her lips and desire sparkled like gold shards in his eyes.

'Again,' he commanded.

She frowned, momentarily unsure and distracted by the play of his hands.

'I want to hear the sounds you make,' he whispered harshly into her ear, as if he were as affected by her pleasure as she was.

She didn't know why it was something she struggled with, keeping her arousal silent, quiet as if it were her own.

'Or do you need me to help you with that?' he asked, his gaze ferocious with anticipation, a slash of red across each of his cheeks. 'Oh, Helena,' he said, before he slipped his finger deep into her, melting her entire body in a single stroke. Her head fell back but she was anchored between his hands. 'You have no idea what the sound of you does to me,' he said, and the thought of it, the want to do that to him, for him...

He added another finger and brushed her clitoris with his thumb and she saw stars. His palm pressed against the curve of her bottom, his fingers a caress, a grip, before pressing between her cheeks, the startlingly wicked play sending a shudder across her entire body.

Gasps fell from her lips unbidden, and victory shone in his gaze. Her breath shuddered in and out in time with the movement of his hands, and in her mind's eye she saw them: Leo wringing pleasure from her, holding her in her most intimate, sacred femininity, herself near mindless under his ministrations.

Her breaths came quicker and quicker, the closer he pushed her towards her orgasm. She both feared it and wanted it more than life itself, because never before had she felt such a crescendo of sensation that her body vibrated with it. He was her anchor in the storm that came for her. He was the one that held her, even as he caused that very same storm—and even, she could barely believe it, as he promised more was still yet to come.

Her breath caught as she was hurled towards the precipice, no longer caring what sounds she made, gasps and cries of pleasure, need and want, carried away on the sea air. She was no longer Helena, but want, desire, a need that couldn't be stopped, a force that couldn't be dimmed. And when her orgasm crashed over her she fell against Leo, utterly spent and overcome.

She was vaguely aware that Leo picked her up as if she were delicate and precious and, slowly, he walked them down to the main deck, past the luxurious living area and back towards the master cabin she had yet to see.

He paused on the threshold, as they both took in the suite that had been prepared for a honeymoon. More peony petals littered the floor, candles in hurricane lamps glittered and flickered from the breeze coming through the open window, displaying dusk at its most beautiful. Sea salt played on the air and she knew in that moment she would always associate that smell with Leo. The breeze pulled and pushed at long net curtains that hung from the ceiling, encasing a king-sized bed in filmy romanticism.

And she realised with sudden, stark clarity that this was all they could have together, it was all they would ever get. Leo tightened his hold on her as if he'd had the same thought. She reached up to him then, and this time it was she who wanted to anchor him, to this moment, to what they'd given in to so selfishly. If they could have one thing, just one, it would be this.

'Stay with me?' she asked.

'For as long as I can,' he promised, truth in his words, refusing to shy away from the constraints that were shaping the rest of their lives.

Leo placed Helena gently on the bed, shocked at having discovered that she was the greatest fantasy he'd never known he'd had. How on earth had he got so lucky and so unfortunate at the same time, as the seconds they had left slipped through the cradle of his fingers?

Ruthlessly shoving that thought aside, he slowly began to undo the remaining buttons on his shirt, his gaze never once leaving her. He took in every detail, every line of Helena's body, the way her breath moved her chest, the way that the silk dress hung off her shoulder, exposing a stretch of unmarred, perfect skin he wanted to lave with his tongue.

As he shucked the shirt from his shoulders, Helena came to kneel on the bed, drawing the silky dress from her body and throwing it aside. She was glorious in her thong and nothing else, her eyes on his, hot, urgent and expectant, the restlessness of her arousal all he wanted to ever see her dressed in.

'You're magnificent,' he said. 'And I am undone,' he finished in Greek.

The yearning in her gaze softened and somehow that hit him harder than anything else that they'd shared up until now. He felt his heart trip, a warning sign he could not pay heed to.

He crossed to the bed, flicking open the clasp on his

trousers, toeing out of his shoes and there, barefoot and barely dressed, Helena looked at him as if she were starving, and damn if it didn't make him feel like a god.

Kneeling at the edge of the bed, Helena reached for him, her hands landing on the waistband of his trousers, gently batting away his hands, her fingers exploring with no shame or embarrassment, simply pure desire that humbled him.

Slowly, she drew the zip down, each tooth grating on his exposed, raw and as yet unsatiated desires. Her gaze was on her hands, but he wanted to see her eyes. He reached down and lifted her chin with his forefinger. The sapphire blue of her gaze was clouded with untamed passion.

'You don't have to do that, *agápi mou*,' he said, looking down into features that drew his heart into a quicker rhythm, but when her lips pulled into a line of wicked intent, it stopped altogether.

'I know,' she replied, and slipped the trousers and his boxers from his hips and helped him out of them before tossing them to the side.

Her hands returned to his hips, to gently caress the hard length of his arousal. His cock bucked against her hand as she wrapped her fingers around the length of him. *Malákas*, he was too ready for this. He was about to pull back, when she guided the head of his penis into her mouth and all thoughts disappeared from his mind in a heartbeat.

It was heaven and hell combined. The soft, wet heat of her mouth encompassed him and this time he did pray to every conceivable god in the known universe. He felt such intense pleasure—heightened only by the knowledge that being with her, joining with her would be even more incredible.

Her tongue swiped the head of his penis and he couldn't hold back the growl of pleasure that burst from his chest. Her hands cupped his backside, and she took him so far into her mouth he was unable to prevent the thrust of his hips—a primal response born of a need so powerful he no longer was sure he could control it.

But when she mewled her own desire-drenched response he could have cried out to the heavens. She was going to be the death of him, but it was a death he would welcome with every ounce of his being.

Her cool fingers against his skin were a contrast to the heat of her mouth, darkness and light, fire and ice—everything about them clashed and contrasted, but all he wanted was her. He gently pulled himself back, unable to resist the lure of finally joining with her, and he reached into the nightstand, where he was sure he would find a condom.

Helena's eyes were glazed with heady desire, clearing only a little when she saw what was in his hands.

'I'm…' she started, before clearing her throat and trying again. 'I'm on contraception.' She bit her lip, the first sign of hesitation he'd seen in her since they'd first kissed. 'I don't want anything between us,' she confessed.

His heart jerked again. And he took a moment. This was a line that couldn't be uncrossed. He'd never shared himself like that with another woman. Never. But Helena's request floored him. He wanted to give it proper thought, needed to, because the raging urge of his desire was scaring him enough.

'I can show you my test results,' he offered eventually, seeing the sincerity and want in Helena's face. 'All negative. If you're in any way—'

'I trust you.'

Her words ricocheted through his heart and into his soul. It was the most precious gift he'd ever been given.

Helena was nervous right until the moment she saw her words land on him. As if they'd settled into his skin, his body, and formed a cord between them, tying them together. A part of her wanted to deny it as much as welcome it—because of what it meant. Of what it would mean for tomorrow and the day after and the day after that. Because they didn't have those days. Not really. They only had this.

As if he'd understood her chain of thought, he came to her, gathered her into his arms and kissed her with a passion that would deny tomorrow—deny the future if he could. He kissed her all the way back until she lay on the bed, surrounded by him, encased in his arms, embraced by his hands and imprisoned not by his body but by his passion. She relished it, because it was not a cage of oppression but bonds of safety and security. She knew that, whatever they shared, he would take care of her, protect her, put her first. He would see her and know her, the deepest truth of her, and that was all she needed, she assured herself, before he nestled between her legs and slowly, exquisitely, entered her, inch by delicious inch.

Her head tipped further back into the mattress as the way he filled her undulated across her entire body. Her hips rose to welcome him further, her chest pressed against his, her fingers wrapped around the forearms braced either side of her head as they joined in a way that made her question where he ended and she began. Her breath filled her chest and she was full...full of him, of her, of them, of joy and passion and fear and future loss, but, above all, love. And love was what pushed her over the edge into the second orgasm that swept her away into bliss.

Helena opened her eyes as the sun stretched its first rays across the line of the sea and cursed herself for having fallen asleep. They only had so much time together and she hadn't wanted to waste a single moment.

She turned in the bed to find Leo on his side, looking down at her, his gaze soft for just a moment before he hid it behind something much more enticing. His hand reached across her stomach, wrapped around her side and pulled her across the bed so that she was nestled into his side. She laughed, unable to help herself, relishing this side of his autocratic nature, relishing his possessiveness.

While it had been unspoken, while they'd not said it out loud, she knew that this was all they would have. This was all it could ever be. Leo wouldn't, and shouldn't, risk the reputation of the company that he had given so much to, that had cost him so much. And really, ensuring Incendia's survival would take all her focus. And if she hid behind these excuses of their day-to-day responsibilities, rather than facing the painful truth that Leo just might not want more than this time, she allowed herself dishonesty. Because if this was the reward, she would take it with both hands. And it would be enough, she told herself. It had to be.

Shoving her thoughts aside, she looked up at the man staring back at her. The close cut of his beard was just a little softer than yesterday, the lure of it so great that she reached up to run the palm of her hand across his jaw.

He indulged her touch, letting her hand drift down the long, thick column of his neck, over the broad curve of his shoulder and across muscular traps and delts that she delighted in. He let her explore his body that morning, her fingers pressing and smoothing over every inch of him, as if she could commit this to memory and live on it for the rest of her life.

He let her lead their erotic dance, as she rolled him onto his back to straddle his hips, finding just the right pace, the right pressure point. She felt as if he might have looked on her with something like awe, but was unwilling and unable to hold on to that thought as yet another orgasm rocked them both into such sweet oblivion.

He gathered her in his arms and took her into the large en suite bathroom. White marble veined with grey and green, gold fittings and a dark wood so rich it hummed with warmth made it feel even more luxurious. He turned on the shower, hand beneath the water until he was happy with the temperature, and when he was, he drew her beneath the spray.

With as much care and attention as he'd shown in their bed, he soaped his hands and ran the suds gently across her skin. Never had anyone shown her such care and consideration. This was touch—not for pleasure, but still pleasureful. It was intimacy, not carnal but still erotic. He didn't say a word the entire time, his dark hair slicked with water, skin slippery with soap, hands roaming all over her body. He was as focused on her as she had been on him earlier, and yet somehow his actions, this, nearly brought a tear to her eye.

In that moment she was the centre of his world and she knew it.

And even if it was just for now, she'd take it.

CHAPTER TEN

'WHERE ARE YOU?' Helena called out from the sun lounger on the main deck.

'I'll be there soon. Just wait.'

But she didn't want to wait, she thought, and nearly laughed at herself. Had he cast some spell? Had they turned back time to when she was an infatuated teenager, desperate to get just one more glimpse of Leo Liassidis? Even though she knew it was more than an infatuation, she told herself that was what it was, what it needed to be. Because she was going to find it so hard to walk away when...

'Ta-da!'

Leo loomed between her and the sun, casting himself and what he was carrying into shadow through her sunglasses. And for a moment it felt like a warning, the cut-out of where he would never be in her life.

She bit her lip, forced a smile to her face, took off her sunglasses and gasped when she saw the tray he was holding.

'You made all this?' she demanded.

'Of course,' he replied, as if outraged that she thought he wasn't up to it.

The platter held bowls of beautiful fruits, yoghurts, nuts and seeds, golden and toasted, flutes filled with mimosas, and even two plates with delicious-looking omelettes.

'Of *course*?' she repeated on a laugh. 'You can cook?' she asked, teasing.

'Is this because I'm Greek or because I'm a man?' he demanded, leaning into one hip and making her laugh even more as his outrage deepened. 'Because I need to know which before I can be offended appropriately.'

'Both?'

A string of Greek curses filled the air and she couldn't help it. She threw her head back and laughed, a deep, stomach shaking, heart resetting laugh that she remembered from her childhood.

'Stop laughing like that,' he mock-complained as if she didn't know how much he enjoyed seeing it.

Over breakfast they talked about what they would do that morning, for lunch, for dinner that evening, as if the spectre of Leander's return didn't hover over their shoulders. As if there would be a hundred tomorrows to come.

Swim, eat, luxuriate. It all seemed so easy and so free. So different to the way that she'd spent the years since she'd last seen him. From the moment her father had passed away, she'd been so focused on working with Incendia, on earning her degree, her master's, on being the best that she could be, hoping, wanting so badly to be someone her father would have been proud of, someone that her mother could…could love.

And somewhere in that, she'd forgotten the girl she had used to be. The one that laughed and played in the sun and the sea. The one who had delighted in the teasing fun offered by the Liassidis twins as much as her father's attention. And it wasn't just she who was learning to relax in this moment.

The Leo she remembered from her childhood unfurled beneath the sun, the smile so far from his lips only a week ago nearly a constant. The heat in his eyes, the promise there, was entirely unfamiliar but utterly thrilling and it left Helena feeling so aware of herself and her sensuality—it was powerful and heady, and terrifyingly addictive.

Leo thrust out an arm to catch Helena around the waist, her skin slippery in the saltwater of the Mediterranean, the swimming costume high on her hips and low on her chest. He'd never forget this as long as he lived.

As he trod water, and ducked to avoid the splash she sent his way, he pulled her against him, his body delighting in the feel of her warmth, her skin, *her*. With the islands in the distance and the sea surrounding them, he racked his brain to find any moment more perfect than this.

He remembered seeing Helena at the bottom of the aisle of the church in her wedding dress. Before she'd seen him, before she'd realised that it wasn't Leander waiting for her, there had been a moment—the length of a heartbeat—when he'd forgotten. Forgotten why he was there, forgotten that she wasn't his fiancée, forgotten the feud with his brother... In truth, he'd nearly forgotten his own name.

She'd had a small smile on her lips, a Mona Lisa smile, hypnotic, cryptic, but alluring nevertheless, and when she'd looked up he'd thought, for just a second, he'd seen recognition in her eyes, delight, hope...before it had turned to horror.

'Earth to Leo,' she whispered into his ear as she twisted in his embrace, their legs sliding against each other as they navigated buoyancy together. 'Come in, Leo,' she finished, the simmering want in her gaze wicked and playful and everything he'd never thought he'd be lucky enough to ever have.

'Well, your wish *is* my command,' he replied as his fingers found the hemline of her costume at her hip.

She squealed in delight, and wriggled, pushing her body further against his, and curses fell from his lips before he claimed hers with his own.

'This is impractical,' he mock-complained against her lips and once again she undulated against him as his fingers found her clitoris. She moaned against him and no amount of cold water could hold back his erection.

'Dangerous even,' he weakly protested, as her head fell back and he anchored her to him and to the surface. He could watch her for ever. He could pleasure her for the rest of his life and it wouldn't be enough.

'Utterly irresponsible,' he tried again as he teased her orgasm closer and closer.

The flush on her cheeks, the gasps of breath on the air, the way she was utterly lost to her own pleasure was almost enough to make him orgasm himself. Her cries grew higher and higher, more urgent, needing, wanting, and he had to try every single trick himself not to follow her over the edge just from watching her come.

Taut lines across her body melted away as she fell into her orgasm and he held her to him, keeping them afloat in the sea, shocked to his core by the single most erotic experience of his life in which he hadn't even orgasmed himself.

Slowly, he drew them back to the boat, pulling her from the sea and into his arms, all the way back up to the main deck, where he washed the saltwater off their skin with the outside shower and wrapped a satiated and smiling Helena in a fluffy white towel.

He drew her to the sun loungers out on the deck. The soft canvas cushion over the wood was comfortable enough for a long laze beneath the rays of the sun climbing too far, too fast, into the sky.

He sat, drawing her between his legs and laying her back against his chest. He couldn't stop touching her. As if his body knew that time was running out and it was desperately trying to take what it could get. All the feelings, all the scents, all the touches.

'So, Ms Hadden,' he began, unable to bring himself to call her by his name. His *brother's* name. 'Curious minds want to know—what is your five-year plan?' he asked in a mock British accent, as if giving an interview.

Only a part of him was interested in the answer, because the other part just wanted to listen to her talk. Or at least that was what he told himself until she hesitated.

'I know that I'm still quite young, and there's so much I'd want to do with Incendia…'

If she managed to succeed in surviving the end of year financial review. He heard her doubt, he knew of her insecurities. But no matter what passed between them here, or in the future, he knew that she would do it. Knew it with a visceral belief in the woman in his arms.

'But one day, in the not-too-distant future, I'd like a family,' she admitted, scrunching her nose.

His heart stopped. Completely and utterly. The high-pitched whine in his ears was like that of a heart monitor flatlining.

'Children. More than one,' she said, her voice stronger the more she entertained her hopes for the future.

As she painted a picture of the family and the life she

wanted one day, he forced his body not to betray the ice-cold hold that had taken him over. He, who had fought with his brother for fourteen years, who had immersed himself in work and business and meetings to fill days that had become increasingly empty the more he tried to protect himself, had never allowed himself to think of a future with a family.

And even if Helena hadn't just 'married' his brother for all the world to see, would he have been able to give her that? The family that she had never had as a child, the kind of love and attention and focus that she deserved and needed? Could a man who had been so ruthless with his twin brother be capable of that kind of love?

'I keep losing you,' Helena complained gently, pulling his attention back to her.

And all he could think was that he'd already lost her.

'What about you, Mr Liassidis? Where do you see yourself in five years' time?' Helena asked, even though she knew that their hearts weren't in the 'game' any more.

'Oh, I think I'll still be sitting at the head of the boardroom, commanding thousands of employees to do my bidding,' he quipped, even though for Helena it was suddenly not at all funny.

His answer was telling, but it was also calculated, and that was what made it worse.

The moment she had told him she wanted a family she had felt something shift between them. Her first thought was that she shouldn't have told him. Shouldn't have confessed her dreams for the future. And then she got angry. Because it *was* what she wanted and it wasn't unreasonable. She wanted the security and love that offered and she wanted to be able to give all the love she had to another human being. To pour it into them.

It wasn't about getting something in return, getting that love back—the kind that she'd never received from her mother or her father—but she wanted so much to share what was *in* her. And there was so much love to give that it almost hurt.

But Leo's retreat, emotionally if not physically, served as a painful reminder that he was not someone who was safe for her.

No, she didn't think that he was the same Leo who had cut her from his life so easily all those years before. She knew—could see—the toll that the separation with his brother had taken on him, and she understood why he had protected himself by creating that separation. Because, deep down, she believed that Leo was just like her. He was someone who had so much love to give and nowhere, no *one*, to give it to.

But he was also very different to her. Because while she still had hope that things could and would be different, it was as if Leo had drawn a line and moved beyond that hope in order to protect himself.

The thought sobbed painfully in her chest. Because she loved him. She loved him deeply and truly and the thought that he wouldn't accept that love, wouldn't allow himself to feel that love was a visceral pain that rended her heart in two.

Forcefully, she pushed back that hurt. There would be time for that later, when Leo was gone and Leander had returned. For now, with desperate hands, she clung to the thread of the present.

She turned in his arms and craned her head to look up at him.

'Kiss me?' she asked.

Distract me. Make me forget that this ends tomorrow.

The staff returned to the boat late that afternoon, after Leo had reluctantly called them back. The car met them at the marina and their return to the villa on the Mani Peninsula was quiet, but the air was heavy with the unspoken words that lay between them.

Leo wanted to rub at his temples, to relieve the pressure that was building there, but didn't want to show such a sign of weakness in that moment. There was a vulnerability between them and he didn't know if it was his or hers.

All he knew was that there was this pressure filling him with a horrible sense of urgency but no direction to go in. Restlessness moved through his entire body, making him uncomfortable in his own skin.

The car took the coastal road back to the villa, each turn offering the most incredible view of the Mediterranean, the classic Greek shoreline, rich green foliage covering sandy white rock, stark against a blue that would remind him of Helena's eyes for ever.

But beyond all the beauty he could see through the window, all he could hear was alarm bells. Ones that had been ringing in his ears ever since that afternoon. No. He couldn't lie to himself, not any more. He'd been hearing them ever since he'd seen her that first time in the church, but they'd been getting louder and louder, warning of danger ahead.

The last time he'd felt like this, he'd ignored it. Ignored all the warning signs that his brother was unhappy. That his brother wasn't as one hundred percent committed to their childhood dream as he'd once been.

Oh, he had done a very good job at convincing himself that he'd not known what Leander was going to do. That it had been such a complete shock to him. But could he still continue to do that? Especially now, when it seemed just as important, if not more so, than it had been then.

Back then, he had done absolutely nothing, because he'd needed to be wrong. Because he couldn't have imagined life, or Liassidis Shipping, without his brother—his other half. And here he was again, feeling that same sense of something, someone slipping through his fingers unable to do a damn thing. That same sense of being unable to imagine his future without Helena in it. And that need, that desperation, scared the hell out of him.

The car pulled up outside the entrance to the villa and, not waiting for the driver's help, Helena left the car without sparing Leo a backward glance, her body a study in taut lines and hard angles, as if she were trying with all her might to hold herself together.

Leo remained behind in the car, his jaw clenched and hands fisted. He needed to staunch the fury, the anger he felt...the *fear* that he wrestled with. It was as if they'd condensed an entire lifetime into a week, and only now was he becoming overwhelmed by the emotions. Only now, when he felt her slipping through his fingers.

He got out of the car, spurred on by that thought, slamming the door behind him, uncaring of who heard or what they thought. He stalked into the villa and found her staring out at the view from the living area. His heart raged in his chest, pounding furiously, protesting against the cage of emotions that had it in such a stranglehold.

For a moment they just stayed like that, Helena desperately holding herself together and Leo desperately holding himself back.

'I think you should go.'

Her statement should have shocked him. Should have cut the ground from under his feet. But it didn't. Just like it hadn't that day when Leander took the money and ran. He'd known. All along he'd known. Then. And now.

'We have time,' he bartered as he looked at the clock. It was barely eight in the evening. 'Hours even.'

She shook her head, her eyes still fixed on some invisible point on the horizon. 'It's better if you leave before your brother gets here, don't you think?'

'No, I don't,' he lied.

He couldn't take it any more. Crossing the room, he came to her side and pulled her round to face him. Her arms stayed crossed around her body, in protection, in defiance, and it hit him hard.

She needed that? Protection? Against him?

'We could find a way to make this work.'

The breath left her lips in a puff of air that sounded painfully like derision. And it cut him deep. Shaking her head, she stared at him, incredulous.

'How?' she asked hopelessly. 'How would we make this work? Secret assignations? One weekend here, an evening there, hoping that no one will notice? Or we could wait, I suppose,' she said, her words falling rapidly from her perfect mouth, one after the other. 'Leander and I were going to divorce after a year and a half. What do you think is a respectable time to wait before I start banging the other brother?'

'*Christós*, Helena.' He hated hearing the crass words in her soft English tones.

'Oh, I think we both know that that is the least offensive way to describe what the world would be thinking and what the press would be printing,' Helena replied, hating the words coming out of her mouth.

She was right. He knew she was right, so why was he fighting this?

Hope. That wretched thing that he had tried to sever all those years ago. Hope that things could be different. The same hope that drove almost everything that Helena did in her life. Somehow, it had sprung back into being, yearning for more than he could have.

He reached for her quickly, so that she couldn't refuse him. The kiss was angry, furious, and all the more passionate for its desperation. He prised apart her lips, his tongue possessing her, taunting her, trying to claim her even as she would evade him. But she opened for him, as she always would. Welcomed him, his anger, welcomed it all and gave back her own desperate helplessness in return. She stroked his tongue with hers and he held her even tighter as she slipped through his fingers.

He stalked them back against the window, his body caging hers between him and the glass, his hands moving over her clothes, desperate to find whatever skin he could claim. Her moan of pleasure drove him wild beyond reason and into chaos. But it was the helpless whimper of need, of want, of so much more than he could give that yanked him back from the brink of madness. They broke apart, heaving breaths between them, Leo nearly buckling beneath the agony of losing her.

'Don't do this, Helena. Don't push me away,' he begged, even though he couldn't offer her anything more than this.

'Away from what?' she pleaded. 'I just married your brother!'

'But you didn't,' he ground out through clenched teeth.

'Do you think that matters? The press announced it across the globe, it made headlines in twelve different countries. How on earth could anything between us *ever* happen? You barely survived one Hadden. You wouldn't survive this. Liassidis Shipping wouldn't survive it.'

The look in his eyes was a shock. The fear, even the idea that he might lose everything he'd worked so hard for—she read it as if it were the lines of a book written on his soul.

It was a lightning strike right into her heart, burning a scar over already damaged tissues. It was the *one* thing she'd never wanted to see. She could have lived with her pain and her loss, telling herself that it was the situation that had come between them. That they had simply been star-crossed lovers. And then she could have still cherished the hope that what they'd shared had meant something, had meant *enough*.

But in that moment she knew. *That* was what she had been trying to protect herself from seeing. That nothing had changed. That she still wasn't enough for him.

The blow to her soul was crushing. It stole the oxygen from her lungs and the ground from beneath her feet. She thought she might have swayed. Leo reached for her, but she batted his hand away.

'Helena—'

'Go. Go now,' she said, shaking her head and turning back out to the view beyond the window, wishing she couldn't see his reflection in the glass and hoping that he couldn't see her tears.

'Helena—'

'No, Leo. It's done.'

Helena held herself together as she watched Leo's head

drop. He had given up. It was what she'd expected, what she'd thought all along, but that didn't mean it wasn't a stab to the heart.

Slowly, the shadowy image in the window turned, and she watched Leo Liassidis walk out of her life for the final time.

Helena woke up, not sure why and confused as to where she was. Her eyes ached from crying the night before and it took a while to prise them open. She was still in the living area. The sunrise must have woken her. Sleep had been her drug again and she should know better. She had barely eaten anything since the boat and that was more hours ago than she cared to do the maths on.

But an empty stomach was nothing compared to the agony in her heart. The force she'd needed to use to hold herself back as she'd watched him leave had bruised her chest. Every time she breathed the pain was a reminder of what had happened.

He'd gone. He'd walked away. She wasn't enough. She never had been.

'It needs to be enough for you, Helena.'

Her stomach clenched so viciously she rolled into a ball to protect herself from the hurt. She hated that he was right. Hated that he had been the one to say it. Nothing she did with Incendia would make her mother feel something she couldn't. Her father was gone and would never be able to give her what she needed. She had to be enough for herself, but right now things were too raw and too painful from the loss of Leo for her to be able to consider it properly or even understand what that would look like.

A sound came from somewhere in the villa. The sound that had woken her.

She rolled her shoulders and swallowed. Leander was due back today. Perhaps that was him calling now, she thought, finally recognising the sound that had woken her as her mobile phone. She'd put it on silent when they were on the yacht, not wanting to have her last time with Leo interrupted by the outside world.

A tear escaped as her heart melted in a painful sob.

She couldn't do this, she thought furiously. She wasn't allowed to collapse, she wasn't allowed to cry. She clenched her jaw and pulled herself up from the sofa.

In the shower she scrubbed every inch of her body and washed her hair, turning the water from scalding hot to freezing. Everything she could think of to give her body the jolt she needed to come back to the present. But somehow, despite everything she tried, she knew that she'd let part of herself, her heart, leave with Leo.

Dressed in a simple shirt dress, with her hair in a towel and her phone buzzing *again*, she finally went to retrieve it from beside her bed and gasped.

Thirty missed calls?

Some from unknown numbers, a worrying amount from Megan, despite the fact that it was six a.m. back home.

What the hell was going on?

Just then someone pounded on the door. 'Helena? Are you in there?'

She walked towards the door on slow, jerky feet.

'Is Leo with you?'

She pulled up short, eyes wide, body tense with shock.

'Why is Leander in California, Helena, and who is the

blonde with him?' another voice demanded as someone tried to peer through the window.

Helena jumped back and then jumped again when her phone rang in her hand. She answered it without thinking.

'Helena? Are you okay?' Megan's voice asked.

'What's…what's going on?'

'They know, Helena. They know that it was Leo with you, not Leander.'

CHAPTER ELEVEN

LEO LOOKED OUT at the Aegean from the coastal path on his parents' island. He'd taken the helicopter and arrived the night before, forgetting that his parents were away visiting friends in France.

But he was thankful for it. He told himself that he *wanted* to be alone. That after seven days of nothing but Helena it would do him good. He told himself that he didn't care that the place felt empty, that he didn't somehow know that *any* place would feel empty now.

He picked up a rock from the ground and hurled it into the sea, where it was consumed by grey, angry waves. He had woken up after a restless night, tossing and turning, to find the sun clawing its way into a startlingly cold and grey morning. The wind whipped cruelly around the island and pulled and pushed at the trees on his parents' estate.

Lonely. He felt lonely.

That's what happens when you turn yourself into an island. Just like the one you're standing on.

His brother's voice had been getting louder and louder and much more frequent in the last week than it had ever been before. Leo's head hurt from the tug between the past and the present, his brother and Helena.

And that's what happens when you don't fight for what you want, the voice taunted.

Leo growled, turning around, half expecting to see his brother striding towards him from the house, but there was no one there. He wanted to fight, to lash out, to get rid of this feeling in him. The feeling of guilt, of shame, of helplessness, because the voice was right.

He hadn't fought for what he wanted. Because, deep down, all along, he'd known that Leander wasn't happy, hadn't he? He'd pretended not to see it; he'd pretended to be shocked by his choice. Oh, it had still been utterly horrifying to experience—his brother choosing the money over him. But he couldn't lie to himself any more. He couldn't afford to.

What Helena had said about Leander was right. Leander would have been utterly miserable at Liassidis Shipping. He was a risk-taker, a daredevil, who would have been suffocated by the company that involved the more grounded and staid work that Leo relished. Because *he* suited *that*.

And why hadn't he fought it? Why hadn't he tried to face Leander all those years ago? Because, deep down, he couldn't shake the feeling that even if he had fought for his brother to stay, it wouldn't have changed a thing. Because he wasn't enough. So it had been easier to paint Leander as the guilty party. As the one responsible for it all. For Leo to emerge blameless, the martyr who had sacrificed all for the greater good of the company.

A sacrifice he'd made all over again.

Helena.

Just the thought of her was a sucker punch to his gut—enough to make him double over in pain. And in that moment he realised that what he'd felt when Leander had walked away was almost nothing in comparison to the earthshattering loss of Helena.

He braced his hands on his knees and groaned, dropping to the ground.

What had he done? He'd let his brother walk out of his life. He couldn't let Helena do that. No, he'd not survive it. He needed her. The montage in his mind of the week he'd just spent with her, of Helena daring him in the art gallery, of her laughing with Leander's friends at the nightclub, or her smiling at the waiter in the small fishing village, and of her looking up at him, playing with that damn necklace that he should have given her himself that Christmas. That Christmas, when she had wanted to give him a present…the one that she'd put in the…

The cubbyhole.

He'd turned back to the house before he'd even realised it and what started as slow steps turned into a jog, driven by an urgency he couldn't name. He shoved through the front door, taking the steps of the staircase two at a time. He came to a stop opposite the painting, imagining a fifteen-year-old Helena outside his room, hearing that she meant nothing to him. *Christós*, his heart buckled in his chest, each beat agony.

With his breath captured in his lungs he lifted the painting, behind which was a small, dusty shelf on which sat a crumpled box wrapped in faded festive paper.

He reached for it at the same time his phone chimed. Once, twice, and then again. With the present in one hand and his phone in the other, he looked at the message beneath his assistant's name.

Check the news. Right now. Then call me.

* * *

Nausea ate at Helena's empty stomach. The moment she had discovered what had happened, she'd called Kate to warn her. And no matter how many times she'd seen the grainy pictures of Kate and Leander passionately kissing, she couldn't stop herself from hoping that somehow the headlines would change.

Twin-Swap Scandal!
Who Married Helena Hadden?
Liassidis Twin Deception!

With shaking hands, she'd scanned an online article written by a blogger who had intended to write an exposé on Californian homes owned by famous Greeks, but had instead stumbled onto an international scandal. He'd identified Leander by spotting him at his home when he'd expected him to be away on his honeymoon and then bribing an usher at a club to photograph Leander with Kate.

Her heart pounded in shock. She'd brought the weight of the world's press down on her two best friends, on Leo; she had ruined *everything*. The guilt was so strong that it blotted out any delight that the two people she had always secretly thought perfect for each other had finally come together.

While reporters had gathered outside the villa, she'd had one harried phone call with her assistant in the UK, and several fraught conversations with the board of Incendia, taking full responsibility for the situation. It was her plan, her choices, that had led the people she cared for most to be caught up in this impossible scandal. All she'd wanted to do was to save Incendia. All she'd wanted to do was to prove that she *could*, that she was worthy to be CEO. That she was *enough*.

But maybe, just maybe, for once there was no fixing it.

It would devastate her to have brought shame to Incendia because of this scandal, but the loss of the money—the issue that would cause them to fail the financial review—that wasn't on her. She had tried to fix it, but it wasn't her fault.

And finally she was beginning to see what Leo had meant.

'It needs to be enough for you, Helena.'

She had tried her hardest. And she had to be okay if that wasn't enough. She *had* to be. Because her mother wasn't going to suddenly be the person Helena wanted her to be. And as much as she could hope that her father would have been proud of her, she had to be proud of herself. And the only way she could still be proud of herself now was to be honest and to face up to the chaos that had happened when people she cared for had tried to help her.

She would put this right as best she could. And there was only one way she could do that. But first she needed to warn Kate what she was going to do.

She picked up the phone and saw missed calls from Leo. She wanted so much to reach out to him, to make sure he was okay. But she couldn't. Not yet. He must be furious at the damage this would do to Liassidis Shipping. Helena could only hope that her plan would deflect as much negativity from him and his company as possible.

She hit call beneath Kate's name on her phone screen.

'Kate?' she asked when the call connected.

'I'm so sorry,' Kate said, her words thick with emotion. 'I've ruined everything.'

'Don't cry,' Helena begged as her best friend's sobs

poured out of the phone. 'Please, Kate, don't cry. This is all on me. I begged you to find him when—'

'You didn't.'

'I did. I was so wrapped up in my own problems that I ignored the signs that something was happening between you and sent you to him,' she said, realising the truth as she said it. While Helena had hoped that both Leander and Kate would find the love that they so very much deserved, she'd ignored what was right in front of her in her desperation to make things right at Incendia.

'Nothing was going on before the wedding, I swear. I never meant for anything to happen.'

'I know you didn't,' Helena said, softly and honestly.

'He's coming back to you today, and—'

'I can't be married to Leander, not now. Tell him to stay in California. It's a feeding frenzy here and it's going to get worse before it gets better because I can't do this any more. I'm calling a press conference. There have been so many secrets and lies and so many people hurt that I can't do it any more. I need to tell the truth and—'

'Helena, don't! You'll lose—'

'I have to. I have to put things right. I've hurt so many people,' Helena confessed, shame unspooling in her chest.

'You haven't. You tried so hard to do the right thing and it was for the best of reasons. I'm the one who's screwed everything up.'

'What happened was inevitable. You and Leander are meant to be together,' Helena insisted, thinking of just how perfect they had looked together in the photos. How much in love they'd looked.

Kate's silence on the other end of the phone reached out to Helena's heart. 'It's over.'

'Oh, my love, I'm sorry,' Helena whispered, devastated that they were both feeling the same pain.

'Oh, Helena. Did it happen for you too?'

Helena could barely confess, 'Yes. And it's over too.' She tried so hard to hold back the tears—for herself, for Kate and Leander... They were her family and she had cost them greatly. 'I wasn't enough for him,' she admitted, pain a slow anguish that tightened around her heart with every beat.

'Helena?' Kate's voice was almost a whisper.

'I'm here.'

'Were the Liassidis twins born unfeeling bastards or is it something they cultivated individually as they got older?'

Helena laughed in the way that Kate had always made her laugh, startled, deep and loving. Helena asked Kate about Borneo, promising to come and visit, also promising *not* to kiss any orangutans. And once the laughter had died down, Helena knew that it was time to say goodbye.

'I'm going to make this right,' she swore.

'Are you sure you want to do this?' Kate asked.

'No, but I have to.'

'I wish I could be there to hold your hand through it.'

'I wish you could be too. Have a safe flight to Borneo.'

'I will. Loves ya.'

'Loves ya too,' Helena replied.

After hanging up the phone, she wiped at the trails tears had left on her cheeks, some from heartache and some from laughter. She knew now with absolute certainty that she was doing the right thing.

Leo's pulse raged in time with the whirring of the helicopter blades. The bottom had fallen out of his world the moment he'd seen the first headline. The intense speculation about why the brothers had swapped, who Leander had been caught kissing and who had Helena actually married made his head spin.

His first thought had been Helena. *All* his thoughts had been Helena.

He'd not been able to get her on the phone, so he'd called his assistant and had him send a security team to the villa. But the moment he'd hung up his phone had exploded with phone calls.

He blocked all unknown numbers, and then ignored calls from the Liassidis Shipping board. He could only imagine how terrified they were of stocks and share prices dropping. They probably were, but honestly? Leo couldn't care less. All he could think about was Helena and making sure she was okay.

They landed about ten kilometres from the villa, unable to get closer because of the news helicopters crowding the airspace. The car Leo had arranged waited on the tarmac and as he slid into the dark, cool interior he pulled out his phone and selected a number he hadn't used in years.

He probably should have thought more about this call, but he knew without a shadow of a doubt that once he got his hands on Helena he wasn't going to let her go. His world-renowned focus would be on her, only on her, for the rest of his life. So he needed to do this now.

The phone rang—and a part of him wanted it to keep on ringing. This entire conversation would be easier if he could just leave a message, but he owed it to his brother, owed it to himself, to face up to his responsibility. Only then could he finally move forward. Hopefully, with Helena by his side.

'Naí?'

'It's me,' Leo said.

The pause was so long that Leo had to force himself to relax the grip on his phone before he broke it into a million pieces. There was so much to say. Too much. But if he could at least say the most important thing…

'I'm sorry,' Leo said, his head hung in shame in the back of the car with no one to see. 'I blamed you for so much. Too much. And I shouldn't have.'

A breath was all Leo heard to let him know that his brother was still on the line. His silence was deserved, Leo had earned that, but at least Leander hadn't ended the call.

'I was…devastated when you chose the money,' Leo admitted. 'I tried to tell myself it was a complete shock to me. That you'd lied to me and that your betrayal was why I was devastated.'

'Leo—'

'Wait, please. I need to say this,' Leo asked, desperate to say his piece. 'The lie was mine, Leander. Because I told myself that I hadn't seen that you were unhappy, that I didn't know you would hate working at Liassidis Shipping, because I was so desperate to cling to our dream. So I pretended that I didn't know, and that I couldn't tell, that it wasn't something you wanted,' he confessed, the dark, furious guilt and anger lessening from telling the truth. 'And I shouldn't have. I'm your brother.'

'Maláka, I worked damn hard to make sure you couldn't tell. Give me credit for something,' Leander said, sounding offended.

Against all hope, Leo barked a laugh, a flicker of love spreading throughout his chest.

'You tried to reach out to me and I… I wasn't ready,' Leo tried to explain.

'But you are now? Because of Helena?'

Leo looked up, tilting his head back, hoping that the dampness in his eyes didn't betray him in his voice.

'Is she okay? She told me not to come.' The concern in Leander's voice was as clear when he was talking about Helena as the distance in his tone when speaking to him.

'I'm on my way to make sure she is, right now,' Leo replied with ruthless determination.

There was another long pause.

'Leo, believe me, I appreciate what you're saying, but right now isn't a good time for me. I'm sorry for dragging you into this mess and please, tell Helena that I'm sorry for letting her down.'

Leo gritted his teeth. He knew that his brother's coolness was justified. Five years of complete silence couldn't be undone in one phone call.

'You cut her off from everything and everyone she knew.'

He had done the same to Leander, his brother, his conscience cried, and guilt opened like a fresh wound across an already battered heart.

'I need to go,' Leander said. 'When I come home we'll talk properly. Okay?'

'Okay. I'd like that,' Leo replied truthfully, thankful for the sliver of hope Leander had created in the darkness.

'So would I,' his brother said before disconnecting the call.

It wasn't the hearts and flowers reunion he might have hoped for, but neither was it an absolute no. It was somewhere to start, and he was okay with that. But it was a very different matter when it came to Helena. As the car took him closer and closer to the villa where he and Helena had arrived only seven days before, Leo grew more and more determined that he would see this through to the end; Helena Hadden was going to be his by the end of the day, no matter what it cost him.

Helena fisted her hand to try and stop her fingers from shaking. The press gathering outside the front of the villa had trebled since the news of her impending statement had been released. She risked a glance through the blinds of the windows that looked out at where they were gathered and felt sick.

A line of black-suited men in dark glasses held back the press, preventing them from trying to gain access to the grounds, as one reporter had done just as they'd turned up. Leo had sent them, she knew it.

But she pushed it out of her mind, pushed everything out of her mind, other than what she was about to do. She steeled herself and the nerves went. Because she knew this was the right thing to do. And she knew that, no matter what the outcome was, she would have done everything in her power to protect those she loved. And that was enough for her. It might not be everything she'd ever wanted, but she was at peace with it.

He had seen her. Leo had. He had recognised her as good at what she did. Celebrated that with her. But he'd been right. No one could give her what she needed. Not him. Not her parents. She had to give that to herself. She had to be enough for *herself.*

Helena smoothed down the dress she had chosen to wear—a simple cornflower-blue muslin V-neck. Her hair, blonde and down, made her feel pretty, feminine and *her.* That was how she wanted to meet the press.

She opened the front door and walked on the grey stone slabs towards the gate to the villa, where one of Leo's bodyguards stood to attention, hands clasped in front of him.

'Ma'am.'

She nodded and he pulled open the gate, and the sudden cry of voices and stuttered flashbulbs hit her like a meteor shower. Drawing on an inner strength she didn't know she had, she walked out into the villa's courtyard, where Leo's other men were holding the press at bay. She waited until the press had calmed themselves, until the camera flashes slowed and the questions halted.

'I'm going to make a statement which will cover as much as possible at this time,' she explained. 'And if you have questions, I will try to answer them honestly.'

A few flashes went off, but predominantly the paparazzi remained quiet.

'Six months ago, I was made CEO of a charity I not only believe in, but personally benefitted from after the sudden death of my father when I was sixteen years old. Incendia raises not only money but awareness, grief support, therapy and research into rare cardiac diseases that are of no financial interest to big pharmaceutical companies. In short, it's a godsend to those who need to rely on it,' she said, a sad smile coming to her lips.

She took a breath. 'Shortly after taking up the position, I discovered that an employee had stolen nearly one hundred million pounds from the charity and disappeared.' She pushed on through the gasp of shock. 'The previous CEO had failed to renew the business insurance and the charity will likely fail the financial review in December.

'But what does all this have to do with the Liassidis brothers?' she asked rhetorically.

She smiled when one reporter cried out, 'Yes!' much to the amusement of many present.

'My father left me an inheritance. An inheritance that will mature when I am either twenty-eight years old or when I marry. I had hoped to use that inheritance to cover the gap in Incendia's finances. I know that this was wrong, but I was desperate for Incendia to keep on doing the good work that it does,' she said truthfully, feeling the damp heat of tears against the backs of her eyes.

'Leander Liassidis offered to loan me the money, but… I *have* the money…or would have it in two years' time, but for an arbitrary bit of wording that would have taken too long to challenge legally. So we decided to marry.

'Please. Let me explain. I love Leander. Truly. But only like a brother. And while no one, not even he, thought he'd ever settle down, he *did* meet someone. A very special someone, whom I love dearly. But that story is theirs to tell.

'When Leander left, Leo Liassidis stepped in so that I wouldn't be humiliated in front of the world on my wedding day. He too wanted nothing more than to help me. And words will never express how much that meant to me,' she said, her throat becoming thick with emotion.

'I assure you that the marriage certificate will never be submitted to the registrar's office and, as such, the ceremony from that day is not legally binding. Leander Liassidis and I are not married.

'I want to make it *very* clear that the Liassidis brothers did nothing but try to help a family friend in trouble. They are two of the most honourable men I have ever met and I am lucky to have them in my life.'

Was lucky, she mentally clarified, the thought striking her silent.

'Are there any questions?' she asked.

'Did he sign his own name, Helena?'

She frowned into the crowed, unsure where the question came from and unable to see from the lights that had been set up to point at her.

'I don't know,' she said honestly. 'I signed first so I didn't see the signature.'

'Was the priest involved?' another faceless questioner asked.

'Absolutely not. Again, to make this clear—this entire mess was of my making. When Leander and I decided to marry, we couldn't have imagined the press interest in the relationship, and from there things spiralled out of control. Please know that I am *solely* responsible for this and the Liassidis brothers have done nothing that I didn't ask them to do first.'

'So you have no feelings—no romantic feelings—for Leander Liassidis?' someone asked, the voice slightly drowned out by other questions, but oddly familiar.

'No,' she confirmed. 'Absolutely not. Nothing has or ever will happen between us in that way.'

'But what about Leo Liassidis?' the same person asked, slowly pushing their way through the throng. Helena's pulse began to pound in her chest, goosebumps rising across the delicate skin on her forearms and the back of her neck.

'Excuse me?' she asked, hesitating for the first time since stepping out into the throng of reporters.

'Do you have any romantic feelings for *him*?' the person prompted again, this time the crowd parting enough for Helena to see Leo Liassidis standing before her—in the middle of a sea of reporters ready to cast the news around the world.

'What are you…?'

Didn't he realise that she was trying to extricate him from this mess? That she was trying to protect him? He was throwing away everything he had for her when all she could do was ruin him.

'Do you,' Leo asked, his eyes locked onto hers, hope and more filling her with every passing second, 'have feelings for me?'

A gasp of shock rippled through the press watching with unabashed interest.

'I…'

'Because I have it on good authority,' he said, to the general laughter of the men and women around him, 'that he has feelings for you. Very strong feelings. In fact,' he said, all cocky arrogance and handsomeness, just like he used to have before the separation with his brother had made him hard, 'I'm pretty sure he's in love with you.'

Her heart soared, breaking through the agony of the last twelve hours. Tears came to her eyes and a sob filled her chest, even as her lips pulled into a shocked smile.

'If you're only *pretty sure*…' she replied with teasing hesitation.

'I love you,' he called out loudly, without question and without any of the cocky arrogance from before. The moment was caught by a billion flashbulbs exploding as they stared at each other across the courtyard.

A feeling of effervescent completeness filled her. It was a high that she would never come down from. He was everything she had always wanted. There had never been anyone else for her, no one had made her feel as wanted, as cherished, as *loved*.

He loved her. He loved her even though she could ruin Liassidis Shipping with the bad press that would surely follow this scandal, and he was smiling at her as if he didn't care.

'I love everything about you,' he confessed. 'I love how much you care, I love how hard you try, and I love how much you inspire me and others to be better than ourselves. You are funny, and sexy and smart and I want to marry you. Again. Under my own name this time,' he said to the laughter of the press. 'I've known you for many, many years, but,' he said, taking something out of his pocket and holding it up, '"*sometimes you have to go it alone to know your own worth*",' he quoted.

Helena shivered—it was the watch, the silly watch she'd bought him all those Christmases ago. The battery must have died long ago, but the inscription she'd asked to be put on the back of the watch probably still clear as day. It was an inscription that had been—at the time—about him and Leander, but somehow was even more fitting for *them*.

'We've both done it alone and we know how strong we are, so now let's find out how unbeatable we are together?'

Leo's breath was locked in his chest.

He could see the tears glistening in her eyes, feel the pounding of her heart in time with his own. He'd meant every word he'd said and he genuinely didn't care if Liassidis Shipping disappeared tomorrow, as long as he was by Helena's side. In seven days she had become his world. She was the light, the sky, the ground beneath his feet, the sun, moon and stars above; she was the only person he would ever need in his life.

Her smile wobbled as she took a tentative step towards him. It was all he needed as he closed the distance between them in a heartbeat, taking her into his arms with a kiss that sent off another thousand sparks. A kiss that would appear on headlines around the world for years to come. A kiss that had many names, but the only one of real importance was theirs: true love's kiss.

'I love you,' Helena pressed against his lips. 'I've always loved you,' she said again.

'I'm sorry it took me so long to get here,' he said, thinking of how long it had taken him to realise how much he lived for her. 'You are the most precious thing in the world to me and I'll not let a single day pass without letting you know that,' he promised.

'Okay,' she said, looking up at him with a love so strong and so sure he could barely believe it.

'Okay?' he asked, unsure what she was agreeing to.

'I'll marry you,' she said. *'Again.'* And through the resounding cheers of celebration from the reporters around them, for the first time in years Leo felt the missing part of his heart return and completeness filled him as he gave Helena his heart, unchecked and untamed.

He kissed her again then, the first of many that would litter their lives like stars in the night sky. Theirs was a happiness proclaimed to the world as true love, from that moment until their very last breaths.

EPILOGUE

Two years later...

LEO LOOKED AT himself in the mirror, fixing his cuff-links, assessing his appearance with a more critical eye than usual. He took in the dark trousers, the morning coat, the waistcoat.

'Tell me again that I'm doing the right thing.'

'You are doing what you *need* to.'

'Am I?'

'Leo, if you want me to talk you out of this, I can,' his brother offered, holding his gaze in the reflection of the mirror.

'Would you?'

'No. Not really. Kate would kill me if I tried to talk you out of this now.'

Leo barked out a laugh. Leander was absolutely right and, while he'd never tell a soul, secretly, he was slightly terrified of his sister-in-law.

'This is what Helena wanted, and I will do whatever it takes to make her happy,' Leo told himself.

Leander slapped him on the back. 'That's the spirit.'

He'd wanted a small ceremony, something quiet and intimate. Helena had done much in the last few years to bring him out of his shell, but Leo was still more inclined to prefer smaller gatherings. But he'd do anything for his future wife, the least of which was having the wedding of her dreams.

Which was why they were in an English Tudor mansion and he was about to put on, of all things, a top hat.

An actual top hat.

'Apparently, she said it made you look handsome,' Leander said, eyeing the damn thing with as much suspicion as Leo felt.

'I don't need a hat to make me look handsome,' Leo replied coolly.

'You keep telling yourself that, brother,' Leander said, with another pat on his shoulder.

'I don't know what you're laughing about. You have to wear one too.'

Leander's face was a picture. A snapshot of a mixture of fear and horror.

'No,' he said, shaking his head, his hand slashing through the air definitively. 'I love you. I do. But not that much.'

Leo couldn't help it. He threw his head back and laughed.

'I'm pretty sure that Kate would kill you if you ruined Helena's wedding,' Leo pointed out when he regained a little of his composure.

Leander glared at the box in the corner of the room, the muscle in his jaw clenching. 'The things we do for these women we love,' he growled and stalked over to the box, opening it and retrieving his own top hat. He practically snarled at the thing.

It had been nearly two years since Leo and Leander had reunited. The phone call Leo had made just before

Helena's press conference had been the start of the road that brought them back together.

That day had changed Leo's life irrevocably. The darkness that had shrouded his life, the heavy weight that he'd tried to pretend had been work and pressure, had lifted. Because he'd finally realised what he needed and wanted from his life, and it had nothing to do with Liassidis Shipping.

Love. Peace. Contentment. *Family.*

When Leander had returned from California they had met and talked long into the night. Both had felt responsible for the separation in their own way, and perhaps it had been partly necessary. They had grown up as two halves of a whole, and had needed to find themselves as individuals as much as twins. But, having done that, they could now appreciate the differences between them as much as the similarities. And their relationship now was based on that understanding and a thousand times stronger for it. The pieces of his life's puzzle had come together to form a picture he'd always wanted.

But it had been complete the moment that Helena agreed to be his wife.

It hadn't been easy—those first few months after the discovery that Leander had been in California and that Leo had been pretending to be him in Greece had caused a lot of anger in the press. Liassidis Shipping stocks and shares had taken a sharp fall and it had been a nail-biting year, watching them slowly come back up as everyone realised that his and Helena's feelings were real. That theirs was the true love story they'd been looking for after all.

Interestingly, Helena's announcement had caused a spike in attention for Incendia, her raw honesty and natural passion as she had spoken about the charity catching the world's imagination.

Donations had started to pour in for the charity from around the globe and within two months they had reached enough to cover a large portion of the money stolen— enough to survive the financial review. Gregory had been found and charged with fraud and financial theft and a slew of other smaller offences.

The trial was due to begin at the end of the following month, the wheels of justice turning painfully slowly. But at least they were turning. Helena was convinced of a positive outcome and had been happy to recover even just half of what had been stolen, the remaining assets lost somewhere in the Caymans was as good a guess as any.

Leander cleared his throat from where he held the door open with one hand, and chucked the top hat at him with the other. Leo caught the brim and, with a huge amount of trepidation, secured it on his head.

'It's showtime,' his brother announced.

Leo stopped at the threshold. 'Thank you,' he said to Leander sincerely.

Leander nodded, for once casting aside the playful persona. He knew how much this meant to Leo, knew that he wanted to honour that for his brother.

'It wouldn't have been the same without you,' Leo said.

'No party ever is, Leo!' he replied, the smile broadening on features that matched his own.

And Leo agreed. Nothing had been right without his brother in his life, but now that he was back it was just as perfect as he remembered from his childhood. That sense of lack, of loss, of something missing, had been found. Not just with his brother but with the woman he was about to marry. If Leander had been a missing piece,

Helena had been his missing heart. And he couldn't wait to declare to the world that she was his, to love, to honour, to protect, to worship and to always, *always*, put first.

Leo had to admit that the Tudor mansion in the Suffolk countryside was spectacular. The thick white stone walls had stood strong against the march of time, and the casement windows punctuating the unique architecture were nothing short of eye-catching. Inside, dark wood panels lined some rooms, while raw stone added rustic features to an already impressive historic building. Four-poster beds welcomed each guest, while open fireplaces and richly coloured carpets added comfort to a luxury that was nothing short of exquisite.

As Leander led him through to the chapel nestled in the gardens where the ceremony would take place he began to feel his pulse picking up. Not for himself, not for the commitment he was about to make to the woman he loved beyond question. But for her. He wanted, needed, this to be perfect for her. With absolutely no doubt about him or his intentions.

Which was why, the night before last, he'd given her a gift—not a wedding gift, no. He had other ideas for that. But as they'd sat in the London apartment where they spent half the year, sharing a glass of wine after dinner, he'd passed across the document he'd asked his lawyers to draw up.

'What's this?' she'd asked. 'You've already given me my birthday present,' she said, smiling saucily.

'Open it and see.'

And he'd watched her read through the document, surprise, delight and love glittering in the sheen that filled her gaze.

'It's not supposed to make you sad, *agápi mou*,' he'd insisted.

It was a document releasing her father's inheritance. The thirty percent shares in Liassidis Shipping. Helena had wanted to marry as soon as they could, but Leo had insisted on waiting until after her twenty-eighth birthday, because whether she needed it or not, *he* did. Because when he married her, he wanted to be the *only* thing on her mind that day.

She'd shaken her head, the smile on her lips purely happy. 'I'm not sad, my love. Not at all. Just happy. Just absolutely, ridiculously happy. Thank you. So much. This means the world,' she'd said before she'd kissed him with one of those drugging kisses that made him lose all sense and reason, and utterly unashamed that he'd not even been able to wait to get her to the bedroom. He'd pulled her across his lap and they'd made love long into the night.

And so it was for the final time that Leo found himself standing at the top of an aisle, waiting for Helena to walk to him.

'Nervous?' Leander asked.

'Not a single bit,' he said truthfully.

'I think we should swap places,' Leander teased. 'Do you think they'd notice?'

'Yes,' Leo replied without a doubt. Because Helena and Kate had *always* noticed—the only two women, aside from their mother, to have ever been able to tell them apart. It was as if he and Leander had always been known, always been loved by the women who had captured their hearts.

Right then, the doors opened and Leo lost his breath.

If Helena had looked amazing two years ago, it was nothing compared to how she looked that day. Dressed in cream silk that clung lovingly to her chest and flared out carefully over the rounded curve of her stomach, she rested the bouquet of pink and white peonies gently on her seven-month baby bump.

A wave of emotion like he'd never felt before swept over Leo. The adoration he felt for her, the worship he wanted to lay at her feet. She was a miracle and he the luckiest man alive.

Kate stepped up beside Helena, having agreed to Helena's request for her to walk her down the aisle, and Leo barely felt Leander stiffen beside him, because all of his renowned focus was entirely on Helena. The true love of his life.

He barely heard the words the priest said that day. And when they signed the register, with Kate and Leander as their witnesses, they all shared a small smile at the memory of how they'd all come together.

But, in truth, Leo didn't need a piece of paper to declare them joined. He had given his heart away years before and nothing would take that away. And this time, when the priest asked if he would take Helena to be his wife, his love, his heart…there was nothing temporary about his answer.

He meant it with his entire soul.

'I do.'

* * * * *

SPANISH MARRIAGE SOLUTION

JACKIE ASHENDEN

MILLS & BOON

To Ajax, King of Scourers!

CHAPTER ONE

ALICE SMITH COULD pinpoint the exact second her life was ruined.

It was the moment she met her brother-in-law.

Five years later and nothing had changed.

Sebastián Castellano, Tenth Duke of Aveira, was still as mesmerisingly beautiful as he had been when Emily had first brought him back to Auckland to show her new husband off to the family. And even now, after all those years and with Emily only two months dead, Alice still felt the same gut punch that she'd always felt every time she was in his presence.

The last time she'd seen him had been at Emily's funeral, in Auckland, and he'd flown all the way from Spain to attend. He hadn't spoken to Alice. He hadn't spoken at all. He'd sat in the back of the church and by the time everyone had filed past the casket and placed on top of it the sprigs of fern frond that Alice had organised, he'd gone.

He'd barely been in the country a day.

Alice's husband Edward's funeral had been the day after, but Alice hadn't been expecting Sebastián to attend that. Why would he? The whole reason Emily and Edward were dead was because they'd both been in the same car that had plunged off the side of a mountain in Switzerland.

Turned out that Emily hadn't been having some 'me time' in Greece as she'd told everyone. She'd been in Switzerland, having an affair with Edward.

Not that the affair was relevant now. The only thing that mattered, or at least the only thing that mattered to Alice, was Diego, Emily's four-month-old son.

Who was not, as it turned out, Sebastián's.

No, he was Edward's. Edward and her sister's, and he was why she was here in Seville, after a nightmare forty-eight-hour journey from Auckland, involving three plane changes and an excruciatingly expensive taxi to the Castellano family's estate, a hacienda, nestled at the base of some rather impressive mountains.

She felt slightly sick with jet lag and the hot, dusty air didn't help, but she took a fortifying breath and shaded her eyes from the intense heat of the midday Spanish sun. She was sweating in the dark suit she'd foolishly decided to wear for the trip and the nerves that had got worse and worse the closer she came to the Castellano estate were now wreaking havoc in her gut.

Sebastián was a difficult man and confronting him wasn't going to be easy, especially about this. But it had to be done. Her nephew was more important to her than anything and she was here to bring him home, back to New Zealand where he belonged.

Ahead of her was the large wooden corral she remembered from previous trips to the Castellano hacienda. The Castellanos had been breeding Andalusian horses for

centuries and were currently the lead supplier of Anda-
lusians in the world. Their bloodlines were highly sought
after, used for dressage, showjumping and other compe-
titions, and Sebastián was a world-renowned talent as a
breeder and trainer.

Alice had always loved visiting the stables whenever
she'd come to Spain, which had been every Christmas
after Emily had married Sebastián. He'd covered travel
expenses for the Smiths and her and Emily's parents
while they'd been alive, which had been very generous
of him. However, the only part of those visits that Alice
had enjoyed was seeing the horses. She'd been a horse
girl once when she'd been small, and a part of her still
thrilled at the sight the magnificent animals. Emily, on
the other hand, had been afraid of them.

Emily certainly wouldn't have liked the magnificent,
glossy black stallion currently trotting around the perim-
eter of the corral on a lead rope. The rope was held by a
figure standing in the middle of the dusty corral circle,
watching as the horse paced around him.

He was exceptionally tall, dwarfing even Alice, who
was five nine in her bare feet, his shoulders wide and
muscular. He had the long, lean shape of an athlete, the
plain black T-shirt and dusty jeans he wore only empha-
sising his magnificent physique.

His raven-black hair was as glossy as the horse's coat
and even though his face was slightly turned away from
her, she didn't need to see it to remember him. That face
haunted her dreams. The precisely carved features of an

aristocrat: high cheekbones, straight nose, and a firm hard mouth. Eyes of dark, smoky gold.

She hadn't told him she was coming. She hadn't wanted him to know why she was here, not until they were face to face. This wasn't the kind of conversation you could have over the phone, and especially not with him. Emily's letter was in her handbag, creased and stained with tears, but Alice needed to show it to him. It was proof of what her sister had wanted in case she ended up having a fight on her hands. She hoped not. She hoped that Sebastián, scion of an ancient dukedom whose history and business dealt in ancient bloodlines, wouldn't want to bring up the child of an affair his wife had had with another man.

He was proud, so Emily had often said, and proud of his family line, so Alice couldn't imagine him welcoming Diego. Perhaps he'd even be glad she was here to take the child off his hands.

When she'd arrived, Lucia, the housekeeper who managed the huge white stucco hacienda that was the Castellano estate, had greeted her like a long-lost daughter and had told her that 'Señor Sebastián' was in the stables looking over a new purchase. Lucia had tried to get Alice to sit down and have something cooling to drink, but Alice had insisted on seeing Sebastián immediately. She wanted to get this over and done with as soon as possible, so Lucia had got Tomas, the stable manager, to bring her to Sebastián.

Which was why she was now standing here in the baking sun, watching said 'new purchase', the beautiful horse, come to a stop directly in front of Sebastián. He pulled something out of his pocket, an apple, and held it out in his palm. The stallion dropped his head, soft mouth closing around the fruit, eating it directly from Sebastián's hand.

It was oddly mesmerising to watching Sebastián reach out and stroke the horse's soft nose. He had a magic touch with the animals, Emily had once told her, pulling a face as she did so. In fact, he'd seemed to like the horses more than he did her, which was a regular complaint from Emily. Alice hadn't taken any notice, which in retrospect had been a mistake. She'd thought it was Emily being dramatic and annoyed at not having attention twenty-four-seven, but apparently it hadn't been.

The stable manager opened the corral gate and went in, going over to where Sebastián stood. There was a brief conversation in rapid Spanish before Sebastián's head turned sharply in Alice's direction.

And as it always did whenever he looked at her, all the air escaped her lungs, and her heart began to race.

It happened every single time.

She hated it.

She'd first met him five years earlier, after his and Emily's whirlwind wedding. They'd come out to New Zealand to meet the in-laws, and it had happened then too, as they'd stood awkwardly on her parents' deck overlooking Waitemata Harbour. The moment his golden eyes had met hers, she'd felt an almost visceral impact. The gut punch of fierce physical attraction, and more than that, for her at least. She hadn't been able to put into words the nature of the emotion that had coursed through her, only that somehow a fire in her had responded to a fire in him, recognising a kindred spirit.

She had no idea why. She didn't know him, had never met him before that day. It was just something about him that had reached inside her and closed its fingers around her heart. But she'd been married to Edward and he'd just married Emily and so there had been nothing to be done about it.

She'd put the feeling behind her, ignored it. Buried it so far down inside her that she could pretend it had never been there in the first place. Easy enough when he and Emily had lived in Andalusia, in the ancient Castellano hacienda. Alice and Edward had seen them only once a year at Christmas.

Alice had become adept at hiding her feelings. At never letting even a hint of what she felt for him show. Yet every time she was anywhere near him, she'd feel that same gut punch, that pull, like a magnet drawing her to him. And perhaps the worst thing about it was that there had been times when she'd catch his eye, and she'd see something glowing in the depths, something that made her think that he felt the same way. But she'd ignored that too, since, even if he did feel the same way, they had both been married.

Out in the corral, Sebastián looked away from her, said something to Tomas and turned his attention back to the horse.

Tomas walked back out of the corral, shutting the gate behind him and coming over to where Alice stood. She was getting sticky with sweat, her suit rumpled and far too constricting.

'Señora Smith,' Tomas said in heavily accented English. He must be new, because she didn't know him and she'd got to know most of Sebastián's employees over the years. 'Su Excelencia is busy. But you may wait in the hacienda until he is able to speak with you.'

A thread of anger wound through her. She was hot, sweaty, and jet-lagged and the longer she waited to talk to him about Diego, the harder it was going to be. Because of course nothing about having to deal with Sebastián was ever easy.

It wasn't that she didn't talk to him. She did. But only when it was impossible to do otherwise, and even then their conversations were short, stilted, and awkward. He was polite to her, but cold and distant, so she tried to avoid him when she could, and when she couldn't, she treated him with icy formality. For a while she'd even entertained the hope that Emily might not notice that her sister and her husband didn't get on.

A false hope.

Emily had soon decided that since it was clear Alice and Sebastián didn't like each other, they needed to be forced into proximity so they could learn to 'get along'.

It had been excruciating and eventually Alice had had to tell Emily to stop. Yes, maybe they didn't much like each other, but they were adults and could handle a bit of dislike without burning things to the ground.

Emily didn't need to know that for Alice the opposite was true.

Alice stared at the tall figure in the corral, but he didn't look back again.

Did he know why she was here? Was that why he'd ordered her to wait in the hacienda? Had Emily told him that Diego wasn't his? Had he known that she was having an affair with Edward before the car accident? Had it been as much of a shock to him as it had to her?

She really should do what he'd said and go back inside the hacienda to wait. She was hot and tired, and it would be better to have this discussion in the cool of the house.

Then again, since she'd started her investment company, she'd become unaccustomed to waiting for men to speak first. Being proactive and taking charge before they even knew they were dealing with a woman was always the best approach. Never let it enter their heads that she was female. That way, by the time they realised who they were talking with, it was too late.

Being female in the world of finance was problematic to say the least. Then again, she'd spent a lot of time trying hard not to be female, which would make dealing with Sebastián a lot less of a problem.

She'd had years of practice at hiding the way she felt about him, at hiding her own feelings, full stop, and that was how she'd go about negotiating this particular situation. She'd tell him logically, calmly, that Emily had sent her a letter about Diego, and that her sister wanted Alice to bring him up should anything happen to her. That was why she was here. To take her nephew back home to New Zealand where he belonged.

And there was nothing Sebastián could do about it.
End of story.

Sebastián tried to focus on Halcón, the stallion, but it was difficult.

He could still feel the hard shock of Alice's unexpected presence echoing through him, and it was proving complicated to get control of himself. Much harder than it should have been, especially after all the years of practice.

He'd learned the art of control early, since his father wouldn't stand for anything less than total self-mastery, and it had come in useful when all his plans, all his dreams for the future, had come crashing down following Emily's death. Then again, he was used to life's body blows.

Meeting Alice for the first time had been one of them.

He hadn't known who she was right away. She'd been standing on the deck at Emily's parents' house, with the views out over the blue water, smiling at something Emily's father had said. Her hair had tumbled over her shoulders in glossy waves, black as a raven's wing, and while her features didn't have Emily's petite, precise beauty, there was something about their arrangement that caught his attention. A strong face, animated and expressive. Not typically beautiful but captivating all the same. Winged black eyebrows, a strong, decisive nose, and a long, sensual mouth. She had skin the colour of dark honey, and when her deep brown eyes had met his, he'd felt a tectonic shift inside him. As if the earth had moved on its axis, changing gravity, changing the seasons, changing the very air he breathed.

Then Emily had introduced them and he'd understood, without a shadow of a doubt, that the worst had happened: he'd married the wrong sister.

Halcón dropped his head and nudged at Sebastián's hand, questing for another treat, but Sebastián wasn't paying attention. He didn't need to turn around to know that Alice hadn't gone back into the hacienda as he'd told her to, and he could feel her watching him, the way he'd always been able to feel it. Even now it still had the power to steal his breath, the way it had done for the past five years.

But he'd made a vow to himself, the day he'd met her, that he'd ignore the change to his life's axis. That he wouldn't let mere physical attraction—because surely that was all it was—affect him in any way.

It was meaningless. She was meaningless. She was his sister-in-law and that was all. He'd already married the woman he intended to spend his life with. He'd made vows to her, promises he'd keep until his dying breath. The Dukes of Aveira the Castellanos, as his father had often told him, had honour in their blood, and, because he was not truly a Castellano, he must learn how to be honourable. And he had learned. It wasn't a lesson he'd ever forget.

So when he heard her say his name, in the low, husky voice that seemed to stroke over his skin and take hold of something inside him, he didn't turn immediately. He directed his attention to the horse, gripping the lead rein and stepping in close.

'Sebastián,' Alice said again. 'I need to talk to you. It's important.'

Of course it would be important. She hadn't flown all the way from New Zealand to arrive unannounced at the Castellano hacienda for nothing, and he suspected he knew the reason she was here. Diego. There wouldn't be anything else that would bring her halfway around the world to his doorstep.

Not even you?

Before he'd met Emily, he'd had many lovers. He was experienced with women. He knew when a woman wanted him, and Alice had wanted him. He'd seen the flare in her dark eyes the moment their gazes had connected. That had made it imperative that he never let slip his own feelings and, so far, he never had.

So no, she wouldn't be here for him, but even if she were, he wouldn't do anything about it. The fact that their spouses had been cheating with each other only made his own determination not to even stronger.

'As I told Tomas, I'm busy,' he said curtly. 'Go into the hacienda. Lucia will give you coffee. I'll be another half-hour.' Without waiting for a response, he gripped Halcón's mane and pulled himself up onto the stallion's back with the casual ease of long practice.

Halcón shifted beneath him, dancing sideways as Sebastián's weight settled.

You know why she's here and yet you think the horse is more important?

Oh, the horse was important. New blood for the stables that were descended from the warhorses of old, that the ancient dukes had once ridden into battle on. But nothing was more important than Diego. His son. And he *was* Sebastián's son, no matter what the DNA tests said. He'd been with Emily when she'd given birth and he'd been the first to hold him. The first to look down into his face, and he'd felt the same shift then that he'd felt when he'd met Alice, as if nothing would ever be the same again.

He hadn't thought Alice would know the secret of Diego's parentage, but somehow she'd found out, and while her visit wasn't entirely unexpected, it definitely wasn't welcome. He needed time. Time to decide what he was going to do about it, about her, and he *was* going to do something. Nobody was taking Diego from him. Nobody.

Sebastián controlled the stallion effortlessly with his knees and laid a hand on the side of the animal's neck. Halcón settled, but Sebastián could still feel the tension in the horse's massive body. A spirited beast, which was good. He liked it when a horse had fire. Not so he could break it—to break an animal's spirit was a tragedy—but to channel it, enhance it.

'I don't want coffee,' Alice said. 'I need to talk to you. Now.'

There was a note of cool authority in her voice, very different from the warmth that had once infused every word. He'd noticed that the warmth had vanished not long after she'd set up her investment company, the same time he'd noticed that the passionate spark that had drawn him so intensely the day they'd met had died. He hadn't wanted to notice, of course, but he had all the same. Some inner light in her had been extinguished and she'd become cool and hard all over, like a field of golden sunflowers slowly being covered with ice.

He didn't know what had happened and he hadn't asked. He never spoke of her with Emily and Emily had learned by then never to bring up the subject of her sister.

Grief and regret twisted in his heart at the thought of his wife, as it had been doing since she'd died, but he thrust away both emotions. He'd failed Emily and he knew it, but he would not fail Diego. Not ever.

Ignoring Alice, he urged the horse into a trot around the corral, assessing its pace. Eventually she would get tired of waiting and do what he'd said. After all, it was hot out here and she must be jet-lagged.

Except she didn't leave.

She stood outside the corral and leaned over the fence posts, watching him. Making it very obvious that she wasn't going to move.

Emily had never come to the stables. She'd been afraid of the horses, which should have been a red flag, but he'd refused to see it. She had been petite and delicate, and even though she'd acted more fragile than she actually was, he'd enjoyed being cast in the role of her protector. That was what he'd been born for, to protect, like the dukes of old.

But Alice had never been afraid of the horses. Every time she and Edward had visited, she'd come to the stables at some point and watch his stable hands. It had been distracting. Eventually he'd had to tell her, curtly, that the stables were out of bounds to visitors.

It seemed she hadn't remembered that fact.

'I can stand here all day,' Alice said as he trotted past her for the second time. 'You can't just ignore me, Sebastián.'

Of course he could. He could do anything he wanted. He was a duke. Still, he was simply being petty now and, more than that, trying to put off the inevitable moment when he'd have to stop and look into her dark eyes. Feel that same kick of desire deep inside him, the same tug of recognition. Knowing that this time there was nothing to stop him from taking what he wanted. What they both wanted…

But that was impossible. Edward and Emily might be gone, he might be a widower and Alice a widow, but there was too much between them now. Too many promises he'd made that he couldn't put aside for the sake of mere sex.

Avoiding her was cowardice and he was not a coward.

After the second circuit, he finally drew Halcón up in front of her. He didn't dismount, instead looking down at her where she stood just outside the corral fence, dressed in a rumpled black suit and fitted white shirt. Her wealth of glossy black hair had been contained in a severe ponytail, not a wisp out of place, and it left her face looking naked. There were dark circles under her eyes, new lines of grief around her mouth.

He couldn't forget that while he'd lost his wife, Edward had meant nothing to him. Yet Alice had lost, not only her husband, but also her sister.

Except that made no difference to the punch of emotion that hit him the moment her gaze met his, the restless, aching want that pulled at him.

There were reasons he didn't speak to her. Reasons he tried never to be in the same room as her, and he'd thought he'd managed to kill the want over the years, but it had never got any easier.

It wasn't easy now, yet he managed to force away the familiar surge of need, steeling himself to meet her level gaze.

Despite her obvious weariness, she didn't seem to have any problems with looking at him, so perhaps she didn't feel it any more. He hoped so. It would make this a lot less complicated.

'I didn't think half an hour was too much to ask,' he said coolly. 'You'd be more comfortable inside.'

'Probably.' There was a determined cast to her chin now and she lifted it, as if he'd challenged her. 'But this can't wait.'

Halcón shifted again, as if picking up on his disquiet, but he put his hand on the horse's neck once more and the stallion settled. He stared at Alice, recognising abruptly something he hadn't seen in her in far too long—a spark.

It was bright, burning and fierce. But, as he already knew, it wasn't for him.

'You're here for Diego.' He didn't make it a question and there wasn't much point pussyfooting around the subject.

Her eyes widened, a ripple of surprise crossing her face. 'How did you—?'

'There's no other reason for you to be here, Alice.'

Slowly, she pushed herself away from the corral fence and straightened, the expression on her face almost imperious. 'No,' she said. 'No, you're right. There *is* no other reason for me to be here.'

He could feel the layers to that statement, but it wasn't worth trying to read deeper into what she was saying. He wouldn't be doing anything about it now, that was for certain, and he wasn't interested in doing so anyway.

'So what?' he demanded. 'What about Diego?'

Her dark eyes met his head-on. 'Emily's lawyers sent me a letter. He's not your son, Sebastián. She wanted me to look after him. So that's why I'm here. I'm here to take him home.'

CHAPTER TWO

ALICE'S PALMS WERE now damp and it wasn't only due to delivering a truth to Sebastián that he didn't want to hear. It was also him.

Watching him pull himself effortlessly up onto the horse's back and then ride without either saddle or reins, as if he and the horse were one beast, one mind, was like drinking a slug of whiskey straight down. It stole her breath then made her feel warm all over, and slightly intoxicated, a little drunk on his competence and the athleticism with which he performed every movement.

She'd seen him ride before, at other visits, and it had always been mesmerising. She didn't know anything about riding, but he seemed a natural to her, and it was clear the horses loved him too. They were always following him around and nuzzling at his pockets for treats, nickering at him and pushing at him with their long muzzles. He was so gentle with them, too. Not at all the cold, proud, arrogant man he was around everyone else, and that had fascinated her. Made her want to know why he was so different around animals. She'd wanted to ask Emily, but talking about him to Emily had felt too dangerous, so she hadn't. Going to the stables had felt dangerous too, and really, it would have been better for her peace of mind not to. Yet she hadn't been able to help herself. She was drawn helplessly there, by her fascination with the horses and with him.

She hadn't known her visits were a problem until he'd told her curtly that the stables were out of bounds to non-employees, and she was disturbing the horses.

It was a good thing, she'd told herself then, ignoring the hurt she'd felt at the time, because she had no right to feel that hurt. Of course, he didn't want her in the stables, especially if her presence disturbed the animals. She didn't work for him, so there was no reason for her to be there after all.

Yet still, watching him now, she felt that same combination of fascination and hurt that she'd felt years ago. The same combination of breathless desire and guilt. Nothing had changed.

God, how she hated it.

He sat on the back of the huge black stallion, his muscular body shifting with the horse's restless movements, automatically adjusting without any seeming effort. His gaze was hard, his smoky gold eyes as cold as she'd ever seen them, so it took her a second to register that he didn't look shocked in the least.

'What?' His voice was deep and dark, his lightly accented English making music of the words. 'You think I didn't know? You think I wasn't aware of Emily's affair? I had the tests done, Alice. So yes, I know he's not my son, not by blood. But he is in every other way that counts and so he's not going anywhere.'

She'd expected to shock him, because she certainly hadn't been aware of Edward's affair with Emily. Oh, she'd suspected that Edward might have been having an affair given his many absences overseas on 'business' trips and the emotional distance growing between them, but not that his affair had been with her sister. Not until the pair of them had died together in that car accident.

She hadn't expected that, not only had Sebastián known about the affair, but he'd also known that Diego wasn't his.

She felt as if the ground had been ripped from under her.

'How?' she asked blankly. 'How did you know?'

He lifted one powerful shoulder. 'That's not important. What is important is that my name is on Diego's birth certificate. I *am* his father.'

Alice felt the world shift again, like the horse between Sebastián's powerful thighs, and her gut churned. Jet lag of course, but also a shock she wasn't expecting to feel to add to the complicated tangle of emotions seeing him had brought back.

She'd thought he wouldn't argue. The Castellanos were an old-world, aristocratic family where blood was everything, and she'd assumed that Sebastián wouldn't want anything to do with a child not of his blood. That, after a period of surprise and anger, he'd have no issue with giving up a child that wasn't his and he wasn't responsible for.

With a supreme effort of will, Alice forced her shock and all the rest of her emotions away and met his steady, hard gaze. 'I don't care,' she said flatly. 'He's my nephew. I have a letter from Emily saying that she wanted me to bring him up and so that's what I'm going to do.' He was all she had left of Emily, all she'd ever have of a family of her own too, but she wasn't going to tell Sebastián that. He didn't know about her terrible miscarriage, but he did know that Diego was all she had left of her sister.

'I sympathise,' Sebastián said, his voice entirely without sympathy. 'Nevertheless, his place is here with me.'

Alice blinked, her nausea still churning, but she'd be damned if she looked weak and sick in front of him, so she reached for the anger instead. The anger that had been burning in her for months now, an anger she'd forced aside because her sister and her husband were dead and being angry with them wouldn't bring them back or change things. Except it might help her now.

She drew herself up to her full height, the way she did at work when men were trying to tell her how things worked. When they were trying to explain the world of finance to her, despite the fact that she knew it far better than they ever could.

'No,' she said icily. 'His place is with me. His aunt. By blood.' She held Sebastián's proud golden stare. 'If I have to get lawyers involved, believe me, I have no problem with that.'

The stallion shifted restlessly and Sebastián once again dropped a hand to absently stroke its glossy black coat. And despite herself, despite everything, Alice found her gaze drawn to that large, strong hand. White scars dotted the olive skin of his long fingers, evidence of a man who worked hard in an intensely physical job, no matter the wealth and power of his position.

She'd tried never to fantasise about him. Tried never to imagine that hand on her skin, stroking her as he stroked that horse, because she'd been married and she'd loved her husband. But sometimes, especially in the years after she'd lost the baby, before Edward had pulled away from her so completely, she'd found herself dreaming of Sebastián's hands on her body, and that hard mouth on hers. She'd always wake up with an aching sense of loss and suffocating guilt.

She still felt that guilt, another thread of pain to add to her grief at losing Emily, even though her sister had been having an affair with her husband. It was just all so complicated and fraught that she had no idea why she would even be looking at Sebastián's hand when she had so many other things to deal with. And even if the situation had been different, she had no idea what Sebastián felt about her. She never had. Nothing, judging from the expression on his arrogant face. It was clear that he wasn't going to give an inch.

'Do that,' he said. 'I also have lawyers. And they have been protecting Castellano interests for centuries. Diego is mine, Alice. And I keep what is mine.'

'Like you kept Emily?' It was a stupid thing to say, and she knew it as soon as the words were out of her mouth. She'd let her anger get the better of her, and that had never been a good thing. If he was going to be difficult about Diego then she needed to get him on her side, not the opposite.

His handsome features hardened even further. 'There is nothing for you here, Alice. Go home.' Then, before she could say anything else, he turned the horse away and set off on another circuit, urging the stallion into an easy canter.

Alice's heart thumped loudly in her ears, sweat trickling down her back, and, much to her horror, she felt tears prickling the backs of her eyes. She must be more tired than she'd thought if she was letting her emotions get to her like this.

Gritting her teeth, she blinked the tears away.

Tears were Emily's trick and one her sister had used often to get her way. Acting weak and fragile, looking like a victim to get attention. It had always worked, too, but Alice had learned early on that it was impossible trying to compete with her beautiful, feminine sister, and so she hadn't.

Instead she'd kept her emotions locked down, hidden away, becoming stoic and staunchly practical. And what had been a cause of pain in childhood became an asset in the corporate world. No one could ever accuse Alice Smith of being overly emotional.

She stood there a moment, getting herself under control.

She'd given herself a week in Spain, thinking that bringing Diego home would be a simple matter, and she still had time. Her lawyer threat hadn't been an idle one—there were some she could call on—but she knew that if Sebastián chose to be difficult about this, then fighting him was going to be hard. She didn't have the resources he did, plus she was unfamiliar with the Spanish legal system. Still, she'd be damned if she went home like a good little dog with her tail between her legs.

She'd already lost one child. She wasn't going to lose another.

He expected her to leave, which meant her only response was to stay. She certainly wasn't going to go without at least seeing her nephew and surely Sebastián couldn't deny her that. Perhaps, if she stayed a couple of days, she might even be able to convince him to change his mind about her taking Diego back to New Zealand.

He is not going to change his mind. He's not going to give that child up and you know it.

Alice took a silent, steadying breath, gazing at Sebastián as he rode another circuit.

Emily hadn't confided much of her marital issues to Alice—now Alice knew about Edward, she could see why—but she had told her that Sebastián could be arrogant and cold, and that he was exceptionally strong-willed. Difficult, Emily had once said, but since he was also amazing in bed—something Alice really didn't want to know—she forgave him his difficulties.

Well, Alice had caught a glimpse of that arrogance and coldness just now, also a ruthlessness she hadn't expected. Though, perhaps she should have. Perhaps she should have called him first instead of thinking this would be better dealt with face to face. If she'd called, she would have known he was going to be difficult and had a backup plan prepared.

Too late for that now. His tone had been hard, as had those aristocratic features, and there was no give in those deceptively hot golden eyes. He wasn't going to budge.

In which case you're going to need to be persuasive, aren't you?

Alice dragged her gaze away from him, turning plans over in her head. She wasn't leaving Spain without Diego, that was the bottom line. Her parents had passed away three years earlier—her mother to cancer and her father to a heart attack—which made Diego her only flesh and blood. And even apart from that, Emily had been very clear in her letter that she wanted Alice to look after her son. Especially now he'd been orphaned.

Sebastián was no relation and he was a hard, proud man. There was no softness in him, no warmth. He treated his horses better than he did people, and she didn't want Diego growing up with a father figure like that.

Children needed love and support and she had all of that to give. After all, she was never going to have a child herself, in which case Diego would be hers.

So getting Sebastián to change his mind might not be easy, but she wasn't going to leave without trying. Her nephew deserved that.

Alice didn't look back again. She turned from the corral and strode along the path through the gardens that led from the stables to the hacienda.

The house was massive, of whitewashed stone and a red-tiled roof, with many terraces and a central courtyard surrounded by colonnades shaded by lush grape vines and brilliant bougainvillea. Green lawns surrounded the house and gardens featuring banks of lavender, along with orange and olive trees and fountains. Out at the back of the house was the lavish pool area that Emily used to live in during the long hot summers, or so she'd told Alice. Alice hadn't been here in summer. She and Edward had only visited in winter, when there was snow on the ground and the hacienda's thick walls would hold in the warmth from the huge fireplace in the central living area.

She loved the estate, though she never let Emily or Edward know how much. She'd even tried to deny it to herself as well, because she didn't want to love anything of Sebastián's. Didn't want any ammunition that would fuel fantasies of how much better suited she was to living here than Emily.

Emily, who was afraid of the horses and complained of the isolation. Who wanted a bright, modern apartment in Paris, not some centuries-old, dark and dusty Spanish estate. Sebastián had duly bought her that Paris apartment and she'd spent a lot of time there, Alice knew. Probably to coincide with Edward's 'business trips'.

But she wasn't going to think of that, not about her sister and her husband. That way lay too much pain and she was barely getting by with grieving their loss, let alone their infidelity as well.

She walked through an archway that led into the central courtyard and then down a colonnaded path that ran down the side of the house before stepping through a door and into the cool of the wide hall.

Her suitcase was still standing beside the big wooden double front doors, as was her handbag. Well, it could stay there. She wasn't leaving.

She went down the hallway and into the huge living area. It was all low ceilings with exposed timber beams and stone flooring covered with thick rugs. Low couches upholstered in faded blue linen with thick white cushions were clustered around the giant fireplace, and dark wooden shelving lined the whitewashed walls.

It was wonderfully cool in here and she was tempted to sit down on one of the couches for a rest, because she was feeling overheated and dizzy, and still faintly nauseous. Then again, if she sat down, she wasn't going to get up again, and that wasn't going to help.

Besides, apart from anything, she wanted to see Diego.

Eventually, she tracked Lucia down in the kitchen. The housekeeper was putting something in the oven and, seeing Alice, she straightened and gave her a smile. 'Did you find Señor Sebastián?'

Alice smiled back. 'I did. But I have a problem, Lucia. I'm here to spend time with my nephew and I was silly. I didn't give either you or Sebastián any warning I was coming. So he's not very happy with me, I'm afraid.'

Lucia raised her hands. 'It's no problem. We have plenty of room. It is just Señor Sebastián and the little one now. And as for him not being happy with you…' She shrugged. 'He will get over it. You are not a stranger, after all.'

No, but she might as well be.

'Are you sure?' Alice didn't care about putting out Sebastián, but she didn't want to make things difficult for Lucia. 'There is a hotel in the village—'

'No, no,' Lucia interrupted emphatically. 'No, Señora Alice. You must stay here. I will not hear of you going to the village. No, absolutely not.'

It didn't matter how many times Alice had told Lucia

to call her just Alice, the housekeeper insisted on calling her *señora*. It made her almost smile. Emily had loved Lucia, because Lucia liked taking care of people and Emily had loved being taken care of. Lucia was warm and motherly, and Alice had liked her too.

'Okay,' she said, feeling relief spread through her. 'I'd love that.'

'Good.' Lucia put down the tea towel she'd been holding. 'Now, I will get a room ready, but first you need food and something to drink. You have had a very long trip here, no?'

'Yes, it was very long.' Alice swallowed, feeling unaccountably nervous. 'Might I...see Diego?'

Lucia's smile became even warmer, the look in her dark eyes softening. 'He is having a nap now. And you, I think, need food, coffee and a rest.'

There was a fleeting moment's disappointment that she couldn't see him immediately, but she didn't want to wake him up, and it was true she'd really love a rest, so she let herself be taken charge of by Lucia instead.

Half an hour later, when Alice was feeling better after some food and a strong cup of coffee, Lucia showed her to one of the guest rooms. Without asking, she'd put Alice in a different room from the one she and Edward had normally used, which Alice was grateful for since she didn't need any more reminders.

It was a pretty room, too, with a terrace that overlooked the courtyard. The dark wooden French doors to the terrace stood open, allowing air to circulate, carrying with it the scent of lavender and the sound of the fountain.

A four-poster bed draped in white muslin was pushed up against one wall and covered in a thick white quilt, a pile of pillows resting against the carved headboard.

Alice sat down on it with some relief. She'd taken off her rumpled suit the moment Lucia had left, and had stepped into the en suite bathroom to have a cool shower. She felt better now, but there was still that deep-seated weariness that felt as if it had settled into her bones. Grief, naturally. It had been two months since Emily and Edward had died, but that exhaustion was still there, tugging at her.

She lay down on the soft quilt and put her head on the pillow, the cotton cool under her cheek. Yes, a rest was a good idea. She certainly was going to need all the energy she could get in order to face Sebastián again. Especially when he found out she hadn't left as he'd ordered her to.

It was only supposed to be a quick nap, but when Alice opened her eyes again, the room was full of the red-gold light of a long, European twilight. She must have slept half the day away and now it would probably be too late to see Diego. Still, she had to admit, she felt a lot better.

A good thing, considering a confrontation with Sebastián was on the cards.

Slipping off the bed, she went to her suitcase to find something to wear that wasn't a suit, only to see that on the low couch at the end of the bed had been laid a loose, cool-looking dress in faded red linen. It wasn't hers, which meant Lucia must have put it there for her.

Alice picked it up. The material was soft and silky, and with the loose style it looked as if it would fit. The faded red was a beautiful colour too. Where had Lucia found it?

Was it Emily's? It probably wasn't, considering it wasn't Emily's colour, but then there were a lot of things she'd thought Emily wouldn't like and apparently had.

After a moment, she slipped the dress on and, indeed, it fitted beautifully, the red linen cool and soft against her skin. It was much less constricting than her suit, and she loved the feeling of the skirts swirling around her legs.

She didn't normally wear dresses. Emily was the pretty, feminine one. The one their father had doted on and their mother had called her 'little princess'. Alice had been the oldest and therefore the responsible one. Too independent and headstrong for their father and too tall and athletic to be anyone's little anything.

No one had called her anything but Alice, not even Edward.

Shaking out her still damp hair, Alice smoothed down the dress, then went to the door and opened it. She stepped into the hallway beyond and went down it to the big, dark wooden staircase that led downstairs.

Still thinking about what she was going to say to Sebastián, she didn't notice the man standing at the bottom of the stairs until it was too late.

He had his arms crossed over his muscular chest and he was watching her with hard golden eyes. 'What are you still doing here, Alice?'

At first all Sebastián could think about was how beautiful the red linen dress looked against her olive skin. How beautiful *she* looked, with her black hair loose and hanging in a glossy midnight tumble over her shoulders.

The dress was designed for comfort, not sex appeal and yet somehow, with her glorious height and Amazonian lines, Alice made it look effortlessly elegant.

He resented that. He resented the fact that she was still here at all.

Lucia had told him that Alice was staying in the way Lucia often did, as if this were her house and he had no say in the matter. And considering how long Lucia had been the housekeeper here, that was partially true. He'd never felt the need to argue with her before, but he did now and he resented that as well.

He didn't like having to pull the duke card with his staff and he wasn't about to start now, especially not when the problem was his sister-in-law.

Who apparently hadn't gone as he'd told her to.

She stopped halfway down the stairs and gave him an imperious look. 'What do you mean, what am I doing here? I presume Lucia told you?'

'She said you were staying. Which was not what I told you to do.'

'No, because I don't take kindly to being ordered around. Especially not after forty-eight hours of travel.'

Anger threaded through him. He didn't want her here. She was too much of a reminder of all the things he'd sacrificed for the past five years, all the things he'd lost. His marriage, his wife, his future.

In Emily he'd thought he'd found the perfect bride. A woman who'd loved him, who'd needed him, who'd appealed to the protector in him and who'd wanted children eventually. And then he'd met Alice and realised he'd been mistaken in his choice. But divorcing Emily hadn't been possible, not for the honour of his family, and so he'd put all thoughts of Alice aside and concentrated on loving his wife instead.

At least, he'd tried. In fact, he'd thought he'd succeeded, until a business associate in Paris had told him he'd seen Emily out and about with her brother-in-law. Not that the signs hadn't been there before that, he'd just chosen to ignore them.

Regardless, Alice's presence brought all of that back and he wasn't having it.

'In that case,' he said curtly, 'you can stay the night. But in the morning, you need to leave.'

She was silent a moment, her guarded dark gaze expressionless. Then she said, 'No.' And folded her arms, mirroring his stance.

The thread of anger pulled tighter. 'What do you mean no?'

'Exactly what I said. I'm here for Diego, Sebastián, I told you that. And I'm not leaving without him.'

'And I told you that—'

'You will let me see him at least,' she interrupted, and there it was, deep in her eyes, that flicker of fire that had drawn him so strongly the moment they'd met. 'He's *my* nephew, Sebastián. He's the only family I've got.'

You can't deny her that.

He wanted to. He wanted to very badly. The longer she was here, the more her presence grated, and he didn't need that, not so soon after Emily's death. His life had already been upended once and he didn't need it happening again.

Then again, family was important, as Mateo, his father, had never ceased to tell him, though apparently that applied only to the Castellanos. And Sebastián was *not* a Castellano, which was another thing that Mateo never ceased to remind him of.

Still, it would be cruel to deny Alice the chance to meet her nephew, not to mention exceedingly petty. Emily had called him cruel once, and he supposed, to her, he had been. It was too late to make any recompense for that now, but he could allow Alice a day at least.

'Very well,' he said. 'You may have tomorrow. I expect you to leave the morning after.'

But instead of being satisfied with this as she should have been, Alice's black brows descended. 'Why?' she asked. 'What does it matter to you how long I stay?'

Good question. Pity he had no answer to give her, or at least not one that wouldn't betray exactly how much it mattered to him.

You're letting her get to you far too much.

Perhaps. Nevertheless, he'd decided.

'It doesn't matter,' he bit out. 'I've made my decision and that's final.'

She was silent again, watching him. Then, after a moment, she came down the rest of the stairs, the skirts of her dress swirling around her. She moved with such economical precision, as if once she had a direction to go in, nothing was going to get in her way.

He found it challenging and exciting in the way watching a spirited animal was challenging and exciting. Thinking about how to harness that animal's spirit, match it with his own, to help it grow and bloom into something magnificent.

You shouldn't be watching her.

No, he shouldn't. Yet he couldn't help himself.

She stopped in front of him, allowing some distance and yet still closer than he would have preferred. Not that he'd ever forget himself and grab her, but he didn't appreciate the temptation. The scent of sweet lavender surrounded him, probably from the soap made from the lavender flowers in the estate gardens that had been put in all the guest rooms. Emily hadn't liked it, preferring the more exotic and expensive scents she'd had made especially for her in Paris. He liked it though, and on Alice there was a sweetness beneath the lavender that made everything male in him sit up and take notice.

It had been a long time since he'd taken a woman to bed. He and Emily had grown apart in the months leading up to the accident and since then, grief and guilt had stolen away anything resembling desire.

But he could feel it now, rising in him as her scent wove around him and he watched the fire flicker in her dark eyes. He knew how badly he wanted to make that fire burn higher, hotter. It was a unique temptation, yet he couldn't give into it. He couldn't.

'You didn't say anything to me at Emily's funeral,' she said. 'Why was that?'

He knew he should step back, put some more distance between them, but he didn't. 'What did you want me to say?'

There was a flicker in her gaze, the glimpse of a temper she'd never displayed in his presence before, or at least not so openly. 'A hello might have been nice.'

But he hadn't said that. He hadn't said anything to her. Which had been rude, but he hadn't been able to bring himself to even approach her. She'd been wearing blue, Emily's favourite colour, in defiant opposition to the black all around her, and loss had been written all over her face. He should have said something, but he'd been so full of anger at Emily for betraying him, and at himself for his failure to make her happy, that he hadn't been able to trust himself to speak to anyone, let alone Alice.

Plus, he'd thought he'd never see her again after that and so what was the point?

'I'm sorry,' he said, knowing he sounded not sorry in the least, but unable to adjust his tone. 'I wasn't fit company that day.'

'Neither was I.'

He didn't like the challenging look in her eyes, not one bit. 'Is there a point to this?' he asked, because suddenly he was conscious that standing here too close to her wasn't a good idea. 'Dinner is ready in the courtyard and Lucia doesn't like people being late.'

Her dark eyes glittered. 'Fine. Let's have dinner. And you can tell me all about why you think Diego is better off here than he is with me.'

CHAPTER THREE

SEBASTIÁN DIDN'T LIKE that and it was obvious. Anger burned in the smoky golden depths of his eyes and his powerful body radiated tension. And heat. She could feel the warmth of him from where she stood; she hadn't realised quite how close to him she'd got, closer than she'd ever been before. She could smell him too, horse and dry earth, sunshine and hay, and under that something spicy and masculine that made her whole body tighten with want.

He was so much taller than she was, his shoulders wide and his chest broad. He made her feel petite and fragile, and while a part of her hated that, another part, the part that had always wanted to be the same delicate, pretty little princess that her sister was, loved it.

Heat climbed in her face, her heartbeat accelerating. A mistake to get so close. She needed to put some distance between them before she gave herself away.

Except he was the one who turned abruptly and strode off in the direction of the courtyard without a backward glance.

Alice swallowed and tried to control her thumping heart. She couldn't get that close to him again. She was too susceptible and if she wasn't careful, she'd end up taking her eye off her goal. It was Diego who was important, and she couldn't forget that.

Emily had wanted him brought home to New Zealand. Emily had wanted him to grow up loved.

In her letter she had written:

I'm so sorry to put you in this position and I know it's asking a lot. You may not ever forgive me for what I did and I'm not asking you to. I wouldn't if I were you. But this isn't about me. This is about Diego. And I'm afraid of what Sebastián will do if he finds out Diego isn't his.

He won't hurt him—he's not violent. But he's cold and proud and blood means everything to him. I want Diego to grow up loved...

Well, Sebastián was certainly proud, but it hadn't been ice in his eyes when he'd spoken of Diego. It had been fire. She could almost imagine him as an ancient warrior with a sword in hand, defending his family, his home, from any invaders who dared cross his threshold.

Emily hadn't said much about their marriage, but Alice had often had the feeling her sister wasn't happy. It was obvious now, of course, since she'd been having an affair with Edward, but Alice wondered what it was that had made Emily so unhappy. Sebastián was a duke, with an ancient lineage and centuries of wealth behind him, and he was gorgeous. Emily liked status and money and a pretty face. She liked having someone being possessive and protective, but...

Why had she thought Sebastián cold? Why did she fear

him bringing Diego up? Was it something to do with their own father? Emily had been his favourite—he hadn't known what to do with tall, stubborn Alice—and he'd doted on her. Maybe that was it. Maybe all she'd wanted was for her son to have a father who doted on him the way their father had doted on her.

Well, whatever her reasons were, Alice was going to have her work cut out for her if she was going to change Sebastián's mind, that was for sure.

She took a breath and followed him into the courtyard.

Outside, under the shade of a trellis trailing bougainvillea, was a wooden table neatly set with a white tablecloth, plates and cutlery, and stemless wine glasses. The heat of the day had faded, leaving behind a warm, pleasant twilight, the air scented with lavender.

Lucia was setting out plates of food that smelled absolutely delicious. Sebastián stood near her, saying something in Spanish that it was clear she did not like one bit. She frowned at him, replying in stern tones as if she was telling him off about something.

Alice tensed. He was already burning with anger, which meant surely Lucia was taking her life into her own hands speaking to him like that.

He glared at her and said something else in a hard, curt voice. Lucia merely shrugged, unbothered. Then, noticing Alice standing there, she said in English, 'It is rude to talk in Spanish when Señora Alice cannot understand us, Señor Sebastián.' She looked at him sternly, and added, 'I have cooked a meal for you both, and you will sit down and eat it. Together.'

Alice blinked. She'd never seen Sebastián be told what to do and for a moment she wondered what on earth Lucia was thinking. His carved features were set in uncompromising lines, his hard mouth unyielding. His golden eyes burned with sullen fury.

Alice waited for him to launch into a verbal attack, maybe even fire his housekeeper on the spot, yet instead he muttered something short and sharp in Spanish, went over to the table, pulled out a chair and sat down.

'Manners, Señor Sebastián,' Lucia murmured.

He muttered another curse, got to his feet, moved over to the chair opposite his, pulled it out and looked fiercely at Alice. 'Please,' he said, his voice like iron. 'Won't you join me for dinner?'

A small shock arrowed down her spine. It seemed that this hard, proud man had not only been roundly told off by his housekeeper, he was also doing exactly what she said, albeit with all the grace of a sullen teenager.

Alice almost wanted to smile.

Lucia, who didn't seem in imminent danger of being fired and obviously wasn't afraid of Sebastián in any way, gave an approving nod, gathered up her trays, and disappeared back into the hacienda.

Sebastián remained standing rigidly behind the chair he'd pulled out. He looked as if he wanted to bite someone's head off.

Alice took another silent breath then moved over to the table. 'I had no idea Lucia was so fierce,' she said as she sat down, trying to keep her voice light.

'She doesn't like it when her meals are under-appreciated.' Sebastián's tone was hard as rock, but Alice could feel the masculine heat of him at her back, smell his delicious scent. It made her mouth go dry.

'Don't feel you have to sit and eat with me,' she said as he pushed her chair in for her. 'I'm sure you have plenty of other things to do.'

'Lucia wants us to eat together.' He came around the table and sat down opposite her. 'The hospitality of the ancient dukes is important to her and we have certain standards to uphold.' He glowered across the table at her. 'Especially to "family".'

This was clearly going to be so much harder than she'd thought. So much. His anger and resentment seemed to reach across the table and wrap around her throat, choking her.

But she wasn't Emily. She wasn't going to crumble and weep in the face of male temper. She often had to deal with that at her company and she'd never let it intimidate her before. She wasn't going to let it now.

Calmly, she picked up one of the snowy white napkins and shook it out over her lap. 'And what? You do everything she says?'

His gaze sharpened, cutting like a knife. 'She has been here for decades and is part of the family. I value her so, yes, on occasion I do what she says.' He said it as if this were self-evident and she was stupid for not understanding. Which of course made her bristle with annoyance.

Except she wasn't going to rise to his bad temper. Men could be so overly emotional sometimes and maybe this was doubly true of Spanish men.

You like his passion. You've always liked it.

In those early days after Emily had first married him, Alice had received lots of glowing emails from her sister about how attentive and protective Sebastián was. Emily had also overshared about his demands in bed and how thrilling that was. Alice had determinedly shoved away her envy, choked her jealousy, and shut down any fevered fantasies about what it would be like to be in Sebastian's arms herself.

She had been married to Edward, who had been loving and attentive with her even after they'd lost the baby. In fact, he'd been very careful and gentle and while she'd been recovering that had been exactly what she'd wanted. But years past the loss—at least physically—what she'd wanted was passion. Desperation. Possession. She'd wanted Edward to be hungry for her, desire her feverishly. She'd wanted to feel as though she was still attractive to him instead of an empty vessel, her fertility gone and her dreams of a family along with them.

But he hadn't been hungry for her, as it had turned out. He'd been hungry for her sister and who could blame him? Emily, petite and feminine and fertile, everything that Alice wasn't.

Edward had been a childhood friend of both her and Emily, and she'd had a crush on him for years. Except he'd only had eyes for Emily. And then Emily had left to go to university in Australia, leaving Edward behind with Alice, and the two of them had grown closer. Alice had been thrilled when he'd told her that he'd fallen in love with her and then asked her to marry him.

Her instead of Emily. Not that Emily had been jealous. No, she'd been Alice's bridesmaid at the wedding and had given the loveliest speech. Except…he'd obviously had second thoughts, hadn't he?

But Alice couldn't bear thinking about that particular past. It was futile. Edward was gone, and so was Emily, and all she had left was Diego.

'Well,' she said in a cool voice. 'Lucia is not here now, so please don't stay on my account.'

Sebastian's gaze didn't even flicker. 'You wanted to talk about Diego.' He made a gesture with one long-fingered hand. 'So. Talk.'

He didn't want to be here. He didn't want to sit opposite her and talk about how Diego would be better off going back to New Zealand with her. He didn't want to talk to her at all.

But Lucia had insisted and he wasn't so petty as to put aside the wishes of a loyal and valued employee. It was only one dinner and he could handle that and, besides, it was probably useful to get the subject of Diego over and done with now.

Then tomorrow, with any luck, Alice could leave.

'Fine,' she said with that irritating cool that got under his skin so badly. 'Why do you want Diego to stay with you?'

He'd already told her his reasons, but if she wanted him to repeat them then fine, he would.

He picked up the bottle of wine on the table and leaned forward, pouring some into her glass before doing the same for himself. 'He is my son. What other reason is there?'

'But…he's not actually your son, is he? He's Emily and Edward's.'

There was no denying that, though Sebastián preferred to keep that secret to himself. Easy enough when everyone thought Diego was his anyway. There had been some rumours, some mutterings about an affair in the elite circles he moved in after Emily had died, but he'd shut them down hard before they could gain traction.

No one was going to take Diego from him and that was final. Of course, Sebastián would tell him when he got older who his parents were and that he could find out more about them. After all, Sebastián wasn't like Mateo, his father, who'd hidden the identity of Sebastián's biological father from him, refusing to tell him anything about him. Sebastián would never be so cruel. But there was no other reason to give him up. Edward had no family and Emily's parents were dead. The only problem was Alice, who seemed to think she had a better claim on him.

'They aren't here,' he said with finality. 'But I am.'

'In case it's escaped your notice, so am I.' Her voice was as level and cool as her gaze. 'Emily's letter said that—'

'I don't care about Emily's letter,' he interrupted, his temper starting to slip the leash. 'Diego was born here, in the hacienda. I was there. I held him. He carries my name. He is my son, my heir, and there is nothing more to be said.'

This time her gaze flickered and she looked down

at her wine, picking it up and taking a sip. Faint colour stained her cheekbones. In the rose and gold of twilight, her skin looked luminous, lit from within, her hair glossy and soft. She was so different from Emily's honey-haired fragility and he didn't know why she appealed to him on such a gut-deep level. It didn't make any sense.

Emily had. He'd seen her on the terrace of a hotel in Madrid, enjoying a glass of wine and laughing with a friend. She'd been so pretty and joyful, and at that point in his life, after his father had so recently died, he'd needed joy. He'd been feeling the weight of the dukedom on his shoulders and, initially, she'd been only an escape for him, a distraction.

But after he'd spent more time with her and she'd told him of her dreams of having a family and a place to put down roots, he'd decided that she would be his new duchess. She hadn't made him feel as if he was missing something vital from his make-up, the way his father always had. She'd made him feel as if he was everything his father had always wanted, the scion of an ancient house. Proud. Strong. Honourable. As if the purest noble blood ran in his veins instead of that of the stable hand his mother had had an affair with.

The stable hand he'd had much more in common with than the man who'd brought him up.

'Emily was my sister,' Alice said. 'And I'm sorry, but there is plenty more to be said.' She reached down, brought out a piece of folded paper from the pocket of her dress, and held it out to him. 'Read this.'

He didn't look at the letter, only stared at her. 'Emily's letter, I presume?'

She nodded.

'And what does it say?' He tried to keep his tone even. 'That she was afraid to leave her son with me?'

'Read it, Sebastián.'

'No.' What was the point, when he knew what was in it already? 'I don't need to. She told you I would make a terrible father, didn't she?'

Alice let out a breath and put the letter down in the middle of the table. Then she fussed with her napkin. 'She said she wanted him to grow up...loved.'

Something twisted painfully inside him, but he made sure nothing showed on his face. He deserved that. They'd never spoken of the hole in the centre of their marriage. Emily had avoided any conversation about it because she hated confrontations, and since confrontations inevitably resulted in Emily weeping, so had he.

But he knew Emily had wanted more from him. She'd wanted love. He'd given her what he could, yet it hadn't been enough. She'd known he was holding something back, and he had been.

His heart. Because the problem was that love, in his experience, was mean and petty and cruel, and he'd wanted nothing to do with it.

Then he'd met Alice and what he'd felt for her, he'd never been able to pin down. He'd never wanted to. It had felt too obsessive, too painful, and so he'd put it aside. Now all that was left was physical desire—somehow that hadn't faded the way the other emotions had. That and the only love he'd ever permitted himself, for a little baby who wasn't even his.

She should have known you'd love him. She should.

No, she shouldn't. Why would she? She'd only wanted what any wife wanted from their husband, and he'd failed her. This letter and the pain that came with it were his punishment.

You should give Diego to Alice and be done with it.

Except every cell in his body rebelled against that thought. He wasn't giving up his son. Diego *was* his. He'd claimed him and a Castellano duke never gave up what was his.

Alice had gone still, watching him from across the table. What she saw he didn't know, until she said, 'I'm sorry. She only wanted what was best for her son and she thought him being in New Zealand was best for him.'

So, he hadn't hidden his grief and pain as well as he thought. He didn't like that she could read him and far more easily than Emily ever had.

She thinks Emily was right, that it's better for Diego to go back to New Zealand with her.

His heart twisted again as if in protest, though, really, why should it matter what Alice thought of him? He wanted her, it was true, and he always had, but all the other powerful feelings she'd managed to evoke had gone. He'd starved them completely. So it shouldn't matter. It shouldn't matter at all.

The urge to explain himself was still strong, but he shoved it aside, reaching for the cold, hard manner that had served him so well in the past. The manner his father had insisted on since that was the manner of a duke, not a common stable hand.

Sebastián leaned back in his chair and met her level gaze. There was a softness in her dark eyes that hadn't been there before. *Dios.* Did she feel sorry for him? Well, there was no need. He wasn't giving up his son—yes, *his* son. Not for anything.

'Why do you want him?' he asked instead. 'What is he to you?'

Her eyes widened slightly in surprise. 'I would have thought that was obvious. He's my nephew, Sebastián.'

Her calm was infuriating. 'So?'

'So?' Finally, as he'd seen out by the corral and on the stairs, fire flickered in her gaze. 'Like I told you, he's all I have left of Emily.'

'Blood is the only reason, then?' he demanded. 'Because your sister was his mother and your husband his father? What do you know of *him* though? Do you know that he takes a little time to settle and that he loves a Spanish lullaby? That he also likes the sound of horses' hooves during the day and will only nap if he can hear them? Do you know that his first smile was three weeks ago and for me? And that when he cries, sometimes only I can settle him?'

Something crossed her face then and it wasn't that cool, calm expression she'd been giving him. It was sharper, flickers of pain and grief.

Do you really think she's untouched by this? That she doesn't care? You know she does.

Before he'd met Alice and shut down all conversation

about her with Emily, his wife had told him about her tall, practical older sister. It hadn't been entirely complimentary and he'd envisaged a stodgy, humourless, dull sort of woman. Except that hadn't been the case. The two sisters had had a fractious relationship, it seemed, and yet it was clear that the pair of them had loved each other dearly despite it.

Of course this would affect Alice and he couldn't ignore that, no matter how much he wanted to.

She is passionate too, remember?

A memory surfaced, making his heartbeat suddenly fast. Of the last Christmas that Alice and Edward had come to the hacienda. It had been Christmas Eve and they'd all been in the living room sipping eggnog. It had been late, but he'd gone out to deal with an urgent matter in the stables, and when he'd come back, everyone else had gone to bed leaving only Alice standing by the fire, staring down at it.

What she'd been wearing, he couldn't remember, but he remembered every contour of her face and how the fire lit her as though she'd been painted with gold. The curve of her cheek. The lush dark fan of her lashes. The fullness of her bottom lip. And the sadness in her expression that had reached inside him and twisted hard.

He'd wanted to know what had made her so sad. He'd wanted to know everything, and then he'd wanted to fix it. And only after that had he wanted to take her in his arms and make her forget whatever it was that had caused her so much grief, wake the passion that he knew was inside her.

Except she hadn't been his and he hadn't been hers and he hadn't been able to do any of those things.

She'd looked up in that moment and their eyes had met. And whatever that thing was between them, the instant connection, the passionate energy, had suddenly sung in the room.

For one long minute they'd stared at one another and he'd seen the look in her eyes catch fire, and he'd known that if they'd both been free to choose, nothing could have kept them apart.

But they hadn't been free, and he was as wedded to his honour as much as he had been to Emily, and so choice hadn't been an option for him.

So he'd turned and walked away.

He wanted to walk away now but… He couldn't. Regardless of how sorry he felt for her, he wasn't going to let Diego go and the sooner she understood that, the better.

'I do care about him,' she said quietly. 'That's why I wanted to take him home. The country his parents came from, to the family that—'

'He was born Spanish. He *is* Spanish. And *I* am his family.'

Her jaw firmed and a spark leapt in her gaze, hot and burning. And he felt the same fire in him respond.

He should look away, he really should.

'I'm not leaving, Sebastián,' she said fiercely. 'I want to see my nephew and I will see him. You're not going to stop me.'

The sun was behind him, sending long fingers of light across her face, bathing it in glory. She wasn't typically beautiful, not as Emily had been. It was her spirit that was beautiful, that caught him by the throat and refused to let go. That made him want to sweep away all the dishes on Lucia's perfectly set table and grab her, haul her over it and into his arms. Put his mouth on hers and finally ease the hunger of years.

But he didn't. He couldn't. Following his own wants and needs had always been a mistake, and he wasn't going to start now. Besides, he had the honour of the Castellanos to uphold, and dukes did not do such things.

What does it matter if she sees him? Dukes aren't petty either, they are capable of justice and magnanimity.

He could do that. He could allow her to stay, and once she'd seen Diego and spent time with him she'd leave. In the meantime, he'd simply keep his distance from her. And if she insisted once again on taking Diego, he'd get his lawyers to deal with her. That way they could avoid any dangerous situations like this one, where anger only fuelled the fire that burned between them.

'Fine,' he said, his voice little more than a growl. 'You have three days. No longer.'

Then he did the only other thing he could.

He shoved back his chair and walked away.

CHAPTER FOUR

THE NEXT MORNING Alice sat in the dim, cool living room of the hacienda, a ball of nervous tension sitting in her gut. Her palms were sweaty and her heartbeat loud.

It was silly to feel so nervous about meeting a four-month-old baby, but she couldn't help it. She'd read all the books she'd been able to lay her hands on about babies when she was pregnant the first time, so it wasn't that she didn't know what to expect. It was only she had no actual practical experience with children, and what if she was terrible at it? What if she dropped him? What if he cried and refused to be comforted?

Emily hadn't called her at all after his birth, but she had emailed, and the only thing Alice had known about him from those emails was that he was a good baby who settled well and hardly ever cried.

'Do you know that he takes a little time to settle and that he loves a Spanish lullaby? That he also likes the sound of horses' hooves during the day and will only nap if he can hear them? Do you know that his first smile was three weeks ago and for me? And that when he cries, sometimes only I can settle him?'

Sebastián's voice from the night before at their aborted

dinner drifted through her head, deep and fierce. His expression had been hard yet the smoky gold of his eyes had shone like pirates' treasure at the bottom of a dark sea.

Her mouth had gone dry then, even as her own anger at him and his intransigence had leapt. He just...burned. He was that warrior with a sword in his hand and a baby in his arms, determined to protect. Determined to keep.

All she'd been able to think about was how hungry she was for a piece of that determination, that possessiveness. Because Edward hadn't had either, or, if he had, he'd never displayed it towards her.

He'd told her after she'd lost the baby, after she'd lost any hope of having a family of her own, that it would all be fine. They could adopt or even have a surrogate, anything she wanted. Yet every time she'd try bringing the subject of a child up again, he'd wave her gently away or agree vaguely, and then never follow up on it. He hadn't touched her the way he once had, either. Sex had become perfunctory, as if he'd been doing it because he'd had to, not because he'd wanted to. And then, in the last year, they hadn't had sex at all.

She'd always had issues around her femininity, largely driven by her parents' constant comparison—even if unconscious—to Emily, and in the last year of their marriage, Edward had made her feel as if she'd actively repulsed him. She'd tried to talk with him about it but he hadn't been interested, and it hadn't been until the car accident and Emily's letter that she'd found out why.

Edward had had a child with another woman. Her sister.

But she couldn't think about that now. It hurt too much

and, anyway, her feelings about the whole thing weren't important. Only Diego was.

She took a breath as Sofia, his nanny, came into the room, a small wrapped bundle in her arms.

Alice got to her feet, resisting the urge to wipe her hands down the front of her denim shorts.

Sofia said something soft in Spanish that Alice didn't understand—Lucia had told her that Sofia didn't speak English—and then put the little bundle into Alice's arms with an encouraging smile.

He was heavier than Alice had expected and warmer too.

She looked down into his face and met Emily's wide blue eyes staring back at her.

Her throat closed, her vision full of unexpected tears, but she forced them back. Perhaps she should have expected the likeness but she hadn't, and the complex wave of grief and joy that swamped her took her by surprise.

And there was joy. This little person was Emily's and, by extension of blood, hers, too, and the emotion that filled her, a powerful love, made Sebastián's ferocity about him suddenly understandable.

He felt this way about Diego too and so… How could she take Diego away from him? Yet also, how could she leave Diego herself?

The baby had settled against her and all her nerves had gone. Not that she knew any more about babies than she had a moment before, she was just even more certain that she couldn't leave him. She wouldn't. Three days, Sebastián had told her, but it wasn't enough. Which meant she was left with two choices: either she initiated proceedings with her lawyers to get Diego home or…she stayed here in Spain until she and Sebastián could work out some kind of custody arrangement.

Slowly, still cradling the little boy in her arms, Alice turned towards the windows and walked towards them. Her nephew's eyes were very wide, looking up into hers, and her heart contracted. She had a life back in New Zealand, but it wasn't much of one, only her, rattling around in the house in Auckland she and Edward had bought. There was her investment company and that was far more successful, but it could keep. She could also work remotely.

What else could she do?

Diego was Emily's and he had her eyes, and, even though Emily had wanted him to be brought back to New Zealand, Sebastián had a point. This couldn't be about what Emily wanted, but what was right for Diego. Not when Emily was dead. Still, her sister was right about one thing: this little boy needed to be loved and while Sebastián was certainly possessive, could he give Diego the love that he needed? Perhaps he could. Perhaps Emily's worries about him were unfounded and unfair. Regardless, Alice was also certain that her nephew needed a mother.

She looked down into his little face, seeing traces of Emily in his nose and in the delicacy of his mouth.

His own mother was gone now, but Alice was here. She could be that for him. She would *always* be that for him. Fathers could be difficult and sometimes harsh, and that needed to be balanced out with someone who could accept him no matter what.

Not that her own mother had been any more accepting of her, but at least she'd shown Alice what *not* to do. All a child really needed was to know that they were loved, and she had plenty of love to give. She would give it to Diego.

She spent a half-hour with the baby, just holding him and getting familiar with him, and when it was time for him to go down for a nap, she let the nanny take him.

As much as she wished she could, there was no point putting off the conversation she needed to have with Sebastián. He had to know immediately that she was intending to stay longer than three days. He wouldn't like it—he'd already made his feelings about her presence here known—but that was too bad. He'd have to deal with it.

After a cursory look around the hacienda failed to locate him, she went down to the stables. But he wasn't there either. Then, as she was coming back to the house, she heard the distinctive sound of helicopter rotors. There was a helipad not far from the house and, since any helicopter around was likely to be for him, she headed in that direction.

Sure enough, she arrived at the helipad in time to see him striding along the path from the house in the direction of the chopper. And despite herself, her breath caught.

He was in a suit today, perfectly tailored to highlight his height and muscled physique. It was of dark blue wool and he wore a black business shirt with it and a blue silk tie. Darkly handsome, phenomenally arrogant and every inch the Spanish duke, his golden eyes smouldering like distant fires, he almost stopped her in her tracks.

Stupid of her. She couldn't let him get to her, especially with the well-being of her nephew at stake.

With an effort, Alice threw off the paralysing effect of his charisma, and called, 'Sebastián! I need a moment.'

He came to a stop and glanced at her as she approached, his gaze raking her from head to toe. She could feel herself start to blush, which was infuriating. Compared to him, all dark beauty and athletic grace, she felt dowdy and frumpy, and she resented it. She wished she'd worn the red dress today, but Lucia had taken it to be washed, and so she'd flung on a baggy pair of denim shorts and a loose black T-shirt. Emily had always dressed herself to the nines because she'd said that Sebastián 'liked it'. What he must think of her current outfit she had no idea and didn't particularly want to know either.

'What do you want?' he asked coldly. 'Be quick, please.'

Alice tried to calm her frantically beating heart. 'We need to talk more about Diego.'

His expression darkened. 'Do we? I thought we said everything we needed to last night.'

'You might have,' Alice snapped, needled by his tone. 'But I didn't.'

Sebastián glanced towards the helicopter then back at her. 'Well, it will have to wait. I'm leaving on a business trip and I need to go now. You can call me when you get back to New Zealand.'

'No, I won't be calling you, because I'm not actually

leaving,' Alice informed him flatly. 'Three days isn't enough time, Sebastián. Diego needs a mother in his life and, since Emily is gone, I've decided to be that mother.'

His hard handsome features remained still, carved out of stone. Only his golden eyes burned. 'That option is not available—'

'I'm staying,' she interrupted. 'I'm not leaving him.'

A muscle leapt in his jaw. 'If I find you still here when I return, I will have you arrested for trespassing.'

Alice's temper began to slip through her fingers. 'Do it, then,' she shot back. 'I'll pitch a tent here on the lawn.'

The pilot of the helicopter appeared suddenly at Sebastián's elbow and said something to him in a low voice. Sebastián nodded curtly then glanced back at Alice. 'I haven't got time to talk about this now. We will discuss it—'

He broke off as Alice turned from him and started furiously towards the helicopter. Because one thing was clear; he was only going to keep fobbing her off or walking away, and she was tired of it. She hadn't come all the way here just to be told what to do by Sebastián Castellano. She had come for her nephew, and they were *going* to talk about him, business trip or not.

A discussion needed to be had, an agreement come to, and they would come to it even if she had to go with him on his stupid business trip herself.

The pilot came rushing after her, but if he'd been intending to stop her he was too late, because by the time he arrived, Alice had already climbed into the helicopter and had belted herself in.

Sebastián halted by the open helicopter door and stared at her. 'What the hell are you doing, Alice?' he demanded.

'Coming with you,' she said, daring him to protest. 'If you won't stay and have this conversation with me here, I'll come with you and have it there.'

'You will do no such thing,' he growled, anger disturbing the ice in his voice, his accent more pronounced. 'Get out of the helicopter right now.'

'No.' Alice lifted her chin. 'If you want me out, you'll have to pull me out yourself.'

Fury burned in his eyes, his body full of a coiled tension that was almost palpable, and for a minute she wondered if she'd made a mistake and if he would actually pull her out himself. Then the pilot said something to him, and he cursed again, low and vicious. Then he said, 'Fine. *Vámonos.*' And got into the helicopter and pulled the door shut.

It was only then that Alice realised that she *had* in fact made a mistake. A terrible one. Because as soon as the door closed, she was locked into the helicopter with him and it was a small space. He was right next to her, the warmth of one powerful thigh almost touching hers, and she was surrounded by his delicious scent; masculine spice, sunlight, and hay.

Her mouth dried and her stomach dipped as he held out a headset without glancing at her.

Okay, so this was actually going to happen, was it? He'd called her bluff and now they were actually going to…

'I… I need to get a bag,' she said, trying not to sound so hesitating.

Only then did he glance at her. 'Too late. We need to leave now because we're going to lose our weather window.'

'But I—'

'You wanted to come, so you're coming.' One black brow rose. 'Or have you changed your mind?'

He wanted her to change her mind; she could see it in his eyes. He wanted her to give in and get out of the helicopter. And maybe she should. Maybe she could wait to have this conversation when he returned.

But he was right. It was too late. She couldn't back down now and she wasn't going to.

Alice held his gaze and grabbed the headset from him. 'No, of course not. So where are we going?'

'Madrid.'

Shutting himself into a confined space for the couple of hours it would take them to fly to Madrid, and then to spend the duration of his business trip with his sister-in-law, was likely to be a mistake, and Sebastián was well aware.

But she'd left him with no choice.

He was hardly going to manhandle her out of the helicopter and even though he would dearly have loved to leave her sitting in it for the next couple of hours, the pilot had been very clear about the window they had for departure. There was a storm coming in over the mountains and they had to go now.

She hadn't been expecting him to call her bluff, that was certain, not given the way her dark eyes had widened as he'd climbed in beside her and shut the door. But she'd covered her shock very well, her chin determined, her expression set, her lush mouth in a hard line.

Maybe it was for the best in the end. They couldn't keep having the same conversation and he was tired of her pushing him on it. He could involve the police to get her removed from the house if she continued to be difficult, but he didn't want to do that. Lucia would be appalled, and Alice was his sister-in-law after all.

She wasn't going to be put off, which meant he was going to have to sit down with her and come to some arrangement about Diego. Some kind of civilised arrangement.

The only problem was that he didn't feel particularly civilised, not with her sitting next to him, wearing only a pair of denim shorts and a loose black T-shirt that was so thin he could see the lace of her bra. Her legs were long and tanned and smooth, and they were sitting close enough that her bare skin nearly brushed the wool of his suit trousers.

He could barely think, and he was furious with himself.

He'd thought he'd made himself clear when he'd walked away from the dinner table the night before. Yet he should have known that she wouldn't meekly do what he said, that she wouldn't stay the requisite three days and then leave. And he thought he'd been smart in taking this business trip over the time she would be staying so he didn't have to have more contact with her. Except it hadn't turned out that way and he still couldn't understand how it had got away from him.

He only knew that he hadn't taken into account her sheer stubbornness and now he was dealing with the consequences. Which were Alice, sitting next to him in a helicopter for two hours, one bare thigh pressed against his, and him as breathless as a teenage boy with his first crush.

The pilot had got in and was spinning up the rotors, and the moment where he could have got rid of her was gone. So, he put on his headset and tried to ignore her as they lifted off smoothly, climbing into the sky, heading for the mountains.

'So,' Alice's voice came crisply through the headset, 'Diego needs a mother, Sebastián. You do know that, don't you?'

He'd been going to work on the trip to Madrid, but with her sitting next to him there was no hope of that. 'We can talk about this when we get to Madrid,' he said curtly.

'If this is a two-hour trip then we might as well discuss it now.'

Sebastián gritted his teeth. 'Diego has Sofia. Until I—'

'Sofia, I'm sure, is a faultless nanny, but she's not his mother.'

'No, his mother is dead,' he bit out. 'And if you'd let me finish, I would have told you that he will have a mother eventually. When I remarry.'

There was a shocked silence that satisfied him far too much and yet made him feel guilty at the same time. It was too soon after Emily's death to even contemplate, but he had to. With his wife gone, he needed to remarry, because Alice was right, Diego did need a mother. Sebastián's own mother had died when he was born so he'd grown up without one, his cold, distant father his only parent. He didn't want that for his son. Not that he had any intention of being like Mateo, but a child should have at least some maternal influence in their life.

Also, he wanted more children. Diego was his heir, despite not being of Sebastián's own blood, which was fine. Sebastián was not Mateo's biological son after all. But he had been an only child and it had been lonely. Diego should have siblings.

'Remarry?' Alice echoed. 'But Emily is only two—'

'Months gone?' he interrupted. 'Yes, I'm well aware. Still, I need more than one heir and you're right, Diego does need a mother. In which case I'm going to need another wife.'

'Emily said you were cold. I had no idea just how much.'

He glanced at her and her dark eyes met his, the expression in them furious. He couldn't blame her. He *was* cold. His heart had always led him astray and so he had to be careful. Mateo had been very clear what was expected of a duke and that was not to allow his emotions to get the better of him.

Yet it was difficult to hear what his own wife had accused him of on more than one occasion coming out of Alice's mouth.

'You're so cold,' Emily had said a couple of times. *'Don't you care about anything?'*

But he had cared, that was the problem. He'd cared too much and, unfortunately for Emily, it wasn't her that he'd cared about, not as intensely as he'd cared about Alice.

'I prefer practical,' he said, wrestling with his own temper. 'I have responsibilities now and I need to keep Diego's future in mind.'

Anger flickered in her eyes. 'Oh? Until you have a child of your own blood, you mean?'

Sebastián stared at her a long moment. Did she really think that was what his issue was? Apparently so. Well, he needed to disabuse her of that notion. 'No,' he said. 'Diego is my heir and will remain so, no matter how many other children I have. But I don't want him to grow up an only child. He should have siblings.'

Alice didn't reply immediately, but her gaze was searching. Did she not believe him? Did she really think he would lie about this?

Are you surprised? She doesn't know you, remember? You can't blame her for having a low opinion of you when you cultivated that yourself.

A shiver of electricity moved through him, though why he had no idea. Because it was true. He'd deliberately made himself unpleasant when it came to her. He was never openly rude but was always subtly cold. Distant. Making sure she never got too close.

No wonder she thinks Diego would be better off with her. And no wonder she believed what Emily told her about you.

'Siblings?' she asked. 'That's really the only reason? Come on, Sebastián. You can't tell me you wouldn't disinherit him in a second if you had a child of your own blood.'

A flicker of pain went through him, though he could think of no earthly reason why, when what she thought of him didn't matter in the slightest. He'd never given her reason to think differently and what was the point now?

However, she still seemed to believe that Diego was unimportant to him and he really couldn't let that stand.

'I see you believe every word Emily told you about me,' he said. 'And that she didn't tell you anything about my history.'

A small crease appeared between Alice's eyebrows. 'What history?'

He didn't tell people about his true origins. His father had guarded the secret jealously and, after Mateo had passed away, so had he. Even now, even after the rumours about him had largely disappeared, only Emily had known the truth. He'd sworn her to secrecy and it was clear she hadn't told her sister a thing. Perhaps he shouldn't let Alice know now. Then again, if he did, she'd understand how he felt about Diego. Perhaps she'd then go home and leave him in peace.

'I am not actually my father's son by blood,' he said. 'A childhood illness left him sterile, but he needed an heir and so when he found out about my mother's affair with a stable hand, and that she was pregnant because of it, he raised the child as his own.'

Alice's eyes widened. 'You?'

'Yes. No one ever knew I wasn't Mateo's son. He made sure of it.'

She looked shocked. 'Did Emily know?'

'Of course.'

'And Diego…'

'Will be my heir. I'll bring him up as my own son and, no, it won't make any difference if I have children of my own blood.'

'So you'll treat him the way your father treated you?'

'No,' he snapped before he could stop himself. 'I would never do that.'

Something shifted in her gaze, though he wasn't sure what it was. Interest perhaps, or curiosity. 'Why? How did your father treat you?'

But he wasn't going to have that conversation, not with her. 'It doesn't matter. All that matters is that Diego will not be disadvantaged because he is not biologically related to me. He will be my son in every other way.'

She didn't say anything immediately, the expression in her gaze unreadable.

'You have my word,' he added, because if she was searching for the truth then he'd give it to her. She needed to know that, while he might have failed Emily, he wouldn't fail Diego.

It had never been a good idea to look into her dark eyes for too long and he knew he shouldn't look now. He didn't want her to see the need burning in him for her. He had to keep it locked away. It would be a disaster if she knew, because then…

Then you might throw caution to the winds? Say 'to hell with it' and take her? Ignore your control and give your heart what it wants instead?

He could. His wife was gone and there was nothing stopping him now. Nothing but the years of denial and guilt and relentless self-control. Nothing but his father's constant, painful example of how love and desire could eat you alive from the inside out and turn you into someone vindictive and cruel and petty.

He wouldn't follow that example. He'd spent years trying to do the right thing, the honourable thing, because he was a Castellano duke and Castellano dukes were always honourable. He couldn't allow those years to be wasted on something so ephemeral and meaningless as sex. And that was all it would be. Just sex and nothing more. *Dios*, if he wanted a woman, he'd find someone else. Someone far less complicated than Alice.

So he kept tight control of himself and it was she who looked away, glancing out of the window, colour staining the olive skin of her cheekbones.

Curious that he'd made her blush, not that he should have noticed.

'You're not who I thought you were,' she said after a moment.

He studied the curve of her cheek and the fan of delicate dark lashes almost resting on it. They were very long, those lashes, and silky looking. 'And who did you think I was?'

'Someone who'd let Diego go easily. I thought that you wouldn't want him because he's not yours.'

He shouldn't keep looking at her, and yet he couldn't stop. The sun through the window was glossing her dark hair. She had it in a low ponytail at the back of her neck and he couldn't help noting that the T-shirt she wore was faded. Old clothes. She really hadn't expected to be going anywhere today, had she?

'Well,' he said. 'You thought wrong.'

Her eyes had widened, and they were even darker, her pupils dilating. Abruptly the tension between them pulled tight, the air in the helicopter filling with a crackling heat.

The colour in her cheeks deepened and a startled expression flickered through her velvet dark eyes, as if she'd read every thought in his head, and that was bad, very bad. He'd wondered, after that Christmas Eve moment in the living room, whether she'd guessed at how he felt about her. Yet that moment had never repeated itself and she'd never said anything, so he'd told himself she hadn't guessed, and it was better that way.

Perhaps she hadn't. She did now, though.

He should have said nothing, should have let the moment pass unremarked. But he didn't.

'No,' he said fiercely instead. 'Don't look at me like that, Alice.'

Her eyes widened even further, the red blush staining her cheeks now creeping down her neck, and that was when he realised things were going to be even more complicated than they were already.

Because Alice felt the same way he did.

CHAPTER FIVE

ALICE'S HEART WAS beating so loud she was surprised it wasn't audible through the entire helicopter cabin, even despite the headset she wore.

He'd told her so fiercely not to look at him that she'd obeyed without even thinking about it, turning to look out of the window instead. Except she paid no attention to the Spanish countryside unrolling beneath them.

All she could think about was the moment when he'd looked into her eyes, and she'd seen something leap in the depths of his golden gaze. Something hot. Something that had felt like a caress of flame over her skin, searing her.

Once, she'd thought she'd seen something similar in his eyes a couple of years ago, on Christmas Eve. Everyone else had gone to bed and he'd disappeared down to the stables. She'd been alone. She'd stood in front of the fire, allowing herself to relax for the first time since she and Edward had arrived, because she never could, not in Sebastián's presence. She'd been thinking that perhaps this would be the last Christmas she and Edward would come to Spain, because it was getting too difficult for her. Emily had been asking her what was wrong and why was she so quiet, and, really, it would have been easier to stay at home. She could hardly tell her sister that it was because of Sebastián. Because his presence made her want things she shouldn't want.

Something had alerted her, as if the air pressure in the room had changed, and she'd glanced towards the doorway. And he'd been there, staring at her, the look on his face fierce with an expression she hadn't understood. His eyes had seemed to burn as golden as the flames in the grate and she'd felt herself catch fire along with them.

But then he'd turned away abruptly and left without a word. Afterwards, she'd told herself it was nothing. That perhaps he'd been looking for Emily and the expression she'd seen on his face was anger that he couldn't find her. Anger that it was Alice in the room instead of his wife.

Perhaps it's anger now.

Alice swallowed, her heart still beating far too loud. Their conversation had definitely been fraught and difficult and, yes, he was angry with her. But…the heat in his eyes hadn't been anger, she was certain. There had been an intensity to it that made her feel as if she were prey under the gaze of a starving wolf.

She shut her eyes and took a deep, soundless breath, trying to get her heartbeat under control. But that only made it worse, because it only made her more aware of his powerful, muscular body sitting next to hers and how tense he was, like a drawn bow just before the arrow was released.

Desperately she tried to think of something to say to ease the weight of the silence, but she couldn't think of a word. All she could think of was that look in his eyes.

The look she'd dreamed of him giving her so many times, even though she knew it was wrong.

He was hungry for her. He wanted her. Maybe she'd imagined it back then on that snowy Christmas Eve. But she wasn't imagining it now.

It doesn't change things.

No, no, it couldn't. Neither of them was bound by marriage vows now, it was true, but he'd still been her sister's husband. And she'd been Edward's wife. She'd loved Edward once and, while he'd been unfaithful to her, she wouldn't use the excuse of his death to jump into bed with someone else only two months after he'd gone. Especially not when that someone was her own sister's husband. Edward might have not been able to control himself around Emily, but she'd been controlling herself around Sebastián for years and she wasn't about to stop doing so now. Also, if Sebastián himself had wanted to do anything about that hunger, he would have done so. At the very least he would have said something, but, since he hadn't, it was obvious that he wasn't about to take any action himself.

It didn't matter. It had never mattered. Neither of them had been in any position to act on their feelings before and they still weren't. There was Diego to consider after all.

Perhaps it would be better to simply ignore the moment as if it hadn't happened. Pretend that she hadn't seen the heat in his eyes, that he hadn't told her to stop looking at him like that.

As if you're just as starving as he is?

She forced the thought away. No, she wasn't starving. She didn't want him. It was better if she convinced herself of that because nothing was going to change between them. Nothing at all.

Slowly, Alice opened her eyes and risked a glance at the man sitting beside her. He had a sleek tablet in his hands and was doing something that must be very important because he was staring ferociously at it as if it were the most fascinating thing in the entire universe.

Her thoughts drifted back to what he'd told her about his father and about how he wasn't Mateo's biological son, that he'd been the product of his mother's affair with a stable hand. That little fact had got lost in the abrupt crackling heat that had sprung between them, but she couldn't forget it.

That had shocked her. It had also made his determination to claim Diego as his own far more understandable, since Diego was the product of an affair, too. Except Sebastián had been adamant that he wouldn't treat Diego the way his own father had treated him. He hadn't elaborated on what way that was, but, given how he'd brushed off her question, it probably wasn't good.

It made her curious, though, and she wanted to know more. But this wasn't the time for yet more difficult conversations, so she left him to whatever work he was doing, staying silent for the rest of the trip and staring out of the window. Trying to distract herself with plans for Diego and how she could find ways to keep herself in his life that wouldn't involve too many confrontations with Sebastián.

It wasn't until they came in to land on the rooftop of a beautiful old building in central Madrid that Alice realised she should have been thinking about more immediate concerns. Such as being in his presence for however long this business trip lasted and just how that was going to work.

As soon as the helicopter's rotors slowed, Sebastián got out, talking in rapid Spanish to a tall, older woman in a black uniform who was waiting on the rooftop. She glanced at Alice then back at Sebastián, nodding all the while. Then, without a backward glance, Sebastián walked away.

Okay, so that was how it was going to be. That was good. Distance was better for both of them.

Alice got out of the helicopter and the woman introduced herself in heavily accented Spanish as Gabriela, the duke's housekeeper, and said that he'd instructed her to show Alice around and to provide anything she might need.

Where the hacienda was full of old-world charm, Sebastián's Madrid apartment was sleek and modern. Inside it was all white walls, black accents, and gold fittings. Gabriela showed Alice to a beautiful bedroom with long gauzy curtains covering the windows and wide white bed scattered with pillows and cushions. Then she asked Alice what she needed in the way of clothes and other 'comforts' since she hadn't brought anything with her.

Alice—uncharacteristically—hadn't remembered that until Gabriela mentioned it and abruptly became aware that she was standing in this beautiful, sleek-looking apartment that had probably cost millions and she was in old shorts and a T-shirt. And not only that, but she also hadn't brought her phone or any money, or even her passport.

She began to explain to Gabriela, but the older woman only shrugged, simply stating that since the duke had instructed that all her needs be met, they would be met. Clothes would be brought for her, as would anything else.

It was going to be difficult to refuse since she could hardly keep wearing her clothes for three days straight, and she had no money to buy any more. However, Alice did insist on finding her own clothes and that an itemised list of prices be kept so she could pay Sebastián back. Gabriela merely shrugged.

The afternoon was taken up with a visit to an incredibly high-end department store with Gabriela, who attended to all the payments. Alice tried to buy a few cheapish items, only to have hangers of beautiful dresses shoved at her by the very insistent housekeeper.

Again, she very much wanted to refuse, but since there was nothing to do in the apartment except sit, and since she was in Madrid and having dresses shoved at her, she might as well try them on, if only to keep herself amused.

Unfortunately it seemed that quite a few of them Gabriela insisted she buy, since 'the duke is paying' and then some matching shoes needed to be bought, also underwear of the lacy, silky variety. Then Alice found herself back in the apartment that evening, surrounded by bags and boxes and feeling a little like Cinderella.

Everything had been astonishingly expensive, and she

was already trying to think of how she would pay for it all, and berating herself for spending so much money. Except she'd never had a shopping trip like it. Even when she and Emily would do a sisters' shopping trip, it had mostly ended up being about Emily buying lovely, delicate, feminine things, while nothing had seemed to fit Alice the way it fitted her sister. She always felt too tall, too large, too ungainly. An Amazon trying to fit into a dress made for a delicate fairy.

But she hadn't been able to resist the dresses that Gabriela had shown her, each one making her feel as if somehow some magic had been employed and she really was the fairy she'd always longed to be.

It was silly to indulge herself like that, not to mention pointless. Because where would she ever wear any of them? At home it was always suits to work and then sweat pants in the evening to sit in front of the TV. Even when Edward was alive, that was all she'd wear. He hadn't seemed to care, which had been nice on the one hand, but, on the other, he'd never mentioned it when she *had* made an effort, so it had also left her feeling unappreciated.

Gabriela hadn't mentioned when Sebastián would be back, which was annoying. She had to force this discussion with him somehow, get some kind of resolution, otherwise what would have been the point of coming to Madrid?

An idea stole through her head, one she'd never contemplated before and shouldn't be contemplating now and yet she couldn't shake it.

There was one way she could get his attention. One

way to *make* him have this conversation with her. One way to bring him round to her way of thinking, even.

She could use the physical chemistry between them, the desire that flared whenever they were near each other. It was maybe a little manipulative, but this was Diego they were talking about and she'd do whatever she had to do for him.

Of course, there was always the risk of such a plan backfiring on her, but it wasn't as if she were going to sleep with Sebastián. She'd already decided that nothing would happen between them. She'd just...toy with him a little, cloud his judgement. It wasn't anything he hadn't been doing to her for the past five years, after all.

Feeling pleased with herself, she showered in the white marble and gold bathroom then carefully chose one of the dresses she'd bought, a beautiful deep red silk number with a plunging neckline and cut on the bias to enhance her curves, before falling from her hips to swirl provocatively around her thighs.

Then she went out to the huge open-plan dining/living area where she sat in grand solitude as Gabriela served her a delicious dinner of a tortilla and salad. No mention was made of when Sebastián would return, but that was fine. She'd just wait until he appeared.

Afterwards, Alice curled up with a book in one of the comfortable armchairs in the small library. On the low coffee table in front of her, Gabriela had put a glass of extraordinarily good Spanish red wine and some squares of chocolate.

It was nice to be looked after, Alice realised, and she

could see why Emily had liked it so much. No thought was required and no energy expended. All she had to do was sit there and have all her needs catered for and for someone like her, who usually preferred to have control over most parts of her life, it was refreshing not to have to do it all herself.

She was just on the point of deciding whether she should have another piece of chocolate or a coffee to keep herself awake, when the door to the library opened and Sebastián walked in.

Instantly all thoughts of sleep vanished.

He stood in the doorway, darkly handsome, intensely attractive, with his tie loosened, the top buttons of his black business shirt undone, his golden eyes widening as he noticed her sitting there.

Her heart began to beat faster, harder, the air in the room getting as thick and electric as it had in the helicopter earlier on that day.

The approach she'd chosen for this conversation was dangerous, which meant she couldn't rush it. She had to do this carefully.

Taking a breath, she put down her wine and the book, slipping from the armchair and getting to her feet.

'Good, I'm glad you're back,' she said into the tense silence, hoping she didn't sound as breathless as she felt. 'We need to talk.'

He hadn't moved, his gaze searing as it scanned her from head to foot, following the curves of the red silk dress and then back up again. And there it was, once more, that hungry look in his eyes, the burning intensity that stole all the air from her lungs.

'Sebastián,' she managed, though what else she'd been going to say, she had no idea. Because that was the moment he finally moved towards her, striding forward as if for battle, as if nothing was going to stand in his way. And she should have done something, followed through with her plan, but she didn't. She stood there, her heart beating its way out of her chest as he stopped in front of her. Then he lifted his hands as if reaching for a prize he'd worked long and hard for, thrusting his fingers into her hair and dragging her head back. And his mouth covered hers and the whole universe stopped.

There was heat and demand and hunger. Years of aching need. Longing and desperation and she was lost to it. All her good intentions fell away, her plan and everything that went with it, all her guilt, all her grief. There was only his hard mouth on hers in a kiss that she'd spent so many years fantasising about, and now was finally happening.

She couldn't control herself. The thought of stopping simply didn't enter her head. Instead, she groaned in sheer relief and melted into him, winding her arms around his neck, leaning into the heat of his muscular body, opening her mouth, and letting him in. And he tasted as good as she'd always imagined he would. No, better. Like dark chocolate and Scotch, and everything delicious and sinful and wrong.

All of this was wrong and yet no power on earth would have pulled her away. His fingers were tight in her hair and he was devouring her as if he were starving. His tongue in her mouth, exploring, demanding, taking.

Then he shifted one hand from her hair down to the small of her back, pulling her hard against him, only the thin silk of her dress and the wool of his suit trousers separating them. She could feel the tensile strength of his body and it excited her. There was so much power there and he was so tall. Taller than Edward. Broader and more muscular, too. She loved that. Loved how it made her feel so delicate and feminine in comparison. She could feel the hard length of his arousal pressing between her thighs, his hunger for her obvious.

It thrilled her down to the bone.

She'd spent so long feeling unattractive and unwanted, and nothing she'd done to make herself more appealing had made any difference to Edward. He'd withdrawn from her so relentlessly and completely that eventually she'd stopped trying.

But now Sebastián wanted her. Sebastián was desperate for *her* and she wanted more than anything in the world to give herself to him.

The kiss went on and on, increasing in desperation until eventually Sebastián dropped one hand from her back and took a fistful of her dress, tugging hard and ripping the silk from her body. She barely noticed. Then she was on her back on the carpet in front of the small fireplace, and he was tearing at her underwear like a madman, shredding the flimsy material and getting rid of it.

His eyes glowed bright like coins, the expression on his beautiful face ferocious with desire. She grabbed at his tie, ripping it away then clawing at the buttons on his shirt, jerking it open to get to the hot skin beneath. She had dreamed of touching him for so long and she felt as if she might die if she didn't right this instant.

He gave a low masculine growl as her hands touched his chest, hot skin and crisp hair and hard muscle. Then he shifted, reaching down to jerk the buttons of his trousers open, shoving her thighs apart as he did so, pressing them wide, opening her up to him.

She was panting now, the pressure and the dragging ache between her legs becoming impossible to fight. The air around them was full of the sound of their panting breaths and then suddenly he was there, the long thick length of him pressing through the soft folds of her sex. Sliding into her so easily, so perfectly, just as she knew he would.

He was made for her. She felt it deep in her heart. In her soul.

She cried out as he settled inside her and arched up into him, the press of his body against hers, the weight of him on her so right. His fingers threaded through hers as he took her hands up and over her head, pressing them down to the carpet and holding them there. And he began to move, hard and deep, golden eyes staring down into hers as if transfixed.

There was fierce desire in them and also shock, as if he couldn't believe they were actually doing this, and she felt the same shock echoing through her.

They were joined finally and at last, and the sensations were indescribable. So much heat and need. Relief and a burgeoning wonder at what was happening. At how good it was to be here together, after so many years.

She wanted to say his name but she couldn't speak, the feelings becoming more and more intense with each passing moment. Her fingers tightened around his as she watched the pleasure glow in his eyes and knew he could see the same in hers. It was an endless feedback loop of ecstasy that only stoked the madness higher.

It didn't last. It couldn't. They'd held back for so long and she was only human.

The orgasm came crashing down on her with unstoppable force far too quickly and with far more power than she'd ever imagined, a wave of pleasure so intense that his name finally burst from her in a hoarse cry. Then he was moving faster and harder until he bent his head and covered her mouth again as it took him too.

Sebastián lay there, the silence broken only by their fractured breathing, for one long moment blissfully free of thought. Reality was the softness of the woman beneath him, the scent of sex and lavender in the air, and a physical contentment he couldn't recall ever feeling.

Then reality crashed in on him.

This was Alice. His sister-in-law. And he'd lost control. Spectacularly. All his good intentions, everything he'd told himself about restraint and being cold, being distant, had gone out of the window the moment he'd seen her curled up in the chair. In that red silk dress that made her sexy enough to tempt an angel.

And an angel he was not.

All day, in the endless meetings he'd attended with his bankers and lawyers, securing Diego's future, and setting in stone that this boy was his son and heir, when he should have been paying attention, he'd been thinking of Alice.

Thinking of that moment in the helicopter, when he'd known in an instant that she'd wanted him every bit as badly as he'd wanted her. But he'd decided that he would not act on it. Could not act on it. And every second of the day he'd told himself the same thing over and over, that desire was a bad thing, it led people down the wrong path. It hurt people. It made them mean and cruel and petty. It made them like his father, and he wouldn't allow that to happen to himself. He was better than that.

He'd purposely stayed later than he'd needed to with his lawyers, just to make doubly sure of his control, and when he'd finally got back to the apartment, he'd been looking forward to settling in the library with a glass of good Scotch.

Except she'd been there, curled in the chair. Her hair loose over her shoulders, wearing a red silk dress that clung to every one of her delectable curves. She'd looked up from the book she'd been reading, and her dark eyes had met his and the moment from the helicopter had rushed back in on him.

Then she'd got to her feet, the fabric of the dress swirling around her, outlining lush breasts and generous hips, and all he'd been able to think about was how much he wanted to rip that dress from her body and finally get his hands all over her. How impossible it was maintaining such control over himself when she was right in front of him, and they were both finally free.

How he couldn't bear it a second longer.

Every step he'd taken towards her had been a mistake, every action as he'd reached for her a grievous error. They'd built on each other, all those mistakes, until he'd been crushed by the weight of them and then nothing had mattered any more.

To slide his fingers through the silken glory of her hair and then feel the softness of her mouth open beneath his had been like finding water in the desert. Such a profound relief. Then having her body press against his... He'd never let himself fantasise about it but the feel of her had been better than anything he could have imagined.

He'd wanted to spend hours exploring her lush body, but there hadn't been any time to spare. He'd been too desperate. And when he'd spread her thighs and finally slid inside her, becoming one with her, it had felt like coming home.

You have made a mistake. A terrible mistake.

He didn't want the cold trickle of doubt to disturb his contentment, but it did all the same, the trickle becoming a flood.

He'd crossed the line he'd drawn for himself years ago, broken the private vow he'd made never to treat her as anything more than his sister-in-law. It didn't matter that Emily had gone. It didn't matter that she'd been unfaithful to him, and that they hadn't shared a bed for over a year. It didn't matter that she'd fallen in love with someone else.

He'd promised himself he would never do anything about Alice, and he'd broken that promise. Now all those years of denying himself meant nothing.

Desire was a terrible force. It had driven Sebastián's mother into the affair that had eventually led to her having Sebastián and then dying. It had fuelled Mateo's jealous rage at being betrayed, which he'd then taken out on Sebastián.

And Sebastián's own desire to belong to someone had driven him to seek out the only man he'd ever felt a kinship with: Javier, who had managed the stables and who'd turned out to be Sebastian's biological father—not that he'd known that at the time.

Desire caused nothing but pain and he'd tried so hard to keep his own in check, but he'd failed. And it was too late to pretend it hadn't happened. Too late to go back and make a different choice.

You didn't even remember a condom.

Yet more ice slid down his spine.

He shifted, pushing himself away from Alice and getting to his feet, putting his clothes back in order. His hands were shaking.

'Sebastián?' Her voice was soft and husky and there was an uncertain note in it that tugged at his heart.

He gave himself a minute to gather the tattered remnants of his control then glanced at her.

She was sitting on the floor, her bra half off one shoulder, her knickers a scrap of ripped lace off to one side, her hair a black smoky storm. Her lips were red and full, and she looked thoroughly ravaged and so utterly beautiful he nearly lost control a second time and reached for her.

Instead, he said the first words that entered his head. 'I didn't use a condom.'

Colour crept through her cheeks, and she glanced away. 'It's fine. You don't need to worry about that.' Her voice had lost the uncertainty, becoming so determinedly neutral, he knew that somehow he'd hurt her.

Of course you hurt her. You took her like an animal and then the first words out of your mouth were about a lack of condom. Nothing about her. Nothing about how beautiful she was or how good she made you feel.

His chest tightened. She was reaching for the remains of her dress and trying to put it on, though it was now thoroughly ruined. Her hands were shaking too.

'Alice,' he said, trying to sound gentler. 'I should have found one—'

'I said, you don't have to worry about that.' She was looking at him now, and he could see a flicker of anger in her eyes.

'Why not?' he asked without thinking. 'Are you on the pill?'

She got to her feet, still clutching the remains of her dress around her, and lifted her chin. Her expression was shuttered and that made his chest tighten even more. 'No.' Her voice was as flat as his had been. 'You don't need to worry about that, because I can't have children, okay?'

He blinked in shock. 'What?'

'I'm not sure how much clearer I can be, Sebastián.' The red silk falling around her half-naked body and the oddly defiant look in her eyes made her look as regal as an empress. 'I had a bad miscarriage a couple of years ago and now I'm infertile. So don't worry, you won't be having any unexpected consequences from this little… mistake.'

She sounded cool and yet he knew now that she wasn't. He'd held her in his arms, been inside her, felt her passion join with his in a bonfire so bright and so hot it eclipsed the sun. He also knew that, no matter how expressionless or cool her voice sounded, the miscarriage had been the thing that had devastated her. Had dimmed that light inside her. And now he'd been thoughtless with a question he shouldn't have asked and it had hurt her. *He* had hurt her. And she didn't deserve that.

'Alice…' He took a breath, running a distracted hand through his hair. 'I had no idea…'

'Of course, you didn't. Why would you? No one knew except Edward.'

'Emily didn't—'

'No.'

'I'm sorry,' he said when she didn't say anything else. 'I didn't mean to hurt you.'

'I'm not hurt.' She tightened the fabric around her. 'Now, if you don't mind, I think I'll go to bed.'

She began to move past him, but his hand shot out before he was even conscious of it doing so, his fingers closing around her arm, her skin warm and silky beneath his fingertips. She stopped in her tracks, looking straight ahead. 'Sebastián, I don't—'

'We need to talk about what just happened,' he said

shortly, because now he was starting to think straight again, they really did. He could, of course, pretend that this had never occurred. Simply ignore it and continue on with their lives, and yet how could they do that when they still had Diego to negotiate?

Her head turned, her dark gaze unreadable. 'Do we? It was a mistake, I think we can both agree, so what more needs to be said?'

'Was it really a mistake to you?' He shouldn't be asking her this, especially when he agreed. But he couldn't stop himself. Couldn't stop his fingers from tightening on her arm, because touching her bare skin was something he'd never get enough of.

She didn't look away, and he could see the embers of the heat between them, still smouldering, ready to burst into flame at any moment. But also hurt and regret and a thousand other things he couldn't interpret.

He felt the same way. It was so complicated, and he knew he shouldn't be pushing her, that it was dangerous. That if he wasn't careful and pushed too hard, he'd lose control of himself a second time and they'd end up where they had been not five minutes earlier. Naked on the floor. And that wouldn't solve anything.

'I…' She stopped then took a breath. 'Of course, it was a mistake. How could it be anything else? It was the grief talking, that's all, and it shouldn't have happened.'

But it wasn't the grief, or maybe not *only* the grief. It had been more than that. When he'd looked down into her eyes as he'd been deep inside her, he'd seen the wonder there, glowing bright.

Except pretending this *thing* between them didn't exist was the lie they'd told themselves for years, the lie they kept on telling themselves in order for them both to have the future they wanted.

A future that had been destroyed by their respective spouses.

Now all they had were the remains: grief and guilt and no answer to either.

He shouldn't make this harder. He shouldn't want to hear her say that it hadn't been the grief, that it had been more, because there was nothing to be gained from that conversation. Knowing it wouldn't make the slightest bit of difference to the distance they had to keep between them.

Perhaps, after all, it was easier if they pretended nothing had happened.

Yes, that was probably for the best.

He dropped his hand from her arm, the warmth of her skin lingering on his fingertips. 'You're right,' he said. 'It was a mistake. I'll let you get to bed.'

Something flickered through her gaze, though he couldn't tell what, and then, without another word, she left the room, leaving him to the silence.

CHAPTER SIX

ALICE BARELY SLEPT. Every time she closed her eyes, she could see Sebastián's face in the darkness behind her lids. The carved lines of his features harsh and fierce with desire, pleasure glowing bright in his eyes. Pleasure that *she* gave him. And then everything he'd given her in return…

Her body pulsed with the reminder of the passion he'd poured into her. The way he'd ripped her dress away and her underwear too, as if he couldn't wait to get his hands on her. Then his kiss, the blinding heat of it…

Restlessly, she turned over in bed yet again, aching, unable to stop thinking, too, of the aftermath. After all of that wonder and pleasure the first words out of his mouth had been 'I didn't use a condom'. As if he hadn't shared any of that wonder and ecstasy with her. As if the only thing that had mattered to him was the possibility that she might be pregnant.

Perhaps she shouldn't have flung the truth of her miscarriage in his face, but it had felt as if he'd taken something special and precious and thrown it in the dirt. She'd felt a momentary sense of satisfaction at the look of shock on his face when she'd told him, and it had been enough to help her walk from the room with her head held high.

But then that satisfaction had vanished and all she'd felt was sick guilt.

She'd showered before she'd gone to bed, even though part of her hadn't wanted to wash away the scent of him on her skin, desperate to hold onto the physical reminders for as long as she could.

But nothing could wash away what he'd said to her and how cheap she'd felt afterwards. Or the knowledge that he'd felt that same guilt too, because she'd seen it in his eyes.

The only way forward, it seemed, was to pretend it hadn't happened. They still had the situation with Diego to negotiate and she couldn't afford to let something as meaningless as sex get in the way of that.

You made a terrible, terrible mistake.

Alice turned over yet again. Yes, so she had made a mistake, but it needn't be catastrophic. If they pretended it hadn't happened, they could move on. They didn't have to let it get in the way of what they needed to do with Diego. It would be fine. In fact, it might even have been a good thing. Perhaps without the sexual tension in the air between them, their negotiations with Diego would go more smoothly.

It was a comforting thought, and yet still she didn't sleep.

Eventually, when the first light of dawn showed around the edges of the curtains, she hauled herself out of bed, gritty-eyed from lack of sleep. She grabbed a white robe from the bathroom and put it on, then went out into the kitchen in search of coffee. Only to find Sebastián already up and leaning against one of the kitchen counters, sipping an espresso.

And it wasn't until that moment that she realised it was going to be impossible to pretend the night before hadn't happened, that all the blazing sexual tension that had always been between them didn't exist. Because it did.

In fact, it seemed to have only increased, because seeing him standing there, dressed in a pair of worn jeans and a loose white shirt, his black hair damp from a recent shower, the shirt open at the neck to reveal the smooth brown skin of his throat… God. He was still just as gorgeous as he'd been the night before.

Now, though, it was even worse. Because now she knew what his mouth tasted like, and how hot his skin felt under her hands. That his eyes glowed bright when he was aroused and when he pushed inside her, it had felt as if he'd been made for her alone.

She didn't know what to do or what to say. The breath had been completely ripped out of her.

Sebastián didn't move as she met his gaze and her mouth dried, her heart once more galloping around in her chest the way it always did when he was near.

'Good,' he said. 'You're up. We need to talk.'

A little shock went through her, though she tried not to show it, resisting the urge to adjust her robe in a nervous movement. 'About Diego, I assume?' she asked with what she hoped was her normal cool.

'About Diego, yes.' He turned, put his cup down on the counter, then went over to one of the cupboards and took out another. 'Among other things.'

Her hands clenched into fists at her sides. 'What other things?'

Sebastián went to the stove and picked up the stove-top coffee maker, pouring some of the thick black liquid into the cup he was holding. Then he glanced at her, the look in the smoky gold of his eyes utterly unreadable. 'Milk?'

'I…uh…yes, please.'

He poured some milk into the cup from a small jug on the counter. 'Sugar?'

The electricity in the air was building again, the tension making her want to tear her skin off or scream, or do something equally inappropriate.

'What is this all about?' she asked instead, struggling to keep her voice even. 'And no, I don't take sugar.'

He came over to where she stood and held out the cup, and her mouth went even drier at his nearness. She could feel his warmth, smell his delicious scent—soap and that musky, masculine spice.

Her hand trembled slightly as she reached for the cup, the way he was watching her not helping. There was something intent in his eyes, something she didn't understand.

She took a desperate sip of the coffee, the hot, strong hit of caffeine settling her nerves a little. 'Well?' she asked after a moment. 'Stop being so irritatingly mysterious and tell me what things you want to discuss.'

He folded his arms across his chest, seeming somehow even taller and broader than he had a second ago. The intensity in his eyes didn't falter.

He seemed…changed. Not angry the way he'd been before, more as if he'd made a decision that he was very, very certain about.

Her heart began to beat even faster.

'There is the matter of Diego, of course,' he said. 'But there is also the matter of you and me.'

Instantly her face heated, which was annoying in the extreme. 'Oh?' She hoped her voice sounded as cool as she wanted it to be. 'Weren't we going to pretend that didn't happen?'

'No. *You* were going to pretend it didn't happen.'

A strange panic filled her. 'But we both agreed that it was a mistake and we were—'

'I've changed my mind.' His eyes glinted in a way that made everything inside her contract.

'What do you mean you've changed your mind?'

The sharply carved lines of his face shifted, his hard mouth almost curving, as if he knew a secret she didn't. 'Drink your coffee. You're going to need it.'

The strange panic inside her began to gather momentum, though she didn't understand what she was panicking about. He was being deliberately vague and it was as annoying as hell.

'What are you talking about, Sebastián?' she demanded. 'Don't be so bloody aggravating.'

'I thought you'd prefer to be fully caffeinated before we have this discussion.' His voice was mild but that glint in his eye was anything but. 'You look like you haven't slept a wink.'

Alice gritted her teeth, trying to hang onto what little poise she had left. 'I slept fine,' she said shortly. 'Just tell me, for God's sake.'

'Drink your coffee.'

She wanted to refuse and perhaps throw his stupid coffee back in his face, but that would be to admit he was getting to her, and she didn't want to do that. He already had far too much power as it was. Besides, she was also desperate for the caffeine. So she downed the small cup in one go then held it up. 'There. I've had my coffee. Happy?'

His mouth curved again for reasons she couldn't guess at. He took the cup from her hand and placed it back on the counter. 'Emily always told me you were stubborn,' he said. 'That will make things…interesting.'

'What things?' Alice glared at him. 'Explain, please.'

'Very well.' He was all calm. 'You remember I told you yesterday that I wished to remarry, that Diego needs a mother?'

'Yes. What's that got to do with anything?'

He leaned back against the counter and folded his arms, his gaze very direct. 'How would you feel about becoming my wife?'

Shock rippled through her, and it was a good thing she wasn't still holding onto her coffee cup otherwise she would have dropped it. 'Be your wife? What?'

'As I said, Diego needs a mother and I need a wife. You want to keep Diego. Getting married would seem a logical solution to both our issues.'

The shock moved slowly outwards, making her stomach twist, and she was aware that beneath the shock, there was also an instinctive thrill of joy. As if being his wife was exactly what she wanted. Which it wasn't. At all. In fact, she was horrified by the suggestion.

'Are you insane?' She stared at him. 'I'm Emily's sister. And she's only two months dead.'

'I realise that. We can wait six months if you prefer.'

'You can't be serious.'

His jaw hardened. 'Oh, I am. Very serious. I want Diego to have a proper family and that includes a father and a mother. I would also like more children.'

Alice struggled to get hold of herself. 'I can't have more children. I told you that last night.'

He lifted one powerful shoulder. 'Not biological children, no, but you can certainly have children in other ways. As you can imagine, blood ties aren't much of a concern to me.'

Of course. He hadn't been his father's biological son, either, as he'd told her the day before. Interest once again flickered through her, belated questions crowding in her head, but since they were the least of her concerns right now, she ignored them.

'You don't need me for adoption,' she said. 'Or surrogacy.'

'The children will still need a mother,' he pointed out.

'What about Sofia? Or another nanny?' She'd told him earlier that Diego needed a mother, and he did, but panic was clouding her thinking.

'A nanny they will certainly have,' he interrupted, relentless. 'But a nanny is not the same as a mother.'

Of course, it wasn't.

Alice swallowed, the panicky feeling intensifying. She couldn't marry him. It was a ludicrous idea. She barely knew him. And she was only just a widow. Why would she rush into marrying someone else so soon, especially him? She didn't love him, and he certainly wasn't asking because he loved her.

'Why me?' she demanded. 'You could have any woman you wanted. It doesn't have to be me.'

He didn't even blink. 'I don't care much about blood ties, as I said, but you do. You're Diego's aunt, his only blood relative. You want to be in his life, yes?'

'I do, but—'

'If you and I are married, you can formally adopt him as your son. All the legal complications will be resolved. There is also one other reason it must be you.' He paused a moment, the intense light in his eyes glowing even brighter. 'I have no intention of divorcing you, and, since I will never be unfaithful, physical desire is vital.'

This time the shock that went through her was hot, making her face flame and her skin tighten. Making her very aware of the night before, of being in his arms, of screaming his name...

'Yes,' he murmured, watching her, reading every single one of her thoughts. 'That is why it must be you, Alice. You and only you.'

Sebastián could barely stop himself from reaching for her, but he managed it. Control at this delicate stage was of the utmost importance.

He knew this would be a shock to her and she needed time to come to terms with it, to think about it.

Marrying Alice...

The solution had come to him in the middle of the night, as he'd lain alone in his bed, every part of his body aching, tormented by thoughts of her and what had happened in that library. Him, losing control. Her, reaching for him, welcoming him. The feel of her better than any fantasy.

She'd wanted to pretend it had never happened and he'd agreed that it had been a mistake. Then he'd started thinking about having to negotiate potential custody issues with her and what they were going to do about it, and how he'd manage to keep resisting the temptation of her...

It had come to him in that moment that there was an answer to all his problems. *Their* problems. He'd known after Emily had died that he wanted to marry again, to give Diego a loving mother at his side.

Sebastián himself hadn't had one and, with nothing to soften Mateo's resentment or to provide even a loving counterpoint, it had been terribly lonely and isolating. And since neither he nor Javier, his biological father, had known of their relationship to each other, because Mateo had kept it secret, he'd felt as if he'd had no one at all to whom he'd truly belonged.

No, he wanted to make sure Diego never felt like that. That he grew up never knowing how painful love was. That he would be accepted, regardless of who he was. That he belonged.

Sebastián knew his own nature all too well, that his emotions were strong and had to be ruthlessly contained and controlled. Which meant Diego would need someone who didn't have to constantly hold themselves back and that someone would be Sebastián's wife. That person would be Alice.

You want her for yourself...don't use Diego as an excuse to justify it.

He was doing nothing of the kind. He knew the dangers of following his heart, of wanting things too desperately, and he kept his passions firmly confined. Yes, he'd lost control the night before, but making Alice his wife should take care of his physical desires. After all, what better solution was there? Alice was Diego's aunt and she wanted him, had been desperate enough to take on a legal challenge to have him. She would be the best mother for him. A lioness to protect him and love him, give him the family he deserved.

Yes, marrying her was the perfect fix for all their issues. Which meant the only issue left he had to deal with was Alice herself.

It was difficult to tell what she truly thought of the idea, because while she'd certainly been outraged, her face had also been flushed, and he could tell that she'd been thinking of the night before. She hadn't slept either—the dark circles under her eyes were proof enough of that.

Those beautiful eyes were very wide now and still full of shock and outrage. Yet not only that. The embers of the passion they'd shared last night were smouldering there too, banked coals just waiting to burst into life again.

It hadn't eased for her as it hadn't eased for him, either. One night would never be enough to satisfy his hunger and, after all, passion was allowed in marriage. He'd shared it with Emily, although he had to admit that what he'd experienced with Emily paled in comparison to what had happened between him and Alice.

You'd give Alice what you could never give to her sister? How is that fair?

But he wouldn't be giving Alice anything more than physical passion, so it was completely fair. His heart would never be involved. That wasn't what he wanted. Love was mean, it was punitive and demanding, and he was done with giving everything he had and it never being enough. Besides, Emily was gone now, and surely she'd forgive him spending physical passion with her sister. After all, she hadn't been faithful and it was too late now anyway. He'd crossed the line already.

'But I... I don't even know you,' Alice said faintly. 'Not really.'

'You know me. You've known me for five years.'

'No, I don't. I don't know the first thing about you. How could I? When you basically treated me as if I had the plague the whole time you and Emily were married.'

Irritation caught at him. While he'd expected her to be reluctant, after last night he'd thought she'd be more receptive to his proposal. Emily's and Edward's deaths were always going to be an obstacle, but still. It wasn't as if he and Alice were in love.

'Are you surprised?' he said shortly. 'It's not as if you welcomed me with open arms yourself.'

How can you say that? When it was you who held her at arm's length? You were cold and distant to her for a reason.

Her chin came up, the light of battle in her eyes, making the dark circles beneath them fade and warm colour stain her cheekbones. Even having no sleep and wrapped in a white robe, her hair tangled over her shoulders, she was so beautiful she stopped his heart. 'You've only got yourself to blame for that, Sebastián. I was ready to wel-come you the day we first met. I couldn't wait to meet you, even. Then you looked at me as if I were dirt.'

He shouldn't admit to what he'd felt for her even back then. It felt wrong. A betrayal of the marriage he'd had with Emily. Yet if he wanted her to accept his proposal, he was going to have to give her the truth. He could see that now.

'Surely,' he said, 'you have some idea about why that was.'

She frowned. 'No, of course I didn't. Why would I?'

Perhaps she hadn't known. Perhaps she hadn't been completely conscious of the electricity that had been be-tween them, what had always been between them. Or maybe she had been, but she hadn't understood what it was. Then again, could she have been that blind? Or that innocent?

Sebastián took a step closer to her. 'I think you do, Alice. I think you know damn well.'

Her cheeks had gone a deep red and he could see her struggle with the urge to step back and away from him, to put some distance between them. Yet she didn't move. She was a fighter, this woman. He liked that very much.

'So, you were attracted to me.' Her chin was held high. 'Is that what you're saying? That's why you were so cold and distant? For five years?'

There was accusation in her voice and admittedly it all sounded petty and ridiculous when she said it like that. Yet…he hadn't been able to do anything else. Not when he knew how susceptible he was to his own reck-less heart.

He'd always been drawn to the stables, the gentle acceptance of the horses soothing something in his wounded soul. Mateo had forbidden him to speak to any of the stable hands, but Javier, the stable manager, had watched him and noted his easy way with the animals, and had told him he had a gift. 'Come to the stables any time,' Javier had told him. 'I can teach you.'

Sebastián had been taught to ride by Mateo as soon as he could walk, but Mateo had been as harsh and exacting with him as he was with the animals. Javier had been different. He'd been gentler, kinder, intuitive and Sebastián had found him a much more knowledgeable and sympathetic teacher than his father had been.

He'd known it was wrong to talk to Javier; his father had forbidden it. But he'd been so desperate for a connection to someone, for attention that wasn't resentment and anger, that he hadn't been able to help himself.

Of course Mateo had found out, and when he had, he'd been furious. And he'd taken out his anger on Sebastián by telling him two secrets that he hadn't known, flinging them in his face like knives.

Firstly, that Javier was his biological father. And secondly, that he'd killed his own mother. She'd died having him.

Then he'd rounded out his vindictive tirade by firing Javier on the spot, then accusing Sebastian of being as faithless and disloyal as his mother and his biological father.

Sebastián had had no answer to that. He'd felt as if his heart had been ripped from his chest, as if Mateo had simultaneously given him something precious before taking it back in the most brutal way possible. And later, in the furious aftermath of the confrontation, watching from his bedroom window as Javier had walked away from the job he'd loved, all he'd been able to feel was the most intense sense of failure. That he'd failed his mother, that he'd failed Javier. And somehow, he'd felt as if he'd failed Mateo too.

When Mateo had died years later, he'd picked up the mantle of the dukedom, determined to make up for his failures, and marrying Emily had felt as if he was firmly putting them in the past. Yet…he'd ended up failing her, too.

He'd given her everything she asked for, attention, physical pleasure, a house in Paris… Yet it still hadn't been enough.

You'd given your heart to Alice. You can't deny it.

No, this wasn't about his heart. His heart couldn't be trusted and he wouldn't listen to it, not again.

'It wasn't mere attraction,' he said, because attraction was too tame a word for the physical hunger he felt for her. 'It was almost obsession, Alice. And you know it. You felt it too. Or was there some other reason that you never let yourself be alone in the same room with me?' The red in her cheeks deepened, her eyes getting darker, and he stared at her, searching her face. 'Or were you afraid of me? Perhaps it was that? Did you think I would do something to you that you wouldn't want?'

'No,' she said quickly. 'No, of course not.'

He knew that wasn't it already. She'd never been

afraid of him, only of the electricity between them, but he wanted her to say it. 'I couldn't get close to you, Alice. You must have known that. And I think you couldn't get close to me for the same reasons.'

She glanced away. The pulse at the base of her throat raced and he was close enough to feel her warmth. She smelled of lavender and sex and, though he wasn't even touching her, he was hard. But he'd already decided one thing: the next move was hers. He'd crossed the line the night before and she'd welcomed him. But now he needed it to be her turn. If this was to work, she had to show that she wanted him every bit as badly as he wanted her.

'I didn't... I never...' She stopped, her fingers fussing with the tie of her robe. Then she looked back at him, her gaze fierce. 'I was faithful to Edward. I always have been.'

'I wasn't implying otherwise. And I have always been faithful to Emily. But you changed everything. You must have known that.' He saw the admission in her eyes. It *had* changed for her too. 'Say it, Alice. I want you to say it. Out loud so I can hear it.'

He took a step even closer, so there were only inches between them. She wasn't as petite as Emily and he didn't have to look down as far. She didn't give off that air of fragility either, the delicacy that Emily had that he'd been so afraid of breaking. He could feel himself get even harder. Sometimes Emily had found his physical passion too much and, certainly in the last year, she'd kept putting him off. Kept telling him she had a headache, that she wasn't 'feeling it', that she was too tired.

But last night Alice had put her hands on him, and she'd been so hungry. He'd almost forgotten what it was like to have a woman desperate for him and he wanted more. He needed it. He wanted a woman whose passion matched his own and the night before Alice had certainly done that. Her body had been all luscious curves and soft skin. A feast he could spend days devouring.

She stared at him for a long moment, and he could see fear in her eyes. She was afraid of admitting what she felt, afraid of admitting what she wanted.

Well, he wasn't going to help her. She either wanted him, wanted this, or she didn't. There was no middle ground. And he wasn't going to force her into an admission. She had to choose it for herself.

'Edward's dead,' she said. 'It's been two months, Sebastián. Just two months.'

'Oh, I understand, believe me. I know all too well how many months it's been. But if you hadn't felt as I did, you wouldn't have reached for me last night the way you did. You wouldn't have kissed me back, and you certainly wouldn't have spread your legs for me so desperately.'

Her jaw hardened, anger leaping in her eyes. 'I would never have—'

'They're both dead, Alice,' he interrupted. 'You don't have to pretend any more.'

Her mouth opened then shut and she swallowed. Took a breath.

Then, before he could move, she reached for him.

CHAPTER SEVEN

HE WAS RIGHT. Even now, despite last night, she was still pretending.

Pretending she didn't want him with every breath in her. Pretending she wasn't desperate to touch him, to taste him. Pretending his physical presence didn't spin her world entirely on its axis.

Pretending had become such a deeply ingrained habit, though, that it was difficult to break. Difficult even to say the words out loud.

You're not alone, though. He always wanted you too.

All this time. From the moment he first saw her. It seemed impossible. He'd been so cold, so distant, and she'd thought the electricity in the air that always seemed to hover around them was only on her side. There had been times where it had felt as if he might feel the same way, that last Christmas Eve they'd all had, for example. But he'd never said anything. Never given her any reason to think that he even liked her, let alone wanted her.

But he had. And last night he'd proved it.

Now, in the kitchen, he was so close, his body hot, and the scent of him irresistible, and she had no idea what to do with his marriage proposal, no idea at all. It was so complicated. The prospect scared her, filled her with guilt and yet at the same time there was also a traitorous joy, as if being his wife was all she'd ever wanted to be.

It seemed easier to reach for him, touch him. Kiss him. Because the only thing that made any sense was the need inside her. That, at least, was simple.

Yet when she lifted her hands to him, his fingers closed around her wrists, holding her at bay, his golden eyes blazing.

'No, Alice,' he said softly. 'Give me the words. I want to hear you say them. You won't get anything until you do.'

She took a shuddering breath. His grip was unbreakable, the force of his will in every line of him. He wasn't going to move until she gave him what he asked for, that was clear. Which meant if she wanted him, she was going to say it, out loud.

Yet even now it still felt dangerous to admit, almost a transgression even though both Edward and Emily were gone, and she was betraying nothing but their memories.

They found each other. Why can't you and Sebastián?

Except Emily and Edward had clearly been in love, and she was not in love with Sebastián. Just as he was not in love with her. And she didn't want him to be. She wasn't ready for love again, not after what her marriage had turned into, and, in fact, she might not ever be ready. Love was far too demanding and required so much, and she didn't have it in her to give anyone that except her nephew. But desire, passion…those she could do.

You need this. You need him. You need to be wanted.

Her heart ached. She did need it. In fact, she couldn't

recall the last time anyone had wanted her the way Sebastián did. His desire healed something painful inside her.

'Well?' he prompted. 'Are you going to say it?'

Her mouth had gone dry at the fierce look in his eyes, her skin burning where he clasped her wrists in a strong grip. He'd given her the truth, surely she could do no less?

'I…want you, Sebastián,' she said huskily, the words feeling forbidden in her mouth and yet also so very right.

The glow in his eyes became brighter. 'How long, Alice? How long have you wanted me?'

She swallowed and gave him this truth too. 'Since I first saw you. When Emily first introduced us.'

His hard mouth curved slightly, but there was no amusement in the smile. Only an intense and very male satisfaction. He released her hands, but didn't otherwise move. He was waiting for her, that was obvious.

It wasn't a choice. Nothing was going to stop her from reaching to take his face between her palms the way she'd wanted to from the moment she'd walked into the kitchen. From relishing his hot skin and the prickle of his morning beard. From staring into his eyes and loving how he stared right back, and the relief that they could do this. That there was no reason to hide any more.

Then she went up onto her toes to press her lips to his. He didn't stop her this time, his mouth opening to greet her, and then the heat between them burst into flames, the feverish intensity leaping high as he took charge and utterly devoured her.

She loved it. She pushed her palms flat to the hard wall

of his chest and kissed him back just as feverishly, just as hungrily, and just as demanding as he was.

Her fingers dropped to the buttons of his shirt, pulling them open so she could touch his bare skin, and then she was stroking him, feeling the iron-hard bands of his muscles flex and release as she traced them. He growled something against her mouth and the rough timbre of his voice thrilled her. Edward had been so unmoved by everything she did that she'd begun to doubt everything about herself, worried that she'd lost her attractiveness along with her fertility.

Yet that was patently not the case with Sebastián. He took her hands and pushed them down to the buttons of his fly, holding her palm against the denim. She could feel him, long and hard for her, making the pulsing ache between her thighs sharp and needy.

He said something rough and demanding in Spanish, but she didn't need any translation. She knew what he wanted.

She gave him a little push back so she had some space, then she dropped to her knees in front of him. It had been a long time since she'd done this—Edward hadn't enjoyed it, or at least that was what he'd told her—and she hadn't insisted. Her sexual confidence had taken a beating after losing the baby and Edward's withdrawal hadn't helped. But…here, now, Sebastián wanted her. He was on fire for her and he wanted to know if she was on fire for him, too.

Well, she'd show him. She'd prove it to him.

With shaking fingers, she pulled open the buttons of

his jeans and released him. He murmured something in his deep voice, his fingers sliding into her hair, caressing. She didn't hesitate, gripping him, stroking velvety hot skin and steel, then opening her mouth and taking him in. He tensed, a low growl escaping him. His fingers flexed and tightened in her hair as she took him deeper.

'Alice,' he murmured, her name sounding like music in his accent. *'Mi cielo...'*

She had no idea what that meant, but she knew it was an endearment of some kind and it wound through her, a thread of gold gilding everything inside her. Edward had never called her anything but Alice, even when they'd first started dating. No sweetheart. No honey. No darling. Not even my love. Just Alice. Plain old Alice.

But then even that thought vanished as she tasted him, loving the sounds she brought from him as his hips flexed and he drove himself into her mouth. She lost herself in that moment. Lost herself to the pleasure she gave him and when he made a low, guttural sound of release, it was her turn to take everything he gave her, and she did.

When he was done, he gave them a few moments then pulled her up and lifted her onto the kitchen counter, so she was sitting on it. He reached for the tie of her robe, tugging at it so the edges of the fabric parted. Then he slid one hand in her hair, pulling her head gently back, and he bent, covering her mouth with his.

Alice shuddered. He tasted of dark coffee and sin and when she leaned into his lips, kissing back hungrily, he made another of those low, masculine sounds that thrilled her so much.

'Slow down,' he murmured against her lips. 'We have plenty of time.' Then he slipped a hand between the parted folds of her robe, his touch a flame on her bare skin, and his kiss became slower, deeper, more intent. His fingers spread, cupping her breast in his palm, his thumb stroking over her hardened nipple, sending waves of shocking pleasure through her.

It felt so good. She couldn't speak, couldn't think. There was only his stroking hand moving over her skin, touching her, tracing her with such care it was as if he was committing every inch of her to memory.

Edward hadn't touched her that way, not even the first time they'd slept together. He'd been attentive, but he hadn't touched her as if she was rare and precious. As if he'd been dreaming of the feel of her skin for years and years.

But Sebastián did. Every caress of his fingers layering pleasure upon pleasure, until she was trembling with the force of it. His mouth had found its way to her throat, tasting the frantic race of her pulse, his hand dropping down between her thighs, stroking and teasing the soft flesh there with such lightness she could barely stand it.

'Oh, my God,' she whispered, her head tilting back, her eyes closing. 'Oh…please…'

'What do you want, *mi cielo*?' His voice was dark and deep as his fingers stroked over the sensitive part of her, making her shudder and shake. 'Tell me.'

She had her hands on his powerful shoulders, her fingertips digging in, her hips lifting against the movement of his hand. 'You.' She had to fight to get the words out. 'I want you.'

'Then look at me,' he ordered roughly.

She opened her eyes, obeying him without question, and there he was standing in front of her, his gaze full of a desire and a possessiveness that stole her breath. He pulled her to the edge of the counter, his fingers pressing hard against her flesh, and her thighs automatically parted to let him stand between them.

He stared at her so fiercely and kept on staring as he pushed inside her, long and slow and deep. She groaned, her whole body trembling, unable to look away from him, his golden eyes inches from hers. It was intensely intimate, as if he could see inside her head and she could see inside his. And he didn't flinch from her stare either. He let her see the fierce passion inside him and how it blazed, and all she could think about was how wrong Emily had been. Because he wasn't cold or distant. No, he burned like the sun. She could barely look at him.

Did Emily make him burn like this? Or is it all you?

But she couldn't think about her sister, not now, not like this. There was no room for Emily. There was only her and Sebastián as he began to move, holding her tightly, the rhythm a dance and both of them in perfect time.

It had never been like this with Edward. Never ever.

The pleasure built and built until there was no keeping it inside and the moment it exploded through both of them, he leaned forward and took her mouth. They shuddered and shook together, the flames consuming both of them.

They remained like that for long moments, locked together, his powerful body pressed to hers, his large, warm hands spread on her hips. She couldn't stop shaking with the aftershocks, the thought of him letting her go almost unbearable.

Finally, an eon later, he lifted his mouth from hers and pressed leisurely kisses along her jaw and down the side of her neck, his hands moving slowly over her hips and thighs, not inciting this time, but soothing.

'Well?' His deep voice was rough and frayed as worn velvet. 'Are you going to marry me, Alice?'

It must have been the effect of the orgasm, she thought later. Or maybe she was simply sick of fighting, and this seemed to be the easiest solution to a very complicated problem. Because all she could think about was that yes, she would marry him. If he could make her feel like this every day, despite the guilt, it would be worth it.

'Yes,' she said thickly. 'Yes, Sebastián, I'll marry you.'

He shouldn't have felt so satisfied at her quiet 'yes' but he did. Maybe it was no wonder. She'd knelt for him, taken him into her mouth, made him feel like a god, and it had been such a long time since he'd felt that way. A very, *very* long time.

It wasn't that Emily hadn't wanted him—she had. At least initially. Yet she hadn't much enjoyed his rougher, earthier passions, and had made that clear, so he'd got into the habit of restraining himself with her.

Then, later, Emily had slowly withdrawn from him, radiating a hurt she wouldn't admit to and that he couldn't seem to do anything about.

They'd taken to sleeping in separate rooms, because

she'd claimed she slept better on her own, but he'd known it was more than that. It was him. It was his inability to give her what she'd wanted: love. He couldn't blame her for finding that with Edward.

The failure had always been his and he couldn't forget that.

Perhaps you will fail Alice too?

No, it would be different with Alice, because he wouldn't promise her anything he couldn't give. And he'd be completely up front about it so there'd be no misunderstandings, no pressure. A legal partnership and a family for Diego, and sharing a bed to satisfy their physical obsession with each other. That was all. It didn't have to mean anything more than that. It didn't have to be complicated.

He shifted, sliding his hands to cup her backside and pulling her even closer against him. She was so warm and she smelled of sex, and he was hardening yet again. He still felt as if he was starving for her and was already desperate to take her to bed yet again, but first, he needed to be absolutely clear on what the rules were for this situation so there would be no mistakes.

Her chin lifted as he gripped her, her dark eyes meeting his. There was uncertainty in them, but she didn't try to hide it. 'I can't help but think you've just manipulated me into saying yes using sex.'

He almost smiled. Things were going to be interesting in his household, since it was apparent that she wasn't going to shy away from difficult subjects. A refreshing change from Emily, who always had.

'That goes both ways, you know.'

'True.' She relaxed into him in a way that made him want to growl with possessive satisfaction. 'Okay, so how is this going to work? We're going to have to wait six months, because I don't want any commentary on how quickly it's all happening between us.'

'We don't have to make a performance of it,' he said, relishing the feel of her bare skin against his palms. 'We can get quietly and legally married at a register office. My parents are dead, so are yours, who needs to know?'

She nodded slowly. 'I suppose I'll have to live with you, then?'

'If you want to give Diego the family he needs, then yes.' He paused a moment then added, because he wanted to acknowledge the fact that she would have to be the one shifting countries, 'I'm sorry, but I can't move to New Zealand. My place is here, on my estate. And I can't move the business either. But I'll buy you a house in Auckland that you can visit whenever you like.'

Again, she nodded, her expression thoughtful. 'I have an investment company, you know that. I don't want to give it up.'

'I would never ask you to. Could you work remotely?'

'Yes, I think I could do something like that.' She paused. 'What about the rest?'

He didn't need to ask what she was talking about. 'You'll live with me at the hacienda. You can have your own room if you want the space and you can live your own life however you choose. But at night you will sleep with me, yes? I won't have a sexless marriage, Alice. And I will be the only man you sleep with.'

This time a flicker of her temper glinted in her eyes. 'You say that like I'm immediately going to go out and sleep with lots of men.'

And he could feel it growing inside him, a certain electric excitement at the thought of having her. Of *finally* having her. In his bed, in his house, in his life. Of having her whenever he wanted her, no need to hide, no need to control himself either. Sure, it was about sex, but he'd also appreciate getting to know her a bit more in a way he hadn't been able to before. She was such a passionate spirit. He couldn't wait to match wits with her. And anyway, shouldn't he know the woman who would be Diego's mother and his wife?

Are you sure that's a good idea? This has the potential to become something more if you're not careful.

No, it wouldn't. Because he *was* careful. He'd always kept his heart guarded and that wouldn't change just because she was in his bed.

'You'd better not,' he murmured, unable to resist teasing her. 'I could get quite unhappy if you did.'

Some of the anger in her eyes eased as she caught his tone, the tension around her mouth relaxing. 'Seriously, though. Have *you* really thought this through? What if we get to the point where we're not attracted to each other any more?'

He squeezed her a little, making her gasp and shiver. 'It's lasted for five years so far. I can't see it getting less any time soon.'

She slipped her hands into his open shirt, sliding her fingers over the bare skin of his chest. 'Perhaps it won't be as exciting if we no longer have to worry about other people.'

He knew what she was doing. She was trying to find excuses, voicing her fears. 'What are you worried about?' he asked. 'That I'll stop wanting you?'

Her stroking fingers paused, her gaze flickering away. 'It happens.'

It did and it had happened to both of them.

'This is about Edward, isn't it?' he asked.

She shifted restlessly, her hands dropping from his chest, but he caught them before they did, pressing her palms to his skin and holding them there.

'Tell me,' he said, because he was tired of not knowing, tired of her being such a mystery to him when all he wanted to know was more. 'Remember, it happened to me also.'

She sighed. 'Yes, it's Edward. After I lost the baby he... withdrew from me. And we...we didn't...' She stopped, a thread of pain in her voice. 'He didn't want me any more.'

Gently, Sebastián reached for a lock of her silky black hair and tucked it behind her ear. 'I can't tell you what was missing for Edward, but I can tell you that the fault wasn't with you. I have wanted you for five years, Alice. And like I said, I don't see that changing any time soon.'

Colour bloomed in her pretty olive skin, deepening the post-orgasmic flush already there, and he watched it, mesmerised. 'They were childhood sweethearts,' she said softly. 'He and Emily. We were all friends at school and I was in love with him for years as a teenager. I never thought he'd choose me. But for some reason, after high school he did, and I was so…happy. Except… I suppose I was always his second choice. He never fully moved on from her, did he?'

Sebastián had been aware of Emily and Edward's history, but he'd never suspected that Emily still had feelings for Edward. It was only after the accident that he'd realised.

'Did you love him?' he asked, unable to stop the flicker of a jealousy he shouldn't be feeling, not when he wasn't in love with Alice, and Edward was dead and gone.

'I thought I did,' she said. 'He didn't love me, though, that was clear.'

That had hurt her deeply, he could see it in her eyes, and of course it must.

'He was an idiot,' Sebastián said bluntly, because she had to know that was the case. 'And if he didn't see or appreciate what he had in you then he didn't deserve you, either.'

'He was always very respectful, very gentle. He was nice to me, so I don't—'

'Nice?' he demanded, oddly angry for reasons he couldn't have explained. 'If he wasn't at your feet worshipping you or spending all night feasting on your body because he couldn't get enough, then he was a fool. If the best you can say about him is that he was nice to you, then your marriage was doomed from the start.'

Alice's eyes widened, shock flickering in them, before that gave way to the familiar glitter of sparks. Her mouth opened, but he found himself saying, before she could, 'Don't defend him. If all he could give you was half-hearted caring and gentleness and *niceness*, then he shouldn't have married you. I have no respect for a man who squandered what he had.'

Says the man who did the same with his own wife.

Guilt ate at him, but he shoved it away.

Again, Alice's chin came up, her temper flaring. 'Are you going to give me more, then?' she demanded. 'Is that what I can expect from you?'

He gripped her tighter. There were things she couldn't expect from him, it was true, but at least he was honest about that. And he wouldn't be a hypocrite. He'd do better with her than he had with Emily. He'd certainly *never* make her feel as if she was anyone's second choice. 'I will *never* squander what I have in you,' he said fiercely. 'I will respect you, care for you, desire you. I will do everything I can not to hurt you. The only thing I can't give you is love, Alice.'

Emotions flickered through her gaze, though what they were he couldn't tell. 'Don't worry,' she said, her voice very neutral. 'In fact, it'll be a long time before I'm ready to love anyone again anyway. I'll settle for what you can give me.'

The word 'anyone' caught at him, as did the word 'settle'. A scrape against his skin and oddly painful. He ignored the sensation. 'If you do happen to fall in love with someone, we can discuss it. I don't want a divorce, but I'm sure we can come to some arrangements if need be.'

Her gaze suddenly became sharper, focusing on him

in a way that wasn't comfortable. 'What about you? What if you fall in love with someone?'

'I won't.' He said it with the utmost certainty, because that was the last thing he'd ever do. 'Any love I have to give will go to Diego and that's all.'

'You didn't love Emily, then?'

The question sounded like an accusation, but then he supposed that was fair since he'd asked her the same thing about Edward.

'I tried to,' he said slowly, and he'd thought he'd managed it until Alice had come on the scene. 'But trying wasn't enough in the end.'

The sharp focus faded from her eyes, replaced with something like sympathy. 'No,' she murmured, regret in her voice. 'It never is, is it?'

She wasn't wrong. Love was never enough for anyone, or at least his wasn't. Not for his mother, not for his father, and not for Emily. Only the horses accepted his and didn't require anything more.

Part of him wanted to know why she thought the same and what had happened in her family to make her think so, because it wasn't just about Edward. Yet, another part of him was done with talking, especially when there were better things to be doing.

'Any other questions?' he asked abruptly. 'I'm hungry and not for breakfast.'

She didn't answer. Instead, she slid her arms around his neck and kissed him. And there was no more talking for a very long time.

CHAPTER EIGHT

TWO WEEKS LATER, Alice sat in the cool of the hacienda's courtyard, under the shade of the bougainvillea, Diego nestled in the crook of her arm. She'd just given him a feed and he'd settled down happily. He was such a good baby.

Alice felt much more comfortable with him now and it eased something in her heart just to sit here like this, in the heat of a Spanish summer with her nephew sleeping peacefully in her arms.

Pity the rest of it isn't so peaceful.

That was an understatement.

In the two weeks since they'd got back from Madrid, Sebastián hadn't wasted any time. He'd taken her to Seville where they'd got married in a quick register office ceremony. She'd felt uncomfortable marking the occasion in any way since it was only a purely legal affair, but had decided at the last minute to wear one of the dresses she'd bought in Madrid, a deep blue silk number that flattered her skin and her figure. She'd wondered initially what the point of wearing the dress was and then seen gold flare in Sebastián's gaze the second he'd laid eyes on her and knew then that *that* had been the point.

The ceremony had been quick and before she knew it,

she was Sebastián's wife. Lucia had then cooked them a special dinner that night and they'd eaten only half of it when Sebastián finally lost patience, pushed his plate aside, pulled her up from her chair and took her to bed.

That was the only part of their relationship that seemed to function on any level. At night they explored each other, learned each other. She found out what he liked and, as it turned out, he liked everything and there was nothing about his body that was off limits to her. She gave him back the same, which he took full advantage of, learning all the things that gave her pleasure and then showing her new ways to experience it. She lived for their nights together.

During the day, though, it was a different story. He was almost a stranger to her, spending most of his time in his office or down in the stables. Mornings and evenings he reserved for Diego and she loved watching him with the baby, seeing him all patient, gentle, and caring. Protective too.

It made her hungry for him, made her want more of him, though she knew that the nights they spent together should be enough. She was almost shocked to find herself a little envious of her nephew, wishing that Sebastián were that way with her, which was ridiculous. She didn't want him to be. He'd been very clear in Madrid that their marriage would be only a physical and legal one, no emotions would be involved, and she'd agreed to it. She couldn't say she hadn't known what she was getting into when she'd said yes to his proposal.

She tried to ignore the feelings though and it was easy at first, since she was busy dealing with transferring her life from Auckland to Spain. She had help from Sebastian's staff, though she knew she was eventually going to have to go back to Auckland to deal with some of the practicalities herself. In the meantime, she'd decided to take a couple of weeks off to spend them as she'd originally planned, getting to know Diego and recovering from Edward and Emily's sudden loss.

Sofia came out to take Diego to put him down for his afternoon nap and, afterwards, Alice sat there in the quiet, listening to the cicadas, knowing she had a mile-long to-do list and that she'd better get onto it, and yet not moving.

It was always like this after Diego was asleep and there were things to do and yet she didn't do any of them. She couldn't stop thinking about Sebastián. About whether this was going to be her life now, living with the stranger who was her husband, about whom she knew very little. Each of them with their separate lives and meeting only at night, in bed, where their hunger for each other remained fierce.

It seemed ridiculous that she knew his favourite sex positions, yet she didn't know how he liked his coffee or whether he preferred movies to books, or what he'd wanted to grow up to be when he was a child.

Remind you of anything?

Alice shifted uncomfortably in her chair then leaned forward to stir her cold tea yet again. She didn't want to be thinking of Edward right now, but she couldn't deny the similarities. They'd stopped talking to each other in the year before he died, becoming virtual strangers to each other, and she hadn't known how to bridge the gap she'd sensed opening up between them.

It had been lonely, and she'd been so unhappy.

And now you're heading down the same path with Se-bastián.

Yes, and if she wasn't careful, she was going to end up having the same life and the same marriage that she'd had with Edward. Only with Sebastián it would be worse, because while she had some of him at night when they were together, she didn't have the whole. Not that she was asking for the whole, but she'd like a lot more than what she had now.

Emily had found living in the hacienda isolating and lonely, Alice remembered, and now she knew why. Because if this was how Sebastián had treated her, no wonder she'd been lonely.

You agreed to the marriage. You knew what you were getting into.

Sadly, true. Emily had solved her issues by staying in the apartment Sebastián had bought her in Paris and then, of course, by having an affair with Edward. But then Emily had always wanted to be chased. Alice was different. She already knew no one was going to chase her and if she wanted to solve this problem, she was going to have to sort it out herself. Clearly Sebastián wasn't going to.

Edward had never wanted to talk, he'd brushed her off every time she'd tried to discuss what was happening in their marriage. And she hadn't pushed. She'd been afraid he'd simply decide she was too much trouble and leave.

She had that same fear with Sebastián. They didn't love each other. Also, he'd made his position clear. He didn't do divorce and he would never be unfaithful, and she believed him. He was very much a man of his word and had strong convictions, and she was certain he wouldn't just up and leave if she pushed him.

Deciding that sitting around thinking about it wasn't going to solve the issue any faster, Alice shoved her chair back and got up, making her way through the gardens to the stables.

Sebastián was with one of the mares, standing outside her stall and talking to Tomas, the stable manager. The mare had her head over the gate and was nuzzling at Sebastián's shoulder. As Alice watched, he lifted an absent hand and gave her long nose a stroke.

Alice shivered, a prickling excitement settling down low in her belly. He was so affectionate with the horses. That was what she'd been drawn to when she'd used to come down here initially, his gentleness and kindness with them so at odds with how cold he was to her. How they would come to him as if they knew he was someone they could love and trust.

She'd never had that, she realised with a sudden lurch. Even with Edward. Emily had been his first love and even though he'd chosen Alice, she'd always wondered if he'd regretted it. If she'd merely been a poor second choice. That doubt had lingered and she'd never been able to shake it. Especially after the miscarriage, as he'd withdrawn from her even more, taking her trust in him along with it.

Of course he regretted it. Why do you think he went and had a child with your sister?

Emily had always been the first choice, the better choice. Even when Alice had been a kid, her parents had prioritised Emily's appointments and play dates, school performances and sports days, and sometimes they forgot about hers. She could never trust that they would think of her first. She'd asked her mother once why that was, and her mother had replied that Alice could look after herself. Emily simply needed more than she did. And it was the truth. Emily always did.

Even now, though, you're not Sebastián's first choice.

No, but she didn't need to be. He, at least, had been honest with her about what he could give and what he couldn't, and, to be fair to him, he'd given her exactly what he'd promised. He'd certainly gone a long way to healing the hurt Edward had dealt to her physical and sexual confidence, so there was that. And as to more, maybe that would come in time.

What about love?

Perhaps she'd find love with someone else at some point. Or maybe this would be enough for her. Somewhere inside her something went stiff with denial at the thought, but she ignored it.

Instead, she waited until Sebastián had finished speaking with Tomas then, after the other man had left, she walked slowly over to the stall.

Sebastián eyed her, his expression guarded. 'Alice? Did you need something?'

Her heart was beating a little too fast, though she wasn't sure why since all he could do was refuse to talk to her and she didn't think he'd do that.

You want more from him than a mere 'talk'.

She ignored that thought too.

He was gorgeous today in casual jeans and a T-shirt that showed off his magnificent physique, and she found it difficult to concentrate on what she wanted to say. It seemed unfair that even after two weeks of gorging herself on him every night, she still struggled to string words together in his presence.

'I think we need to talk,' she finally managed.

He lifted one black brow. 'Talk? Talk about what?'

Alice took a steadying breath and folded her arms over her thundering heart. 'Our marriage, Sebastián.'

His expression betrayed nothing. 'What about it?'

'It's just… Is this how it's going to be from now on? You and I living completely separate lives except at night?'

He frowned. 'I'm not sure quite what the issue is. That's what I told you would happen, and you agreed.'

'Yes, I did. I just didn't realise I was expected to live here and be happy with you completely ignoring me.'

The mare nickered and nudged at his shoulder, and he reached up once more to stroke her nose. His gaze was dispassionate as he stared at her, and Alice was reminded yet again of what Emily had said about him seeming to care more for the horses than for her. Perhaps he did. Why that thought should feel so very disappointing she didn't know.

Are you sure you don't know? You want him to care for you and you always have.

No, she didn't want that. Why would she? She'd already been in love with one husband who'd seemed indifferent to her and she didn't want to fall for another. Sebastián wasn't indifferent at least, but she knew that was all about their physical chemistry, despite what he'd said back in Madrid about it being more than that. If it had been more, he wouldn't have distanced her, so clearly he'd been mistaken.

'You can live somewhere else if you'd prefer,' he said. 'You're not a prisoner here, Alice. You can go wherever you like.'

The inexplicable disappointment deepened into hurt. So not only did he not want to talk to her, he was also completely happy for her to leave.

He told you what to expect.

A physical marriage, that was all. And back in Madrid, on a high from the sex they'd had, she'd been fine with that. But now the reality of her situation was becoming apparent, she realised that actually she wasn't fine with that.

But there was no point in telling him she was hurt or making a fuss about it. That was what Emily had done. Either that or running away, and she wasn't going to do that either. Instead, she reached for her anger, because that at least made her feel strong.

'And if I did?' she asked shortly. 'What would you do at night without me in your bed?'

A muscle ticced in the side of his jaw, a sure sign of his own temper rising. 'I would survive.'

So, after the intense passion they'd shared and then insisting on a full marriage, he was now completely happy for her to move out?

The hurt inside her deepened, a knife twisting in her gut. It was so much a reminder of her marriage to Edward that it was painful. Edward might have chosen her, but he hadn't fought for their relationship, and he hadn't fought for her. When he'd been unhappy, he'd turned around and gone after her sister instead.

'Okay, so you're absolutely fine with me living somewhere else, then.' She knew she was starting to sound shrill and yet she couldn't help herself. 'And you don't apparently care whether I'm around or not. I get it. But I did think the whole point of this marriage was to create a family for Diego.'

The muscle in his jaw leapt again. 'It is. I'm not the one threatening to live somewhere else.'

Her anger twisted hard. Did he really not understand? Perhaps he didn't. Yet that would mean having to tell him that she was lonely. That she wanted more than this. More from him. How could she though, when she didn't even know what more she wanted?

Then again, if she didn't tell him, how would he know?

'It's isolating, Sebastián,' she said, trying not to sound as pathetic as she feared she might. 'And it's lonely. I uprooted my whole life to come here and yet for the past two weeks I've been alone with nothing but Diego for company. Which is fine, but he's a baby. He can't exactly have a conversation with me.'

Something shifted in Sebastián's eyes, a flicker of what looked like surprise, but it was gone before she could read it. 'What do you want, then?' he asked. 'I'm busy during the day and you get plenty of attention at night.'

'I'm not talking about sex,' she snapped. 'Some adult conversation might be nice.'

'Fine. What do you want to talk about?'

He didn't want to talk to her. He really couldn't be clearer.

The needle of hurt dug deeper. Again, this felt like what had happened with her and Edward, her constantly pushing and him retreating, giving her what she wanted and yet always in ways that felt placating. It had always felt false. She hated it.

Suddenly her appetite for argument vanished, leaving her with a bone-deep emotional exhaustion that had nothing to do with lack of sleep and more to do with spending two weeks fighting grief and an intense desire for a man who apparently wanted nothing from her but sex.

'Forget it,' she said, abruptly turning away. 'I've changed my mind.'

The air felt tight around him, as if her entering the stables had somehow tipped the oxygen right out of it. She had on one of the loose summer dresses she'd taken to wearing around the hacienda, this one in a deep golden yellow, and it made her skin look gilded, her eyes like the darkest espresso, and her hair as if there were threads of gold running through the glossy black strands.

She was so beautiful. She was also hurt and angry, and all thanks to him.

He should let her walk away, let her take that hurt and anger with her, but while he could stand her temper, he couldn't bear to hurt her. Emily had told him the same thing about life at the hacienda being lonely and isolating, yet it hadn't been time with him that Emily had wanted. She'd wanted to go back to the city, to shop and eat at fancy restaurants, and go out to nightclubs and parties. Oh, she'd wanted him to come with her and he'd gone a couple of times, but those things weren't to his taste. He preferred the quiet of the countryside, spending time with the horses, going riding and hiking in the mountains, or simply sitting in the hacienda courtyard with a good book.

Alice wasn't asking for any of the things Emily had. All she'd wanted was some conversation. It wasn't much, and yet she couldn't have asked for anything more dangerous. Mainly because he'd been trying to set boundaries around their marriage for the past two weeks.

He'd realised not long after they'd returned from Madrid that he was on a precipice. That the more time he spent with Alice, the closer to the edge he got and if he wasn't careful, he was going to let his desire for her carry him straight over it.

The fantasies he'd had of being able to have her whenever he wanted and no one to stop them this time had been heady and intense, and also too much. So he'd decided that keeping himself distant during the day and only letting the leash off at night, in bed, was the answer. Made sure it all stayed about sex and nothing else.

There had to be clear boundaries. His emotions always led him astray and then he'd end up failing the people who mattered to him, the way he'd done with Mateo and Emily, and he wasn't doing that again. He couldn't. He didn't want to give Alice any false expectations either.

So yes, he should let her walk away and yet he found

himself reaching for her all the same, his fingers closing around her bare arm and holding on tight, stopping her from leaving. 'Wait,' he said in a low voice.

She halted and turned back to him, and, even though she was trying to hide it, he could see the hurt glinting in her dark eyes.

Dios. He'd been a bastard to her.

'I'm sorry,' he said, hating her hurt and wanting to give her the truth, because she deserved it. 'I know what you gave up to come here and marry me, that it was a sacrifice. You did it for Diego and I appreciate that. He is the most important thing in the world to me, and knowing you will be a mother to him is the best outcome I could have hoped for.'

She stared up at him, her lush mouth losing the hardness around it, the glint of hurt in her eyes easing. Her skin was so warm beneath his fingertips, and he could feel his desire for her begin to coil like thick smoke in his veins.

'But I've been deliberately putting distance between us these past two weeks, Alice,' he went on. 'And yes, it's because of you.'

Surprise flickered over her face. 'Why?' Then the surprise faded, leaving yet more hurt behind it. 'What did I do?'

Look at you. You failed Emily and now you're failing Alice.

No, he wouldn't. He couldn't hurt her the way he'd hurt Emily. He tugged her closer. 'You did nothing,' he said. 'The problem is me.'

She gave him a searching look. 'How?'

It was going to be difficult to articulate the complicated need he had for her. The strange compulsion that had gripped him the moment he'd first seen her, that had caused him to constantly crave her presence even though he was married to her sister.

He knew it wasn't love. He'd already experienced love and it was cruel. Love had made his mother betray her vows and caused his father's bitter resentment. Love had made him a target for Mateo's anger and been the reason Javier had lost his job. Love wasn't something he'd ever wanted to give anyone else, though he'd tried to give Emily a facsimile of it and it had caused her nothing but heartache.

He couldn't make that same mistake with Alice.

'When you're around I…can't think,' he said slowly. 'I can't do anything but imagine you beneath me and it's… consuming. It interferes with everything. I told you, it's an obsession, and there has to be some boundaries, understand? It's easier to keep my distance.'

'Easier for you, you mean?'

He could deny it, give her some lie and then walk away, but he couldn't do that. It wouldn't be fair, not to either of them. 'Yes,' he said bluntly.

'So what about me? Am I supposed to…what? Just accept that I can't even talk to you? Is that what you're saying?'

'Alice—'

'How is that fair? I'm not asking for your heart on a plate, Sebastián. Only a conversation.'

His fingers tightened on her arm, frustration coiling

through him. 'It will never be just a conversation, that's what I'm trying to tell you.'

'So? What are you so afraid of?'

'You,' he said before he could stop himself. 'I'm afraid of falling for you.'

The words crashed into the silence like stones through a window, shattering the nice little lie he'd told himself that this was all about physical obsession.

He didn't want to fall for her. His first wife was only two months dead and he'd failed her.

Just as you failed your father. Just as you failed Javier.

And that was the truth, wasn't it? He hadn't been his father's son and he hadn't been Javier's, even though he was Mateo's by adoption and Javier's by blood. He'd been nobody's. And so nothing he'd done had ever been good enough.

It won't be good enough for her either...

Alice pulled her arm from his grasp and took a small step back, her eyes still wide and dark. The flickering emotions in them made his breath catch.

She shook her head. 'That's...not... I can't...'

'Of course not,' he said, so she didn't have to explain. 'It's too soon after Emily's death and now I have Diego.'

She glanced away, lifting a hand to her mouth, her fingers trembling. 'You said it was nothing more than sex.' Her voice was slightly hoarse. 'That's what you said in Madrid.'

He'd shocked her, he could see that. And it was clear that love wasn't something she wanted either. A part of him was satisfied by that and yet another part found it...

No. He couldn't think about that. It would lead him one step closer to the precipice and he wasn't going to do that. 'Yes,' he said reluctantly, 'I did.'

Her dark eyes came to his again. 'So maybe…we need to find out once and for all. Maybe if we have no limits, no boundaries, we can…keep doing whatever we want until this…obsession is all gone.'

The idea had merit. In Madrid, she'd said that perhaps part of the appeal had been how forbidden each of them had been to the other, and even though he'd denied it at the time, maybe she hadn't been wrong. In which case putting limits on his hunger would of course make her even more appealing to him.

So…perhaps if he took the limits off completely, indulged in every single one of his fantasies whenever and wherever he liked, not just at night but during the day too, that would make his own hunger less intense. It was worth considering.

Maybe if he spent time with her, if they lost themselves totally in each other, they'd discover that what this instant chemistry between them had been all along was only physical attraction and the allure of the forbidden. An illusion giving the impression of a depth that wasn't there.

'Are you sure that's a good idea?' he asked.

Slowly Alice lifted her chin. 'I don't want to fall for you any more than you want to fall for me, because you're right. It's too soon. I lost my sister and Edward, and Diego is more important than anything. How can we give him the family he needs when we're so consumed by what we feel for each other anyway? We need to know. We need to find out. Or at least get rid of the…want. Neither of us want love, Sebastián, so perhaps it will work out.'

She was right, especially about Diego. This constant uncertainty when it came to her and what he felt wouldn't be a good foundation on which to build the kind of family he wanted for his son. They needed to burn out their need for each other and do it without distractions, so they could then decide what their marriage would be like going forward. And with Diego front and centre.

His heartbeat was suddenly loud, desire rising inside him, relentless and all-consuming. Her, with no boundaries, no limits… They hadn't had a honeymoon—he hadn't thought they'd need one, but perhaps that had been a mistake. Perhaps a honeymoon was exactly what they should have, and away from the hacienda. Away from the memories of Emily and Edward and the Christmases they'd spent here. Away from the ghosts of his own marriage and his failure.

A honeymoon where there were no memories. Where they could find out what *their* marriage looked like in a place that was theirs and only theirs.

'If you could go anywhere in the world,' he asked abruptly, 'where would you go?'

Alice blinked. 'What? What's that got to do with anything?'

'We didn't have a honeymoon and I think that was a mistake.'

She gave him a wary look. 'So, you're saying we should have one?'

'Yes. Away from the hacienda and the memories here.

Away from everything. If we know what we don't want, then we can decide what we do.'

She nodded slowly. 'Okay. But we do it together. You don't make decisions like putting distance between us for me and I don't make them for you.'

That was fair. He should have said something to her about that, he should have been clearer.

Already you're failing.

No, no, he wouldn't, not this time. Not with her.

'So,' he said, allowing the need that was strangling him to deepen his voice. 'In the interests of making decisions together, tell me where you want to go.'

Something lit slowly in her eyes and he felt warmth settle just behind his breastbone in response. It had been a long time since he'd put that light in anyone's eyes, in fact the last time had been when he'd bought Emily her Paris apartment. Then there had been a bitterness in him at the gift, because what he'd actually been giving her was his absence, and that was what had made her look so pleased. Not with Alice though. A honeymoon meant time spent in each other's presence and it was clear that was exactly what she wanted.

She wanted to spend time with him.

Her mouth curved and the warmth deepened. This was the first time he'd made her smile. 'Okay, well, I like sun and I like swimming. Nice food obviously. I also love beaches and being on the ocean.'

Good. He liked all of those things too. 'No sightseeing?'

'I don't know if that's the point of this, is it?'

No, it wasn't. The point was seeing each other, not other things.

'Fine. Will you leave the decision to me?'

She tilted her head slightly, her mouth curving even more. 'I like how you're not really giving me the option.'

There was a teasing note in her voice, only slight, but it was there, and it made the warmth spread through him, thawing parts of him that had been frozen for a long time. Perhaps even since his father had made it very clear just how wide the gap between them was and how it was up to him to bridge it. He wasn't actually Mateo's son after all, so *he* had to be the one to do the work.

And suddenly he couldn't stand the distance between them. If there were no limits and no boundaries, if they were going to test what this thing actually was between them, then he didn't have to fight any of his urges. In fact, it was better if he actively indulged them.

So he crossed the space separating them and pulled her into his arms. 'Do you want the option?'

'No,' she said without hesitation, her palms coming to rest on his chest. 'In fact, you can arrange everything if you like.'

The warmth was changing now, becoming the kind of heat it always did whenever he was touching her, whenever he was even near her. A fire, a blaze, all-consuming, devastating.

'Good,' he said. 'And this honeymoon? It starts now.'

Then he bent his head and took her mouth like a man starving.

CHAPTER NINE

ALICE LAY ON the blanket on the sand and watched Sebastián stride from the sea, magnificently naked, drops of water and brilliant sunshine delineating every hard-cut muscle of his powerful body. His tan had deepened, providing a rich foil to the smoky gold of his eyes, the colour standing out even more as he came towards her across the sand.

Her stomach clenched. Everything clenched. He was so beautiful and he was her husband. Hers.

Your husband who doesn't love you.

That was true, but they'd already decided back in Spain that love wouldn't feature in their marriage. There were too many reasons why it wasn't a good idea. They'd both lost their spouses and her heart was still broken and bleeding, and she couldn't risk giving it to someone else. Especially someone who didn't want it anyway.

What about later? When the grief has eased? What about then?

Alice pushed the thought out of her mind. There was no point thinking about the future and she didn't want to anyway. Not when the present was so much better. The present with *him* filling every moment of it.

She could hardly believe how much she wanted him. In fact she seemed to have an endless capacity. A hunger that didn't seem to be getting any better no matter how many times they indulged it, and they'd indulged it *a lot* since they'd arrived.

Sebastián had kept their final destination a surprise and it wasn't until they were in a smaller plane from Belize City and flying over the Belize Barrier Reef in the Caribbean that Sebastián had told her where they were going.

A villa on a tiny, private and very remote island. There were no other people on the island, and, apart from a small cottage on a neighbouring island that housed the staff who managed the villa, there was no one else within miles.

The island had the most beautiful white sand beaches surrounding it and the villa itself was sprawling and open-plan, with massive floor-to-ceiling windows that doubled as doors so one entire wall could be opened up. There were lazy fans and dark wooden floors and the master bedroom had a huge four-poster bed hung with gauzy white curtains.

It was the most utterly perfect place she could imagine.

The first couple of days were spent entirely sating themselves physically with each other, neither of them holding back. They didn't talk, but talking hadn't been the point, at least not initially. That could wait until their physical hunger was at least at a reasonable level.

After the intensity had eased a little, they explored the island, spending hours in the water and lying on the beach. There was a small boat for their use and Sebastián piloted it out to the nearby reef where they snorkelled amongst multicoloured coral and fish. It was astonishingly beautiful.

He refused to let her do a thing, cooking for her and bringing her treats, making sure her every wish was catered to, and she loved it. Her and Edward's honeymoon had been spent in Italy and, while she'd enjoyed it, even then she'd had the nagging feeling that Edward had been far more interested in sightseeing than in spending time with her.

She had no such doubts about Sebastián. She was what interested him, and he made no secret of it. She'd never felt so desired. Except his interest seemed to be limited to the here and now, what they were doing that day and what she'd like for dinner and whether she'd like having her hands tied to the headboard of the bed as he made love to her.

Perhaps he was waiting to talk more until later, or perhaps he was waiting for her to broach the topic first. Either way though, it made a subtle tension run through her, a nameless doubt she couldn't shake.

He came up now to the blanket she was lying on, beneath a pavilion hung with shade cloth to protect them both from the sun, water dripping from his magnificent body as he picked up a towel and dried himself off.

She made a cursory protest as water scattered over her bare skin, but she didn't really mind, not when she was enjoying watching the play of water on his tanned skin. He dropped the towel and lay down on his side beside her, his head propped on his hand. When he smiled, her heart turned over in her chest.

'I'm afraid of falling for you,' he'd said back in Spain.

She hadn't been able to get it out of her head. He'd been honest, his gaze fierce, yet there had been a grim note in his voice when he'd said it.

A shiver at the memory went through her. She'd been shocked. Firstly that he'd been anywhere close to falling for her, which she hadn't known, and secondly, that her initial reaction had been one of pure, unadulterated joy.

In fact, if she thought about it now, she could still feel the warmth of that joy, like the Caribbean sun blazing in her heart. She'd struggled to cover it because there had been no joy in his face, no joy in his voice either. He'd said it as if falling for her would be the worst thing in the world.

That had hurt, made the knife twist hard inside her, but she was good at masking her emotions, so she'd made sure that hurt didn't show. It was fine if he didn't want to love her. Love had always been a fraught emotion, full of high expectations and crushing disappointments, of giving and giving and getting nothing in return. Of feeling as if she wasn't good enough for anyone. Not for her parents, not for Edward. And maybe in the end, not enough for Emily either. Because if she had been, would Emily have had an affair with Alice's husband?

Really, she was better off without it, and most especially from him.

Yet no matter what she told herself, she could still feel that joy inside her. The bright spark of possibility that refused to be ignored. And looking into his eyes now, she couldn't help the rogue thought that whispered just how good it would be to be loved by him. To have all his fierce passion directed on her, and not just the physical passion. The emotional intensity that had had him claim Diego and refuse to give him up.

You want that. You want to be claimed. You want to be loved and loved passionately. You're hungry for it.

Her throat closed with longing. Well, who wouldn't be hungry for it? But it didn't have to be with him. She could find some other man like him who didn't have all the baggage and who was ready to love and be loved in return.

But there are no other men like him and you know that.

She tore her gaze away from his mesmerising smile. It wasn't true. There were plenty of men like him. Men with smoky golden eyes and fierce passion and intensity. Men who blazed with desire when she touched them. Men who wanted her just as fiercely as she wanted them…

The strange grief in her throat got worse. No, she was lying to herself. It was true. There were no other men like him. He was the only one. And she could tell herself all she liked that she'd find someone else and fall in love with him, but the truth was that wasn't going to happen.

No. Because you're in love with him and you have been ever since the day you met him.

Cold prickled all over her skin, her stomach dropping, and she had to stare hard at the brilliant turquoise of the lagoon to control her expression. Her heart was thundering in her chest so loud she could barely hear anything else.

Love at first sight. The lightning bolt from the blue. She'd never believed in it. She hadn't loved Edward at first sight. That had grown over the years he and she and Emily were at school. Maybe that was why she hadn't recognised what she'd felt for Sebastián when it had happened. Because she hadn't believed it would ever happen to her and yet… It had. She was in love with him, completely and utterly and she had been for the past five years. But she'd been married so she'd minimised it, told herself it was just some strange attraction she didn't understand. Yet it had never been that.

He doesn't want to love you in return.

She tried to ignore the lump of pain and grief that choked her. She couldn't let that matter. She had to pretend that all of this was just sexual attraction and nothing more, because maybe if she did, it would go away. She certainly couldn't tell him how she felt, not when doing so might ruin this special time together. And especially not when he'd been perfectly clear about what he wanted and what he didn't.

'Alice?' he asked, his voice full of concern. 'What's wrong?'

Forcing away her emotions, she swallowed hard and braced herself before glancing back at him. Somehow she managed to produce a smile. 'Nothing. Only…sometimes you're just too gorgeous to even look at.'

He laughed, which made everything worse, because the sound was so warm and so devastatingly attractive. She could listen to him laugh until the end of time. 'I know the feeling,' he said, his gaze turning molten as it ran over her in blatant appreciation. 'Though I think I can force myself.'

Inevitable arousal moved like a tide through her veins. God, how she loved the way he looked at her. She was as naked as he was and the obvious delight he took in her nakedness had gone a long way to boosting her confidence in her body. She'd even come to enjoy wearing nothing, especially since it meant he wore nothing too.

Yet another reason to love him.

She fought to keep the smile on her face, to not let any trace of her thoughts show. Luckily his attention had dropped to her stomach. He frowned slightly then reached to trace her surgery scar. She'd been very aware of it initially, the first time she'd been naked with him, but he hadn't made any comment about it or drawn attention to it, and gradually she'd lost her self-consciousness.

Now though, as his fingers brushed over the thin white line just above her pubic bone, she tensed.

He glanced up immediately. 'You don't want me touching you here?'

She swallowed again, trying to relax. 'No, it's fine.'

'It's not fine. You're tense.'

'It doesn't hurt, if that's what you're asking. It's just…'

'Painful in other ways,' he finished for her.

What could she say other than the truth? 'Yes,' she said simply. 'It is.'

He kept his hand where it was, his fingertips tracing the line of her scar with such gentleness that the full, aching feeling already in her heart became heavy and raw.

'I'm so sorry this happened to you,' he murmured. 'You wanted children quite badly, didn't you?'

She didn't know why he was choosing now to talk about this, and, given how emotionally fragile she felt already, she should have found both his question and his touch intrusive. Yet she didn't. He was so gentle and maybe that was why her heart hurt so much. Because she could hear the sympathy in his voice, as if what had happened to her was important to him, as if it mattered.

Yet another reason to love him.

For some inexplicable reasons tears prickled in her eyes, though she fought them back. 'I did,' she said huskily. 'And it wasn't just the baby and its future I lost, but also any possibility of having another and all the futures that went with it.'

His gaze was warm, his fingers still tracing her scar gently, as if he were soothing it and her. 'When did it happen?'

'About two years after Edward and I got married. It was my...first pregnancy.'

He glanced down at the scar. 'I saw a light go out inside you at some point. I always wondered what happened. Now I know you were grieving.'

A little shock ran through her that he'd noticed the change in her because no one else had apart from Emily. But yes, he was right, she'd been grieving.

'Edward wanted to move on,' she said, even though it felt disloyal to say. 'He was kind, don't get me wrong, but he thought the sooner we put it behind us, the better. He didn't want to discuss it either. He mentioned surrogates and adoptions initially, but...' She stopped, stripped bare by the pain of the memories even though it had been years ago, and by another, somehow deeper pain that had only just occurred to her. Sebastián wanted more children yet she would never be able to give them to him. She would never carry his baby. Never.

The knife in her heart twisted.

'Alice,' Sebastián said, his expression full of concern. 'We don't have to talk about it if it's too painful.'

She set her jaw, forcing away the hurt the way she always did. 'No, it's okay. It's been years and I'm over it.'

He said nothing for a long moment, looking at her, the compassion in his eyes making her want to weep despite everything. 'Were you ever allowed to grieve properly?' he asked softly. 'Were you ever allowed to mourn?'

The question felt as if he were twisting in the knife even harder, yet there was nothing but understanding in his expression. Grief was no stranger to either of them, she realised, and he knew loss when he saw it.

'No,' she admitted. 'I don't think I was. I don't think I...let myself grieve. Edward was patient with me but...' She swallowed, wanting to say it even though, again, it was another disloyal thought. 'I always had the impression that he wasn't as upset about it as I was and that he didn't think it was as important as I did. Even later, he never followed up on adoptions or anything.' She took a breath, suddenly weighed down by grief. 'I'll never be able to have your child, Sebastián. Never.' She hadn't meant to cry and yet there were tears in her eyes, and then his hands were reaching for her, pulling her close, his arms folding around her.

He didn't speak, only held her, and somehow the warmth of his presence and the strength of his arms had her weeping into his chest as the pain cut its way through her heart. He remained silent, holding her tightly, giving her space to grieve for the baby she lost and all those futures. For her failure of a marriage and for the husband who hadn't really loved her. And for her sister, whom she'd loved even though she'd betrayed her.

Eventually her sobs ran dry and he kept holding her, stroking her hair and murmuring soft words in Spanish that were inexplicably comforting.

Another reason to love him.

Her eyes were scratchy and her throat was sore and her heart ached and ached. She wished passionately that the day she'd met him she'd been true to her heart and recognised the feeling for what it was. That she'd been honest with her husband and left him instead of fighting for something that neither of them had wanted any more.

But she hadn't. And now all she was left with was her broken, shattered heart that somehow still managed to beat for a man who thought the worst thing in the world would be to love her back.

She had no idea what she was going to do.

'I could tell you that I don't care that you won't have my child,' Sebastián said after a long moment, his deep voice rumbling in her ear. 'I do care. But I also care about you and your pain. But you know that Diego will be our child in every way there is. And we will have more, I promise it.'

It *did* matter to him. It did. That was what she'd wanted from Edward, just some sign that he felt the loss too, yet Edward had never given it to her. But Sebastián had. And it felt good to know he felt the same way, and also that he felt all wasn't lost.

Of course they would have Diego and others, too.

She lifted her damp face from his chest, and looked up at his hard, carved features. His expression was fierce, as was the burning look in his eyes. It was clear that this was a promise he intended to keep.

Yet another reason to love him.

She wished she didn't keep thinking that. She wished her heart would stop reminding her that this man was the only one for her.

'What about Emily?' she asked, her voice still thick with tears. 'Did you want children with her?'

He reached to gently brush the tears from her face. 'Yes. But she didn't, not right away. She wanted to wait a few years. That was okay with me initially, because I was busy in the stables. I didn't insist either, because I wanted to give her time to adjust to our marriage and to living in Spain.' He pushed a curl behind her ear. 'Like Edward, she didn't want to have the discussion about children. She kept avoiding it. And then Diego arrived.'

'You really thought he was yours?'

'I had no reason to believe otherwise. And when I did find out, it genuinely made no difference to how I felt about him. In fact, after I found out I became even more certain that he would be my son.'

'Why? Because of your father?'

'Yes. I couldn't let any child grow up the way I did. Mateo was resentful of me for not truly being his. I was the evidence of my mother's faithlessness and that needled him but, since I was also the only way he'd ever get an heir, there wasn't much else he could do.'

The aching grief in her chest had gradually subsided and all she wanted was to lie here in his arms and ask him questions about his childhood. She was hungry for information now.

'Did he hurt you?' she asked, concerned.

'No.' Sebastián gently stroked the crease between her brows. 'Don't worry, *mi cielo*, he didn't. Not physically. He was…exacting. Demanding. A jealous man too. I used to love visiting the stables, because I loved the horses, and I spent a lot of time with Javier, who was the best stable manager we ever had. Javier didn't know I was his and I didn't know he was my biological father, not then. I just knew I liked being with him. Mateo became very jealous of the time I spent with him and eventually he fired Javier and told me that Javier had lost his job because of me. Because I was disloyal and ungrateful.'

Her heart seized at the blunt words. 'That sounds… awful.'

His eyes glinted as he looked at her. 'Mateo already had an unfaithful wife, and he drew the line at having an unfaithful son. Especially when that son was actually the son of his wife's lover.'

'Still,' she said. 'That doesn't excuse him being awful to you. It wasn't fair of him to treat you like that. It wasn't your fault that you weren't his. It's not as if you were allowed to choose your own father.'

'No,' he agreed. 'But then being Javier's son wasn't the only reason he resented me.'

'There was another reason?'

'Yes.' The glitter in his eyes became sharper, harder. 'He told me that I'd killed my mother.'

Alice's eyes went wide with shock and concern. He'd been too blunt but that was exactly what Mateo had told him and in just that way. Making him feel like a murderer.

He shouldn't have said anything about it, of course, but she'd asked and there was no reason not to tell her. She should know about his bitter childhood so she'd understand what he hoped to avoid with Diego.

She was beautiful here, lying naked against his chest with the warm Caribbean salt-scented air feathering over both of them. Her hair was a wild tangle over her shoulders, and she still had the flower behind her ear that he'd put there that morning, a hibiscus blooming pink and gold and red.

Her eyes were red from her moment of grief for her lost baby and her lost fertility, the tracks of her tears still shiny on her skin. The sight of them made him ache.

He shouldn't have made their first discussion about that loss, not when it was obviously still so painful for her, but when he'd come out of the water and dropped down beside her, that scar on her belly was all he could see. He knew what it was and he hadn't wanted to say anything about it earlier, and yet after spending days making love to her, knowing it was there and knowing what it meant... He couldn't keep ignoring it.

Her lost child, her lost fertility, her lost marriage were all things they needed to talk about, just as they needed to talk about their future and their own marriage. Everything had remained so unspoken between them for so long and they couldn't keep doing that.

So he'd touched that scar gently, tracing the line of it over her warm skin.

She hadn't held back when he'd asked her about it and when she'd starkly said that she'd never have his child, and he'd seen the grief in her eyes, he'd felt the same grief inside himself too. Both at realising that, yes, he wanted her to carry his child, and yet knowing she never would.

That it felt painful to him meant that the edge of the precipice was even nearer than he'd thought, and that he'd have to be careful. Yet he'd pulled her into his arms to comfort her instead, unable to stop himself.

Years ago he'd wanted to do the same thing when he'd seen the light inside her go out, but back then it hadn't been his place to do so.

He was her husband now, though, and it was definitely his place, and, regardless of whether it was a good idea or not, he was going to give her comfort and space to grieve however he could.

They had to be able to talk to each other in order to build a healthy relationship between them. A relationship that would provide the best environment for Diego to grow up in.

Now, Alice was looking up at him, her eyes dark. 'What do you mean you killed her?'

He tried never to think about that day in his father's office. It had been a long time ago, yet, despite the years, it still felt as if his father with those words had reached inside his chest and gouged out his heart. The simple cruelty of it, to an eleven-year-old boy, still bothered him.

Another reason why you can't fall in love with her.

Of course not. He'd seen the true face of love that day and it was petty and cruel and jealous. He wanted no part of it ever again.

'Mateo never told me how my mother died,' he said. 'And no one knew that I wasn't Mateo's son. And until the day he fired Javier, not even I knew.'

Alice look aghast. 'What? You mean he kept that all from you, only to dump it all on you then? Why?'

His father's face had been red with fury and Sebastián had been bewildered as to why. He'd thought that his spending time with the horses was what Mateo wanted, especially learning from Javier, the most experienced of the stable hands.

'Mateo was jealous,' he said. 'And vindictive. And he was furious that I'd spent more time with my biological father than him. He accused me of being as faithless and ungrateful as my mother. Then he told me that she'd had an affair with Javier, that I was Javier's son and that my mother had died having me. And he told me all of that for no other reason than to hurt me.'

'Oh, Sebastián,' Alice breathed, her expression full of deep sympathy and a flickering hurt that he knew was for him. 'I'm so sorry.'

He wasn't sure why the rest of the words spilled out, given what they revealed, but they did. 'He told me I was a poor replacement for her, that I wasn't who he would have chosen for a son. But I was all he'd had to work with and so I'd have to do.'

Her hands had pressed flat against his chest, the look in her dark eyes making him ache. 'What a terrible thing to say to a child. And how cruel.'

Yes. Mateo *had* been cruel and vindictive, and needlessly petty. But Sebastián knew why. He'd loved his wife and she'd been unfaithful to him and had a child by another man. Sebastián's mere presence hit Mateo in a place where he was most sensitive—his male pride.

Another reason why you can't love her, no matter how understanding she is. No matter how much you want to.

It was true. He didn't know if his mother had loved Javier, but they'd clearly formed enough of a bond that she'd been unfaithful to her husband for him. And he had been the result. Just as he was the cause of his mother's death.

After his father had told him the bitter truth, he hadn't known what to do. All he'd known was that he was the cause of so much unhappiness and so the only way forward seemed to be trying his hardest to make up for it.

Except Mateo had made it very clear that nothing Sebastián did ever would.

It still doesn't.

'I got over it,' he said, pushing the thought away.

'Though my father made it very obvious that nothing I could do would make up for her loss. He wasn't very good at hiding his resentment or his jealousy, and I think if I hadn't had the horses I might have eventually decided it wasn't worth it and left. But they were what kept me there.'

Her fingertips were warm on his skin, her gaze dark and deep, piercing him right through. She'd always seemed to see more than he wanted her to. More than Emily had. He hadn't told Emily about his father, for example, mainly because Emily had never asked.

'That's why you care about the horses,' Alice murmured. 'Why you love them. They accepted you.'

How she somehow knew that, he wasn't sure, but it was true nonetheless.

He stroked his thumb across her cheekbone, relishing the feel of her skin. 'They did. They were much more accepting than my father ever was. All a horse needs is some good hay, clean water and kindness, and maybe an apple now and then. They don't require anything else and they don't need you to be anything else.'

'I understand,' she said. 'No wonder you spent a lot of time with them.' She paused a moment, her dark brows drawing together. 'You know that your father was wrong, don't you? And that the horses were right. He should have learned from them. He should have accepted you the way you were, just like you accepted Diego.'

A thread of impatience wound through him. He didn't want to keep talking about this, because what was the point? The past was immutable. He couldn't change it now even if he wanted to.

'Perhaps,' he said, dismissive. 'But he didn't. And in his mind, my mother's death was my fault and so how could anything I do ever make up for that?' He'd been bitter once, but he'd lost that over the years, because there was no reason to dwell on it. Mateo hadn't accepted him and had continued to blame him right up to the day he died, and it was what it was.

Alice reached up and took his face between her hands, her fingertips cool on his cheeks. 'You're not supposed to make up for it,' she said. 'You were a child. A baby. You didn't do anything to anyone.'

'I know that,' he said. 'But he blamed me for it anyway.'

'He shouldn't have,' Alice said insistently. 'He might have been grieving and angry, and all of those things, but that was *his* issue. He shouldn't have made it yours.'

But there must have been something bad about you, something wrong. Why else would he have been so cruel? Why else would you have caused such unhappiness to so many people?

Something twisted painfully in his heart, as if she'd touched on an old wound, an old doubt that had festered even though he'd tried to forget it.

'Perhaps I should have helped him,' he said, even though he didn't want to say it. 'Perhaps there was something I could have done to make it better.'

Alice's fingers pressed a little harder. 'Tell me,' she said, that light in her eyes that had drawn him to her so powerfully flickering. 'If Emily had died having Diego, would you have told him the same thing eventually? That he killed her? Would you expect him as a little boy to make it up to you?'

A shock went through him, bringing with it a ferocious protectiveness. 'No,' he said flatly before he'd even thought it through. 'Never.'

'No,' she echoed. 'And there was no excuse for him to treat you like that, either. You didn't deserve it, Sebastián.'

There was so much conviction in her voice, so much warmth in her eyes that he teetered on the edge of the precipice, the wind threatening to take him over. It would be so easy to fall, so very easy. To name what he felt for her as love and let it take him.

But he couldn't. He already had one person in his life that had a claim on his heart—Diego. The thought of potentially failing him was crushing enough. He didn't want to add any more weight to the one he was already carrying.

'Whether I deserved it or not doesn't matter,' he said. 'But now you know why I will put Diego and his happiness before everything else. Why I want him to have a mother as well as a father. Why I want him to have a family, somewhere safe where he feels he belongs.'

Her gaze flickered, as if something about his response had disappointed her, though he wasn't sure what it had been.

This is how it starts. Failing her.

No, he wouldn't. This time it would be different, he'd

make sure of it. Love wasn't a possibility but he'd give her everything else. A home. Children. Comfort. Companionship. He'd support her career too and anything she chose to do. She could have just about everything she wanted.

They could have it.

And if she wants more?

But she didn't want more. She'd told him back in Spain that she didn't want love, that she felt the same way he did about it, and besides, she'd agreed to marry him. He'd told her what to expect and she'd still said yes.

Doesn't she deserve love, though? After everything she's lost?

Oh, she did. She deserved to be loved completely and utterly, but he wasn't going to be the one to give it to her. And if that meant she'd eventually leave him and find someone else who would, then he'd have to deal with that. He would never get in the way of her finding happiness, even if that was with another man.

Even if that thought makes you feral with rage.

He ignored the thought, shoved it away. That was a thought his father would have, one of those jealous, vindictive thoughts and he wouldn't be like him. Ever. If Alice wanted to leave him, he'd let her go, but... That didn't mean he couldn't make the decision a difficult one. In fact, he'd make it as hard for her to leave him as he could.

He turned her in his lap so she was facing him, her thighs spread on either side of his hips, the soft, damp heat of her sex pressing against his aching shaft. She gave one of those delicious little shivers that she always did whenever she was aroused, the darkness of her eyes seeming to glow and get molten.

'Of course you do,' she murmured. 'I want all those things for him too.'

'I know you do.' He settled one hand on her hip while he slid the other between her thighs, stroking the hot, soft folds he found there, making her gasp. 'But that doesn't mean that there can't be anything for us.'

She moaned, her hips flexing, arching against his hand. She was already wet for him, her nipples hard, her skin flushed. 'Such as?' she asked, her voice husky.

'This.' He moved his hand and gripped her other hip, sliding into her in one long, slow, deep thrust. 'And it's not just sex, *mi cielo*…my sky.' His voice had roughened at the tight clasp of her sex around his. 'It *is* more. We have a connection and it's not only physical.'

She slid her arms around his neck, her lovely body pressing hard against his. Her eyes had gone very dark, inches from his own, and he was captivated by the currents in them, light and shadow like the sun moving over a dark river.

'What else is it, then?' she asked softly. 'Tell me.'

He couldn't look away from the emotion shifting in her gaze. He began to move, watching as the building pleasure became part of those currents, turning into something powerful and deep, glowing in her eyes. 'It is emotional too,' he said, his voice even rougher. 'And I will be there for you, understand me? I will give you everything you need to be happy. Because your happiness is as important to me as Diego's.'

She stared back at him, unflinching, those currents in her eyes shifting and swirling. But she didn't speak, she only leaned forward and kissed him, her mouth hot and open and sweet. Yet he could also taste desperation, though he wasn't sure what she was so desperate about.

Are you certain? Are you certain you don't know?

But he pushed that thought aside as the pleasure began to get deeper, wider, and soon he wasn't thinking at all. There was only the rhythm between them and the friction that drove him out of his mind, the heat and the blazing passion that always seared both of them down to their souls.

And if a small, nagging doubt crept into his heart, it was soon lost under the relentless tide of ecstasy, as it washed over both of them and carried them away.

CHAPTER TEN

ALICE WALKED SLOWLY over pristine white sand still warm from the heat of the day, her hand held securely in Sebastián's as he walked beside her. They'd taken to having evening strolls along the beach to watch the sunset, sometimes talking idly about their day, sometimes not speaking at all and just enjoying each other's company.

It was peaceful and usually she relished this time with him. But tonight was their last night on the island. Tomorrow they'd be returning to Spain, and she couldn't shake the tension that coiled inside her.

All this would be ending and she didn't want to think about how it would be between them once they returned to the hacienda. Back to her life as Sebastián's wife in every way, except one.

Abruptly, he came to a stop and let go of her hand, bending to pick something up off the sand. 'For you, *mi cielo*,' he murmured and held it out to her.

It was a shell, polished by the sea and the sand, gleaming in the light of the setting sun, its smooth white surface stained pink and gold and red.

'Oh,' she breathed, taking it from him and turning it over in her palm to examine it. 'It's beautiful.'

He smiled, genuine and warm, his eyes full of the familiar heat that always stole her breath clean away. 'Yes,' he said, 'it is.'

But he wasn't looking at the shell. He was looking at her.

Her heart ached in her chest and her throat closed. She'd never get enough of the compliments he gave her, never. And when he gave them, she always felt as beautiful as he told her she was. For the first time in years.

Will he say those things to you back in Spain, too? Will he still look at you the way he's doing now? Or will that heat in his eyes grow colder? Will he stop looking at you at all...?

Alice tore her gaze from his, directing it out over the ocean instead, the agonising pressure of all that love in her heart like a weight, crushing her.

It had become even worse after that day on the beach when he'd told her about his father and the terrible things he'd said to Sebastián. How he'd made a lonely little boy feel as if he'd failed. She'd hurt for him so much. She knew what it was like to believe that you weren't enough, to feel as if you'd disappointed people.

It wasn't fair and it wasn't right, and she'd wanted more than anything to help him understand that he hadn't deserved it and that nothing he did was a failure. That he couldn't blame himself for his mother's death or his father's inability to accept him.

He hadn't brought up the subject again, so perhaps she hadn't succeeded.

'If I didn't know any better,' she said with forced lightness, shoving the drag of grief away, 'I'd say you were a romantic, Sebastián Castellano.'

He didn't seem to notice the effort in her tone, his fingers threading through hers and drawing her close with gentle insistence. 'Apparently, there are many things you don't know about me.' He leaned forward to brush his mouth over hers. 'Perhaps a few lessons will be in order.'

The ache inside her intensified. She'd love to know more about him and not just the pain of his childhood, but about the things that brought him joy. That made him happy. That made him laugh. She wanted to know *everything*.

'And perhaps I might even like that.' She leaned into his warmth, trying to concentrate only on this moment with him and not on the fact that they'd be leaving the next day. 'I'd very much like you to teach me to ride, too.'

'Of course.' He stroked his thumb over her knuckles, a wicked glint in his eyes. 'Though you don't appear to need much teaching. You have a natural talent for it.'

Despite the ache and the tension clutched around her heart, she couldn't help smiling. 'That's the most blatant double entendre I've ever heard.'

'I could be more blatant if you like.' The wickedness in his eyes gleamed brighter, hotter, his mouth curving. 'I could even give you your first lesson here and now.'

She wanted to. Wanted to lie down with him on the hot sand and let his touch take away the knowledge of their impending departure, if only for a brief time. Wanted to keep teasing him, keep flirting with him, since being able to was new and special, and she liked it. But that would only make things worse. Deepen her longing for what she couldn't have, what he'd already told her he would never give her, and quite frankly she wasn't that much of a masochist.

'Hold that thought,' she whispered, going up on her toes to give him a quick kiss back in promise. 'For when we have a mattress instead of sand.'

'That didn't seem to bother you yesterday.'

She leaned against him, her hand on his broad chest, feeling the strong beat of his heart, relishing this peaceful moment. 'Maybe I just like saying no to you.'

Amusement lit his eyes. 'You have a natural talent for that too.'

Her chest tightened even further. She liked him teasing her in return and she couldn't resist responding to it, spreading her fingers wide to feel the heat of him through his T-shirt and the hard band of muscle beneath the fabric. 'And you like it.'

He laughed, the sound travelling through her like sunlight, turning her knees weak with want. And he lifted his free hand to push a lock of hair the wind had blown over her face behind her ear. 'I do, my lovely wife. God help me, but I do.'

Looking up into his beautiful face she almost said it, almost let slip what was in her heart. But at the last moment she bit it back. She wasn't going to ruin this night by giving him a truth he didn't want to hear, no matter how desperately she wanted to tell him how she felt.

Instead, she went up on her toes and brushed his mouth with hers. 'Good,' she whispered. 'Because I do too.'

Later, on the rooftop terrace of the villa, her hands on the pale stone of the parapet, Alice watched the rest of the sunset flaming over the ocean. The air was still warm and scented with salt and jasmine, and the turquoise of the lagoon looked as if it had been turned to flame by the setting sun, all reds and pinks and golds.

She should be enjoying the spectacle, but the ache in her chest that had begun during their evening walk had settled in. She was so tired of it. For the past few days she'd managed to push the fact that they were leaving aside, trying to exist only in the here and now, because the here and now was so wonderful. Yet as the hour of their departure loomed, she couldn't fight the pull of grief. And not, this time, for her sister or Edward, or even the baby she'd lost.

It was grief for the present that she was losing. Him, available whenever she wanted him. Ready to touch her, talk to her, hold her. Walk beside her along the sand and give her seashells. Show her some new delight in the rock pools near the beach or at her side as they snorkelled in the lagoon. His thoughtful, incisive conversation as they discussed politics and the state of the world, books and movies and everything in between over dinner. His strong arms holding her when the grief hit as it sometimes did, letting her know that she wasn't alone, that he was right there beside her.

And grief for the future that she wanted so badly and would never have.

Somehow her heart had known the moment she laid eyes on him that he was perfect for her in every way, and he was. A true soulmate. Except for the fact that he didn't feel the same way. He'd been very clear about that.

And it hurt, the thought of leaving here, of going back to their life and the reality of their marriage. He'd told her that day on the beach, when she was in his arms, that their connection was deep and emotional, that her happiness was important to him, and she'd tried to tell herself that that was enough.

But it wasn't. They'd promised to be honest with each other and yet she was terrified of telling him her deepest truth: that she was madly, passionately in love with him. Which was the one thing he didn't want. Telling him would change things between them irrevocably, because once that secret was out, she could never take it back. How it would change things, she didn't know, but she was very sure it wouldn't be for the good.

Besides, he might distance her and she'd already had that once before, and she'd hated it. She couldn't go back to it, especially now, after having these past two weeks with him. It would be like going from having everything to having nothing at all.

Still, she was tired of holding onto her secret. Tired of pretending she didn't feel it.

A footstep came from beside her and Sebastián was there, putting down a flute of champagne. He'd gone to open a bottle so they could toast their last night here.

She glanced at him and, as it always did, her breath caught. He was as gorgeous as ever in a loose white shirt and black trousers. His black hair looked as if there were threads of amber in it from the light of the setting sun, his eyes molten gold.

Her heart clenched and reflexively she looked away in case her heart was in her eyes.

'So,' Sebastián said. 'To our last night?'

Alice took a silent breath then reached for her flute and forced herself to meet his gaze. 'Our last night,' she echoed, her voice huskier than she wanted it to be, and raised her glass.

He toasted her, the glasses making a soft chiming sound as they knocked together.

She took a larger gulp of champagne than was probably wise, trying to moisten her dry throat and control the intensity of her emotions that suddenly felt choking. She wanted to leave right now, get this over and done with so she could get on with trying to figure out how to be in a marriage where she was desperately in love with her husband, while he wanted no part of that love.

'Something's wrong,' Sebastián said after a moment, watching her. 'What is it?'

Alice took another gulp of champagne, trying to resist the urge to drain her glass completely. 'Nothing.' She tore her gaze from his and stared out at the sunset. 'Sad to go home, I suppose.'

Sebastián was silent a moment. Then she felt his finger beneath her chin as he turned her face relentlessly towards him. The deep gold of his eyes held hers. 'It's more than sadness, Alice. What is it? Are you having doubts?'

His gaze was difficult to hold and she was desperate to pull away. But he'd know something was definitely wrong if she did, so she stayed where she was. 'I suppose so. Is it going to be like this when we get back home? I mean, are we going to be together like we are here back in Spain? Or are you going to put me at a distance again?'

His black brows drew down. 'No, of course I'm not going to distance you. We both decided that wasn't a good idea. The whole point of this honeymoon was to decide what kind of relationship we did want.'

'So what did we eventually decide?' She was sounding demanding and she didn't want to. She didn't want to let her doubt ruin their last evening, and yet she couldn't help it. 'I don't think we actually discussed it.'

'It's going to look like this,' Sebastian said. 'Like what we have here.'

'And what is that?' She was getting shrill now, and she hated that too.

Remind you of something?

No, it wasn't the same as her marriage to Edward. With Sebastián it would be different. He talked to her at least and he definitely wanted her. He cared for her too, that was clear. He said he would do anything to make her happy…

Anything except love you.

She could cope with that. She would have to. He'd promised her everything else so why make a drama out of it? She wasn't her sister to weep and pout if she didn't get what she wanted.

But you want more and it matters.

She hadn't thought it would, but now… Her heart twisted. Would her marriage turn into the kind of marriage she'd had with Edward? Where there was doubt and lack of communication, and one-sided uninterest?

'Isn't it obvious?' A thread of tension had entered Sebastián's voice. 'We have passion, mutual respect, interest in each other, and caring. You're important to me, Alice, you know this. I told you this. I want to make you happy. It won't be the same as before.'

She should say it was okay, that that was enough. She wanted to smile and kiss him, and make their last night a night to remember. To not ruin it by making a big song and dance about their relationship, or by pushing him into something he didn't want to give. Yet she had promised him honesty.

'I know,' she said, her voice husky. 'We do have all those things.'

His gaze turned sharp, scanning her face. 'But that's not enough, is it?'

She swallowed, her throat aching. He was too close, his scent around her, the warmth of his body a fire she wanted to warm herself against. He had become so familiar to her, so necessary…

Don't be a coward. Tell him no, it's not enough, that you want more. Tell him that what you want is his heart.

That terrified her. Every time she'd asked, she'd been refused or rejected, or simply ignored. Her parents had always prioritised Emily, and Edward had simply refused to engage. Why should Sebastián be any different?

Yet… He'd spent two weeks taking care of her, giving her pleasure, holding her when she cried and giving her little pieces of himself. He'd told her she was important to him, and he'd made her feel it too.

He was important to her. He was everything to her. She had to be honest with him. She had to. And she couldn't pretend that she was okay the way she had with Edward, the way she had with Emily and with her parents. Pretend that he didn't matter to her and that she didn't feel anything for him. Pretending was all she'd been doing for years and, yes, she was tired of it.

She didn't want to do it any more and maybe the time had come to stop.

They could have more than this if only she had the courage to ask for it.

Alice pulled away from him and took a couple of steps, putting some physical distance between them.

He frowned in puzzlement, his beautiful face lit by the setting sun, turning his hair glossy, gilding him with amber.

Her heart beat hard against her ribs. She couldn't not say it. She owed it to him and to herself. 'No, Sebastián,' she said. 'No, it isn't.'

He didn't move and yet his whole posture tensed, his face hardening. 'What more do you want?'

It was too late to back down now. She'd said the first words and now she had to say the rest of them.

Alice swallowed and lifted her chin. 'I know back in Spain I said that I didn't want love, but… I lied. I lied, Sebastián. Because that's when I realised I was in love with you.'

Something bright and intense leapt in his eyes, then it was gone. His expression hardened even more, becoming set. 'Alice. That's not what we agreed on.'

Of course he wouldn't want this. She'd known that already, but his response was proof. The small, precious hope she'd been nurturing for longer than she could remember shrivelled up and died. It was strangely freeing.

He didn't want this. He didn't want her. Which meant she could say anything she liked to him without fear of upsetting the delicate balance between them. Because it wasn't just upset, it had been destroyed.

'I know,' she said and lifted a shoulder. 'But it happened anyway.'

He stared at her, his mouth a hard line. 'This changes things. This changes everything.'

'Really?' Anger was starting to rise up inside her and she let it. 'And how, exactly, does it change things?'

He took an abrupt step forward. 'You know I can't hold you to our marriage now, don't you? You know I can't keep you.'

'Why?' Her anger leapt higher. 'Why does it make any difference at all?'

'Because I don't want love, Alice. In fact, I specifically said that our marriage would not feature love in any way.'

'So?' she flung back. 'That sounds like a you problem, Sebastián. And it certainly doesn't mean I can't love you.'

'So for how long?' he demanded, his own temper glittering in his eyes now. 'How long will this last if love is any part of it? You'll get tired of it. You'll get tired of me withholding something from you that you want. Then you'll stop wanting our marriage and you'll go behind my back with someone else.'

Hurt knifed through her. 'No,' she said furiously.

'That's *not* going to happen. How dare you think that I'd ever do something like that?'

'I thought Emily wouldn't, but she did,' he said flatly. 'Because I couldn't give her what I can't give you.'

'Couldn't or wouldn't, Sebastian?' She took a step towards him too, staring up into his furious amber gaze. 'Be clear on which it is, because that sounds awfully like a choice to me.'

He stared at her. 'Yes, you're right. It's a choice. I couldn't give her what she wanted, because I'd already given it to you.'

There was shock in her eyes, and she was staring at him as if he'd just started speaking Greek. She looked magnificent, as she always did, especially when she was in a fury. Her eyes deep and dark and full of hot temper, her hair wild and dark down her back. She wore the sexiest white dress, a halter neck that cupped her breasts and hugged her hips before swirling out into full skirts. The ends of the halter tied behind her neck and fell down her back, just begging to be pulled.

She was so beautiful and yet everything inside him was clenched tight with disappointment.

She loved him. Even though he'd told her that love could never be a part of their relationship. Even though he'd warned her. And now he could give a name to the feeling that clawed at his own heart every time he looked at her.

He loved her too. He had loved her the second he'd seen her. And he'd been telling himself lies all this time, because he'd already had a wife and he'd made promises to her. He'd wanted to be a good husband just as he'd wanted to be a good son. Telling himself that it wasn't, couldn't be love, that it was something else, something powerful and compelling and passionate, but definitely *not* love.

It was love, of course.

When he'd told himself he wasn't going to fall over that precipice, he hadn't realised he'd already fallen.

That was why it was so very disappointing. Why, even if he didn't want it to, it changed everything. Why he couldn't hold her to their marriage and wouldn't.

She'd told him it was a choice, and it was. She'd taken his heart, there was nothing he could do about that, but he could choose not to take hers in return.

'What do you mean you'd already given it to me?' Alice said softly, her anger giving way to surprise and a dawning hope.

But he couldn't allow that hope. It would be better for her if he crushed it completely, if he failed her now before he failed her at some later stage, when it would hurt her even more.

And he would fail her. He'd failed his mother, his father, and Emily, and he didn't see how it was possible not to fail Alice. Diego would take everything he had to give, and he didn't have anything left for anyone else. His son would have to come first; he had to.

She never wanted to be anyone's second choice.

No, and it killed him that she would be. But it had to be this way. With any luck, she'd understand.

'My heart, Alice,' he said roughly. 'You had it the moment I saw you and so I had nothing to give Emily.'

'What?' She'd gone pale. 'So it's my fault? Is that what you're saying?'

'No, *mi cielo*, that's not what I'm saying.' He wanted to hold her, but he couldn't allow himself that. He could never allow himself anything, that was clear. He'd thought he'd be able at least to have her in his life and at his side, but he couldn't, and he'd been selfish to think so. 'You weren't to blame for anything. As you said so eloquently, it's definitely a me problem. Because I loved you, I couldn't give Emily what she wanted, what she needed, and what I should have done was let her go. But I didn't. Selfishly, I wanted to prove that I could be a good husband, but I ended up proving the opposite.'

Mean and petty and cruel. Just like your father.

'No,' Alice breathed, the colour rushing back into her face. 'No, that's not true. You were a great—'

'I was not,' he interrupted flatly. 'Just like I wasn't a good son. My father was jealous and vindictive, and I made him worse. I got Javier fired. I didn't love Emily the way she should have been loved and ended up causing her so much pain.' His jaw ached but he made himself go on. 'Love is cruelty and pain. And everyone I love I fail. So I'm choosing now not to fail you. Do you understand?'

She was shaking her head, still staring at him in shock. 'No, Sebastian. No, I don't understand. You haven't failed anyone.' She took another step, getting close to him and he had to take a step back. He didn't want her near. She was too much of a temptation to him already and he was too weak when it came to her.

'I love you, Alice,' he said, allowing himself the luxury of saying the words once, out loud, because he would never say them again. 'But I'm not letting my heart make my choices for me, not this time. I'm going to give everything I have to Diego. Everything. He is the one person I have no choice about and he's only a baby. You will find someone else, another man who—'

'Are you serious right now?' Bright sparks of anger leapt in her eyes. 'Are you really saying that I need to turn around and look elsewhere?'

'I'm not choosing you, Alice,' he said roughly. 'That's what you always wanted. You wanted to be someone's first choice and I can't give you that. I can't give you anything but hurt and disappointment.'

'Do you really think I want to be put ahead of Diego?' Her voice was fierce, hot. 'Do you really think I'd demand that you put me ahead of my four-month-old nephew?'

'No, but I—'

'You're damn right, I wouldn't,' she interrupted furiously. 'And you're a coward for even thinking that I would. A coward for using Diego as an excuse.'

He stiffened in outrage. 'I'm not using him as an excuse!'

'Aren't you?' Abruptly she stormed up to him, her dress sweeping out behind her, all the fierce passion of her soul blazing in her eyes. 'You're using him as a reason not to even try, Sebastian. And all so you can avoid the possibility of failing.'

His own temper leapt high. 'I'm not afraid!'

'You are!' She drew herself up to her full height, magnificent as a goddess in her anger. 'You're afraid. And you're afraid because even now, even after all this time, you're still trying to make it up to your father.'

'No,' he said furiously. 'That was years ago.'

'So why are you still doing it? Why is failure the only thing you can think of when you look at me? Do you think I'm demanding? Is that it?'

'No, love is demanding, Alice.' This time he took a step, getting close to her, letting her feel his hopeless rage. 'It's vindictive and cruel and it expects everything from you. And I have nothing to give. *Nothing.*'

She didn't back away, she just stared right back at him. 'You're wrong,' she said flatly. 'It's not love that's vindictive and cruel and demanding. That was all your father. *He* was the issue, not love. And not you. Never you. I don't know why you get the two confused, but what I do know is that it's not me you're protecting, it's yourself.'

'I'm not—'

'I don't want to hear it.' The darkness of her eyes stared into his, the strength of her spirit shining through. 'I waited five years for you, and I'll be damned if I let you fall at the first hurdle, just because you're afraid. I'm also not going to leave so you can take the easy way out.' Her expression blazed with something passionate and intense. 'I love you. I loved you the day I met you. And now I've spent time with you, got to know you, I love you even more. You're the most amazing, intelligent, caring and passionate man I've ever met and what we have together is special, Sebastián. What we have is unique. I let my first marriage go without a fight, without a protest, but I'm not going to do it with you.'

She lifted a hand to his cheek, rooting him to the spot. 'I will fight for you. I will fight for what we have, because you're worth it. *We* are worth it. We *deserve* it.' Then she dropped her hand and stepped back. 'Let me know when you change your mind because I'm not leaving this place until you do.'

Then she walked right past him and off the terrace.

CHAPTER ELEVEN

ALICE STORMED DOWNSTAIRS, absolutely furious. She'd bared her heart to him, told him what she wanted, and all he'd given her in return were excuses. He had good reasons to believe them to be truths—his experience of love had been terrible, after all—yet they were excuses all the same.

He was afraid and she understood that, but she'd hoped that what they had would be greater than his fear. She'd hoped that he'd give love another chance, yet it seemed he wasn't going to overcome this.

By the time she got downstairs though, all her anger had evaporated, and as she stepped into the lounge, the tears she'd been fighting all this time finally streamed down her cheeks.

A part of her wanted to run, find the boat they'd been using and turn it out into the open sea and let it go. Let it take her far away from the island where she'd been so happy, and far away from him.

But she knew if she did that she'd be losing yet one more thing. She'd lost her baby and her marriage, her husband and Emily. She couldn't bear to lose Sebastián too, and she damn well wasn't going to.

She couldn't force him to look at himself and what he was doing, to see what she saw in him, which was a loving, generous, passionate man who'd been told nothing he could do would ever be enough to be accepted and loved. No wonder he thought love was a terrible force. No wonder he didn't want it. It must feel like mountains crushing him.

Still, she wasn't going to walk away from this. She wasn't going to accept whatever scraps he was willing to give her and she wasn't going to do what she'd done with Edward and let him withdraw from her either. She wanted to fight for him, fight for the relationship they were just starting to build, and if that meant waiting for him to be ready, to face his fear, then she'd wait.

But she wasn't leaving.

She wanted him more than she wanted her next breath and so she was going to stay here to fight for him whether he wanted her to or not.

Sebastián stood for a long time on the rooftop terrace, watching as the sun disappeared beneath the horizon. Every muscle in his body was tense and his heart felt as if it had shattered in his chest.

He couldn't give her what she wanted. He couldn't. He didn't have it in him. He had *nothing* left.

She's right. That's the excuse you use because you're afraid and you're protecting yourself.

What was wrong with wanting to protect himself, though? His father's terrible revelations had gutted him, and even though he'd tried hard afterwards to be a good son, nothing he had done had made any difference. Mateo had resented him until the end.

Could she really blame him for not wanting to open himself up to that kind of pain again? For not wanting to visit that pain on anyone else? Especially after what had happened with Emily.

When he'd married Emily, he'd been determined to be a good husband. He'd pushed aside his longing for Alice, tried to forget about her, tried to channel his passion into his wife instead of into his obsession with her sister.

But he'd failed and he'd hurt her badly enough that she'd gone looking for someone else. She'd broken her vows to him, yet he couldn't blame her. He hadn't loved her the way he should have.

He didn't love anyone the way they should be loved, because it was such an intense, powerful emotion. It caused great harm and he only had to remember Alice's white face and her dark eyes full of passion and fury to know that.

She loved him and it had brought her nothing but pain.

Yet she's still going to fight for you, for what you both could have together. Why aren't you fighting for her in return?

Why would he? When love was a never-ending grind of keeping your emotions tied down and held back, of trying to give someone enough to make them happy and failing?

The shattered edges of his heart ground against one another, pain spreading through him.

A coward, Alice had called him.

It's true. You don't want to try, because you don't want to fail. And you don't want to fail because she was right when she said you were still trying to make it up to your father. That's all you've been doing for years...

His muscles ached, everything ached. The sun was sending up its last flaring brilliance and he couldn't drag his gaze away. But he wasn't looking at it. There was only Alice standing in front of him, throwing the truth in his face, because it *was* the truth. He could see that now. That was exactly what he'd been doing and for years now, letting his father's anger and resentment colour his life. Still trying to prove himself to a man who'd died years ago.

A man who wasn't his father, he knew suddenly, because a father wouldn't do that to his son. He could see that now, because he wouldn't do that to Diego. He *loved* Diego.

And you love Alice too.

He did. And the past two weeks with her hadn't been a grind. They'd been the happiest he'd ever had and she had been happy too. Turning towards him, her face shining, smiling at him, her dark eyes full of light.

You made her happy.

Yes, he did. That was all him. And she made him happy too. Diego also made him happy. Was it as simple as that?

'It's not love that's vindictive and cruel and demanding. That was all your father...'

That was what she'd told him and...maybe she was right. Alice loved him and she'd never been cruel or petty.

No, all she'd given him was happiness. So…was love happiness? Was it…acceptance?

She accepts you. She always has. She got to know you and she's still here, fighting for you. Wanting you. How can you give her nothing in return?

He couldn't give her nothing. That was it, wasn't it? That would be repeating his marriage to Emily, and he knew abruptly that the answer wasn't to walk away. Alice wasn't walking away, she was standing and fighting, and he couldn't let her be the only one. He had to fight for her too, because she deserved it. She deserved everything he could give her and that meant giving her *everything*.

His mind. His body. His heart and his soul. They were all hers.

Sebastián pushed himself away from the edge of the terrace and turned, striding down the stairs and into the living area. She wasn't there.

He went through the sliding doors and out into the front garden that sloped down to the sea and there she was, standing staring at the horizon, the last rays of the sun outlining her in gold.

'Alice,' he said quietly. *'Mi cielo.'*

Slowly she turned and their eyes met the way they had all those years ago, and he could feel it then. He let it in, fully and completely.

It was what it had always been. Love at first sight.

'What did you choose?' Her chin was still lifted and he could see that she was still prepared for a fight.

But she didn't have to fight now, not any more.

'You were right,' he said. 'When you said it was my

father who was the problem, not love, you were right. These past two weeks with you have shown me what love truly is and it's...happiness, Alice. And it was you who showed me that.'

Her eyes were liquid with tears and the expression on her face put the setting sun to shame, but he went on, because nothing was going to stop him from saying the rest now. 'So, Alice Castellano, my beautiful wife. I have made my choice, and my choice is love. My choice is you. It was you five years ago and five years from now it will still be you. Those years we spent waiting were too long and I want more. I want everything. I want for ever.'

'Really?' She took a shaky breath, staring at him as if she didn't quite believe it. 'As simple as that?'

'Yes,' he said. 'As simple as that.' And then he opened his arms and she ran into them, and she was finally there, where she should have been right from the start.

In his arms.

Close to his heart.

EPILOGUE

THE HACIENDA LOOKED beautiful tonight. There were strings of lights wound all through the courtyard and the bougainvillea was magnificent. Guests filled the space, and the air was full of the buzz of conversation and the sound of classical guitar.

Alice saw him then, across the courtyard talking with Diego's new father-in-law. He was dressed in a dark suit, with a gold silk tie the colour of his eyes and, even after all these years, he was still the most beautiful thing she'd ever seen.

Apart from Diego, of course. And his new bride. And his sister, Giselle, whom they'd adopted not long after Diego and who at eighteen was growing up into the most gorgeous young woman. And of course the twins, Emily and César, whom they'd had via a surrogate, and at ten were still terrorising their poor parents. César in particular was a carbon copy of his father and he was going to break hearts one day, while Emily had decided that boys were ridiculous and she was going to be Prime Minister instead. Alice had no doubt she would be.

Their children were in the crowd somewhere, along with Diego's bride's family and a few of Alice's colleagues and Sebastián's. But mainly it was full of the children, both past and present, who'd come to the hacienda to heal.

A year after they'd got back from the island, Sebastián and Alice had decided to open their home and the stables to children from traumatic backgrounds, who could find acceptance with the horses, just as he had.

Alice considered every one of those kids her children too.

They were all here on this night to celebrate Diego's wedding, but right in this moment, Alice only had eyes for her husband.

He looked up from his conversation and their eyes met, as they'd once done long ago, and she felt it now as she'd felt it then, the thunderbolt. The lightning strike.

He was older now, with white at his temples, but the lines around his eyes and mouth were from laughter and joy. He smiled at her, then said something to Diego's father-in-law, and started towards her.

At the same time as she started towards him.

They met in the middle of the courtyard and when he held out his hand, she took it.

'*Mi cielo,*' he murmured. 'I think I've seen you somewhere before.'

'Oh, I don't think so,' she said, pretending. 'Are you sure?'

'Oh, yes.' He drew her close. 'I'm sure. In another lifetime. Or maybe many other lifetimes.'

He was so familiar to her and yet every time he touched her, the same excitement flared. She looked up at him from beneath her lashes. 'Perhaps we'll see each other in future lifetimes too?'

His smile was the whole world. 'We will. We have so much to look forward to.'

It wasn't too much of a stretch to believe him.

Theirs was a love that had been written in the stars.

It always had been.

And it always would be.

* * * * *

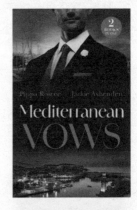

COMING SOON!

We really hope you enjoyed reading this book.
If you're looking for more romance
be sure to head to the shops when
new books are available on

Thursday 4th July

To see which titles are coming soon, please visit
millsandboon.co.uk/nextmonth

MILLS & BOON

MILLS & BOON®

Coming next month

ITALIAN'S STOLEN WIFE
Lorraine Hall

'I am very well aware of who you are, *cara*.'

His smile felt like some kind of lethal blow. Francesca could not understand why it should make her feel breathless and devastated.

But she had spent her life in such a state. So she kept her smile in place and waited patiently for Aristide to explain his appearance. Even if her heart seemed to clatter around in her chest like it was no longer tethered. A strange sensation indeed.

'I am afraid there has been a change of plans today,' he said at last, his low voice a sleek menace.

Francesca kept her sweet smile in place, her hand relaxed in his grip, her posture perfect. She was an expert at playing her role. Even as panic began to drum its familiar beat through her bloodstream.

'Oh?' she said, as if she was interested in everything he had to say.

No one would change her plans. *No one*. She narrowly resisted curling her free fingers into a fist.

'You will be marrying me instead.'

Continue reading
ITALIAN'S STOLEN WIFE
Lorraine Hall

Available next month
millsandboon.co.uk

LET'S TALK
Romance

Follow us:

Millsandboon

@MillsandBoon

@MillsandBoonUK

@MillsandBoonUK

For all the latest titles and special offers, sign up to our newsletter:

Millsandboon.co.uk

afterglow BOOKS

Afterglow Books is a trend-led, trope-filled list of books with diverse, authentic and relatable characters, a wide array of voices and representations, plus real world trials and tribulations. Featuring all the tropes you could possibly want (think small-town settings, fake relationships, grumpy vs sunshine, enemies to lovers) and all with a generous dose of spice in every story.

♪ @millsandboonuk
⊙ @millsandboonuk
afterglowbooks.co.uk
#AfterglowBooks

For all the latest book news, exclusive content and giveaways scan the QR code below to sign up to the Afterglow newsletter:

Never Date A Roommate
PBO 9780263322897 £8.99
Ebook 9780008938420 | Audio 9780263324860
For publicity enquiries please contact
millsandboonpressoffice@harpercollins.co.uk

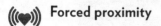

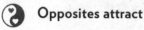

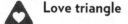

OUT NOW!

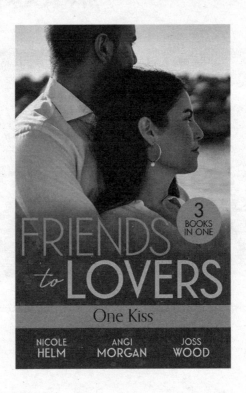